THE PHANTOM OF RUE ROYALE

Jean-François Parot is a diplomat and historian. His Nicolas Le Floch mysteries have been published to much acclaim in French. The first two novels in the series, *The Châtelet Apprentice* and *The Man with the Lead Stomach*, were enthusiastically reviewed on publication in English

Howard Curtis's many translations from French and Italian include five novels by Jean-Claude Izzo, four by Marek Halter and three by Gianrico Carofiglio, as well as works by Balzac, Flaubert and Pirandello.

Praise for Jean-François Parot

'The period detail is marvellously evocative, Le Floch is brave and engaging . . .' *Economist*

'Parot succeeds brilliantly in his reconstruction of pre-revolutionary Paris, in splendid period detail.' *The Times*

'A solid and detailed evocation of pre-revolutionary France – the poverty and squalor, side by side with the wealth and splendour, are brought lovingly to life. And the plot has all the twists, turns and surprises the genre demands.' *Independent on Sunday*

'Jean-François Parot's evocation of eighteenth-century Paris is richly imagined and full of fascinating historical snippets.' *Financial Times*

'. . . the superb Parisian detail and atmosphere . . . truly beguiles.' *The Times*

'An interesting evocation of place and period.' *The Literary Review*

THE

PHANTOM OF
RUE ROYALE

Also by Jean-François Parot

The Châtelet Apprentice
The Man with the Lead Stomach

THE

PHANTOM OF RUE ROYALE

JEAN-FRANÇOIS PAROT

Translated from the French by Howard Curtis

GALLIC BOOKS
London

Ouvrage publié avec le concours du Ministère français chargé de la culture – Centre national du livre.
This work is published with support from the French Ministry of Culture/Centre national du livre.

A Gallic Book

First published in France as Le fantôme de la rue Royale by Éditions Jean-Claude Lattès

First published in Great Britain in 2008 by Gallic Books, 134 Lots Road, London SW10 0RJ

A CIP record for this book is available from the British Library

ISBN 978-1-906040-15-4

Typeset in Fournier by SX Composing DTP, Rayleigh, Essex

Printed in the UK by CPI Bookmarque, Croydon, CR0 4TD

2 4 6 8 10 9 7 5 3 1

For Monique Constant

CONTENTS

Dramatis Personae   xiii

The Phantom of Rue Royale   1

Notes   348

Background to *The Phantom of Rue Royale*

For those readers coming to the adventures of Nicolas Le Floch for the first time, it is useful to know that in the first book in the series, *The Châtelet Apprentice*, the hero, a foundling raised by Canon Le Floch in Guérande, is sent away from his native Brittany by his godfather, the Marquis de Ranreuil, who is concerned about his daughter Isabelle's growing fondness for the young man.

On arrival in Paris he is taken in by Père Grégoire at the monastery of the Discalced Carmelites and on the recommendation of the marquis soon finds himself in the service of Monsieur de Sartine, Lieutenant General of Police in Paris. Under his tutelage, Nicolas is quick to learn and is soon familiar with the mysterious working methods of the highest ranks of the police. At the end of his year's apprenticeship, he is entrusted with a confidential mission, one that will result in him rendering a signal service to Louis XV and the Marquise de Pompadour.

Aided by his deputy and mentor, Inspector Bourdeau, and putting his own life at risk on several occasions, he successfully unravels a complicated plot. Received at court by the King, he is rewarded with the post of commissioner of police at the Châtelet and, under the direct authority of Monsieur de Sartine, continues to be assigned to special investigations.

DRAMATIS PERSONAE

NICOLAS LE FLOCH : a police commissioner at the Châtelet

MONSIEUR DE SARTINE : Lieutenant General of Police in Paris

MONSIEUR TESTARD DU LYS : Criminal Lieutenant of Police in Paris

MONSIEUR DE SAINT-FLORENTIN : Minister of the King's Household

PIERRE BOURDEAU : a police inspector

OLD MARIE : an usher at the Châtelet

TIREPOT : a police spy

RABOUINE : a police spy

AIMÉ DE NOBLECOURT : a former procurator

MARION : his cook

POITEVIN : his servant

CATHERINE GAUSS : a former canteen-keeper, Nicolas Le Floch's maid

GUILLAUME SEMACGUS : a naval surgeon

CHARLES HENRI SANSON : the public executioner

LA PAULET : a brothel-keeper

LA SATIN : a prostitute

PÈRE GRÉGOIRE : the apothecary of the monastery of the Discalced Carmelites

MONSIEUR DE LA BORDE : First Groom of the King's Bedchamber

CHRISTOPHE DE BEAUMONT : Archbishop of Paris

PÈRE GUY RACCARD : the diocese exorcist

LANGLUMÉ : a major in the City Guards

THE DUC DE RICHELIEU : a Marshal of France

MONSIEUR BONAMY : the city historiographer and librarian

KING LOUIS XV

MADAME DU BARRY : the King's mistress

RESTIF DE LA BRETONNE : a writer

MADEMOISELLE GUIMARD : a dancer

CHARLES GALAINE : a furrier, aged 43 years

ÉMILIE GALAINE : his second wife, aged 30 years

JEAN GALAINE : his son from his first marriage, aged 22 years

GENEVIÈVE GALAINE : his daughter from his second marriage, aged 7 years

CHARLOTTE GALAINE : his elder sister, aged 45 years

CAMILLE GALAINE : his younger sister, aged 40 years

ÉLODIE GALAINE : his niece and ward, aged 19 years

NAGANDA : a Micmac Indian, Élodie's servant,

LOUIS DORSACQ : an assistant in the Galaines' shop, aged 24 years

MARIE CHAFFOUREAU : the Galaines' cook, aged 63 years

ERMELINE GODEAU (known as MIETTE): the Galaines' maid, aged 17 years

I

PLACE LOUIS XV

What should have been a day so fair
Becomes a day of mourning.
The smell of death pervades the square
Before the next day's dawning
ANON. (1770)

Wednesday 30 May 1770

A sneering face topped by a red bonnet appeared at the door of the carriage, and hands with blackened nails clutched the lowered window. Beneath the grime, Nicolas recognized the already wizened face of a little boy. This sudden apparition took him back almost ten years to a certain Carnival night just before Monsieur de Sartine, the Lieutenant General of Police, had given him his first case. The masks that had surrounded him then had remained in his memory as death's heads. He dismissed these thoughts, which merely added to the gloom he had been feeling since the morning, and threw a handful of coins into the air. Delighted with the alms, the apparition disappeared: leaping backwards from the running board of the carriage, it landed on its feet and made its way through the crowd in search of the coins.

Nicolas shook himself like a weary animal and sighed, trying to shrug off his nagging sense of melancholy. It was clear that the past two weeks had exhausted him: too many sleepless nights, constant watchfulness and the nagging fear that he might be caught unawares by some unforeseen incident. Since the assassination attempt by Damiens, security had been tightened around the King and his family. It was an endless struggle to remain vigilant, and for nearly ten years the young Châtelet commissioner had been in the front line of this struggle, closely involved with matters of state, often secret matters, on whose mysteries he had thrown light. Monsieur de Sartine had entrusted him with keeping a close watch on the royal family on the occasion of the wedding of the Dauphin and Marie-Antoinette, archduchess of Austria. Even Monsieur de Saint-Florentin, Minister of the King's Household, had urged him to give of his best, reminding him, affably, of his past successes.

Beyond the Vaugirard toll-gate, serried ranks of people filled the roadway, frequently impeding the disorderly stream of carriages. Nicolas's coachman kept yelling warnings, punctuated by sharp cracks of his whip. From time to time, the carriage came to a sudden halt and tipped forward, and Nicolas had to reach out a protective hand to stop his friend Semacgus from smashing his nose against the partition. He could not have said why, but nothing had ever caused him as much anxiety as this unruly multitude converging on Place Louis XV. A wave of impatience seemed to run through this great mass of people, like a nervous shudder through the flank of a horse, as they hurried towards the celebration, eager for the pleasure they had been promised: a great firework display organised by the city authorities in honour of the Dauphin's wedding. Rumours were rife, and Nicolas was listening out for what people around him were saying. The provost of the merchants, who was providing the festivities, had announced that the boulevards would be lit up after the display. As if he had read his neighbour's thoughts, Semacgus belched a few times and woke up, then pointed at the crowd and shook his head.

'Look at them, so confident in their provost's generosity! Let's hope they're not disappointed!'

'What makes you think they might be?' Nicolas asked.

After all these days of anxiety, it had been a pleasure for him to go and fetch Dr Semacgus from the depths of Vaugirard. He knew that the doctor was fond of such great occasions, and had invited him along to Place Louis XV to watch the festivities from the colonnade of the new buildings on either side of Rue Royale. Sartine was expecting Nicolas to report on the event, even though, for once, the city authorities had not called on the services of the police.

'Jérôme Bignon is not known for caring much about the populace, and I fear these good people may be bitterly disappointed by the celebrations. How times change! You can't imagine the feasting when the father of our present Dauphin remarried. The provost at the time sent out wagons carrying horns of plenty overflowing with sausages, saveloys and spicy leeks, not to mention the drink . . . Damn it, people knew how to live in those days, and they really indulged themselves, I can tell you!'

Semacgus clicked his tongue at these pleasurable memories, and his face, already naturally ruddy, turned quite purple. He ought to be careful, Nicolas thought. The man was still true to form, still greedy for the pleasures of life, but he was becoming a little fatter with every year that passed and tended to doze off more and more frequently. His friends were starting to worry about him, although they did not dare to offer him advice. In any case he would never have consented to lead a more careful life, a life more suited to his age. Nicolas measured his friendship for Semacgus by the degree of anxiety the old man caused him.

'It's very kind of you, Nicolas, to have come and fetched this old bear from his den . . .' He raised his big, bushy eyebrows – increasingly white these days – in a gesture of interrogation or puzzlement. 'But . . . you seem to be in a sombre mood for such a festive day. I'd wager you're worried about something.'

Beneath his dissolute exterior, Semacgus concealed an acute sensitivity towards his fellows and a great concern for their welfare. He leaned towards Nicolas and placed a hand on his arm.

'You mustn't keep things to yourself,' he said in a graver tone. 'You seem to have something on your mind . . .' Then, reverting to his usual manner, 'Some pox-ridden beauty who left you a souvenir?'

Nicolas could not help smiling. 'Alas, no, I leave that to my more boisterous friends. But you're right, I am worried. Firstly, because I'm about to attend a great public gathering merely as an observer, with no mission to accomplish, and no means at my disposal, and secondly—'

'What do you mean?' Semacgus interrupted him. 'Is the finest police force in Europe, held up as an example from Potsdam to Saint Petersburg, at a loss, with its hands tied, incapable of doing anything? Couldn't Monsieur de Sartine have sent his best investigator – what am I saying, his extraordinary investigator – into action? I can't believe it!'

'I see I shall have to tell you everything,' Nicolas replied. 'Naturally, Monsieur de Sartine is somewhat anxious – quite rightly, since there are precedents . . .'

Semacgus looked up in surprise.

'. . . Yes, when our Dauphin's father married the Princess of Saxony. I heard it, of course, from Monsieur de Noblecourt. It happened in 1747, and he was there. There was a firework display in the Place de l'Hôtel de Ville, which went well, but, because there was an unexpectedly large number of spectators, the streets became congested with carriages and many people died, crushed and trampled. Monsieur de Sartine, who's always sending for files from the archives, must have read about this and drawn the obvious conclusions.'

'Of course! So what's the problem?'

'The problem is that nobody is prepared to take drastic action.'

The carriage swerved to avoid an old man who was singing, hopping on one foot and accompanying himself on a bird-organ. He was surrounded by a small crowd, who took up the refrain:

We shall give subjects to France
And you will give them kings

Someone in the crowd whistled, and a brawl broke out. Nicolas was about to intervene, but the culprit had already fled.

'My deputy, Bourdeau, often says Parisians are capable of the best and the worst, and when their patience . . . Anyway, His Majesty decided to ignore Monsieur de Sartine.'

'The King is getting old and so are we. La Pompadour used to watch over him. I don't know if the new concubine is so thoughtful. He's in decline, and that's a fact. Last year, when he reviewed the French Guard, everyone was struck by how changed he was, bent over his horse – he used to be so upright. In February, he had a bad fall while hunting. These are difficult times. But how to account for such a strange decision?'

'He was anxious for the wedding celebrations to pass off without incident. There are too many sinister omens hanging over this marriage. Have you heard about the horoscope by the Tyrolean astrologer, Dr Gassner?'

'You know I'm a philosopher. Why should I concern myself with such nonsense?'

'He cast the Dauphine's horoscope when she was born, predicting a terrible end for her. And there have been some curious incidents. Our mutual friend Monsieur de la Borde, First Groom of the King's Bedchamber, told me that the pavilion in Kehl intended to welcome the princess was decorated with a Gobelins tapestry depicting the bloody wedding of Jason and Creusa.'

'A remarkably tactless thing to do, to say the least. A deceived woman who takes her revenge, Creusa burned to death by a magic tunic, and Jason's two children with their throats cut.'

'Well, Sartine was hoping – since it is his prerogative – to have control over the Parisian part of the celebrations. But Bignon had already engineered it so that the responsibility fell to him. The King didn't want to antagonise the magistrates of a city he hates and which feels the same way about him.'

'All the same, Nicolas, we shouldn't judge the city authorities too harshly before seeing them in action.'

'I admire your confidence. Provost Bignon, whose motto is *Ibi non rem*,[1] has a reputation for being incompetent, vain and stubborn. Monsieur de Sartine told me that when he was appointed the King's librarian, his uncle, Monsieur d'Argenson, is supposed to have said, 'What an excellent opportunity, nephew, now you can learn to read.' The fact that he's now a member of the Academy has of course only added to his conceit. But that's nothing compared with how little thought has gone into the preparations for these festivities.'

'That's as may be. But are things so bad that you must get into this terrible state?'

'Judge for yourself. Firstly, these gentlemen of the city haven't taken any security measures. The whole thing is potentially like a rush of blood to the heart of the capital. Nobody's even thought about how the carriages are going to gain access, whereas for the least performance at the Opéra, we carefully regulate the traffic on the approach roads. Remember when the new auditorium was inaugurated? We were there together. Remember all the measures we took to avoid congestion and disorder? The French Guards stationed all the way from Pont Royal to Pont Neuf? Traffic flowed easily all the way up to the immediate vicinity of the building. We had thought it all through, down to the smallest detail.'

Semacgus smiled at this royal 'we', encompassing both the Lieutenant of Police and his faithful deputy.

'And secondly?'

'Secondly, the architect given the task of building the structure for the fireworks didn't even bother to level the area, which was a building site not so long ago. In places, there are still trenches in the ground, and that's very worrying. The crowd could easily fall

7

in. Thirdly, no provision has been made for allowing the distinguished guests – the ambassadors, the aldermen, the city authorities – to gain access. How will they get through this flood of people? And lastly, in defiance of custom, the provost has refused to grant a general bonus of a thousand crowns to the French Guards. So the streets are left to the City Guards, whose one concern over the past few days has been to show off the spruce new uniforms they've been given for the occasion by the municipality.'

'Come now, don't get so worked up. It may not turn out as badly as you think. The people will probably end the evening making merry on the victuals and wine provided by the provost.'

'Alas, no! That's another thing. According to my sources, the city authorities, in their anxiety to put on a firework display even more lavish than the King's at Versailles, first tried to skimp on the food and drink and finally decided to do away with it altogether.'

'No food and drink for the people! How stupid can they be?'

'Instead, there's to be a fair on the boulevards, but the stallholders have had to pay dearly for their pitches in order to meet some of the cost of the fireworks. You know how expensive such displays are. In short, the omens are not good. What annoys me is that I'm powerless to do anything. I'm here to report on what I see, nothing more.'

'What on earth is the provost for, anyway?'

'Not very much. Ever since His Majesty's grandfather created the post of Lieutenant of Police, he has lost most of his prerogatives. He has a few trifles left, above all managing city property and taking out loans. He also cuts a decorative figure at ceremonies, with his red satin robe, his split gown – half red, half tan – and matching hat.'

'I see!' Semacgus said. 'He's like one of those pins or nails that are considered absolutely essential for holding together the parts of a building, but which in themselves are probably worth precisely nothing.'

Nicolas laughed heartily at this jibe. A long silence ensued, during which the noise of the carriages, the cries of the coachmen and the shuffling of the advancing crowd filled the carriage like the sound of rising waves in a storm at sea.

'You haven't said anything about the past two weeks, Nicolas. Nor have you told me what impression our future queen made on you.'

'I accompanied His Majesty to Pont de Berne, in the forest of Compiègne, to greet the Dauphine.' He lifted his head somewhat boastfully. 'I rode beside the royal coach, and even received an amused smile from the princess when my horse reared and I almost fell. The King cried, "Steady, Ranreuil, steady!" as if we were out hunting.'

Semacgus smiled at his friend's youthful enthusiasm. 'Hard to find anyone more in favour than you!'

'On the evening of the wedding, there was gambling in the King's apartments, and the firework display was postponed until the following Saturday because of the storm. It was a great success, a dazzling sight. Two thousand giant rockets and an equal number of bombs. The whole park was lit up, all the way to the Grand Canal. There, a structure a hundred feet high representing the Temple of the Sun, exploded into a thousand extravaganzas. There was an enormous number of spectators, and the official responsible for the ambassadors had to settle endless quarrels of precedence among the notable guests on the balconies of the palace.'

'And what of the Dauphine?'

'She's still a child. Beautiful, yes, but unformed. A graceful gait. Lovely blonde hair. Rather a long face with blue eyes and a magnificent porcelain complexion. I'm less fond of her mouth: her lower lip is too thick and droops. Monsieur de la Borde claims she is quite slovenly and that the Dauphin is rather uncomfortable with that . . .'

'All very courtly of you, Nicolas!' Semacgus laughed. 'I sense the policeman in you rather than the private man. And the Dauphin?'

'Berry is a very tall, gangly young man, quite abrupt in his manner. He sways as he walks and gives the impression that he hears and sees nothing, or that everything is strange to him. On the wedding night, the King strongly advised him to . . . well, to think of the succession . . .'

'First Minister Choiseul does not spare our future king,' Semacgus observed. 'According to him he's incompetent. And they say the Dauphin won't even speak to Choiseul because of an offensive remark he once made to his late father.'

'A remark amounting almost to lese-majesty: Choiseul begged heaven to spare him from having to obey the future king!'

The carriage stopped suddenly, pitching them forward. Straightening up, Nicolas opened the door and jumped out. A traffic jam, he thought. What had happened, in fact, was that a berlin emerging from Rue de Bellechasse had tried to join the long line of vehicles in Rue de Bourbon. With some difficulty,

Nicolas made his way through the gathered onlookers. If only he had listened to the wise counsel offered by Semacgus, who had suggested crossing Pont de Sèvres and reaching Place Louis XV via the right bank of the Seine. He had insisted on taking a more direct route via the left bank and Pont Royal. He finally broke through a circle of onlookers who were looking down at a distressing sight on the ground.

An old man, who must have been knocked down by the berlin, was lying in his own blood, his face white and his eyes rolled upwards. His wig and hat had slipped off to reveal a smooth skull the colour of ivory. An old woman in bourgeois clothes was kneeling by the body, her cape in disarray, weeping silently and trying to lift the wounded man's head. Unable to do so, she began gently stroking his cheek. The crowd stood motionless, contemplating the scene. Before long, voices rose in anger, followed immediately by threats and insults to the coachman who had tried to enter Rue de Bourbon. From inside the carriage, an arrogant voice gave the order to push the rabble aside and carry on regardless. The coachman was already urging the horses forward when Nicolas seized one of them by the bit to stop its progress and said something in its ear, a method he often used with his own mounts. With his finger, he massaged the animal's gum, and the horse quivered and moved back. Turning his head, he saw Semacgus leaning over the wounded man, feeling his neck and holding a small pocket mirror in front of his lips. The surgeon helped the old lady to her feet and looked around for help. Two men appeared, carrying a table on which they carefully laid the victim. A man dressed all in black brought up the rear. Semacgus said something in his ear, and he took charge of the old woman.

Nicolas felt a blow on his shoulder. The horse shied in fright and almost fell backwards. He turned to discover a glittering mass of bright gold stripes, and recognised the blue and red uniform of an officer of the City Guards. A broad, crimson face with cold little eyes, the very image of rage. It was the passenger from the carriage, who had got out and angrily struck Nicolas with the flat of his sword.

'At the King's service, Monsieur,' Nicolas said. 'You have just struck a magistrate, a commissioner of police at the Châtelet.'

The crowd had moved closer and was following the scene with noticeable annoyance.

'At the city's service,' the officer replied. 'Move aside. My name is Major Langlumé, of the City Guards. I am on my way to the Place Louis XV to make sure that the festivities organised by the provost are proceeding in an orderly fashion. In accordance with the King's decision, Monsieur Sartine's people are not involved.'

The regulations were categorical: it was out of the question for Nicolas to cross swords with this brute, even though he was itching to do so. He suddenly saw the onlookers closest to them, including some with especially sinister faces, gathering stones. What followed happened so quickly that nothing and nobody could have prevented it. A hail of stones, even a piece of rubble from a house under construction, fell on the carriage and horses. The major was hit on the temple, resulting in a gash. Shouting and swearing, he quickly got back into the carriage and resigned himself to having it move back into Rue de Bellechasse. Through the broken window, he waved a vengeful fist at Nicolas.

'I admire your capacity for making friends,' said Semacgus,

who had approached. 'Our victim will be fine with a plaster. He'd only fainted from a cut to the head, but he lost a lot of blood, which is always dramatic! I handed him and his wife over to an apothecary, who will do what's necessary. What were they thinking of, at their age, running around the streets like young-sters, with all this upheaval going on? I've seen some pretty dubious-looking characters here, and my watch nearly ended up in someone else's hands.'

'I'd have got it back for you!' Nicolas said. 'The day before yesterday, at a grand supper given by the Emperor's ambassador at Petit Luxembourg, I unmasked a criminal who had somehow wormed his way into the party and was trying to steal a watch from the Graf von Starhenberg, Maria Theresa's former ambassador in Paris. The Graf was kind enough to write to Monsieur de Sartine and compliment him on the excellence of his police force, "the finest in Europe", as you called it just now. I've also seen some doubtful behaviour here. It makes me worry about what's going to happen next. What a coincidence – the person responsible for security at the festivities is that same jumped-up individual who was just now trying to pick a quarrel with me.'

'Bah! Those people aren't professionals. They're a bourgeois guard who can buy their way in.'

'And there's a great deal of competition between them and the men of the watch. One day we'll have to do something about it. The divisions between these various forces have rendered them powerless, and they're more interested in scoring points off each other than in serving the public. But I'm wandering from the point. Think of it – the man in charge isn't even in position yet to keep order in this great throng of people!'

Nicolas sank back into his thoughts. Their carriage finally managed to get onto Pont Royal, where a motley mixture of pedestrians and a tangle of vehicles gave the impression of an army in flight. The Quai des Tuileries was no easier to negotiate than the rest of the route. Two turbulent streams – one coming from the left bank and another, just as large and just as disorderly, emerging from the Quai des Galeries du Louvre – came together and tried, with a great deal of pushing and shoving, to share the roadway.

'The road seems to be blocked at Pont Saint-Nicolas.'

That was enough to set Semacgus off again. 'There's not even a vessel of the line to delight the Parisians. When I was a child – the Duc d'Orléans was still regent – my father took me to see a Dutch ship with eight cannon moored there.'

Nicolas was becoming impatient, tapping with his fingers on the window. It was almost completely dark by now, and the coachmen were stopping to light lanterns, which merely added to the chaos and slowness of the convoy. When they reached Terrasse des Feuillants, Nicolas gestured to his friend that they should abandon their carriage. He ordered the coachman to go back to the Châtelet: they would find their own way back after the festivities, and, besides, they were supposed to be having supper at the Dauphin Couronné in Rue du Faubourg-Saint-Honoré, the house run by their old acquaintance La Paulet. Their progress through the crowd, which was getting denser all the time, was something of a miracle. Several times, Semacgus drew Nicolas's attention to a number of threatening-looking characters mingling with the throng in little groups. Nicolas shrugged his shoulders in a gesture of powerlessness. They found themselves sucked into an eddy of people. Jostled, crushed, half-carried, they somehow managed to reach Place Louis XV. Here, too, two swollen streams of people and carriages met, one coming from the Quai des Tuileries and the other from the Cours-la-Reine promenade. Standing on tiptoe, Nicolas noticed that more and more carriages had parked on the *quai*, unchecked by any representative of authority.

Pushed as they were in opposing directions, they found it a real struggle to get to the ambassadors' mansion. What made Nicolas especially anxious was the realisation that there were no guards to be seen anywhere. Fortunately, he thought, no member of the royal family was due to be present at the display. They made their way, not without difficulty, past the structure that had been built in front of the statue of Louis XV: a Temple of Hymen with a magnificent colonnade. A kind of parapet ran all the way round it, at the four corners of which were dolphins ready to spew forth whirls of fire. The four sides of the temple were covered with symbols of rivers, also destined to spurt fire in sheets and cascades. The whole structure was surmounted by a pyramid with a globe on top. Semacgus criticised the proportions, finding them deeply flawed. Nicolas noted that most of the initial elements of the display had been placed around this structure, while behind the statue, on the side closest to the river, was a bastion from which the grand finale would be launched.

At the ambassadors' mansion, they were greeted by Monsieur de La Briche, secretary to Monsieur de Séqueville, and the man responsible for presenting the ambassadors to the king. He seemed to be beside himself and was finding it hard to catch his breath.

'Ah, Monsieur Le Floch, you see me under constant attack by harpies . . . I mean, by the ministers accredited to His Majesty. Despite my pleas, the city authorities have distributed more reserved places than actually exist. The ambassadors' bench is overflowing. As for the *chargés d'affaires*, I'm going to have to seat them on each other's knees. Monsieur de Séqueville had the same problem at Versailles during the wedding celebrations . . .'

He paused to scold two pages who were banging a newly painted wall with the bench they were carrying.

'I keep adding more benches. How can I be of help to you, Monsieur Le Floch – where is my head? – Monsieur le Marquis?'

'Le Floch will suffice,' Nicolas said with a smile.

'Madame Adélaïde[2] calls you nothing else, Monsieur, and you are her favourite hunting companion. I don't know where I'm going to put you and Monsieur, Monsieur . . .?'

'Dr Guillaume Semacgus.'

'Dr Semacgus. Your humble servant, Monsieur. Any privilege sets these people off. The least little minister or hospodar from the Ottoman court would prefer to be chopped to pieces on the spot rather than give up the place he thinks is due his rank. And Monsieur Bignon has thoughtlessly scattered invitations to every last alderman, official, monk, professor and God knows who else!'

A fat man in a grey and gold coat suddenly interrupted them and began speaking very loudly to Monsieur de La Briche, who responded with an abundance of promises. The man strutted off.

'Can you imagine? That plenipotentiary, who represents the Palatine Elector, keeps yelling at me that he can't accept this insult to his sovereign and that he will be in trouble back in his court when it becomes known. I ask you, is it my custom to insult a sovereign?' He shook his head. 'They simply won't listen to reason.'

'I don't want to overburden you,' Nicolas said, 'but if it were at all possible to have a general view of the square . . .'

'Say no more. Monsieur de Sartine would never forgive me if I did not make every attempt to satisfy you.'

'If it came to that, I would plead your case; you can count on it.'

'You're most kind. Would it be convenient for you to go up on the roof? It looks like being a fine evening, you'd have a perfect view from up there and . . . you would get me out of a spot, for I really don't know where else I could fit you in.'

He called a footman, and handed him a large key.

'Take these friends of mine up to the roof by the small staircase. Leave the door open and the key in it, in case I have to put anyone else there. Oh, Lord, I must go, here comes the Conde de Fuentes, the Spanish ambassador. I can't deal with his arrogance any longer – he can find his own seat!'

La Briche did an about-turn and skipped off. Nicolas and Semacgus followed the footman through a series of crowded drawing rooms. Major Langlumé, a piece of taffeta on his temple, was holding forth in the midst of an admiring circle of women. He looked daggers at the commissioner as he passed. After climbing several staircases, they at last reached the attic and then the roof.

The sky had grown darker and the first stars were out. The spectacle unfolding before their eyes left them speechless. In the distance, towards Suresnes, the last rays of the setting sun bathed the horizon in purple, the outlines of the hills around the capital drawn against the sky as if on a length of Chinese silk. The city lights glittered on the waters of the Seine. They were struck by the number of spectators gathered in Place Louis XV. A space had been cleared around the central monument, but it was overrun every time the crowd pushed forward. The gaps that appeared here and there corresponded to trenches that had not yet been filled with stones. Nicolas, always alert to the revealing detail, noted anxiously that the number of carriages and horses on the Quai des Tuileries and in the immediate surroundings was still increasing.

Semacgus was the first to speak. 'It's going to be a long and difficult process, dispersing all these people after the display. They all came at different times, but they'll want to leave together. There's bound to be congestion.'

'Guillaume, I admire your sagacity and I'm grateful for the unofficial zeal that makes you aware of the dangers. I pray to heaven that Monsieur Bignon has thought of all this and has a specific evacuation plan in mind. I think our friend Monsieur de La Briche will have a few problems with all Their Excellencies in a hurry to get home.'

Nicolas walked over to the right-hand corner of the roof, stepped across the balustrade, much to Semacgus's consternation, climbed onto the ledge and, supporting himself with one hand, leant over to look down at Rue Royale, which was so crowded that no one seemed able to advance.

'Don't stay there,' Semacgus said. 'One false move and there's nothing to stop you falling. My legs are shaking just to see you.'

He held out his hand. Nicolas grasped it and jumped nimbly over the low columns.

'When I was a child, I loved to scare myself by playing on the ochre cliff of Pénestin in a high wind. That was much more dangerous than this.'

'You Bretons will never cease to amaze me.'

They fell silent again, captivated once more by the grandeur of the spectacle, which, as darkness fell, was concentrated on Place Louis XV.

'Have you seen the Dauphine's coaches? All of Paris is talking about them. It's said that they do credit to the taste of Monsieur de Choiseul, who ordered them and took a close interest in their manufacture.'

'Yes, I've seen them. Their splendour is somewhat calculated for my taste, but the present is at least as good as the future.'[3]

'Ah!' Semacgus said. 'I shall remember that one.'

'They're four-seater berlins, one covered in crimson velvet with the four seasons embroidered in gold, the other in blue velvet with the four elements, also in gold. All extremely fine and exquisite, and topped off with gold flowers painted in different colours, which sway at the slightest movement.'

'They must have been expensive.'

'You know what the comptroller replied when the King asked him anxiously how much the celebrations would cost.'

'Not a bit. What did the Abbé Terray reply?'

'"Priceless, Sire."'

They were laughing at that when a muffled explosion announced the beginning of the display, followed by a joyous cry. The King's statue in the centre of the square was surrounded by girandoles, and further explosions startled the sleeping pigeons, making them rise in a great mass from the Tuileries and the Garde-Meuble. But these were not followed by the dazzling sights that were expected, and when the failure was repeated several times, the crowd gradually passed from cries of admiration to murmurs of disappointment. Some of the rockets rose into the air without exploding: with faltering trajectories they fell back to earth or else fizzled out with a dry crackle. There was a moment's silence, during which Ruggieri's pyrotechnicians could be heard with unusual clarity, shouting orders, then their cries were smothered by the sharp whistle of a rocket, which also came to nothing. This unfortunate attempt was forgotten when a fan shaped like a peacock's tail, studded with gold and silver, hung over the vast assembly and seemed to restore some impetus to the spectacle. The crowd applauded wildly. Semacgus, though, was grumbling: Nicolas knew that, like many elderly Parisians, he was easy to please, but equally quick to criticise.

'Launches badly synchronised, no rhythm, a performance that doesn't build. If there were music, it would be out of time. The people are complaining, and they're right. They can't be deceived by sham; they feel swindled.'

'Yet according to last Monday's *Gazette de France*, Ruggieri has been preparing the display for a long time, and connoisseurs have been comparing him favourably with his rival, Torre, at Versailles.'

The launches continued, alternating successes, false starts and fireworks that fizzled out. A rocket rose into the air, followed by a plume of light. It seemed to stop, then tipped over, nosedived, and exploded on the pyrotechnicians' bastion. At first nothing happened, then wreaths of black smoke appeared, and immediately afterwards, flames began to shoot up. The crowd surrounding the monument recoiled instantly, a movement that spread like a wave through the rest of the spectators. There followed a series of ever louder explosions. Then the bastion appeared to split in half and fire spewed out.

'The reserves and the pieces for the grand finale have caught fire prematurely,' Semacgus observed.

Place Louis XV was lit up by a cold white light, as if it were the middle of the day. The Seine was transformed into a frozen mirror, reflecting this luminous stream that fell as silver rain. Startled by what was happening, the crowd looked on, unsure about what to do or where to go, as the fire transformed the Temple of Hymen into a huge inferno, from which a few weary rockets still rose. Minutes went by as they watched. The spectators' uncertainty was palpable: heads turned in all directions as they questioned each other incredulously. The fire was spreading. The display had come to an end with all the convulsions of a dying organism. Leaning over the balustrade, Nicolas peered down into the square with an expression of anguish on his face that scared Semacgus.

'Nothing is being done about the fire,' he said.

'I fear the people may think this is a new kind of display, and that its unexpected end was all part of the festivities.'

All of a sudden, everything seemed to start moving, as if some perverse genie had fermented disorder in the crowd. To the noise of the explosions and the cracking sound as the structure collapsed were now added cries of anguish and calls for help.

'Look, Guillaume, here come the pump wagons. But the percherons are panicking at the noise and bolting!'

Several wagons had indeed appeared from the two streets that ran parallel to Rue Royale – Rue de l'Orangerie on the Tuileries side, and Rue de la Bonne-Morue on the Champs-Élysées side – but the heavy horses that drew them had broken into a gallop and were trampling everything in their path. What followed would remain forever in Nicolas's memory, and he would often relive the successive stages of the tragedy. The sight reminded him of an old painting he had once seen in the King's collections at Versailles, showing a battlefield on which thousands of figures moved, the face, uniform, armour, actions and expressions of each one clearly detailed. He had observed that by isolating a small area of the painting, he could pick out hundreds of perfect miniature pictures. From the roof of the ambassadors' mansion, no episode of the tragedy was lost on him. The situation was evolving with every minute that passed. Groups of spectators had been forced back by the horses, and some had already fallen into the unfilled trenches. Nicolas recalled that the site had only been cleared on 13 April of that year. Semacgus pointed to another area, where the guests who had watched the display were starting to leave the building. Their carriages, which had been waiting in a disorderly mass on the Quai des Tuileries, were now flooding onto the square, and the coachmen were laying about them with their whips to force a way through the crowd. Caught between the pumps and the coaches, many spectators stumbled and fell into the trenches. To add to this, a number of dubious characters bearing swords were attacking the terrified citizens and relieving them of their belongings.

'Look, Nicolas, the crooks have come out of the *faubourgs*.'

'Right now, I'm more worried by the fact that no one can get to the Quai des Tuileries, and that Pont du Corps-de-Garde, which leads to the Tuileries gardens, is closed. The only way out is through Rue Royale. The stage is set for a massive collision.'

'But look at all the people trying to get onto the *quais*! The only way to avoid being crushed is by river. My God, I've just seen at least a dozen people fall in! The net at Saint-Cloud[4] will be full tomorrow, and the Basse-Geôle, too.'

Panic had spread. There was a terrified surge away from the centre of the disaster. Those members of the crowd at the perimeter of the square did not seem to grasp the seriousness of the situation and were advancing calmly, inexorably, towards Rue Royale, thinking they would get through that way to the boulevards to enjoy the illuminations and the attractions of the fair. Meanwhile, those who had been in the middle of the square, unable to move, were now converging on the same street, unaware of the trap closing on them. Their way was obstructed by carriages, and Nicolas could already hear screams, but these premonitory signs of the disaster to come were drowned by the noise of several tens of thousands of spectators.

Nicolas, still at the corner of the building, leaned over once again to look down at Rue Royale, and what he saw there was worse than anything he might have feared. He shouted to Semacgus, who was holding back from the edge, 'If nothing stops the crowd moving, disaster is inevitable. There's no room to circulate. Everyone who's trying to leave the square is coming into this one street. It's packed with people all the way to the

Marché Daguesseau. The crowds on the boulevards are trying to get back to the square.'

At that moment they heard a long chorus of screams and cries. Horrified, Nicolas watched the two contrary movements growing in volume and increasing in speed like two opposing groundswells. Those who found themselves stuck in the middle of the roadway could neither advance nor retreat, because the street narrowed at this point, forming a kind of tunnel where houses that had not yet been demolished jutted out. As if the unfilled trenches were not bad enough, freestones lying on the ground made the road even more difficult to negotiate. Nicolas now saw bodies sliding into the trenches, immediately covered by others. By the light of lanterns, he could see open mouths crying out in terror. Men, women, children, squeezed and jostled, stumbled and fell and were instantly trampled by those who followed. Some people, crushed standing up, had blood spurting from their nostrils. The trenches were soon as full as communal graves. Like a Moloch, Rue Royale was devouring the people of Paris. The King's statue in the middle of the square seemed to be sailing on a sea of lava: the still-glowing embers of what was left of the festivities.

'We have to get help to those people,' Nicolas said.

Followed by Semacgus, he rushed to the small door that led to the attic. It resisted their efforts. The evidence was incontrovertible: it had been locked from the other side.

'What are we going to do?' Semacgus asked. 'It's well known that you can climb walls like a cat, but don't count on me to follow you.'

'Don't worry, I don't think I'd be able to get down the wall except with a rope. But I have other strings to my bow.'

He searched in his pocket and took out a small instrument equipped with several blades. He introduced one into the lock and tried to move the bolt, but it hit an obstacle. He kicked the door frame angrily, then stopped for a moment to think.

'If that's how it is, I'll have to use the chimney – there's no other way out. But there, too, I'd need a rope. Let's have a look all the same.'

They went back up onto the roof and Nicolas climbed a cast-iron ladder to the top of one of the monumental stone chimneys. He struck a light and, with a sheet from his notebook, made a small torch which he dropped into the void. The shaft descended vertically and then seemed to become almost horizontal.

'There are clamps in the stone; I'm going down. At worst, if I can't get through, I'll come back up. Guillaume, you stay here.'

'What else could I do? My paunch wouldn't let me get down that thing.'

The noise rising from the square was increasingly punctuated by cries and moans. Nicolas quickly took off his coat and shoes.

'I don't want to get snagged. Keep these. It makes me sick to feel so powerless with all that's happening down there . . .'

Before giving his coat to Semacgus, he took from the pocket – the surgeon, wondering what on earth would come out next, was greatly amused – a short candle, which he placed between his teeth. The clamps, put there to help the work of the chimney sweeps, made the descent easy enough, but Nicolas thought anxiously of what lay ahead. He was no longer a child, but a man in his thirties, and with quite a full figure. Catherine and Marion's cooking had left its mark, as had the meals in taverns with his deputy, Bourdeau, who like him loved good, cheap food. He reached the bottom of the shaft. There were two pipes to choose from, the opening of one hidden inside the entrance to the other. He chose to take the less steep of the two, judging that it would take him to one of the fireplaces on the upper floors of the building. Unable to hold the candle in his hand, he lit it and fixed it between one of the clamps and the wall. He would have to plunge blindly into the darkness.

The risk of getting stuck in the narrow passage made him sick with apprehension. It suddenly occurred to him that the folds of his shirt might hinder his progress, and he took it off. From somewhere above his head, Semacgus was dispensing advice in a voice ashen with anxiety, which echoed down to him, distorted. He caught his breath and thrust his legs forward. He felt as though he were sliding into some kind of greasy material, and for a moment he lost all notion of time and space, before making a painful return to reality. Too bulky for the space, he had got stuck and could descend no further. For several minutes he stretched like a cat, lifting first one shoulder then the other. He remembered the grotesque movements of a contortionist he had seen at the last Saint-Germain fair. At last he managed to force his way through and continue his descent. He felt as if he were being sucked down into a vacuum. Almost immediately, he fell onto a pyramid of logs in a huge fireplace. The pyramid collapsed noisily under his weight, and his head hit a bronze plaque which bore the arms of France. He was surprised not to be knocked senseless. He got up carefully and checked the condition of his joints. Apart from a few grazes, he was unharmed. He looked at himself in a huge pier glass crowned with floral decorations in stucco: a stranger, black with soot, face like a scarecrow's, britches torn and tattered. He walked across an unfinished, undecorated room which looked as if it belonged in a barracks rather than a palace. He opened a door and found that he had come out on the floor where the drawing rooms were. Here, the guests were crowded around the balconies. There was as much bustle as in an overturned hive. Some people had gathered at the windows, where they jostled for a view of the square, others were holding forth. Nicolas had the feeling that he was watching some absurd spectacle, a comedy or ballet in which automata endlessly repeated the same gestures. Nobody paid him any heed, even though his filthy appearance should have attracted notice.

He got back to the staircase leading to the attic. As he climbed it, he heard Semacgus's solemn tones alternating with the sharper voice of Monsieur de La Briche. They were both coming downstairs so quickly that they almost fell into Nicolas's arms. With the disaster on the square increasing in scale, Monsieur de La Briche had tried to send for Nicolas, only to find the lock of the door that led to the roof obstructed by a mysterious object in gilded metal, a kind of spindle, which he now gave to the commissioner. The key itself was lying on the ground. Clearly, someone had been playing a practical joke on the spectators on the roof. He would see to it that the culprit was found – probably an insolent footman, or else one of those pages in blue who, in spite of their youth, considered themselves entitled to do anything because they were close to the throne.

'Commissioner,' said Monsieur de La Briche, 'you must help me to restore a little order. The crush is terrible, and we have so many injured we don't know what to do with them. They're being brought in all the time. The City Guards are nowhere to be found. When things started to go wrong, their leader, Major Langlumé, went off to give orders to his men, and that's the last anyone saw of him. On top of that, I keep hearing that there are bandits among the crowd attacking honest citizens.' He lowered his voice. 'Many of our guests have been drawing their swords to force their way through the crowd. A lot of people have been killed that way, not to mention those run down by carriages. The envoy from Parma, the Conte di Argental, has had his shoulder dislocated, and the Abbé de Raze, minister to the prince-bishop of Basle, was knocked down and is in a terrible state.'

'Has Monsieur de Sartine been informed of what is happening?' Nicolas asked.

'I dispatched a messenger to him. By now he should be acquainted with the gravity of the situation.'

Two men entered, carrying an unconscious woman in a frilly dress, one of whose legs was hanging at an odd angle. Her bloodstained face had been so flattened that it no longer looked human. Semacgus rushed to her, but after a brief examination he rose and shook his head. Other bodies were arriving, equally devoid of breath. For a while, they helped to receive the injured with the meagre means at their disposal. Nicolas was waiting for the return of the emissary who had been sent to Sartine. When he did not reappear, Nicolas retrieved his coat and went outside in order to get a clearer picture of the disaster. He took Semacgus with him.

After making their way through the crowds of people coming in and out of the building – some of them, they were annoyed to observe, mere idle onlookers – they emerged on Place Louis XV. The great noise of the festivities had died down, but cries and moans rose on all sides. Nicolas ran straight into Inspector Bourdeau, his deputy, who was giving orders to some men of the watch.

'Ah, Nicolas!' he exclaimed. 'We don't know if we're coming or going! The fire has been contained, the water pumps from La Madeleine and Saint-Honoré market have seen to that. Most of the criminals have scattered, although some are still trying to strip the dead of their belongings. The victims are being removed, and those bodies that have been identified have been taken to the boulevard.'

Bourdeau seemed overwhelmed. The vast esplanade looked like a battlefield at night. An acrid black smoke rose into the air, whirled about, then, blown back down by the wind, fell again, shrouding the lights beneath a lugubrious veil. In the middle of the square, the remains of the triumphal structure stood like a sinister scaffold. Wreathed in smoke, the bronze monarch looked down at the scene, unruffled and indifferent. Semacgus, who had noticed Nicolas looking at the statue, murmured, 'The Horseman of the Apocalypse!' To their right, in Rue Royale, people had started to lay out the dead against the wall of the Garde-Meuble and were searching them in order to determine their identities and putting labels on them so that they could be recognised more easily by their families. Bourdeau and his men had restored a semblance of order. The area had been cordoned off with some difficulty and groups of volunteers were going down into the trenches on Rue Royale. A chain was starting to form. As soon as the victims had been brought out, an attempt was made to determine which of them were still alive so that they could be taken to the improvised emergency posts. There, doctors and apothecaries who had come

29

running did whatever they could to treat them. Nicolas noted with horror that it was no easy task to bring up the bodies; those who lay at the bottom were crushed beneath the weight of those on top, and it was difficult to disentangle the various layers. He noted, too, that most of the dead belonged to the humblest classes. Some of them had wounds which could only have been caused by deliberate blows from canes or swords.

'The street was claimed by the strongest and richest,' Bourdeau muttered.

'The criminals will get the blame,' Nicolas replied. 'But the cabs and carriages played their part in the slaughter, and those who forced their bloody way through even more so!'

They worked all night, helping to sort the dead and injured. As the sun was rising, Semacgus drew the commissioner and Bourdeau to a corner of La Madeleine cemetery where a number of bodies had been gathered. He had a puzzled look on his face. He pointed to a young girl lying between two old men. He knelt and uncovered the upper part of her neck. On each side were bluish marks that appeared to have been left by fingers. He moved the dead girl's head. Her mouth was twisted and half open, and let out a sound like sand.

Nicolas looked at Semacgus. 'That's quite a strange injury for someone who's supposed to have been crushed.'

'That's my impression, too,' the surgeon agreed. 'She wasn't crushed; she was strangled.'

'Have the body put to one side and taken to the Basse-Geôle, Bourdeau, we'll have to tell our friend Sanson.' Nicolas turned to Semacgus. 'You know, he's the only person I'd trust with an operation like that – apart from you, of course.'

He made a preliminary search of the body. The victim had nothing on her except her clothes – of high quality, he noted. No bag or reticule, no jewellery. One of her hands was clenched: he prised it open to reveal a small pierced pearl, of jade or obsidian. He wrapped it in his handkerchief. Bourdeau returned with two porters and a stretcher.

As they stared at the young victim's distorted face, they were overcome with exhaustion. It was out of the question that they would go to La Paulet's and eat now. The sun rising on this grim, bloodstained morning could not dissipate the damp mist which presaged a storm. Paris was shapeless and colourless, apparently finding it hard to awaken from a tragedy that would gradually spread to city and court, districts and *faubourgs*, and, when it reached Versailles, would cast a shadow over the waking moments of an old King and a young couple.

II

SARTINE AND SANSON

Sic egesto quidquid turbidum redit urbi sua forma
legesque et munia magistratuum.

Thus emptied of its turbulence, the city recovers its usual form, its laws
and its magistrates with their practice.

TACTITUS

Thursday 31 May 1770

Nicolas moved through a suspended city, a city surprised by its
own suffering. Everyone had his own version of the events to
peddle. Little groups conversed in low voices. Some noisier ones
seemed to be pursuing a long-standing quarrel. The shops, usually
open at this hour, were still closed, as if observing a state of
mourning. Death had struck everywhere, and the spectacle of the
wounded and dying being brought back to their homes had spread
the news of the disaster throughout Paris, made all the worse by
the false rumours inevitably aroused by such a tragedy. People
seemed struck by the fact that this catastrophe had happened
during the celebrations for a royal wedding. It was a bad omen,
and it made the future uncertain and vaguely menacing. Nicolas
passed priests carrying the Holy Sacrament. Passers-by crossed
themselves, took off their hats or knelt before them.

Rue Montmartre lacked its usual animation. Even the familiar, reassuring smell of freshly baked bread coming from the baker's shop on the ground floor of Noblecourt's house had lost its enchantment. Breathing it in, he immediately remembered the terrible, musty odour of wet fire and blood hovering over Place Louis XV. An officer of the watch had lent him a mare, a cantankerous animal which snorted and pulled back its ears. Bourdeau had remained on the scene to help the commissioners from the various districts who had come running as reinforcements.

Nicolas's first impulse had been to gallop to police head-quarters in Rue Neuve-Saint-Augustin. But he knew all too well that, despite the gravity of the moment, Monsieur de Sartine would not have tolerated anyone appearing before him with a soot-blackened face and dishevelled clothes. He had often experienced the apparent insensitivity of a chief who did not accept any weakness in himself, and hated having to deal with that of his subordinates. The King's service was all that mattered, and there was no particular advantage in being injured, bruised and dirty. On the contrary, such a lapse in the proprieties would have brought disfavour on anyone who dared to appear in that way. To Monsieur de Sartine, it would have demonstrated neither courage nor devotion, but rather a contempt for all that his office represented, a licentiousness that went against everything he believed in.

The bells of Saint Eustache were chiming seven o'clock as Nicolas handed the reins of his nag to a young baker's boy who stood gaping in the doorway. He went straight through to the servants' pantry where he found his maid, Catherine, slumped beside her stove, fast asleep. He surmised that she had not gone to bed but, having heard of the tragedy, had decided to wait up for him. Old Marion, Monsieur de Noblecourt's cook, whose age excused her from heavy work, slept later and later these days, as did Poitevin the footman. Noiselessly, he went out to the courtyard and washed himself at the pump, as was his custom in summer. Then he tiptoed upstairs to his room to change his clothes and brush his hair. For a moment he considered telling the former procurator that he was back, but when he thought of the detailed account he would have to give, and the thousand questions that would follow, he changed his mind. He missed being greeted by Cyrus, the little, grey, curly-haired water spaniel. The days were long gone when the dog would jump up and yap excitedly when he arrived. The animal was now quite old and stiff, and only the slow movements of his tail still showed how pleased he was to see Nicolas. He spent all his time on the tapestried rug, from where he observed events surrounding his master with eyes that were still alert.

Nicolas thought about the passage of time. Soon, it struck him, he would have to bid farewell to this witness to his first steps in Paris. The idea occurred to him that the compassion he felt for Cyrus was a way of avoiding having to think of other imminent farewells which were just as inevitable. He gently placed a short note of explanation in Catherine's lap and left the house without a sound. He went back to his restive mount, and the baker's boy smiled and handed him a brioche, still hot from the oven. Remembering that he had not had dinner, he wolfed it down. The buttery taste was a delight to the palate. 'Come on,' he said to himself, 'life isn't so bad. *Carpe diem*!' It was a phrase constantly repeated by his sybaritic friend Monsieur de La Borde, who loved female dancers, fine food and works of art, and was currently writing an opera and a book about China.

In Rue Neuve-Sainte Augustin, an unusual amount of activity indicated that the night's events had left their mark. Nicolas climbed the steps four at a time. The elderly manservant greeted him with a flustered look on his face. He was an old acquaintance, for whom Nicolas was almost part of the furniture.

'Here you are at last, Monsieur Nicolas. I think Monsieur de Sartine is waiting for you. I'm very worried: it's the first time in years he hasn't asked to see his wigs. Is the case so serious?'

Nicolas smiled at this reminder of his chief's innocent obsession. Contrary to the custom of the house, the servant led him to the library. He had only once before had the opportunity to enter the beautifully proportioned room, with its shelves of white oak and its ceiling painted by Jouvenet. He remembered admiring the work of this artist when his guardian, Canon Le Floch, had taken him one day to the parlement of Rennes, and every time duty called him to Versailles he would gaze in awe at the splendid tribune of the royal chapel, which was decorated by the same painter. He tapped softly at the door and opened it. He thought at first that he was alone, until he heard a curt voice he knew well. Monsieur de Sartine, in a black coat and powdered wig, was perched at the top of a stepladder consulting a red Morocco-bound book embossed with his coat of arms: three sardines.

'Greetings, Commissioner.'

That gave Nicolas pause. The Lieutenant General only addressed him by his rank when he was trying to master his anger – an anger directed less at his men than at the general inertia or obstinacy of things.

He was looking up at the figures on the ceiling, apparently deep in thought. Nicolas respected his chief's silence for a few moments, then decided to begin his report. He gave the number of dead which, by early that morning, had been approaching a hundred. Nevertheless, in his opinion, this figure could well be much greater, even by as much as ten times, since many of the injured were unlikely to recover.

'I know what you did, you and Bourdeau. Believe me when I say that it is a comfort to me to know that you were there to bear witness for our force.'

It occurred to Nicolas that Monsieur de Sartine was ill, and that his illness went deeper than anything he might have imagined. His manifestations of satisfaction were so rare that they were seen as events, and, besides, he never came out with them when a case was in progress. Nicolas saw him opening and closing his book mechanically, as if unsure what to say or do next.

In a low voice, as if speaking to himself, Sartine resumed, '"This man has marr'd my fortune, and manhood is call'd foolery when it stands against a falling fabric . . ."'

Nicolas smiled inwardly and recited aloud, '". . . The tag whose rage doth rend like interrupted waters, and o'erbear what they are used to bear."'

Monsieur de Sartine slammed the book shut, slowly descended the stepladder, then turned and looked at Nicolas with ironic severity. 'You allow yourself to improvise on my words, I think!'

'I step aside in favour of *Coriolanus* and continue his.'

'So, my Shakespearian friend, what is your opinion of last night? "Paint me Nicolas distraught amid these horrors . . ." '

'Lack of preparation, improvisation, coincidence and disorder.'

He gave a brief account of the night's events, without going into details which Sartine surely knew, since Sartine always seemed to be well informed, in some mysterious but effective way, about anything, whether happy or tragic, that happened in the capital with whose care he was entrusted. He mentioned the incident with the major from the City Guards, and described the layout of the area, the absence of any organisation, the initial episode with the fireworks and the disaster that had been its inevitable consequence. He did not fail to mention how certain privileged individuals had distinguished themselves on this battlefield by laying about them with their canes or even their swords and sending their carriages rushing through the crowd, nor how circumstances had left the field clear for crooks and thugs from the *faubourgs*.

Sartine had sat down in a *bergère* covered in crimson satin and was listening with his eyes half closed, his chin on his hand. Nicolas noted his pallor, his drawn features, the dark patches on his cheekbones. When he had met Sartine for the first time, it had struck him that he looked older than his age – a fact the Lieutenant General played on to assert his authority when confronted with older interlocutors who might consider him a young upstart. He did not deign to look at Nicolas until the latter's account of his adventures as a chimney sweep. At that point he looked sharply at his deputy's clothes, confirming to Nicolas that he had done the right thing in changing them. The satisfied smile that lit up his chief's face for a fraction of a second was highly gratifying.

'Yes,' Sartine said, 'it's as I feared . . .'

He seemed to feel a kind of bitter joy in observing that, once again, events had justified his anxieties. He brought his fist down on the beautiful inlaid backgammon table before him.

'I did, however, indicate to His Majesty that the city authorities were not in a position to control an event of that size.' He thought for a moment, then went on, 'Eleven years with no disasters, no mistakes, and now this Bignon, this cheap, stupid, powerless provost, usurps my authority, poaches on my territory and cuts the ground from beneath my feet!'

'We'll soon be able to apportion blame,' Nicolas ventured.

'Do you really believe that? Have you ever had to deal with these snakes? At court, the war of tongues can be deadlier than a battlefield. Calumny . . .'

Nicolas's body still ached in places, bearing witness to the risks he had taken and the dangers he had confronted, which were just as real as those with which the Lieutenant General was now faced. 'Monsieur,' he said, 'your past, the confidence that the monarch—'

'Balderdash, Monsieur! Favour is by essence volatile, as our drawing room apothecaries and chemists say! People always remember the bad things we are supposed to have done. Do they ever take into account our efforts and our successes? Well, that's as it should be. We are the King's servants, for better or worse, and whatever it may cost us. But that this ridiculous provost, who has used his alliances and relationships to advance himself and who has obtained everything without having to make any effort, and certainly without deserving it, that such a man should be the cause of my disgrace, that's something I can't get over. He's the kind of person who's puffed up with pride when he mounts a good horse, or sports a plume in his hat, or wears fine clothes. What nonsense! If there's any glory in those things, it should go to the horse, the bird or the tailor!'

Again he struck the gaming table. Nicolas, astonished by this uncharacteristic outburst, suspected a touch of play-acting in his chief – and suspected, too, that his last words had been a quotation, although he could not immediately identify it.

'But we're straying from the point,' Sartine went on. 'Listen carefully. You've been with me for a long time now and you are the only person I can tell these things. The reason I feel so strongly about this affair is that beneath such struggles for influence, major interests are always at play. You know that I am friendly with the First Minister, the Duc de Choiseul. Even though they had their disagreements and didn't always trust each other, by and large he was close to Madame de Pompadour . . .' He broke off. 'You had dealings with her, didn't you?'

'I often had the privilege of speaking with her and serving her, when I first started working for you.'

'And even, if I remember correctly, performing some signal services for her.[2] The last time our poor friend received me, she was no more than a shadow of her former self . . . She was burning hot and complained of being frozen, her face looked drawn, and her complexion was pale and mottled . . .'

The Lieutenant General broke off, as if the memory was too painful to evoke.

'I'm straying from the point again. My relations with the new favourite are quite different. She has neither the contacts, nor the political grasp, nor the subtle influence of the lady of Choisy,[3] who was distinguished by her education, her studied elegance, her sure taste in arts and letters, and her native charm – well, she was born under the sign of Pisces. This one's a decent enough girl, but she's been thrown into the subtle ins and outs of the Court without preparation, apart from the wrong kind, perhaps.'

He lowered his voice, and looked around at the shelves of his library.

'The worst of it is, whatever's been achieved during the day she undoes at night. By arousing the old King's senses she ensures her influence. Choiseul is obsessed with getting his revenge on the English. As he's unsure how long he'll keep his position, he's in such a hurry to achieve this end that he has a tendency to rush in and make stupid blunders. He's antagonized the new mistress or, more precisely, he resents her for having succeeded where his own sister, Madame de Choiseul-Stainville, failed – God knows she put her heart and soul into it! What's all this to do with me, you will ask. I've been dragged into this quarrel against my will. Keep this to yourself: on the King's orders, I had to go to Madame du Barry and protest my loyalty. I had to promise her, almost on my knees, that I would do everything I could to prevent the publication of scandalous writings, which, unfortunately for me, have multiplied and spread – the work of journalists and printers paid for by Monsieur de Choiseul himself.'

'I recall, Monsieur, your ordering me to track down a lampoon called *The Nocturnal Orgies of Fontainebleau*. But where does Provost Jérôme Bignon fit in to all this?'

'There's the rub. He's wooing Madame du Barry. You see, my

dear Nicolas, the regrettable position in which last night's events place me, apart from my sadness at any example of bad administration by the city authorities. I'll be held responsible, because no one knows that the celebrations were taken out of my hands.'

'And yet the marriage of the Dauphin does seem like a genuine success on Choiseul's part. Everyone sees it as his crowning achievement. He always wanted to forge an alliance with Austria.'

'You're right, but nothing is closer to a precipice than a summit. You now have all the inside information I can give you – except for one other thing. Last night, His Majesty and Madame du Barry went to Bellevue to see the fireworks from the terrace of the chateau. They didn't know anything of the tragedy at the time. On the other hand, the Dauphine and the King's daughters went to Paris. On Cours-la-Reine, they were admiring the illuminations when they heard cries of terror that got them all aflutter. The coaches did an about-turn, with the princess in tears . . .'

He stood up, checked the position of his wig and readjusted it with both hands.

'Commissioner, here are my instructions. They must be followed to the letter. You will use every means necessary to draw up a report on the events in Place Louis XV: how they started, who was responsible, who was at fault, who interfered. You will try to determine the exact death toll. Don't let anything stand in your way. People may try to obstruct you. We should be prepared for the worst: they may even threaten your life. You will report only to me. Should I fall out of favour and be unable to use my authority, or should I lose my life, then speak to the King on my behalf. You have the necessary access, since you hunt with him. This is a personal service I am asking of you, and I would be grateful if you would perform it with the rigour you have always demonstrated. Naturally, all this requires absolute secrecy.'

'Monsieur, I have a request to make.'

'You want Inspector Bourdeau to assist you? Your wish is granted. His past record speaks for him.'

'I'm very grateful. But I had something else in mind . . .'

Monsieur de Sartine appeared impatient, and Nicolas sensed that he had no desire to prolong an interview in which he had been forced to reveal a number of secrets and confess to a certain helplessness.

'I'm listening, but be quick.'

'You know my friend Dr Semacgus,' Nicolas said. 'He assisted me all night and, as we were looking over the victims who had been taken to La Madeleine cemetery, our attention was drawn to the body of a young woman who seems not to have been crushed or otherwise injured in last night's disaster, but strangled. I'd like to pursue the case.'

'I should have known! It would have surprised me if in the midst of so many dead bodies you hadn't managed to find one for your personal delectation! Why are so interested in this particular victim?'

'It could be, Monsieur, that one tragedy is being used to conceal another. Who knows?'

Sartine was thinking. Nicolas had the feeling that he had touched the right chord.

'And how do you propose to pursue this case, Commissioner?'

'I'd like Sanson to open up the corpse in the Basse-Geôle. We need to determine if the death occurred as the result of last night's disturbances or if it was a domestic crime. Finally, may I suggest that this investigation could usefully serve as a cover for the more discreet general investigation you wish me to conduct into the tragedy of Place Louis XV? No one will be able to see the wood for the trees.'

It was doubtless this last argument that swayed the Lieutenant General of Police.

'You present your case so skilfully that I cannot refuse you. Let us hope it doesn't drag you into one of those criminal imbroglios whose mysteries you love to complicate even further, so that we never know where they may lead us! With that, Monsieur, I bid you farewell. I suspect the King and Monsieur de Saint-Florentin are waiting to hear my explanations. After all, I'm supposed to be keeping order in the capital of the Kingdom.'

Nicolas smiled inwardly at this refrain. He had heard it many times before, whenever he had had to force Sartine's hand to let him loose on a case. Monsieur de Sartine turned on his heels and quickly walked out of the library, leaving Nicolas to reflect on the surprising things he had heard and the delicate mission with which he was now entrusted. For a moment he stood there, motionless, staring into space. By the time he got back to the stables, a coach was already speeding out of the building. Through the window he caught a glimpse of his chief's sharp profile, the very image of despondency. He had never seen him in such a state, he who was always so in control of his emotions, and so anxious not to lose face before his visitors. He seemed weighed down with anxiety, and it was not only, as a superficial observer might have supposed, because he feared for his position. Nicolas knew him too well to think that such selfish matters were all that preoccupied him. He had been wounded by the King's decision. That this decision had had fatal consequences the previous night merely increased his profound sense of abandonment. He was right to feel aggrieved by this absurd chain of events, so alien to his sense of duty and his total devotion to the monarch whom he had been serving selflessly for so many years. Sartine enjoyed the exceptional privilege of a weekly interview in the small apartments at Versailles, often in that secret study, which even those close to the King knew nothing about, where the monarch studied his agents' dispatches and reports. In one night, this whole world had come tumbling down like a house of cards. To Nicolas, it seemed as though the image of an infallible chief had disintegrated, to be replaced by that of an unhappy man, a man worthy of pity. This merely strengthened his own determination to see this thing through. Yes, he would do all he could to find those responsible for a tragedy which the city authorities should, in the normal course of events, have anticipated and avoided.

He chose a frisky young chestnut gelding, which stretched its slender head towards him, and had it saddled by a groom. The streets had recovered a little of their animation, but everyone still looked grim and groups were forming. The air, matching the mood of the day, was oppressive. Nicolas could feel his clothes sticking to his body, and his horse gave off a strong odour, as if it were overheated. Slate-blue storm clouds were gathering in the sky. It was almost dark by the time he rode in beneath the archway of the Grand Châtelet. As he was handing over the reins of his mount to the stable boy, a familiar voice hailed him.

'Ah, there's my Nicolas, in a hurry as usual!'

He recognised the individual who was addressing him with such familiarity as his fellow countryman, a Breton called Jean, better known on the streets by his nickname, 'Tirepot'. He was a singular character, a godsend to a populace deprived of privies. He carried two pails that hung from a bar resting across his shoulders. This contraption, hidden beneath a length of tarred canvas, allowed his customers to relieve themselves unseen. Nicolas often used the services of this friendly helper, who was always well informed.

'What's new, Jean? What are they saying this morning?'

'Oh, certainly not good things! Everyone's licking their wounds and mourning the dead. They're saying this marriage has got off to a bad start. They're blaming the watch and' – he lowered his voice – 'cursing the police and Monsieur de Sartine for not doing their job properly. People are complaining and gathering together, but things won't go far – the poor have seen it all before!'

'Is that all?'

The man scratched his head. 'I was in Place Louis XV, doing my job . . .'

'And?'

'I quickly put down my trinkets and lent a hand. I heard some things, I can tell you!'

'Really? What?'

'Men from the city accusing Sartine early this morning. According to them, he's to blame for the tragedy.'

'From the city, you say? Aldermen?'

'No. City Guards in all their finery. A lot of them were coming out of taverns, hardly able to stand, stinking so much of wine they could have killed flies with their breath. One big fat fellow, who seemed to be their officer, was urging them on, getting them all stirred up.'

Nicolas rewarded him with a crown, which Tirepot caught in mid-air, at the risk of dropping his pyramid.

'You could do something for me,' Nicolas said. 'Go back to the Saint-Honoré district and try to find out where those guards spent the night. As you can imagine, I'm really interested to know that.'

Tirepot winked, loaded everything onto his back, adjusted it and disappeared beneath the archway. For a long time his voice could be heard receding into the distance, yelling his insistent cry: 'Come one, come two, you all know what you need to do!'

Nicolas was still thinking about Tirepot's words as he entered the commissioners' duty office. Bourdeau sat slumped at the table with his head on his arms, snoring loudly. He looked at him tenderly. There was someone who never spared himself! He called Old Marie, the usher, who immediately fetched two cups of coffee liberally laced with Lambic beer, which he smuggled in and which smelled of cider apples. It was this smell that woke the inspector. He shook himself, seized one of the cups, and drank the coffee noisily because it was piping hot. A long silence followed.

'Methinks,' said Bourdeau, in a mockingly pompous tone, 'this coffee is merely an invitation to more solid refreshment.'

'Methinks,' Nicolas said, 'I'll follow you on that path. I've had nothing in my belly since midday yesterday except a brioche. I'm all ears. What do you propose?'

'The usual place we go when we're hungry and we don't have

much time, in Rue du Pied-de-Boeuf. I think that's the perfect choice.'

'I'm hungry, therefore I follow you. That's my *cogito* for this morning.'

'Especially as I've been to see Sanson,' Bourdeau went on. 'He'll join us in the Basse-Geôle on the stroke of noon for the opening of the corpse. Not something to watch on an empty stomach – it might give us the hiccups . . .'

He laughed, and Nicolas shuddered at the thought of this grim prospect. He agreed, though: opening a corpse was like a journey by sea – both required a full stomach.

Their usual tavern was only a short distance from the Châtelet. The proximity of the Grande Boucherie, although a source of sanies and foul odours, also offered the advantage of fresh products. As soon as they entered the low, smoky room, Bourdeau called to his old friend – they were both natives of a village near Chinon, in the Touraine – and asked him what the kitchen could offer them at that hour of the morning. The fat, ruddy-faced man smiled.

'What can I possibly serve you?' he said, giving Bourdeau a dig in the ribs that would have knocked over anyone less steady on his feet. 'Hmm . . . What do you say to a calf's breast pie? I just made one for a neighbour of mine who's christening his baby. I'll go and heat it up for you. With two pitchers of red wine from our region, as usual.'

Nicolas, who loved inside information, asked him the recipe for this promising-sounding dish.

'Only because it's you, Commissioner. Otherwise, I wouldn't say a word, even under torture. Here goes. You cut a decent piece of calf's breast – choose it well: it has to be plump and pearly. Then you cut it up into slices, which you lard with one or two pieces of fat. Make a crust pastry out of lard and lower it into the pie dish. Put in the slices of veal, after seasoning them with bacon, salt, pepper, cloves, nutmeg, herbs, bay, mushrooms and artichoke ends, and cover the whole thing with pastry. Two good hours in the oven. You take it out and, just before serving, you cut a little hole in the top and carefully pour in a white sauce made with lemon juice and egg yolks.'

'That seems to me perfectly adapted to the emptiness of our bellies,' said Bourdeau with a gleam in his eye and his lips all aquiver with anticipation.

'And, to whet your appetite, I'll serve cherries, the first of the year, cooked in cinnamon wine.'

'Ideal for a little eleven o'clock meal,' Nicolas said ingratiatingly.

A pitcher of purple wine was quickly brought. They drank many glasses, calming their raging hunger with a salad of beans mixed with slices of lard. Nicolas informed Bourdeau of the night's events as he and Semacgus had experienced them, as well as the gist of his interview with Monsieur de Sartine, emphasising the fact that it was their chief who had appointed the inspector to assist him in this delicate case.

'Let me see if I've got this right,' said Bourdeau, turning red with pleasure. 'We're going to concentrate on the case of the strangled girl in order to divert attention from what we're really up to.'

'Exactly. But the credibility of our alibi will depend on the result of the autopsy. The marks on her neck could have been caused by attempts to free the body from where it lay with the others.'

'I don't think so. Nothing in the state of her clothes or her appearance indicated that there had been any kind of struggle to free her.'

Nicolas was convinced that it was a good policeman's duty to obey his instincts. From snippets of information, sometimes unformulated impressions, clues, coincidences and assumptions, a policeman used his common sense to organise all the elements of a case. He needed an open mind, a good memory for precedents and the barely conscious ability to refer to a whole collection of human types and situations. Beneath his good-natured appearance, Bourdeau had all these qualities, as well as a remarkable sensitivity. How many times had one of his apparently innocuous remarks sent an investigation along a new line of inquiry which had not previously been explored in depth?

The smell of veal simmered in its spices drew Nicolas from his reflections. Carefully, their host placed his golden pie on the uneven wooden table. He disappeared, only to reappear immediately with a small pan that had seen better days, having been seasoned by hours of exposure in the oven. From it he took a sharp knife and nimbly cut a small hole in the pastry. Steam rose through it, enveloping them in its aroma. The innkeeper gently drizzled white sauce into this opening, so that it soon reached the smallest crannies of the pie. He put down his pan, picked up the dish, moved it from side to side, and set it down again. Nicolas and Bourdeau were already leaning forward when he stopped them.

'Go gently, my lambs, let the sauce do its work. It has to imbue the meat with its aroma and make it tender. The thing to remember is that I call it calf's breast pie, but to make it particularly mellow and plump I add a little cartilage. And the sauce! It'll make your mouth water! It's not like that miserable stuff that tastes like plaster, put together in a hurry by kitchen boys. It takes hours, gentlemen, for the flour to rise. I may be an insignificant little innkeeper, but I put my heart into my work, just like my great-grandfather, who was sauce chef to Gaston d'Orléans under the great Cardinal.'

Inspired no doubt by this glorious memory, he served them ceremoniously. The dish and its flavours lived up to his introduction. The hot crust, crisp with caramelised meat juices at the edges, enclosed meat perfectly tender from the sauce melted over it. They spent a long time savouring this piece of work so simply and eloquently presented. The cooked cherries were refreshing, acid and sweet at the same time. The two men were overcome with a pleasant drowsiness, made all the stronger by brandy served in porcelain bowls as a precautionary measure. They blissfully let this infringement of the regulations pass without comment. Their host had no licence to serve spirits, the sale of which was reserved for another guild. His modest business allowed him only to supply wines from the cask, not from sealed bottles. Bourdeau, always alert to detail, suddenly realised that they did not have any snuff. It was an old joke between them. They always resorted to snuff when attending autopsies, in order to blot out the musty smell of decomposition pervading the Basse-Geôle. The host obligingly lent them two earthen pipes reserved for his customers, and a proportionate amount of snuff.

Back at the Grand Châtelet, they went straight to the torture chamber adjoining the office of the clerk of the criminal court. It was in this sombre Gothic room, on one of its oak tables, that bodies were opened up. The operation was still fairly uncommon: the regular doctors attached to the court refused to perform it unless specifically ordered to do so and, even when that was the case, they did not follow the rules, thus rendering the examination imperfect and completely useless from the point of view of an investigation.

A man of Nicolas's age, dressed in a puce-coloured coat, breeches and black stockings, was laying surgical instruments out on a bench. They glittered in the torchlight. Daylight never entered this room: the casement windows were fitted with metal hoods to prevent screams being heard beyond the walls of the fortress. Charles Henri Sanson was an old acquaintance of Nicolas from his earliest days in Paris. They had begun their careers at about the same time, and both served the King's justice. An unexpected sympathy – one quite unhoped-for by Sanson – had drawn the young commissioner to this shy, temperate, highly cultured man. Nicolas always found it hard to imagine him as an executioner. He thought of him more as a doctor of crime. He knew that Sanson had been given no choice, but had been forced to take over the family profession. Nevertheless, he accomplished his terrible task with all the care of a compassionate man. Sanson turned, and his grave face lit up when he recognised Nicolas and Bourdeau.

'Greetings, gentlemen,' he said. 'I am at your disposal. My one regret is that the pleasure of seeing you again has only been afforded me by last night's tragedy.'

They shook hands, a custom on which Sanson always insisted, as if this simple gesture admitted him back into the community of the living. He smiled when they lit their pipes and started puffing on them. Semacgus suddenly made his entrance, and his ribald laughter introduced a touch of joviality into the heavy atmosphere of the crypt. The two professionals carefully lined up their instruments and examined them one by one, checking the cutting edges of the scalpels, scissors, stylets, straight knives and saws. They also put out curved needles, string, sponges, tenacula, a trepan, a wedge and a hammer. Nicolas and Bourdeau observed how precise their gestures were. At last they all gathered around the large table on which the unknown girl lay. Sanson nodded towards the commissioner and gestured towards the corpse.

'Whenever you wish, Monsieur.'

Nicolas began: 'We are in the presence of a body brought to La Madeleine cemetery on Thursday thirty-first May 1770, presumed to have perished in the disaster of Rue Royale.'

Bourdeau was taking the minutes.

'It was noticed by Commissioner Le Floch and Inspector Bourdeau on the stroke of six. Their attention was drawn by what were clearly marks of strangulation on the victim's neck. In these circumstances, the order was given to transport the body to the Basse-Geôle, where, at' – he consulted his watch before putting it back carefully in the fob of his coat – 'at half past twelve on the same day, Charles Henri Sanson, executioner to the viscountcy and generality of Paris, and Guillaume Semacgus, naval surgeon, proceeded to open it in the presence of said commissioner and inspector. First, the clothing and objects belonging to the victim were examined. A loose dress of good quality, with a straw-coloured satin bodice . . .'

Sanson and Semacgus undressed the body as Nicolas spoke.

'. . . A white silk corset, very tight over the hips, fitted with whalebones and laced at the back . . .'

The corset was in fact so tight that Semacgus had to use a penknife to cut the lace.

'. . . two petticoats, one of thin cotton and the other of silk, with two pockets sewn inside the first . . .'

He searched them.

'Empty. Stockings of grey yarn. No shoes. No other objects, no jewellery, no papers, no clues of any kind seen on the body. Apart from . . .'

Nicolas took a handkerchief from his pocket and carefully unfolded it.

'. . . apart from a black pearl of a mineral resembling obsidian, which was found in the victim's clenched hand when the corpse was discovered in La Madeleine cemetery. We seem to be in the presence of a young girl of about twenty, of slender constitution and with no distinguishing marks, except for those previously noted at the base of the neck. The mouth is twisted and the face contorted. The blonde hair is clean and very well groomed. The rest of the body is equally clean. Gentlemen, you may now proceed.'

Nicolas had turned to Sanson and Semacgus. The two

practitioners approached and meticulously examined the pitiful, recumbent body. They turned it over, observed the purplish tinges on its back, then laid it flat again. Nodding, Semacgus passed his hand over the stomach and looked at Sanson, who bent to do the same. He turned to pick up a probe for a more intimate examination.

'You're right, there's no doubt about it.'

'The clues speak for themselves, my dear colleague,' Semacgus said, 'though we'll know more after we've opened her up.'

Nicolas looked at both of them questioningly.

'This maiden of yours,' Semacgus said, 'was a maiden no longer. In fact, there's every indication that she had already given birth. Further observations are sure to confirm that.'

Sanson now also nodded. 'It's beyond dispute. The disappearance of the hymen proves it, even though some authors say this is not infallible proof. In addition, the fourchette is torn, as is almost always the case in women who have had a child.' He again bent over the body. '*Gravis odor puerperii.* There's no doubt about it, labour only took place a few days ago, and perhaps even more recently than that. These stretch marks on the stomach show how distended it was.'

'Not to mention this brownish line from the pubis to the umbilicus,' said Semacgus, pointing at what he was describing. As for the swollen breasts, they also speak for themselves. We still have to do a detailed examination. Hold her head steady.'

'Notice,' said Sanson, 'that the joint with the first cervical vertebra lacks normal mobility.'

Nicolas tensed as the scalpel entered the flesh. It was always the same: at first, you found it hard to watch, and you would drag desperately at your pipe or frantically take snuff, but gradually your profession would gain the upper hand over the horror of the spectacle. Curiosity was a strong incentive to succeed, to shed light on the shadowy areas of a case. The body was no longer a human being who had lived, but the object of precise, painstaking labour, with its strange sounds and its colours uncovered by the stylet or the probe. It was an unknown world in which the body was a machine, and the inner drama of a life was offered up for view like meat on a stall before the corruption of the flesh obliterated everything.

Without exchanging a single word, understanding one another by look and gesture only, the hangman and the naval surgeon proceeded. Then, after what seemed like a long time, they put everything back in its place. The incisions were sewn up, the body was cleaned and wrapped in a large sheet which, once closed, was sealed with wax by Nicolas. When they had finished, they rubbed their hands with vinegar, and carefully dried them, still in silence: neither wanted to be the first to speak.

'Monsieur,' Semacgus said at last, 'you are at home here. I won't encroach on your jurisdiction.'

'Unofficially, Monsieur, unofficially. I consent, but don't hesitate to interrupt me. Please do me the honour of supplementing my words.'

Semacgus bowed. 'I shall, with your permission.'

Sanson assumed that modest, calm air of his, which made Nicolas think of a Lenten preacher.

'I know, Commissioner, that you would like to obtain as quickly as possible the information which will be of most use to your investigation. I think you will benefit from what we have been able to ascertain. Let me therefore sum up the basic points.'

He took a deep breath and folded his hands.

'We have here a member of the female sex, about twenty years of age . . .'

'Quite pretty, by the way,' Semacgus murmured.

'Firstly, we ascertained that she had been strangled. The state of her trachea, the contusions and internal haematoma due to loss of blood – everything clearly pointed to that. Secondly, the victim recently gave birth to a child, although we are unable to fix a precise date.'

'Undoubtedly no more than two or three days ago,' said Semacgus. 'That much is clear from the state of the organs, the breasts and other details of which I shall spare you the description.'

'And, thirdly, it is difficult to ascertain the exact time of death. Nevertheless, the condition of the body encourages me to make a cautious estimate: between seven and eight o'clock yesterday evening.'

'In addition,' Semacgus said, 'when we cleaned the body, we found . . . some traces of hay.'

He opened his hand. Nicolas took the strands of hay and put them in his handkerchief next to the mysterious black pearl.

'Where did you find them?' he asked.

'More or less everywhere, but especially in the hair, which is why they were not noticed, given that the subject's hair is long and fair.'

Nicolas was thinking. As always when he wanted to get to the bottom of things, he resolved to play the devil's advocate.

'Is it possible, even if the time of death were much earlier than the tragedy in Place Louis XV, that you could be mistaken – forgive me – and that the wound to the neck, the apparent cause of death, was due to the removal of the body?'

'No,' Sanson replied. 'We're positive that the wound was inflicted prior to death, and was indeed the cause of it. I shan't bore you with details, but the evidence is irrefutable. And the clothes are intact, which would be unlikely if the opposite were the case.'

Semacgus expanded on this. 'It would also be hard to explain the facial expression and the presence of black blood in the lungs.'

'From what you can see, was the labour normal?' Bourdeau asked. 'In other words, is there any possibility that there was an attempt at abortion?'

'Hard to say. The folds in the skin of the abdomen are undoubtedly similar to those found on a woman who has given birth. However, the marks resulting from a late abortion are generally the same as those following labour, especially when the pregnancy is advanced.'

'So,' Bourdeau concluded, 'there's nothing to prove that there wasn't a late abortion?'

'That's right,' Sanson said.

Nicolas began thinking aloud. 'Were we right to move the corpse and perform this unofficial procedure? If we'd left her where we found her, a spy could have stayed there and informed us if anyone recognised her. We may have interfered with the normal order of things and made our task more complicated . . .'

Bourdeau reassured him: 'We'd have arrived on her family's doorsteps with our accusations, and can you imagine the fuss they would have made? Forget about an autopsy! They'd simply have told us she was crushed in the disaster. And, what's more, we wouldn't even have known the poor girl had given birth! I prefer the truth I find for myself to the truth other people expect me to believe.'

This vigorous outburst dispelled Nicolas's doubts.

'And besides,' Bourdeau concluded, 'as my father, who looked after the dogs for the King's boar hunts, would have said, at least now we can be sure we won't mistake the front of the prey for the back. Still, the case doesn't look as if it's going to be easy.'

'My friends,' Nicolas said, 'how can I thank you for all the useful information you've given me and for the light you've thrown on this case.' Then, addressing Sanson, 'I'm sure you know that Monsieur de Noblecourt has long wanted you to dine with him, and you've long refused.'

'Monsieur Nicolas,' said Sanson, 'the mere fact that he has thought of me is a great honour, which fills me with joy and gratitude. Perhaps a time will come when I can accept.'

He left Semacgus and Sanson deep in an animated discussion on the comparative merits of Beckeri[4] and Bauzmann,[5] two precursors of the new science of forensic medicine. The commissioner and his deputy walked in pensive silence to the gateway of the Grand Châtelet. The storm had finally broken, and the roadway was inundated with streams of muddy water carrying rubbish along with them. Bourdeau sensed that something was troubling Nicolas.

At last the commissioner spoke. 'There's one thing that puzzles me,' he said. 'Why did the young woman lace up her corset so tightly?'

III

THE DEUX CASTORS

The past is gone, the future yet lacks breath,
The present languishes 'twixt life and death
J.-B. CHASSIGNET (1594)

Nicolas whistled for a cab. They had to get back to Place Louis
XV, more specifically to the place where the corpses had been
gathered together, to find a grief-stricken family searching for a
young girl – or young woman, although the corpse lying in its
sack at the Basse-Geôle bore no ring.

Their carriage reached Rue Saint-Honoré by way of the *quais*
and the cesspools of Rue du Petit-Bourbon and Rue des Poulies,
which ran alongside the old Louvre. Nicolas looked out at these
foul clusters of hovels, so close to the palaces of the kings and so
conducive to every sickness of body and mind.

The western end of Rue Saint-Honoré consisted of a long row
of shops selling fashion, shops which dictated style in the city. At
the beginning of each season, the master artisans of this luxury
trade dispatched porcelain dummies all the way to distant
Muscovy in the north and to the very interior of the Grand Turk's
seraglio in the south. These dummies bore the latest wigs and
were carefully dressed in the season's novelties. The other half of
the street, towards La Halle, was given over to more down-to-

earth pleasures, such as the Hôtel d'Aligre, a celebrated temple of delicacies, which had been open for a year, its window filled with hams and *andouilles*. One evening, Bourdeau had given him a fashionable new *ragout* to taste: *choucroute* from Strasbourg. This dish, which was now much in demand, had won acclaim from the Faculty, which had declared it 'refreshing, a cure for scurvy, producing a refined, milky liquid that makes the blood bright red and temperate'. The establishment's trout *au bleu* came directly from Geneva in their own *court-bouillon*, and rumour had it – a rumour confirmed by Monsieur de la Borde – that the King himself sometimes delayed his dinner if this special delivery was late in arriving at Versailles.

Already the wet slate roofs of the Capuchin monastery near the Orangerie flashed grey on their left. The fiacre turned into Rue de Chevilly, then briefly into Rue de Suresnes, and at last neared the cemetery belonging to the parish of La Madeleine. Here, it slowed down, blocked by a dense, silent, grim-looking crowd, which was itself barred from the parish and its dependencies by a cordon of French Guards. Nicolas banged with his fist on the front of the box to stop the vehicle and stepped out. A man in a magistrate's black robe, whom he recognised as Monsieur Mutel, Commissioner of the Palais-Royal district, came forward and shook his hand. The two men with him bowed. One was Monsieur Puissant, the police official responsible for performances and lighting, and the other was his deputy, Monsieur Hochet de la Terrie. Both were old acquaintances.

'My dear colleague,' Mutel said. 'These gentlemen and I have been organising the identification of the bodies. There's so little space that, if we let it, the crowd would come rushing in and we'd have a new disaster on our hands. I assume Monsieur de Sartine has sent you to help us?'

'Not exactly, although we are at your disposal. We're here to carry out a preliminary investigation following a suspicious death noted last night. We need to consult . . . I assume you have lists?'

'We have three. A list of bodies having means of identification on them, a second list of those already identified by their nearest and dearest and a final list with descriptions of missing persons to help our assistants try to find the relative or friend in question. But the faces are often terribly disfigured, which makes it quite difficult to recognise anyone. What's more, there's a storm brewing and we won't be able to preserve the bodies for too long . . . Even the Basse-Geôle couldn't contain them all!'

The commissioner came closer to Nicolas and, in a low voice, enquired after Monsieur de Sartine's state of health.

'Well, you know him, my dear fellow, *simplicitas ac modestiae imagine in altitudinem conditus studiumque litterarum at amorem carminum simulans, quo uelaret animium.*[1] But without touching his wigs . . .'

Both men were fond of the classics, and occasionally, when they needed to be discreet, they enjoyed conversing with the help of Latin quotations.

'*Bene*, that's certainly an interesting symptom! I'm reassured, though. This is a grave crisis, but he'll get through it. The truth will out, and sooner rather than later. We just have to let the stupid and the envious stew in their own juice!' He winked. 'Don't worry, anything I find out about last night's incompetence I'll pass on to you.'

Nicolas smiled and made an evasive gesture with his hand. His brilliant entry into the corps of commissioners at the Châtelet in 1761 had impressed his colleagues. By now, most had learnt to appreciate him for his particular qualities and readily opened their hearts to him about their problems, confident that he would be able to bring pressure to bear on the Lieutenant General. Without exaggerating his natural charm, Nicolas had been able to honour some of the older veterans with his services.

The registers had been laid out in the church. All around them rose the cries and weeping of the families. They shared the task among themselves. After a moment, the inspector pointed out a line to him.

'. . . a frail young girl,' Nicolas read aloud, 'in a pale yellow satin dress, fair hair, blue eyes, aged nineteen . . .'

He questioned the police officer who was keeping the register.

'This entry is at the end. It can't have been long since these particulars were given. Do you remember the person who gave them?'

'Yes, Commissioner, it was only a quarter of an hour ago. A gentleman of about forty, accompanied by a young man. He was looking for his niece. He seemed in a very emotional state and gave me a seal from his shop so that we could reach him in case we found the girl.'

He noted the number of the entry and looked through a cardboard box in which various papers were being stored. 'Let's see . . . number seventy-three . . . Here we are!' He took out a leaflet. 'At the sign of the Deux Castors, Rue Saint-Honoré, Paris, opposite the Opéra. Charles Galaine, furrier, manufacturer and purveyor of furs, muffs and coats.' The girl's name was apparently Élodie Galaine.

The decorative seal showed two beavers facing each other. Their tails framed an engraving representing a man in a fur coat and hat reaching out his hands towards a fire. The commissioner wrote down the address in pencil in his little black notebook.

'Let's not waste time,' he said. 'We'll go straight there.'

As they were getting back into their carriage, Tirepot appeared and held Nicolas back by a button of his coat.

'Here's what I can tell you. The City Guards were having a merry time of it last night. They happily got through a lot of bottles in the taverns round about, celebrating their new uniforms. They went to lots of different places, but in particular to the Dauphin Couronné. La Paulet will be able to tell you more. She asked me to tell you and Monsieur Bourdeau that she waited for you, that your food got spoilt, but that she realised what was happening. She went on and on about a piece of news she said was sure to please you. She's expecting you tonight at about ten; it'll be worth your while . . .'

Nicolas was once more about to climb into the carriage when Tirepot again detained him.

'Not so fast! Have a look at what they've been hiring people to distribute. The city lot are behind this. I heard from a proofreader who was using my convenience that it was produced in a work-shop that prints adjudication announcements for the aldermen. Sorry about the state of it!'

He handed the commissioner a stained poster. Nicolas threw him a coin, which he made as if to refuse, while seizing it in mid-air. The lampoon was crude and obscene. Its target was Monsieur de Sartine and beyond him, the First Minister, Choiseul. They certainly were not losing any time at the Hôtel de Ville, thought

Nicolas. As a loyal subject of the King and a magistrate, he was shocked by these accusations. Not that he wasn't used to such hate-filled writings: he had been hunting them down for ten years, under two royal mistresses. He kept seizing them and destroying them in disgust, but the hydra possessed a hundred heads and was constantly reborn.

Their carriage set off and again went through the cordon of French Guards. Nicolas had the coachman ask an officer for permission to go along Rue Royale. The cab slowly moved those few hundred fateful yards. Nothing remained of the previous night's tragedy except for scraps of clothing and scattered shoes, which would soon provide a harvest for the second-hand clothes dealers. The rain that had fallen during the storm was gradually erasing the brown stains on the ground. In the crude afternoon light, the immediate causes of the tragedy were like so many accusing witnesses: trenches, blocks of stone, the unfinished street. Place Louis XV was emerging from the disaster, and teams had already started to clear the remains of the structure from which the fireworks had been launched. The ambassadors' mansion and the Garde-Meuble stood resplendent in all their hieratic solemnity. The wind was chasing away the last miasmas of the night. Tomorrow, everything would be back to normal, as if nothing had happened. And yet Nicolas could still hear the cries of agony. As they went past the Garde-Meuble and along Passage de l'Orangerie to Rue Saint-Honoré, he thought with anguish of how the evening's merriment had turned sour. Before long, their carriage stopped near the corner of Rue de Valois, outside a fine-looking shop with the sign of the Deux Castors. The window, in its frame of carved wood, displayed scenes of trappers and savages hunting animals native to the various continents. The glass was protected by a grille with gilded points in the shape of pine cones. Through it, in the gloom of the shop, a number of stuffed animals could be seen. Nicolas pointed out some naked dummies to Bourdeau.

'At the end of spring, the hides and garments are taken down into cool cellars fumigated with herbs to protect them from insects.'

'You're very knowledgeable about these things. Some lovely lady, I suppose . . .'

'And you're very nosy . . .'

A small bell tinkled as he opened the door. They were struck by a strong smell, which reminded Nicolas of a certain wardrobe in the Château de Ranreuil in which, as a child, he had often played, burying his face in the fur clothes that belonged to his godfather, the marquis. A brown-haired woman stood by the light oak counter. She was still young, wore a grey taffeta dress with large lace oversleeves, and was studying a piece of paper with a stern expression on her face. She lifted her head – Nicolas admired her pale complexion – and looked angrily at a young girl, little more than a child, in a maid's cap and apron, who was shrinking into herself, her head lowered like someone caught in the act. The girl had an angular, unprepossessing face and the mulish expression of a small, hunted animal. The two men approached in silence.

'Miette, my girl, either someone stole it from you or you stole it yourself.'

'But, Madame . . .' the girl moaned.

'Quiet, you hussy, you're getting on my nerves!'

While the maid fiddled with a corner of her apron, the woman's eyes came to rest on the girl's feet.

'Where have you been? Look at your shoes . . . Your face is dirty, your clothes are a mess! Who would think, in a respectable house – ' Suddenly she noticed Nicolas. 'Get out of my sight, you wicked girl! Gentlemen, to what do I owe your visit? We have some wonderful bargains at this time of year. Hats, pelisses, cloaks, muffs. Buy now for the autumn. Or else, for your lady, a fresh consignment of sables just in from the North. I'll call my husband, Monsieur Galaine – he can tell you everything you need to know about his hides.'

The woman disappeared through a side door with bevelled glass panels.

'There's someone who's not too worried about her niece!' Bourdeau muttered.

'Let's not jump to conclusions,' said Nicolas in a conciliatory tone. 'We're still not sure who the unknown girl is. The lady simply has a good head for business.' He always guarded against first impressions, even though experience told him they were often accurate.

The lady in question reappeared and invited them into a kind of office. Behind a wooden table, covered in samples of hides, were two men. Both seemed on their guard. The older of the two was sitting with his arms folded. The other stood leaning with one hand on the back of the armchair. Nicolas, alert as ever to fleeting impressions, detected a smell he knew well, the kind given off by an animal at bay or a suspect during interrogation. This smell, imperceptible to anyone other than him, was super-imposed on the acrid stench of furs pervading the shop. There

66

was something about the two men that did not suggest honest merchants getting ready to vaunt the quality of their merchandise. The older of the two was the first to speak.

'You gentlemen no doubt wish to take advantage of our bargains? I have some articles here which might interest—'

Nicolas interrupted him: 'Are you Charles Galaine the furrier? Did you go to La Madeleine cemetery this morning and leave a description of your niece, Élodie Galaine, aged nineteen?'

He saw the man's hand tighten so much that it turned white. 'That's correct, Monsieur . . .?'

'Nicolas Le Floch, commissioner at the Châtelet. This is my deputy, Inspector Bourdeau.'

'Do you have news of my niece?'

'I'm sorry to have to inform you that I myself found a body answering the description you gave to a police officer at La Madeleine cemetery. It would therefore be advisable, Monsieur, if you could come with me to the Grand Châtelet to help identify the body in question. The sooner, the better.'

'My God! How is it possible? But why to the Grand Châtelet?'

'There were so many victims that some have been transported to the Basse-Geôle.'

The younger man bowed his head. He looked like his father but with softer features; small, deep-set blue eyes; a broad nose and light chestnut hair. He was biting the inside of his cheek. His father, whose features were more virile, showed no particular emotion, apart from two beads of sweat at his temples, just below his wig. They were both wearing light-brown coats.

'My son Jean and I will go with you.'

'Our carriage is at your disposal.'

As all four were leaving, a large, mannish-looking woman in a chenille,[2] her head bare and her features distorted, threw herself at the merchant, grabbed the lapel of his coat and harangued him in a shrill tone.

'Charles, tell me everything. Where is our bird, our beauty? Who are these people? You're hiding something, aren't you? This is unbearable. We've never counted for anything in this house, unlike . . . It'll be the death of me, yes, the death of me.'

Charles Galaine pushed her away gently and sat her down on a chair. She burst into tears.

'Forgive her, gentlemen. My elder sister, Charlotte, is upset by her niece's disappearance.'

He turned to his wife, who was watching the scene impassively. 'Émilie, give our sister a little orange blossom water. I'm going with these gentlemen; I shan't be long.'

Émilie Galaine shrugged her shoulders, but did not say a word. They left and got into the cab. Whether because he wished to spare his family's feelings, or because he was indifferent, Nicolas noted that Monsieur Galaine had said nothing of where they were going. He assumed that Madame Galaine was his second wife: how else could she have a son only a few years younger than herself? All the same, her indifference was quite surprising. As for the son, he could barely conceal his anxiety – which might be brotherly concern or might just as easily be something else. The father, on the other hand, was controlling himself to perfection, which made him seem rather insensitive to the possibility that one of his nearest and dearest had died. In truth, Nicolas knew nothing about the family. This investigation had already provoked a great many questions. But the priority was to identify the body. A heavy silence descended on the carriage. Nicolas, sitting opposite the son, saw him mechanically picking at the upholstery on the door. Bourdeau pretended to doze, but in fact he was observing Charles Galaine through half-closed eyes. The merchant sat motionless, staring obstinately into space.

As soon as they reached the Grand Châtelet, things moved quickly. Leaning on his son's arm, Charles Galaine hesitantly descended the stone staircase to the old prison. All at once they were face to face with the sheet which Nicolas had sealed that very morning, and which had been carried in from the adjoining cellar. The commissioner removed the sheet from the dead girl's face, then turned his back on the visitors. He heard a dull thud: the son had fainted. Old Marie was called. He poured a few drops of his usual revulsive between the young man's lips, and for good measure gave him a couple of hearty slaps. The treatment was effective: the younger Galaine came to his senses with a sigh. The usher took him up to the courtyard for a little air. Charles Galaine made as if to follow, but Nicolas stopped him.

'Please, Monsieur. Old Marie knows what he's doing; he's seen it all before. He'll take care of your son. The important thing right now is that you confirm to me this girl's identity.'

The merchant looked at the body with alarm, his eyes wide open and his lips quivering. 'Yes, Monsieur, this is, alas, my niece Élodie. How terrible! But how am I going to tell my sisters? They were so fond of her. She was like their own child.'

'Your sisters?'

'Charlotte, my older sister, whom you've met, and Camille, my younger sister.'

They went back to the duty office where Monsieur Galaine's identification was duly written down by Bourdeau.

'Monsieur,' said Nicolas, 'I have a painful duty to discharge. It falls to me to inform you that Mademoiselle Édolie Galaine, your niece, was not crushed during the disaster in Rue Royale. She was murdered.'

'Murdered! What do you mean? What are you saying? Why would you add an extra burden to a relative already devastated by such terrible news? Murdered? Our Élodie? Murdered? My brother's daughter . . .'

As a great lover of the theatre, Nicolas judged the tone false. A noble father's indignation was a common feature of the current repertoire and was very familiar to him.

'What I mean,' he said, more curtly, 'is that an examination of the body' – Nicolas avoided the shocking word 'autopsy' – 'proves beyond doubt that this girl, or woman, was strangled. Was she married? Engaged?'

He had no intention of mentioning the victim's condition, preferring to keep that card up his sleeve, ready to play it when the moment was right. Galaine's reaction convinced him of the rightness of this decision.

'Married! Engaged! You're out of your mind, Monsieur. She was a child!'

'Monsieur, I'm going to have to ask you a few questions. There are certain things we need to confirm. We know for a fact that a crime has been committed, and the procedure will be set in motion as soon as I have presented my conclusions to the King's Procurator, who will then refer the case to the Criminal Lieutenant.'

'But, Monsieur, my family, my wife . . . I must tell them . . .'

'That's out of the question. When did you last see your niece?'

Monsieur Galaine seemed to have come to terms with the situation. He reflected for a moment.

'As a member of the furriers' guild – one of the great trade associations, as you know – I'd been invited to the city festivities. We first met at the house of one of our number, near Pont Neuf. I saw my niece that morning. In the evening, she was due to go to Place Louis XV to see the firework display with my sisters and our maid, Miette. As for me, I got to the square rather late, when the crowd was already very large. In the crush I was separated from my colleagues. I was trapped beside the swing bridge in the Tuileries, and I looked on as the disaster developed. Then I helped with the search for victims until early this morning. When I got home, I was informed of my niece's disappearance, and I set off for La Madeleine cemetery.'

'Right,' said Nicolas. 'Let's go through that in order. What time did you get to Place Louis XV?'

'I couldn't say for certain. We were quite merry, having drunk a few bottles during our banquet. It must have been about seven.'

'Could the other members of your guild confirm your presence at that banquet?'

'You only have to ask them: Monsieur Chastagny, Monsieur Levirel and Monsieur Botigé.'

Nicolas turned to Bourdeau. 'Take the addresses, we'll check. Did you meet any other acquaintances during the night?'

'It was so dark and there was so much excitement that it was almost impossible to recognise anyone.'

'One more thing. Do you have any idea how your niece died?'

Monsieur Galaine looked up, and an expression of something like bewilderment crept over his face. 'What am I supposed to say to that? You haven't told me anything about the circumstances of her death. All I saw was her face.'

It had been a deliberate ploy on Nicolas's part to only uncover the dead girl's face thereby concealing the marks of strangulation on her neck. 'All in good time, Monsieur. I simply wanted to know what you felt. One more point and we're finished. When you got back to Rue Saint-Honoré early this morning – about six, I think you said – who was in the house? Naturally, your answer will help us to draw up a list of occupants.'

'My son Jean, my two sisters, Camille and Charlotte, my daughter Geneviève, who's still a child, Marie the cook, our maid Miette and . . .'

It did not escape Nicolas's notice that he hesitated a moment before continuing.

'My wife and also . . . the savage.'

'The savage?'

'I see I'm going to have to explain. Twenty-five years ago, at our father's request, my older brother, Claude Galaine, went and settled in New France. The idea was to dispense with middle men and buy furs directly from the trappers and the natives. That way we reduced our expenses and were able to lower our prices in Paris, where there's fierce competition in the field of luxury goods. But I'm straying from the point. My brother got married on Île Royale, also known as Louisbourg, in 1749.'

Now that Galaine was talking shop, he had become a great deal calmer.

'The English attacks on our colonies grew more frequent. My

brother decided to return to France with his family. His daughter Élodie was just a baby. He obtained a passage on a vessel in the squadron of Admiral Dubois de La Motte, but it was attacked and in the confusion he was separated from his daughter. The return voyage was a disaster. Decimated by illness, ten thousand sailors died before the squadron reached Brest.[3] My brother and my sister-in-law did not escape this calamity. My niece, though, survived, and a year and a half ago she was brought back to me by an Indian servant carrying a copy of her birth and baptism certificates. For seventeen years she had been raised by nuns. Since then, she's been like a daughter to me.'

'And what about this native? What's his name?'

'Naganda. He's from the Micmac tribe.[4] He's a sly one; I don't know what to do with him. Just imagine, he got it into his head that he would sleep across the doorway of my niece's room! As if she had anything to fear from our family! We had to put him in the attic.'

'Presumably he's still there?'

'It's perfectly all right for him, though I'd have preferred to put him in the cellar.'

'I imagine that's where you keep the hides,' said Nicolas curtly.

'I see you know the demands of my trade.'

'I'm going to ask you to step into the antechamber. I need to speak to your son.'

'Couldn't I stay? He's a very sensitive boy, and I'm sure he's very upset about his cousin's death.'

'Don't worry, you'll see him soon enough.'

Bourdeau accompanied the witness into the room next to the office of the Lieutenant General of Police, and returned with

Jean Galaine. The young man was very pale and was sweating profusely. Nicolas knew from frequent observation that excessive sweating denoted an imbalance of humours, but that it could also be produced by exhaustion or anxiety. When Nicolas told him his cousin had been murdered, he grew even paler, and for a long time he was speechless.

'Are you Jean Galaine, son of Charles Galaine, master furrier, residing in Rue Saint-Honoré?' Nicolas asked at last. 'How old are you?'

'I'll be twenty-three on Saint Michel's day.'

'Do you work in your father's shop?'

'Yes. I've been learning the trade. I'll be taking his place one day.'

'What were you doing last night?'

'Walking on the boulevards, looking at the fair.'

'What time was that?'

'From six till late at night.'

'Weren't you interested in the firework display?'

'I'm scared of crowds.'

'There were plenty of crowds on the boulevards. Can anyone testify to having seen you last night?'

'About midnight I had a few glasses of beer near Porte Saint-Martin, with some friends.'

'What are their names?'

'They were just casual friends. I don't know their names. I'd drunk a lot.' He took out a huge handkerchief and wiped his brow.

'Indeed? And was there a particular reason why you were so thirsty?'

'That's my business.'

Despite his mild appearance, Nicolas thought, this young man was proving to be distinctly uncooperative.

'You are aware that we are dealing with a murder and that the smallest detail may be of major importance? Do you have an alibi?'

'What does that mean?'

Nicolas was struck by his interest in the detail while being apparently unconcerned about the overall picture.

'An alibi, Monsieur, is proof of someone's presence in a place other than where a crime has been committed.'

'So that means you know when and where my cousin was killed.'

The young man was certainly demonstrating an unassailable logic and a great deal of composure. He was perceptive and quick-witted, and probably a lot craftier than he had at first appeared.

'That's not the question here. You'll learn these details in due course. Let's get back to your whereabouts last night. What time did you return home?'

'About three in the morning.'

'Are you quite sure of that?'

'My stepmother can confirm it for you. A cab dropped her off and she got into an argument with the coachman. He was telling her that at three in the morning the fare was double. Then . . .' He bit his lip. 'Nothing that would interest you.'

'Everything is of interest to the police, Monsieur. Does it have some connection with your stepmother's late return? You won't tell me? That's up to you, but we'll find out everything in the end, believe you me.'

The interrogation could have been pursued, but Nicolas was impatient to learn more about this family. The young man could wait.

They rode back to Rue Saint-Honoré in grim silence. Nicolas was going over the answers the two Galaines had given him. He was surprised at their lack of curiosity about the circumstances of their relative's death. The father had not insisted, and the son had asked no questions. It was nearly six by the time the carriage stopped outside the Deux Castors. Nicolas had forbidden the two men to converse with the other members of the family, and had decided to lock them in the office. He had to strike while the iron was hot, without giving any of them the opportunity to consult each other or to agree on a story. It occurred to him for a moment that he might be jumping the gun. After all, there was nothing to indicate that he was dealing with a domestic crime, with one of the Galaine family as the culprit. And yet his intuition told him that this was the right way to go, and the mystery of a hidden or aborted child strengthened that belief. Unless he was attempting to conceal his niece's dishonour, the uncle showed no sign of being aware of the situation.

Was it a question of honour? Nicolas Le Floch had often had to deal with matters of family honour during his career in the police force. Among the nobility, an arrogant obsession with the purity of the blood could lead the finest souls astray. Was he not himself the bastard child of this outdated concept? In bourgeois houses, too, honour was invoked whenever there was any offence against the rules of civility, any transgression of the established order, any possibility of censure from prying neighbours that could lead to a whole family being tarnished for the sins of one of its members. Was that what had happened here? Some magistrates issued warrants for arbitrary arrests in broad daylight. From this point of view, the *lettre de cachet* was an advance, for it was only issued once every precaution had been taken to avoid scandal. Whereas a judicial arrest inevitably caused a fuss, a *lettre de cachet* preserved a family's honour, as the wrongdoer was removed from the world, and his or her ignominy disappeared into some secret dungeon or convent cell. The family whose honour had been offended allowed the Lieutenant General of Police to pry into its secrets, and in return the King buried the sin forever. Had Élodie Galaine died because of an exaggerated conception of honour? Had someone been so perverse as to prefer her death to her salvation?

Bourdeau roused him from his reflections. The carriage had stopped outside the Deux Castors, where a crowd was milling about before the window. A police officer known to Nicolas was barring the door to an angry group of women who had been joined by a throng of onlookers. Nicolas jumped out and elbowed his way through the crowd to ask the officer what was going on.

'What's happened, Commissioner, is that a maid from this house, a skinny young girl, ran out half-naked, in fact naked as the day she was born. And there she was, jumping, shaking, falling to the floor, foaming at the mouth and screaming! People gathered to look, some laughing, some concerned. I got here just in time to stop these women stoning her as if she were a mad dog. That was a whole other story. She was as stiff as a piece of wood and tried to bite me. God be praised, her mistress brought out a blanket, and we rolled her in it, took her inside and put her to bed, where she fell asleep.'

The crowd was yelling more loudly than ever. A stout woman shoved Nicolas out of the way with her stomach. Hands on hips, she harangued the crowd.

'Is it any surprise they want to stop us drowning the witch? Are you planning to stand in our way? Don't think we haven't recognised you – you're Sartine's henchman!'

'That's enough!' cried Nicolas. 'Be quiet, woman, or you'll end up in the Hôpital.[5] As for the rest of you, I order you in the name of the King and the Lieutenant General of Police to disperse immediately, or else . . .'

Impressed by Nicolas's authority, backed up as it was by Bourdeau's robust presence, the crowd withdrew, although not before greeting this mention of Monsieur de Sartine with jeers, which gave Nicolas pause for thought. The two policemen escorted Charles and Jean Galaine from the carriage and into the shop. They were met by Madame Galaine, looking very pale in the candlelight. There ensued a silent scene during which Bourdeau pushed the men into the office, while Nicolas turned to the woman.

'Madame . . .'

'Monsieur, I must see my husband immediately.'

'Later, Madame. He has identified the body of your niece by marriage. She was murdered.'

Émilie Galaine showed no reaction. In the flickering light of the candles, her face remained impassive. What did this absence of feeling mean? Nicolas had occasionally encountered such self-possession before, and knew that it often concealed great emotion.

'Madame, can you account for how you spent yesterday?'

'There's no point in questioning me, Commissioner, I have nothing to say. I went out, I came back.'

'Madame, that doesn't tell me much. Do you expect me to be satisfied with that?'

'I don't care – that's all you're going to get from me.' The colour was returning to her face, as if the blood had begun circulating more quickly beneath her skin. 'You've come into this family to bring us bad luck. I've answered your question: I went out; I came back. There's no point insisting.'

'Madame, it is my duty to warn you that as soon as a case of homicide has been referred to the Criminal Lieutenant in charge of criminal investigations, the King's justice will be able to use various means to make you talk, whether you like it or not.'

He was aware of the futility of what he was saying. He had never believed in torture. His long conversations with Sanson and Semacgus had convinced him that confessions obtained under torture were worse than useless, since those who made them would say anything to save their lives.

'What happened to your maid?' he resumed. 'Do you refuse to answer questions about that, too?'

She nodded stubbornly.

'Very well. Would you be so kind as to call your sisters-in-law? I want to question them. Perhaps *they*'ll talk. As for you, I'd like you to go into your husband's office.'

Émilie Galaine walked to the far end of the room and abruptly pulled open a door to reveal two women huddled behind it, clearly eavesdropping. Nicolas recognised the taller of the two as

Charlotte, the elder sister, who was biting a handkerchief as if to stop screaming.

With her head down, the shorter of the two trotted up to him. She was dressed in plain, dark colours, combining black lace and jade necklaces. She looked like her elder sister, but her features were stretched more tightly over her withered face. With her thin lips, she smiled humbly, but this humility was somewhat belied by the mobility of her grey, prying, unfriendly eyes. Her dull hair had been laboriously arranged into powdered curls – a hairstyle that seemed to have no connection with her overall appearance, which was as unattractive as could be imagined.

'Commissioner,' she said quickly, 'we heard everything. Oh, my God, is it possible? As I was telling my older sister, that's her behind me, looking so upset . . . Anyway, as I was telling her, she should have got dressed earlier, but everything's upside down . . . Imagine, Monsieur, the cat is so old and infirm, it usually keeps close to the edge . . . But let's keep to the point. I don't think those furs should have been taken down so early. Did you notice how late winter was this year? And how much it rained? . . . That unfortunate marriage which caused us so much unhappiness. What can he do, poor man? Always led . . .'

Nicolas was struck dumb by this uninterrupted flow of words, which was so incoherent as to make him doubt Camille Galaine's sanity. The elder sister, her hair as dishevelled as when they had first met, was dressed in brighter clothes, but they were dirty, creased and torn.

'Please, Mademoiselle, calm down. As you heard, I need to question you about the circumstances surrounding your niece's unlawful death. And I have to speak to the two of you separately.'

Charlotte began crying and sniffling more loudly. The door to the office opened and Bourdeau put his head round it, looking panic-stricken. Nicolas made a sign to him that all was well. The sisters had formed a couple again, the black wrapped within the scarlet, their distorted faces pressed together. He realised that he would not be able to separate these Siamese twins and that, at least to begin with, he would have to tolerate their strange ways and question them together. Into his mind came the fleeting image of a jar containing a tangle of foetuses, one of the rarest items in Monsieur de Noblecourt's cabinet of curiosities.

'When did you last see your niece?' he began.

Camille, the younger of the two, did not hesitate. 'Yesterday afternoon. We helped her to get dressed, didn't we, Lolotte?'

'Yes, yes,' said the other, 'and we even—'

'We even scolded her, because her clothes were too light in colour for an evening out. The idea!'

Nicolas had the clear impression, from the look of alarm in the elder sister's eyes, that her sibling was interpreting her thoughts very freely.

'How was she dressed?'

Her little eyes kept darting about, never meeting Nicolas's gaze. 'A yellow satin dress and a fur hat with yellow ribbons.'

'Did she have a bag?'

'No, no,' said Charlotte. 'No bag. But a very pretty Venetian mask. So white, you'd have thought there was powder on it.'

'You're confused, that was at Carnival. You have such a bad memory! My sister means she had a reticule with a few *écus* in it. Isn't that right, dear?'

The other assumed a stubborn, disappointed air. 'If you say so.'

'I don't just say it, I'm sure of it. Oh, Commissioner, my sister's such a scatterbrain. Just imagine, the other day her canary, say what you like but I say it's a canary, perhaps even a chaffinch . . . What was I saying? I read in a travel book that they've discovered a new species, Kirschner's wagtail . . . But that's not yours—'

Nicolas again interrupted these ramblings. 'What time did your niece leave?'

'I couldn't tell you. Our poor heads! She left with our maid, Miette. Naganda the savage wanted to go with her and we had to lock him in. We stayed at home, played *bouillotte* and had a light supper. We went to bed just before midnight.'

'What about you, Mademoiselle, can you confirm that?'

Charlotte, still sulking, shook her head without a word.

He would learn nothing more from the nonsense being spouted by these two terrified women. They were doubtless playing a trick on him in their way, a trick intended to mislead him in his search for the truth. The younger sister's incoherence and verbosity however, seemed too natural to be feigned. He called Bourdeau, and had Charles and Jean Galaine brought back in. Addressing the father, he asked to speak to Naganda. The man left the room, and returned a few minutes later looking embarrassed.

'Commissioner, we locked him up, but he's not there!'

'I think you'd better explain.'

'I've just been up and the door was locked, but when I opened it, there was no one there! He must have escaped over the roofs. They're as agile as cats . . .'

'Not ours,' said Camille. 'You don't know the tomcat—'

82

Nicolas cut her off shamelessly, hoping to avoid the flood of words that would follow. 'Let's go up to the attic, shall we? Show me the way.'

Galaine hesitated for a moment, then led him along a corridor, at the end of which was a staircase. On the third floor, which was reached by a stepladder, a door stood open onto an attic room. Through the open skylight, the twilit sky could be seen. A straw-bottomed chair had been placed below the skylight. It seemed to Nicolas that you would need considerable strength to hoist yourself up by your arms and get out through an opening that was so hard to reach. He had some experience of such exercises . . . The furniture was Spartan, the bed consisting of bales of straw beneath a large blanket with a strange pattern. Clothes hung in a neat row from a rope strung across the room. Many were native, but he noticed a brown greatcoat and a big, wide-brimmed black hat.

'That was what he usually wore when he went out,' Charles Galaine said. 'We made him wear them, otherwise people got scared at the tattoos on his face and his long black hair.'

'Are there any clothes missing, as far as you can see?'

'I have no idea. I don't keep count of the savage's rags. Isn't it enough that I've been feeding him for more than a year?'

Nicolas continued his search. In a small wooden casket, he found a few amulets, some small figures carved out of bone, a doll with the head of a frog, several bags filled with some unknown substance, three pairs of moccasins and a few obsidian pearls identical to the one found in Élodie Galaine's hand. He quickly seized them before her uncle could notice. They went back downstairs in silence. The rest of the Galaine family were waiting, as motionless as when he had left them. Nicolas warned them to stay within the walls of the capital: instructions would be given to the officials at the tollgates to have them arrested if they infringed this order. A perfectly illusory measure, but they did not need to know that.

Night was falling by the time the two policemen found themselves outside in Rue Saint-Honoré. Nicolas decided to accept La Paulet's invitation. Dr Semacgus had presumably not been informed of the renewed offer, so he suggested to Bourdeau that he go with him instead. The inspector declined with a smile: Madame Bourdeau was waiting for him and, besides, he was the father of a large family. But he had a question for his chief.

'May I ask why you didn't interrogate the servants? There's that Miette, and an old cook.'

'It's too early, Bourdeau. We don't want to panic the whole household. Domestics always have a lot to say, but you have to approach them carefully and gently. Our first harvest hasn't been so bad, though . . .'

Bourdeau bade him farewell and got into the cab. Nicolas set off for the *faubourg* where the Dauphin Couronné was located. Once again, those familiar premises would play a part in an investigation. What did La Paulet have to tell him about the previous night's disaster? And what was the good news she wanted to announce? As he walked, he went over the interrogations in his mind and made some notes in his little black notebook. The son did not seem especially surprised by the murder, but he alone had shown genuine emotion when confronted with the body. The father had said that the sisters were supposed to accompany Élodie to the firework display, but they had not confirmed this. Other details played on his mind: the reference to a Venetian mask; the mention of a marriage, which could have been the marriage of the Dauphin, but could just as easily have been Charles Galaine's second marriage. And, finally, those obsidian pearls, which certainly cast suspicion on the Micmac Indian who had vanished somewhere in the city. Nicolas was not worried about him: if he really was wandering around Paris, he would be apprehended as soon as the watch and the spies were supplied with his highly unusual description. Incidentally, what language did he speak?

One last thing intrigued him: although the younger sister was impeccably dressed, the elder seemed slovenly and neglectful. How could there be such a startling contrast between two people who were so close? There was also Madame Galaine's silence, and the fact that no one had mentioned Élodie's condition. Yes, the case was turning out to be more difficult than Monsieur de Sartine had imagined when he had allowed him to pursue this investigation in order to conceal another. There was also little Miette. What was that attack all about? It was some years now since a number of people had gone into convulsions over the grave of a Jansenist deacon at the Saint-Médard cemetery.

IV

TWISTS AND TURNS

The care this great man takes will calm the rage
Of your most bitter foes;
The promises he keeps will then assuage
The deadliest of blows.

RACINE

Standing outside the door of the Dauphin Couronné, Nicolas raised his hand towards the worn old bronze knocker, the noise of which would echo through the sleeping depths of the house of pleasure. His gesture came to an abrupt end. What was this wrought-iron door doing here, with its intermingling of satyrs and golden vine branches? What had become of the old, worm-eaten oak door, the top of it given a patina by years of being pushed and the bottom spattered with mud from the street? A carved handle hung there provocatively, presumably corresponding to a mechanism on the inside. Everything pointed to the fact that the premises had recently undergone a transformation. The supper planned for after the festivities in Place Louis XV, he recalled, was to have been his reunion with an old accomplice he had not seen since the autumn of the previous year. After a brief hesitation, he pulled the handle. A bell jingled inside, and no sooner had the sound died down than the door opened. A tall figure stood there, looking him up and down and smiling. Definitely, he thought, time was passing. It was hard to recognise in this apparition the little black girl he had known in the past. A beautiful, dark-eyed young girl was nodding her head, her languid air accentuated by her Turkish-style attire. She greeted him with a lisping warble – that at least had not changed – curtseyed and moved aside to let him in. The surprises were not yet over for Nicolas. The long hall with its geometric frieze and its great chandelier was gone. Gone, too, the partition walls, and the room where once, in darkness, he had killed his first man. Farewell mirrors, gilded cornices, ottomans in pastel colours and saucy prints in frames.

He found himself in a vast circular room, and all around its edge were intimate little alcoves behind heavy brocade curtains. Here and there about the room were chairs and console tables in a harmonious arrangement. The alcoves were furnished with charming little settees on bases carved with the shapes of pearls and ribbons. Some unity was given to the whole by the repetition of a flowered pattern on a number of small, moulded armchairs with oval backs. Nicolas, who had once been a notary's clerk, had done enough inventories after people's deaths to be able to estimate the cost of these furnishings at several million *livres*. Had he come to the wrong house, or did the place have a new owner? And yet the black girl was still here. He was still puzzling over these things when a familiar voice, at once throaty and hoarse, reached his ears.

'Damnation, girl, don't just stand there gaping. Pay attention. I'll go over it again. First you get a cask of Spanish wine at Tronquay's. Then take the burgundy back to Jobert et Chertemps

– it tastes like vinegar. If the scoundrels complain, tell them they'll lose my custom. These merchants will be the death of me!'

This was followed by several sighs.

'That's the wine dealt with! What a bother – it'll kill me, I tell you! Next, go to the perfume seller. First of all, I need some beef marrow pomade with orange blossom for my poor hair. For the girls, a dozen bars of scented Naples soap, and some of those small marble bars as well. Don't forget the virgin milk. My, that's well named! Are you laughing, you little devil? How dare you?'

He heard a fan strike flesh.

'You asked for that! We also need a bottle of kidney vetch in liquid form for La Mouchet who collapsed into the bed twice last week and, what's worse, she was with a bishop at the time! Admittedly, he did ask her to . . . Oh, you'll learn about these things in good time. Anyway, we still need some of those little sponges for . . . Well, I know what I mean. Now get on with you – I hear someone.'

The maid – a small girl – withdrew. Nicolas had approached. There indeed was La Paulet, that monster of flesh, sprawling across a chaise longue, and buried in a grey silk dress from which her huge arms emerged. Her face, which seemed to have shrunk, was covered as usual with ceruse and rouge applied like plaster. What was new was the blonde wig, with its serried ranks of curls.

'Well, well, it's our commissioner! That rascal Nicolas, who kept his old friend waiting all night! I'm joking, I know that when duty calls, you policemen have better things to do than amuse an emaciated old thing like me.'

'You underestimate yourself,' Nicolas said. 'There's still plenty of flesh on your bones and, what's more, I find you in a palace of such splendour as to leave me breathless.'

If it had not been for the thick plaster covering her face, Nicolas would have seen her blush.

'So,' she simpered, 'you've noticed the change? I've been in a whirl for the past month. The devil take these guilds and artisans! Twenty times I thought I was going to die, and the money I had to spend to feed them all! But I'm no fool: I'd never let anything be done in my house without having my say. Nobody's going to swindle La Paulet. But what has to be done has to be done! All the same,' she went on with a learned air, 'what do I know? Sometimes, our own opinions aren't the best. Ah, I see your eyes light up at the thought of cornering your old friend and finding dishonest reasons for this prosperity. You're so good at wheedling things out of me. You don't believe for a moment that I've discovered treasure.'

Nicolas smiled. 'Certainly not, but I must admit I'm surprised by such magnificence.'

'Ah, my good sir, there is a God, and he looks on those with pure hands, not full ones. You know how sweet and innocent I am. Well, he filled them for me.'

'Filled what?'

'My hands, my hands! Do you remember I once treated you to a ratafia from the West Indies given to me by an old acquaintance? My taste buds are still tingling. You were mad about it. It was that time when my parrot Sartine – it still makes me cry – died of shock after the violence you inflicted on us.'

'It was in a good cause, my dear.'

'Yes, to make me talk. But that's all in the past and I never bear grudges. I was perfectly happy with our arrangement and you can testify that I've kept to it. We'll talk about that later.'

'I'll gladly give you that testimony. But what about this fortune?'

'I'm coming to it. This acquaintance of my youth – God, how I loved him in those days – died and I didn't even know. Communications with the West Indies had broken down because of the war with the English. Anyway, six months ago this rascal appeared. Despite the layers of powder on his wig, he stank of writs and seizures and *lettres de cachet* and other nasty things. When I saw him there, all dressed in black, I said to myself, "Paulette, this means trouble!" I even thought he might be a new agent of the Lieutenant General's. Can you imagine? I was afraid they'd taken my Nicolas from me!'

She gave him a wink, which caused two or three pieces of her make-up to fall off, making her right eye look bigger.

'Anyway, I put on my most welcoming air. The fellow opens a portfolio. Turns out he's a notary, and a posh one, too – you just have to see his coach to know that. Straight out, he tells me that, Fortune being the daughter of Providence, my old friend, a rich planter, has died and, having no children, has made me his heir.'

'His heir?'

'Knowing that I wouldn't cross the seas – even thirty years ago I refused to do that – his business manager sold his property, and the notary had come to inform me that a huge sum was waiting for me at a Paris bank. I pocketed the windfall, convinced that good fortune is no sin and that, if you don't want to become a miser, you need to know how to spend.'

'Always a good girl.'

'More than you know! I'm getting on in years; there's nothing

I can do about that. This house is not a bauble; someone has to run it. These days, the girls don't respect authority like they used to. If you ever give in to them on anything, everything goes out the window. The profession has changed, and keeps changing. Once, you came up out of the gutter and, as long as you had brains and common sense, you could end up quite well off. I started as a flower girl. Oh, you should have seen me: I was a lovely girl, always happy, able to play hard to get when I had to, discreet when I needed to be. It didn't take me long to realise that the reason we have two ears but only one mouth is because we need to listen more than to speak. I found an old beau, a bit over the hill, but very neat and tidy, very gentle with me and willing to turn a blind eye to my younger suitors.'

'Old men can be like books,' Nicolas said. 'Full of excellent things, even though they're often worm-eaten, powdery and poorly bound.'

They both laughed.

'Gradually I made enough money to put together a nice little nest-egg. I built up a discreet but well-to-do clientele. That's how I managed to build this house. But the wind turns and, like I said before, the profession isn't what it was. We feel it, we mother superiors. As I'm sure you know, there are more and more girls working in isolation, most of them riddled with the pox. Our houses are well maintained, but we need to adapt to change. Wealthy customers are always looking for something new. They want "novelties". Our houses have always survived on force of habit, but luxury and refinement are the necessary commodities today. Well, I've embraced this way of thinking. I've invested part of my inheritance in adapting this place to modern tastes. But

I'm getting older, and my legs are so swollen they won't carry me any more. I can still look after the beginners, and I can keep order among the girls, even though they're so wild these days – they're getting harder and harder to select! So I'll stay in the house to keep an eye open for trouble, but I've decided to pass on the torch.'

'And who is the rare bird who's to succeed you?' asked Nicolas sternly. 'Don't forget, we have a say in the matter.'

'There he goes, playing the stern taskmaster! But I'm quite certain you'll be delighted with my choice, Commissioner. She's going to be my heir; she'll have everything that's mine, provided I'm pleased with her work and she takes care of me when I'm old. She's someone who's been through hard times. She's not some flighty young thing – she has a head on her shoulders. The Lord tempers the wind to the shorn lamb, thank God. The only thing that worries me a little is that she's too soft-hearted, but no one's perfect, and she'll get harder. As for me, if everything works out well, I'll retire to my property in Auteuil. You have to know when to let go. My experience and all this novelty does not make for the best mixture. Blend Suresnes wine with burgundy and I guarantee you'll get a disgusting brew.'

'Are you going to tell me the name of your find?'

'She's right behind you,' came a soft voice from somewhere close to Nicolas.

He immediately recognised it: it was a voice he had never forgotten. How many times had he heard it whispering passionate words in his ear? The memory of La Satin[1] had always remained precious to him. Their relationship had lasted for a long time, but the unease, not to say the fear, he felt at the work she did and the

92

life she led had eventually distanced him from her. He turned. My God, how beautiful she was! Even more beautiful than he remembered. With serene, tranquil eyes, she was looking at him tenderly. The silky curls of her hair were lifted at the back, leaving her neck and shoulders bare, and he remembered how he used to devour that neck and those shoulders with kisses so ardent that she would complain of the marks he left in her flesh. Her breasts swelled above a bodice of Alençon lace. A loose pigeon-blue silk dress gave her figure an air of languor. All her old charm was still there, but as if purified. She came to him and put her arms round his neck. He quivered when their lips met.

'Well, my doves,' said La Paulet. 'Now that's what I call a nice reunion!'

She clapped her hands. The African maid reappeared, and with a dancing step drew back the curtains of one of the alcoves. There was a table there, and on it stood a cooling pitcher of almond-green porcelain containing a number of bottles of Champagne. Beside the table, a circular bed promised other delights.

'My children,' La Paulet went on, 'I'll leave you to it. I need to go upstairs and tend to my legs. I'm sure you have a lot to talk about! The meal will be small, but refined. Those who gorge themselves, as a duke of my acquaintance says,[2] are not true gourmets, and nothing is more dispiriting to the talent of a cook than his master's gluttony.'

'That's the wisdom of Comus!'

'To begin, fresh melon from my garden in Auteuil. Not one of those horrible, flabby, washed-out things your Sartine bans by the cupboardful every year. No, one of those orangey honey melons, as juicy and tasty as anyone could wish. After that, a dish fit for a king, perfectly prepared by my cook: a fattened chicken from Angoulême. It'll make you lick your lips . . .'

She gave a salacious laugh.

'I'd love to know how it's prepared,' said Nicolas.

'I should have known it! Well, you have to get hold of a fine chicken, raised with love, corn-fed. All the fleshy parts you sprinkle generously with flakes of truffle. Then, by hand, you fill the body of the chicken with slices of truffle that you've baked in the oven with grated bacon and spices.'

'And then straight into a casserole?'

'No, no, my dear, as in love you have to lead up to things gradually. You wrap the chicken in paper to let the truffles and the spices blend. Three days later, you remove the paper and wrap the bird in slices of calf leg and bards of bacon. Then, and only then, you lay it down, just like your sweetheart, in a braising pan of exactly the right size, on a bed of sliced carrots and parsnips, mixed herbs and spices, salt and pepper, and two onions stuck with cloves, and pour a bottle of Malaga over it. Then let it simmer gently for at least two hours. Finally, you cut the fat off, sprinkle it with a handful of finely ground truffles, reduce the sauce by simmering and thicken it with crushed chestnuts. Fit for a bishop, I tell you!'

'And the dessert!' sighed La Satin.

'Glacé pineapple straight from the greenhouses of the Duc de Bouillon. And after that . . . well, just don't make too much noise!'

'Another duke! Our Paulet really has changed!'

Nicolas was letting himself go, aware that he had fallen into a trap but unwilling to stop himself. The atmosphere had changed. La Paulet was talking to him more familiarly, certain of her own impunity. He was agreeing to an evening that promised to be full of delights, thanks to this unexpected reunion. For a long time, he had had no means of escape. The constant tension of his work, exacerbated by the daily obligations of the Dauphin's wedding, had left him no respite. This evening, he would let himself go like a horseman who drops exhausted by the side of the road. But then, in a flash, he remembered something which made him sit up: Tirepot had told him to expect some revelations from La Paulet. The woman never did anything in a direct way. You always had to worm information out of her, as not only was she always keen to gain advantages and privileges from selling her services, but she also took pleasure in holding out on the police.

'That's all well and good,' said Nicolas, 'but before letting you rest I'd like to ask you a few questions. According to our friend Tirepot, you had some interesting things to tell me.'

She pulled a face and collapsed heavily onto her chaise longue. 'This one certainly never forgets which way it is to the Châtelet!'

'Never! Especially as I'm as eager to sample your news as your cooking. The sooner we get it over with, the better. So tell me all about the evening of the disaster. So much has happened – it seems like days ago, but it was only last night.'

'Alas,' sighed La Paulet, 'if I have to, I have to. I was making preparations for the dinner we had planned in your honour and that of Dr Semacgus when the bell started ringing as if a thousand devils were pulling it. When I eventually opened up, there were about thirty City Guards, threatening to break everything. Those beanpoles were all spruced up, and wanted to have a party to christen their new uniforms. They were shouting and screaming, demanding wine and girls. I don't like to be put under pressure . . .' She threw a glance at Nicolas. 'La Paulet's a good girl, but you mustn't provoke her. I gave them a piece of my mind, but since I had no choice but to serve them drinks, I took out a vinegary burgundy, which certainly can't have done them much good, and –'

'What time was this?'

'Eight o'clock exactly, before the firework display. It even occurred to me that, what with the celebrations and the crowds and all that crush on the boulevards, they ought to have had better things to do than get drunk in an honest house.'

'And how long did all this go on for?'

'Until two or three in the morning. My legs had doubled in size. The rascals cleaned me out of my last stocks of ratafia. They had some officers with them. Someone even came looking for the major because of the disaster. He laughed and said he'd just come from there and was sick and tired of it, and that Monsieur de Sartine would sort it all out.'

'What did this major look like?'

'Tall, fat, red-faced, with wicked little eyes like boot buttons. A shrill, nasty voice. But he doesn't frighten me. I'll find him again for you!'

'My dear friend, I thank you. Don't let us keep you; go and look after your legs. We have to preserve you – you're too valuable to us.'

'Oh, he's a crafty one, a smooth one! Now he's suddenly in a hurry to get rid of La Paulet! All right, I understand, you can't wait for your juicy chicken, ha ha!'

And with an eloquent smile, La Paulet rose and left the room, sighing in pain with each step she took. La Satin and Nicolas looked at each other. Just like the first time, he thought, in that cubby hole where he had found her when she was working as a maid for the wife of a President of the Parlement. A rape and a subsequent pregnancy – he had briefly thought that he was the father – had led La Satin into the business of trading her charms for money. But she had been lucky to end up at La Paulet's, and thus escape the riff-raff and the General Hospital. Their relations had become less frequent, and it had been a long time since their paths had crossed.

'I've never forgotten you, Nicolas,' she said. 'Oh, be quiet, I know how you felt . . . The times I waited under the archway of the Châtelet, just for the joy of catching a brief glimpse of you. You were always in a hurry, and passed like a shadow . . .'

He did not know how to reply.

'And your child?'

She smiled. 'He's beautiful. He's at school now, a boarder.'

What followed was a happy interlude for Nicolas. Constantly at the mercy of events as he was, only rarely granting himself a moment of respite between the end of one activity and the beginning of another, he now abandoned himself to the carefree pleasures of the here and now. The maid brought the food, took the cork from the wine, merrily filled the flutes and withdrew, singing a languorous chant which she accompanied with a slow swaying of her hips. Nicolas relaxed. La Satin delicately boned the chicken and handed him the best pieces. The air in the alcove was filled with the aromas of the meal and heating bodies. Well before the glacé pineapple, Nicolas had drawn his friend onto the bed. There, buried in the sheets, he was back among the gentle slopes and deep ravines, the roads a thousand times travelled. The ardour of their renewed desire sealed that night's reunion before they sank, exhausted, into sleep.

Friday 1 June 1770
Languidly, Nicolas pressed himself into the hot sand. He must have dozed off in the sun on the shore at Batz. Someone was muttering above him, unconcerned that he was trying to sleep. Much to the displeasure of his guardian, the canon, who always worried about the risk of naked bodies coming into contact with water, which was reputed to contain all ills and inspire all perversions, he loved to run in the summer with other rascals his age and throw himself into the waves, surrounded by fishing boats. He groaned: a hand was shaking him. He opened his eyes, saw a brown nipple, a tangle of rumpled sheets and, at a slight distance, the mocking face of Inspector Bourdeau. He disentangled his legs from La Satin, who was sleeping peacefully, wrapped himself in a sheet and looked sternly at the intruder.

'Pierre, what are you doing here so early?'

'A thousand pardons, Nicolas, but duty calls! They've found the Indian.'

'Good Lord. What time is it?'

'The stroke of nine.'

'Nine? I can't believe it – I could have sworn it was midnight! I was sleeping like a child.'

'Like a child, really?' said Bourdeau, stealing a glance at La Satin's body.

'Bourdeau, Bourdeau! Come on, you have to help me. I remember there was a fountain in the backyard of this house of perdition.'

'Come now, don't speak ill of good things!'

Muttering, Nicolas pushed the inspector aside, and went and splashed himself with cold water from the pump. He caught the black maid ogling him shamelessly from the pantry window. He wagged a threatening index finger at her, and she disappeared. Once he was dressed, he joined Bourdeau in the cab. He left a moment's silence, as if closing a door on the past night, then began questioning his deputy.

'I was sure we'd find the man soon enough.'

'We had a bit of luck. Just imagine, he was trying to get back to New France – or rather, what we called New France until 1763.[3] What could be more obvious for an innocent native than to get to the river and find a ship? After he escaped from Rue Saint-Honoré, he followed the streams, wandered for a while in the warren of the Louvre, and finally found himself on the Quai de la Mégisserie. You know the reputation of the place.'

'Of course. The Lieutenant General is constantly battling with the Ministry of War about it. But, as you know, it is the Duc de Choiseul himself who holds that portfolio. Order, in this case, feeds disorder, and necessity is law. How many times have I heard our chief deplore the misdeeds of those crimps who use every trick in the book to enlist inexperienced young people, and frequently resort to violence.'

'Every inexperienced peasant who ends up on the river bank is ensnared by them. And it's always the same refrain . . .'

'"My master needs a servant, and you're the right build. I'm sure he'll take you, as long as you obey his orders." They give the poor wretch a little brandy and then take him to see a soldier in disguise who, instead of hiring him as a domestic, gets him to sign up.'

'We could almost be there,' said Bourdeau, amused by the pitiful tone Nicolas had adopted.

'Go ahead and laugh, my dear fellow, but it happened to me when I first arrived in Paris. My Breton accent would have proved my undoing if I hadn't shown them a letter from Monsieur de Sartine. But we're getting off the point.'

'Anyway, our man was approached. His strange appearance – naked except for a loincloth – and the fact that he looked lost attracted one of these soldiers of fortune, who tried to entice him, offering him a passage to the New World for a deferred payment. In fact, he was enlisting him, and the bird was caught in the trap. When the patrol came and tried to take him to the barracks, he realised what had happened. That made him furious and, as he's built like Hercules, he knocked five men to the ground before they got him under control. The watch were called to the rescue, and they led him in chains to the Châtelet. I tried to find you in Rue de Montmartre. Everyone was asleep, except Catherine . . .'

Nicolas thought with a smile of the time long gone when, as a young man and the cherished child of the house, his least delay had caused anxiety. Since then, everyone had grown accustomed to his erratic comings and goings. Only Catherine, whose unyielding loyalty was equalled only by the affection she had for her saviour, always feared for Nicolas's safety.

'And your sagacity led you to the Dauphin Couronné?'

'I assumed you were in retreat here. With the mother superior.'

Nicolas laughed. 'Oh, that's good, I'll leave you the last word.

The doctor is always right.'

Back at the Châtelet, they went straight to the prison. A clerk of the court admitted them to a dungeon so dark that Nicolas demanded a lantern. It was just possible to make out a human form, bound hand and foot, squatting on a squalid bed of rotten straw. The man's long black hair covered his face. He was wrapped in a jute blanket which must have been used for generations of prisoners. His feet were black with a thick layer of dried mud. His bare legs seemed to be affected by spasms, the muscles and tendons standing out as if the skin had been flayed. Nicolas reached out his hand to touch his shoulder. The man raised his head suddenly, throwing his hair back to reveal intense, expressionless black eyes. The commissioner was astonished to see a number of scars close to his temples. The face was long, with a hooked nose and the regular features of a pagan idol carved in stone.

'Monsieur, I am a police commissioner. I want to help you. Do you understand?'

'Monsieur, I was educated by the Jesuits. "He believed the advice of a power so blind, and is punished enough by his rigorous fate."'

'"For only the innocent suffer this state." Nicolas smiled. 'I didn't know the verses of Monsieur de La Fontaine were so popular in New France.'

The face, which had lit up, now clouded over. 'Why do you call it New France? We were abandoned by our King. As for me, I've been shamefully deceived and mistreated here in Paris by a family I would have liked to be able to respect, in memory of a dead man. Monsieur, I appeal to you for protection. I would like to be untied and to wash myself. Alas, I had to leave a hostile house without my clothes, which had been stolen anyway . . .'

'You have our protection,' Nicolas assured him. 'You are blameless in that deplorable incident of which you were the victim. But I need to question you about another matter. Clerk of the Court, unchain this man, and bring him a pail of water for his ablutions. Bourdeau, have a look in the clothes cupboard and see if you can find something for him to wear for the moment.'

They left the prisoner and went to the duty office.

'Now that's what I call a very urbane native!' said Bourdeau.

'And a first class witness. I can't wait to interrogate him. He seems intelligent. We still have to determine how best to tackle the subject that most interests us.'

Nicolas reflected on this while Bourdeau searched through the clothes the two of them had patiently accumulated, to be used as disguises whenever they needed to blend into the Parisian crowd for the purposes of an investigation. The inspector finally found what he was looking for, and went out. The Micmac seemed determined, Nicolas was thinking, and undoubtedly had a good command of French. He was probably skilful at concealing his thoughts and, through them, any awkward truths – that at least was what was often said about the natives of New France. Tackling him head-on would only put him on the defensive and lead him to keep silent about the most important things. Therefore it would be better not to conduct the interrogation too rigidly. It was often through being vague and approximate that a word, a phrase, an inflection emerged, which allowed the investigator to gain a foothold, verify his assumptions and take the interview where he wanted it to go, just as the men of a frigate getting ready to board another had to approach cautiously, and find the right place to throw their grapnel. Nicolas did not like witnesses who were too smooth, so that the strict rhetoric of his questions slid off them – 'like water off a duck's back' as Bourdeau put it.

The Micmac made his entrance. The pitiful old clothes supplied by Bourdeau could not conceal the strangeness of the man. He refused the straw-bottomed stool indicated by the inspector and remained standing with his arms folded and his hands under his armpits – much to Nicolas's displeasure, as he was always alert to the language of hands. A heavy silence fell.

'I'm sure you have many things to tell us, Monsieur,' the commissioner said at last.

He was talking for talking's sake. He thought he glimpsed a gleam of irony in Naganda's eyes.

'I had the feeling, Monsieur,' Naganda replied, 'that you yourself had much to tell *me*. Perhaps you will oblige me by satisfying my curiosity. Incidentally, please accept my gratitude for getting me out of that difficult situation. It was only my ignorance of your people's customs that got me into it.'

'Let's begin at the beginning, shall we?' Nicolas said. 'Please don't take this amiss, but perhaps you could enlighten us as to your presence in Paris. You are a long way from the snows of your country!'

The irony in Naganda's dark eyes intensified. 'I fear the words so pleasantly vouchsafed by Monsieur de Voltaire may have clouded your judgement. My country does have "acres of snow", yes, but the summers are very hot. I will, however, answer your question. I was twelve years old when my father died in an English ambush. He worked as a guide to Monsieur Galaine – that was Monsieur Charles's older brother. Monsieur Galaine was a good man, a just man. He took responsibility for me and paid for my education. When things turned bad, he decided to return to France. We were supposed to join the French naval squadron. An attack by Indians in the pay of the English forced us to scatter. I was carrying Monsieur Claude's daughter, Élodie. I managed to hide, and eventually reached Quebec, where I was able to entrust her to the Ursulines. They took me at my word, as I had papers with me from her father. For seventeen years, I practised various trades, which made it possible for me to accumulate enough money to pay for a passage to France and take Élodie back to her parents, whom I believed were still alive.'

'How old were you when the tragedy happened?'

'I was fifteen and Élodie a few months.'

'I've interrupted your story. Please continue.'

'Despite the curiosity aroused by an Indian escorting a young girl and an old nun the sisters had insisted I take with me as a chaperone, the voyage passed without incident. The Galaine family were not very welcoming. Although they subsequently adopted Élodie as if she were their daughter, their treatment of me did not improve. What could I do, alone, isolated, without friends or family, treated as less than nothing not only by the Galaines, but also by their servants, who were frightened by the way I looked?' He gestured towards his face, and Nicolas noted the clenched fists. 'I am the son of a chief. Naganda is the son of a chief.'

It was as if he were trying to convince himself. He folded his arms again and fell silent. What Nicolas had heard had touched him, taking him back several years to his own arrival in the capital of the kingdom. He, too, had been aware of his own solitude. A terrible feeling of abandonment seized him again at the thought.

'Now I'd like you to explain in detail how you came to be half naked and got into difficulty on the Quai de la Mégisserie.'

'Naganda is not a spirit who can be locked up. The day before yesterday – Wednesday, I think it was – Élodie told me she wanted to be present at the great celebration being held on Place Louis XV, in honour of the King's grandson. She wanted me to go with her, as much to protect her – the streets are not safe, and young men too forward with a young girl in such a mixed crowd – as because she wanted me to see fireworks for the first time. I'd heard of them – the English used them to celebrate their victory over the French, but I'd refused to see them at that time. It was a nice idea, but her aunts objected. My duty, they said, was to protect the house. Élodie protested, but they wouldn't listen to her. As for me, I had made it my policy never to oppose the wishes of her family, knowing that if I did so I would immediately find myself out on the streets, and would be unable to keep the promise I had made her father to always watch over her. But I had made up my mind to ignore the ban, to escape in secret and follow her from a distance to make sure she was safe.'

'And your clothes?'

'What clothes? After the midday meal, I felt drowsy and fell fast asleep in the attic. When I woke up, my clothes had vanished and I was locked in. What's more . . .'

'What's more?'

'What's more, I realised that a whole day had gone by!'

'What do you mean? You'll have to explain.'

'I have a watch, or rather, I had a watch given me by Monsieur Claude. When I looked at it just before falling asleep, it said three in the afternoon. When I woke up, it was one o'clock and the sun was high in the sky. I came to the conclusion that I'd slept nearly twenty-four hours. Will you believe me if I say that I still have no idea how?'

Bourdeau, who was sitting behind the Indian, shook his head doubtfully. 'Do you expect us to believe, Monsieur, that you slept an entire day?'

'Believe what you want – it's the truth.'

'We'll look into that,' said Nicolas. 'Personally, I like the truth rather better when I find it for myself than when someone else shows it to me. What happened next?'

'Next, I stood on a chair and opened the skylight. I managed to pull myself out and get onto the roof of a neighbouring house. From there, I went across a series of sloping roofs, until I came to a tree and climbed down. After wandering for a long time, I noticed some seagulls and observed the direction of their flight. That led me to the river, where I hoped I might find a boat about to leave. A man came up to me and offered me work. The money would pay my passage, he said. I accepted, and he took me to a low tavern where another man with stripes on his arm, a somewhat unfriendly man, made me sign a paper. As soon as I had, some soldiers appeared and jumped on me. I defended myself, but had to yield to superior numbers. Then, thanks to you, I was freed.'

He saluted Nicolas with a certain nobility, and the commissioner was taken aback by this witness from two worlds, whose refined language was in such marked contrast to his appearance that it was hard to know what to make of the man. His story was all well and good, but sounded a bit too much like a tale from the *Arabian Nights*.

'Could you describe the clothes that disappeared?' Nicolas asked.

'Tunics and trousers made of hide. A large brown cloak and a black hat, which I often wear to conceal my face lest it frighten the fainthearted in the street.'

Nicolas took a handkerchief from his pocket, carefully unfolded it on his desk, and held up the obsidian pearl he had found in Élodie Galaine's clenched hand at La Madeleine cemetery.

'Do you recognise this pearl?'

Naganda leaned forward. 'Yes, it's from a necklace that belongs to me, which I'm very fond of. It was taken along with my clothes.'

'And your watch?'

'When I put my hand under my bed, I found it there.'

'Where is it now?'

'The soldiers took it from me.'

'Monsieur Bourdeau will check that. Let's get back to this pearl. You say the necklace has disappeared. Very well. Why were you so fond of it?'

'It was a souvenir of my father, and Monsieur Claude put an amulet on it.'

'You claim a talisman was given to you by the elder Monsieur Galaine? Wasn't he a Catholic? A good Christian?'

'Of course. I'm just telling you what happened. When he gave me that little square of leather, he told me never to let it out of my sight. I can still recall his words: "When Élodie marries, open it and give her what it contains.'"

'So you never opened it?'

'Never.'

Nicolas felt in his pocket for the broken necklace he had found in the attic in Rue Saint-Honoré. He held it out to the Indian. Naganda made a quick gesture, as if to grab it, and the commissioner just had time to pull back his hand.

'I see from your reaction that this object is not unfamiliar to you.'

'Yes, it's mine, and for the reasons I've told you nothing is dearer to me. Where did you find it?'

'Excuse me, I'm the one asking the questions. So you say this necklace is yours? You recognise it? You confirm that this pearl belongs to this necklace? Is that correct?'

The Indian nodded. It seemed to Nicolas that the moment had come to tell him the news of Élodie's death.

'I'm sorry to have to inform you that this pearl, which you recognise as being part of a necklace belonging to you, was discovered in the clenched hand of Mademoiselle Élodie Galaine, whose dead body was found among the victims of the disaster on Place Louis XV. All evidence points to the fact that this death was the consequence of a criminal act, and it is also my duty to tell you that you are one of the suspects.'

Nicolas was expecting some strange manifestation of grief: a howl, a dance to the sound of a savage chant, just as he had read in accounts by missionaries. There was none of that. The only thing that betrayed any emotion or surprise in the Indian was that his coppery skin seemed to turn grey, and his eyes sank even more deeply into their sockets.

'You don't seem either surprised or upset.'

The man's answer left him speechless. '*Quam cum vidisset Dominus, misericordia motus super eam, dixit illi: Noli flere.*'[4]

'You feel nothing at the loss of a person to whom you have devoted part of your life, and for whom you have cared most diligently?'

'"The pain which dare not speak is all the stronger."'[5]

He certainly loves jousting, thought Nicolas. But when it came to quoting Saint Luke or Racine, he could give as good as he got, and was not deceived by this kind of response, which concealed too much.

'"The law in all its might / Divides two hearts whom misery did unite."[6] What was your relationship with Élodie Galaine?'

'She was the daughter of my master and benefactor. I swore to protect her, and I failed.'

The man had a gift for prevarication.

'How did you think of her?'

'She was . . . she was like a sister to me.'

Bourdeau and Nicolas looked up. They had both noticed the hesitation, a kind of stutter – strange coming from a man who had shown no emotion so far. Nicolas felt a pang in his heart: the bitter-sweet memory of his own half-sister, Isabelle de Ranreuil, came back to him.[7]

'Let me make something clear. A suspect you may be, but you are entitled to our protection. In return, we hope and expect that you will be completely honest with us. If you know something, if you suspect something, you must tell us.'

Naganda looked at Nicolas and opened his mouth, but no sound emerged. He lowered his eyes.

'You're free to remain silent, but think about what I've just said. You're alone, and a suspect. You'll be taken back to Rue Saint-Honoré, where you will remain at the disposal of the law.'

Bourdeau called a police officer. Naganda bowed and followed the man out.

Nicolas remained silent for a moment. 'I don't think he's lying,' he said at last, 'but he's hiding something important.'

'Why are you sending him back?' asked Bourdeau.

'My friend Père Grégoire once explained that when certain substances are brought into contact with one another, they can produce some very surprising reactions. We may well see such a phenomenon in Rue Saint-Honoré. The people there would like him to be a long way away. Well, we're going to throw him back among them and just wait to see what happens!'

'What do you make of that story about his long sleep?'

'It seems suspicious to me, and not very believable. We need to get to the bottom of it. I'm sure that, like me, you noticed in passing where he contradicted the other testimonies. We'll have to look into all that. But for the moment we need to concentrate on the other affair that concerns us. It's urgent that we gather the elements of the report that Monsieur de Sartine asked for.'

'We already know the festivities were left unsupervised because of the incompetence of the City Guards.'

'We have to identify who's responsible and establish the death toll. The Lieutenant General will be received by His Majesty on Sunday evening, as usual. Send one of our men out to gather information. A letter must be dispatched to the twenty district commissioners. We need to consult the doctors, the apothecaries, the bonesetters, the coffin makers, the parish registers for the number of funerals, the gravediggers. Question everyone. Get everything you can from our spies. Let everything be recorded and communicated to me as soon as possible.'

'Yes, indeed,' a curt voice echoed through the duty office. 'And let the report be given to me as soon as possible!'

The two colleagues turned to discover Monsieur de Sartine dressed in his black magistrate's robe with the white bands, his head adorned with a large wig. He stood looking them up and down rather coldly. Nicolas, himself surprised by this apparition, imagined what effect it might have on the *vulgum pecus*. Despite the great man's reputation for affability, Nicolas knew from experience that his smooth tone could conceal a sharpness of which only those who knew him well would be aware.

'Didn't I foresee all this?' cried Sartine. 'Wasn't it crystal clear in my mind? Didn't I keep telling myself that your little obsessions were bound at the very least to cause conflict and scandal, as usual? That in trying too hard to untangle things which you yourself had tangled, you would confound us?'

'Monsieur, to what do I owe this volley of scathing remarks?'

'And, what's worse, he feigns ignorance! Monsieur Le Floch, I have just come from the office of the Criminal Lieutenant, who regaled me with a lesson on procedure which I had to endure through clenched teeth. He didn't hold back on the pompous phrases, I can tell you. He really encroached on my territory for fear that I wouldn't understand what he was saying.'

'Monsieur—'

'Quiet! Accustomed as you are – and the guilt is mine for tolerating such things, and even lending a hand – to conducting extraordinary operations on the fringes of convention, and undertaking adventurous personal initiatives, you have thrown yourself headlong, without any thought, into a criminal investigation. Don't deny it – I've heard all about it: conceal-ment of a corpse, encroachment on other people's procedures, an autopsy performed by unappointed individuals, threats to respectable citizens. All that just to serve as a screen for the vital investigation with which I entrusted you! What do you have to say to that?'

'I say that there is nothing in all of this which should upset you, Monsieur. I'm sure that, confident of your own rights and the legitimacy of the actions of your representatives, you have, as usual, duly defended them and countered the attacks of the Criminal Lieutenant. Moreover, I think Monsieur Testard du Lys too honest a man to have long resisted your gentle but firm insistence.'

Monsieur de Sartine stretched out his leg and admired the glittering silver buckle on his shoe. 'Oh, really? My gentle but firm insistence? I'm pleased to know that my subordinates give me full marks. Well, they will benefit from my indulgence of their perspicacity. Have you at least made any progress? I don't want speeches, I want facts. Go on.'

'Monsieur, we've established that the young woman was murdered. We've also discovered a probable infanticide. The family situation is extraordinary, and no hypothesis can be ruled out. It would be most annoying if a case that has been started should be taken away from you, and that other, clumsier hands should interfere with what is already a promising inquiry.'

'Promising, eh? I need more than promises, and fast! And what of our other subject of interest?'

'I'm making progress there too, Monsieur. Everything confirms what we had already guessed.'

'Never mind about guesswork. Come and see me with a detailed report tomorrow evening. After that I'm going to spend the night at Versailles, where I shall see the King in his small apartments after Mass. You're to come with me, Nicolas. His Majesty is always happy to see young Ranreuil.'

Sartine straightened his wig, did an about-turn and walked out of the duty office with his usual dignity.

'Ha!' said Nicolas. 'I think I need to pay a visit to the Criminal Lieutenant. Then I'm off to see my tailor.'

V

AFFAIRS OF STATE

Artifice always fails and does not long
produce the same effects as truth.

Louis XIV

The office of the Criminal Lieutenant was in another part of the
Grand Châtelet. Nicolas was introduced immediately: clearly, he
was expected. A small, sly-faced man in a grey wig greeted him
less than cordially and proceeded to give him a lesson in
procedure, throwing in a number of bitter-sweet observations on
the presumptuousness of certain subordinates in the lower
echelons of the police. This outburst was received with coolness,
patience and humility, at which the magistrate's attitude softened
– so much so that he complimented the commissioner on his good
reputation, which had even reached the doors of the high
department of justice over which he reigned. Little by little, he
agreed that in the heat of an investigation urgency had to prevail
over an absolute respect for legalities. Therefore, he concluded,
given the good relations he had built up with Monsieur de Sartine,
and with the clear understanding that Monsieur Le Floch would
not engage in any machinations hostile to his ministry, he
consented to pass over, for now, the errors that had been noted,
and authorised him, contrary to the usual practice, to continue

with his inquiries and interrogations. From now on, he was convinced, the commissioner would observe the necessary caution, share information and show the required reverence which all power, all . . . Nicolas interrupted this ever-lengthening oration with a humble bow and retreated, barely able to contain his laughter. He hurtled down dark staircases to the entrance archway, where he had the servant on duty call him a sedan chair.

Summer was on its way, and the good weather lightened the commissioner's constantly shifting thoughts. A stall at the corner of a street attracted him with its pyramid of bright, yellow-skinned cherries. An old woman sold him quarter of a pound, and he immediately devoured this unexpected gift of the streets. Without thinking, he began to send the stones flying just as he used to do when he was a child, but a sense of the dignity of his office soon stopped him. The taste of these 'pigeon's breasts' lingered pleasantly in his mouth. By the time he had finished the cherries, he found himself in Rue Vieille-du-Temple, where Master Vachon, who had been his tailor for ten years – and who also happened to be Monsieur de Sartine's – had his shop and made sure the rules of his profession were strictly observed, while embracing successive fads and fashions, whether he liked them or not.

In his lair at the far end of an oval courtyard, in a shabby building where the daylight barely penetrated, Master Vachon held court, true to form as ever. His tall figure stooped a little now, but his emaciated face, although paler than before, still expressed the same ardour in condemning the present day, supervising and reprimanding his assistants as they bent over wooden counters that had acquired a patina after years of use.

Perhaps he also leant more heavily now on his long, old-fashioned cane.

'How's business?' asked Nicolas.

'Ah, my dear Commissioner, I'd need several heads to deal with all these innovations! Look, here's the latest.' He waved a shapeless piece of lace. 'Just take a look at this. It makes my blood boil. The simple elegance of a woman's *fichu* is no longer enough, we must add to it – overburden it, more like! Farewell the beauty of the white cambric or muslin *fichu*, whether flat or fluted! And look at this hood, held upright on the shoulders. How? you may ask. By the complicated means of a length of trimming shaped like a hoop. You'll never guess the name of this brainwave! They call it a *rise-to-heaven*. May it please God we get there! That's for the women. As for us men, we're inspired by Germany, especially its sense of economy. No sleeves on the jackets. Here's a jacket and waistcoat. It makes my head spin. Everything is novelty! Now here's something for you, with your love of classic styles and the colour green. This is a specimen that'll never go out of fashion, a coat *à la Sanson*, which would suit you down to a T . . .'

'*À la Sanson?*'

'Yes, *à la Sanson*. Didn't you know – I thought he was a friend of yours – that he has long been a leader in fashion? Before his marriage, he was a giddy young fellow – quite a ladies' man, too.'

This information surprised Nicolas. 'Charles Henri Sanson, the public executioner?'

'The very same!' cried Master Vachon, delighted that for once he could tell this man from the Grand Châtelet, with his fearsome reputation, something he did not know. 'He frequented high society and was known as the "Chevalier de Longval", after a property belonging to his family. He had an insatiable taste for hunting. Not content with assuming a dubious name and title, he carried a sword and dressed in a blue coat, which is the prerogative of the nobility. They even say that he was called to order by the King's procurator, who loudly disparaged him for being nothing more elevated than an executioner. After this angry outburst, Sanson is said to have adopted green as a colour and had his coats tailored to a particular cut, which was so unusual that it drew the attention of the Marquis de Lestorières, the self-styled arbiter of elegance at Versailles. The fashion spread, and soon everyone was dressing *à la Sanson*. Isn't that a pleasant story?'

His tall body bent with laughter. Then, with a furious glance at his apprentices, who were all listening, he came closer to Nicolas.

'They even say he had a weakness for Jeanne Bécu,[1] the current concubine. Her uncle, the Abbé de Picous, was close to his family. Sanson used to tend his rheumatism with the fat of a hanged man! But I'm getting on your nerves with my ramblings. What can I do for you?'

He rushed over to one of his assistants and twisted his ear.

'Ah-hah! I caught you, working with long stitches. Do it again and you'll see. You'll be fined! You'll be fined!'

Nicolas took a small shiny object from his pocket and handed it to Master Vachon. 'What do you make of this?'

The tailor adjusted his spectacles, turned the object over and moved it close to a candle so that it gleamed several times. 'Pah!' he said. 'A brass tag designed to finish off a cable stitch. A novelty object for a novelty uniform. In fact, I'd wager . . .' He walked over to a cabinet made up of a number of drawers stacked side by side and searched in one of them. Before long, he brought out a handful of similar objects. 'I was sure I'd seen them somewhere before. As I'm sure you know, I have some very high-class customers, both at court and in town. Well, this little brass article is a trifle added, unnecessarily I'd say, to the new uniform of the City Guards, so unhappily worn for the first time during the festivities organised by the provost in Place Louis XV.'

'Just what I wanted to know. Could you further indulge me by telling me the names of the customers who bought this article?'

'I can't refuse you anything. Let's see, there was Barboteux, Rabourdin . . .' He consulted a dog-eared register. 'Tirart and . . . Langlumé. He was the major, the most demanding and the most . . . arrogant, I must say.'

Before he could take his leave, Nicolas still had to feel a few new fabrics offered by the tailor. Once outside, he walked, lost in thought, through streets he knew well from having lived here when he first arrived in Paris. He passed the house in Rue des Blancs-Manteaux, which had been the scene of his first exploits. God, how long ago it all was! But the present was proving equally full of surprises. Master Vachon had revealed an unknown side to his friend Sanson. Could it be that Monsieur de Sartine's police force did not know these things, or was it simply that he himself had never sought to discover them? People were so various in the image they presented to others. They opened different drawers depending on who they were talking to or, like mirrors, reflected what was expected of them. So that unassuming man of proven qualities – erudite, pious, if not devout, sensitive and compassionate, always trying to make the most of the scientific knowledge he had acquired from the suffering of the tortured and condemned – could also be light-hearted and concerned about his appearance, quite unlike the shy figure in his puce coat who officiated in the semi-darkness of the Basse-Geôle. Well, everyone had a right to his freedom, and perhaps this was a way for Sanson to exorcise the horror he confronted daily in his work. Nicolas was suddenly annoyed with himself for passing judgement. He had to give credit to a man he considered a friend. Those who benefited from this appellation should not be judged: they had to be taken as they were, in all their light and shade.

Nicolas got into a cab in Rue Saint-Antoine. So he had not been mistaken: the object which had blocked the door leading to the roof of the ambassadors' mansion did indeed come from the uniform of a City Guard. And who else apart from Major Langlumé could have had access to a building reserved for the provost's special guests? He alone, for reasons still to be explained, could have nurtured a plan to keep a police commissioner up on the roof. It was not Nicolas personally who had been targeted, even though they had been involved in an unpleasant altercation a few hours earlier, but the representative of Monsieur de Sartine, the man the Lieutenant General had sent to keep an eye on the festivities. To put obstacles in the way of his mission – that, in a nutshell, had been the major's intention. He would have to discover the motives, which were not unconnected with what happened after the disaster. Perhaps things might have turned out differently if Nicolas had not had to waste so much time escaping through the chimney and had been able to act sooner.

But Nicolas's curiosity had been aroused on another matter,

and he resolved to consult the Châtelet's archive. It was a collection read by few, but full of surprises. The information in it came from various sources, some from police spies, some from the operations of the *cabinet noir*. So strong was his desire to check the archive that he went straight there as soon as he got back to the Châtelet. Helped by the ancient clerk of the court who was the curator of the collection, he soon discovered an imposing bundle devoted to the Sanson family. In it was a profusion of papers and files, untidy but chronological. He finally found a recent document which seemed to provide a useful summary:

Charles Henri Sanson, born in Paris, 15 February 1739, son of Charles Jean-Baptiste Sanson and Madeleine Tronson, executioner. Courts women and visits prostitutes. Stakes his claim by carrying a sword and using the name Chevalier de Longval. Settles down after his marriage. Is considered a sorcerer and bonesetter. Met his wife, Marie-Jeanne Jugier, daughter of a market gardener in Rue Montmartre, while hunting, a favourite occupation of his. One of his witnesses is Martin Séguin, manufacturer of fireworks for the Kings' celebrations, living in Rue Dauphine in the parish of Saint-Sulpice. Owns a house at the corner of Rue Poissonnière and Rue d'Enfer, and a farm at Brie-Comte-Robert. Acquainted with J. B. G. D. D. L. d. B., and is said to have slept with her. On very good terms with Commissioner Le Floch, who asks him to perform clandestine autopsies in place of qualified doctors (see attached complaints).

There was nothing in all this to surprise Nicolas, who was

amused to see himself included. As for the mysterious initials, they clearly denoted Madame du Barry. Nor was there anything here that might have made him see Sanson in a less favourable light. Nicolas reflected on the subterranean life of the archive, which underlay and reinforced the work of the police and the law. He worked all afternoon, thinking and writing, while receiving emissaries bearing messages both written and oral from his colleagues in the twenty districts of the capital. The hours went by without his being aware of them. It was only when hunger began to gnaw at his vitals that he looked at his watch. He gathered his papers and walked to Rue Montmartre.

Night was falling on a glittering city. Only the previous year the street lighting had been poor, provided by ill-conceived lanterns hung across the roadway and only lit between twilight and two o'clock in the morning. After much consultation, Monsieur de Sartine had devoted his energies to the installation of street lights. A way was found to fix the lanterns in position and to improve the delicate mixture of oils in order to increase combustion. The artists Argant and Quinquet, renowned for the invention and manufacture of lamps for interior lighting, had participated in the enterprise. Not only was the street lighting now on all night, but the main road from Paris to Versailles was lit, too, providing security and wonder to the occupants of the coaches travelling at night between the city and the Court.

When Nicolas got to Monsieur de Noblecourt's house, he went straight to his apartment, which seemed larger now that he had added a small desk and moved all his books to beautiful shelves of white leaded wood. The pleasant smell of cooking suggested that the supper would be a fine one. He assumed that the master of the house had guests. Apart from such special occasions, the former procurator was, more often than not, condemned to a meagre portion by Marion, his elderly housekeeper, who wanted to spare her master, so attracted to the good things in life, a resurgence of his gout. Nicolas changed his coat and tied a fine lace cravat round his neck. Thus elegantly attired, a reflection of Master Vachon's classicism, he went down to Monsieur de Noblecourt's floor.

For a moment he waited in the shadow of a display cabinet in order to get an idea of the evening's guests, and noted that the former procurator was speaking to one of them in a more deferential tone than was his custom with his table companions.

'I am pleased, Monseigneur, to find you in such perfect health. The last time I had the honour of receiving you in my humble abode, you were suffering from a most irksome increase in the humours . . .'

'More than that, my dear Noblecourt, much more than that. A real plague, and your reminder makes me realise that I don't invite you often enough for supper. I was covered in scurf. It was the veal that saved me. They put veal on me every day. On my own initiative, I decided to bathe in almond milk and to drink distilled wine in an infusion. In Bordeaux, they said I was taking milk baths and getting my arse cut to restore my face! But it purged me for the rest of my life, like a universal cauterant supplied by Mother Nature. Since, I've had nothing but slight upsets.'

'The years roll off you like water off a slate roof.' Noblecourt let out a sigh. 'The same cannot always be said of men your age. I am only four years your junior, and alas . . .'

'My dear fellow, it may be a foible of mine, but I give credence to a prediction based on an examination of the stars, which puts my death in the month of March.[2] Like Caesar, I become gloomy at its approach, but once it's over I can be sure that I have a whole year ahead of me. So at the moment I'm at the high point of my annual cycle!'

Nicolas decided it was time to make his entry. He recognised the lively old man as the Duc de Richelieu, Marshal of France. He had often seen him at Versailles where, as First Gentleman of the King's Bedchamber, he was part of the monarch's intimate circle. The former procurator made the introductions, and Nicolas bowed. Richelieu was a short man. He wore a blue coat, his face was covered in ceruse and rouge, and his wig was so heavily powdered that every time he moved he was enveloped in a small cloud. The study was hot, and the smell of scent that pervaded it, mixed with the aromas of the food and wine, was almost nauseating.

'Ah! Young Ranreuil, with whom the King is so besotted, and who spends his time helping Sartine. Delighted to see you, Monsieur, delighted.'

Noblecourt, doubtless worried about Nicolas's reaction, hastened to say, 'Yes, he provides security for us, a living proof of the excellence of the finest police force in Europe.'

He turned to the other guest, a man dressed in black whom Nicolas had barely noticed.

'Monsieur Bonamy, city historiographer and librarian and my companion in the administration of the parish of Saint-Eustache.'

Richelieu laughed. 'And a friend of Provost Bignon, my companion in the French Academy.'

'Monseigneur, Monsieur, I am overwhelmed by the honour you do me,' said Nicolas, bowing again.

'Honour be hanged!' the marshal exclaimed. 'Sit down, young man. We're on the meat course.'

'Monseigneur,' said Noblecourt, 'has sent me his cook, who uses a particular technique to treat meat, which makes it easily digested.'

The duke laughed, 'But not very tasty – you might as well say it.'

'Monseigneur,' Noblecourt went on, addressing Nicolas, 'has had a carriage made which he calls his "sleeper". He can rest inside it as if he's in his bed, and as he doesn't like eating in inns – or at his friends' houses – his carriage has a stove tied to the bottom, filled with heated bricks, for cooking meat.' He turned to Richelieu. 'In truth, I don't think there's ever been a man who's gone to such lengths to enjoy life's comforts, or who has been obeyed more punctiliously than you.'

'That's as may be,' the marshal grumbled. 'I succeed in everything, everything obeys me and everyone yields to me. I have the favour of His Majesty's small apartments, but I, who was once page to his ancestor Louis the Great, have never been admitted to the Council!'

'Surely a hero like you should be above such vanity!'

'Vanity! Vanity! I'd like to see your reaction if you were in my position! You don't know anything about it – you're only a lawyer!'

Nicolas felt sorry that Noblecourt, the most courteous and

generous man in the world, should have to swallow such an affront. He knew the marshal's pride was boundless and that he was never able to resist a witticism, however cruel and unpleasant it might be to his friends. Everyone knew that his ambition was 'to be more of a Richelieu than the great Cardinal' and to add the prestige of a statesman to his own military glory by becoming First Minister. He had an implacable hatred of Choiseul, and made no bones about saying so. He had encouraged the King's new favourite – although he denied it – and counted on the fact that Choiseul's hatred of the English would lead the King to dismiss him in order to avoid a resumption of hostilities. The ageing monarch was tired and had not yet recovered from the impact of the disastrous war of 1756. All these elements came into the marshal's calculations.

'So,' he went on, too shrewd to dwell on his disagreeable remark and anxious to change targets, 'Sartine's wings have been clipped, have they? Quite a success for a Lieutenant of Police, to let one half of Paris crush the other half to death! Such incompetence! His Majesty is angry, and Madame du Barry likes Provost Bignon. Excellent conditions for seeing the mighty fall.'

'May I be allowed to remark, Monsieur,' said Nicolas, 'that the Lieutenant General was in no way responsible for security at the festivities?'

Monsieur de Noblecourt glanced uneasily at his companions and, without calling for his servant Poitevin, filled their glasses with a cherry-blue burgundy.

'That's good,' said the marshal approvingly. 'The young rooster defends his chief. I like that in such a charming young man.'

He was looking intently at Nicolas. His love of women did not exclude other tastes, which the fair sex is fully entitled to frown upon, and it was rumoured that one of his first mistresses, the Duchesse de Charolais, reproached him for paying too much attention to one of his vergers, a handsome young man.

'Monseigneur,' Monsieur Bonamy intervened, in a cracked little voice, 'I feel I may contradict you, having known you for more than forty years. The responsibility for maintaining order during the festivities in Place Louis XV lay entirely with the provost. I have worn out my poor eyes looking for genuine precedents, but those I found pre-date the creation of the post of Lieutenant General of Police by the great King to whom you had the honour of being page. No need to go as far back as Charles V to know that!'

'Now Bonamy butts in to refute me! Forty years ago, I would have ignored the edicts on duelling – if, that is, you'd been in a position to hold a sword.'

'It would have been presumptuous of me to cross swords with the finest warrior in Europe,' the city historiographer replied calmly.

'Not at all, Bonamy. I wasn't that yet, and you're forgetting the Maréchal de Saxe.'

'Only true glory can recognise its fellow,' declared Noblecourt.

'Oh,' said Richelieu, 'on the day of the battle of Fontenoy, the marshal was bloated with a remedy intended to purge him of a stubborn pox – he was the only army general to ever be deflated by glory. The whole of the King's household witnessed it!'

They laughed and drank as the dessert was served. The

marshal dipped a parsimonious spoon into the redoubt of a blancmange, which he then bombarded with a drop of jelly.

'I'm glad to see, my dear Noblecourt, that you still cling to the old traditions and don't spoil the end of your meals with those cream salads or sultanas with spun sugar that stick to the teeth! Not like those lunatics besotted with novelties which seem to me quite absurd, where everything is so overloaded with decoration that you really have no idea what you're eating.'

The noise of a horse and carriage could be heard from the street.

'But it's getting late, and even the best company must break up.' He rubbed his hands with a ribald air. 'The night is still young for a Richelieu! A thousand pardons, Noblecourt. Your humble servant, Monsieur Le Floch. Bonamy, if you'd like to take advantage of my coach, I can drop you anywhere you like.'

Bonamy bowed. Noblecourt seized a five-branched torch, which Nicolas immediately took from his hands for fear that the weight might make him stumble. The group walked the marshal to the coach entrance, where a carriage was waiting, with a coachman and two footmen, for the victor of Port-Mahon.

Back in his apartments, Noblecourt collapsed into a *bergère*. He seemed overcome with fatigue. He groaned several times, sunk in gloomy reflection. Nicolas opened the door to the cabinet of curiosities and immediately a pitiful shape panting with gratitude rubbed against his feet.

'What is Cyrus locked up for?' said Nicolas, taking the dog in his arms.

'The marshal doesn't like dogs, or, rather, he can't stand other people's dogs. And when I say he can't stand them . . .'

Noblecourt looked at Nicolas. 'I'm sorry for the exhibition I made of myself; you must have thought me very sycophantic. But I am of a generation for which friendship, not even friendship, just so much as a glance from a duke and peer of the realm was part of a family's precious inheritance. He's not as bad as he likes to appear, but he thinks only of himself. This evening, being something of a freethinker, he insisted on meat even though it's Friday. He spurned the Normandy sole so divinely cooked by Marion and Catherine. You can imagine how upset they were!'

'I find him quite insolent.'

'What can we do? He used to make even Madame de Maintenon laugh! You judge him harshly because he attacked Sartine. But his quarrel is not with the Lieutenant of Police, it's with the friend, or supposed friend, of Choiseul. He judges others only through the prism of his own interests and his own glory. Even in his private life, scandalous as it is, ostentation prevails over sentiment. His love of sensuality is part of his pride, and as women have always been boundlessly generous to him, they have confirmed him in his attitudes.'

He rang, and Poitevin appeared.

'Bring the sole for Nicolas. At least I can be certain that he'll appreciate it.'

Monsieur de Noblecourt was recovering his taste for the here and now.

'In the middle of an investigation, I presume? While you eat, tell me whatever you can, provided it's not a secret. It'll distract me.'

Nicolas set about the fish, which he washed down with red wine: white wine was banned in Noblecourt's house because of his gout – and his lack of will power. He gave a detailed account of the two investigations in which he was engaged. For a while, Noblecourt remained pensive.

'Once again,' he said at last, 'you are involved in a very delicate case. What you have to understand is that you are trapped between conflicting forces. Of course no one suspects the provost of having engineered the disaster on Place Louis XV himself. But nor is anyone stupid enough not to realise that he'll do everything in his power to shift the blame on to someone else.'

'Does he really have the power to do that?'

'Make no mistake, the new concubine, who's all the more dangerous in that she has permanent access to the King and feels threatened by the arrival of the Dauphine, will do her utmost to bring down those thought to be supporters of Choiseul. And, unfortunately, Sartine is seen, rightly or wrongly, as his friend.'

'You know how highly I prize your judgement. It's always been of benefit to me. What is your feeling about the crime in Rue Royale?'

'That Indian of yours interests me. I'm pleased that a native from the untamed depths of the New World knows our language. He sounds like an honest man to me, although he may well be hiding something vital from you. As for the rest of them, there are often domestic wars within families and, when they are discovered, new light is suddenly thrown on what appear from the outside to be tranquil households. It also seems to me that, beneath their eccentricity, the Galaine sisters are quite crafty. Those are my first impressions. With that, Nicolas, I really must go to bed. The evening has been quite taxing. I shall leave you alone with the fruits of Neptune and bid you good night.'

Cyrus slipped from Nicolas's arms and languidly followed his master. Nicolas was too exhausted to linger and, after dispatching the two sole and emptying the bottle of wine – much to the satisfaction of Poitevin, who ran to tell the two cooks – he went upstairs to bed. For a long time he tossed and turned, mixing the elements of the two cases, trying to seize certain details that escaped him. As sleep overcame him, everything became confused in his mind, and his last image was that of three dice rolling, hitting each other but never stopping.

Saturday 2 June 1770

After washing and donning a sober but elegant dark-grey coat, Nicolas put on his wig. He hated wearing a wig, especially now that the weather was getting warmer. He breakfasted on soft rolls and a *bavaroise*,[3] and enquired after the health of Monsieur de Noblecourt, whose weariness the previous evening had struck him. According to Catherine, the old man had got up early and after a light breakfast had decided to follow his doctor's advice. The famous Tronchin of Geneva, whose best-known patient was Voltaire, had been consulted through the intermediary of the great man about the former procurator's condition. He had recommended a personal visit, but in the meantime had prescribed a diet and a daily walk. Monsieur de Noblecourt had therefore decided to begin the day by taking Cyrus for a stroll along Rue Montorgeuil, where he could stand and gape like a true Parisian at the stalls and the passing parade of the city. Marion was afraid only of one thing, that he might be tempted by the ali babas – delicate saffron-flavoured pastries – sold by Stohrer, the Queen's pastry cook.

Nicolas enjoyed these morning conversations. He was sitting in the servants' pantry when there was a knock at the door. After a few moments, one of Monsieur de Sartine's footmen was admitted by Poitevin. The Lieutenant General's coach was waiting for him at the door. They had to leave for Versailles immediately. Nicolas had the presence of mind to go back upstairs and get his tricorn. Then he ran down to join his chief.

'You nearly kept me waiting, Commissioner,' said Sartine by way of greeting. 'We need to get to Versailles as quickly as possible. The King has brought forward to Saturday morning the audience he usually grants me on Sunday evening. He's a creature of habit, so that's an ominous sign. Apart from that, His Majesty having learnt, I don't know from whom' – his expression grew sterner – 'that a young commissioner witnessed the scene, he wants to hear you describe the evening of which you spent, God damn me, a good part down a chimney! What I'm saying is that my patience is being tried, especially when I read all these pamphlets and songs full of untruths, which try to fool the people with manufactured news! And, to make matters worse, I then have to wait for you in Rue Montmartre!'

Nicolas listened with a smile. He knew that Sartine was trying to purge himself of his own anxieties with this flood of words.

'Monsieur—'

'No! May I remind you, Monsieur Commissioner at the Châtelet, secretary to the King in his counsels, that your office demands taste, an aptitude for work, precision, uprightness, fairness of mind, equanimity of character, propriety in conduct . . . Who do you think I'm describing, Monsieur?'

'Why . . . you yourself, Monsieur.'

131

Sartine turned to Nicolas, and only a slight pursing of the lips revealed that he could barely contain his laughter. 'And what's more, he makes fun of me! But you're not mistaken, Nicolas. That was the description of a good policeman, for which I, being the chief, am indeed the model.'

At Porte de la Conférence, beside the Tuileries Gardens, they were brought to a halt by an angry gathering. A wagon had spilt its load, blocking the roadway.

'Look at these people,' said Sartine pensively. 'The most amiable in the world, but the quickest to become aroused. We need to know our territory – as indeed you do – the better to contain any disorder into which they could all too easily be led. Above all, we mustn't show weakness where we need to display energy. But we must always act with tact and caution, taking care not to offend public opinion, knowing how to defuse and restrain human passions, which are so harmful to society as a whole.'

With these powerful words the Lieutenant General offered his snuffbox to Nicolas, who declined. He only used snuff during autopsies at the Basse-Geôle. Semacgus, as a former naval surgeon, was amused by this habit, borrowed from the officers on galleys who were sickened, up on their 'coach',[4] by the heavy stench rising from the rows of oarsmen. Nicolas had noted at a glance that the snuffbox was a gem, with a portrait of the King set in a circle of diamonds. A series of sneezes followed, which seemed to procure Monsieur de Sartine the greatest pleasure. They rode in silence as far as Sèvres. These silences were also marks of confidence, and Nicolas took them as such. They crossed the Seine, and as they passed beneath the hill on which the Château de Bellevue stood. He remembered Madame de

Pompadour, as he always did at that point. The same thought had occurred to Sartine.

'Many unpleasant things were said when our beautiful friend died . . . If you ever hear them, don't let them go without comment. The King is a good master – we have to defend him.'

'I assume, Monsieur, that you are referring to the accusations of indifference made against him when the marquise's body was transferred to the church of the Capucines in Paris. Her cortege passed within sight of the chateau . . .'

'You assume correctly. In fact, the King was very affected by her death, although he made an effort to conceal his grief from everyone. But that evening, when your friend La Borde went to close the shutters, he found the King with his other groom, Champlot, who told me that the King had stood in the rain, watching the cortege until the last carriage had disappeared. He had come back into the room, his face covered in tears – tears, not rain – and murmured, "These were the only respects I could pay her! . . . A friend of twenty years!"'

With this confidence, Sartine turned away and did not break the silence again until they reached Versailles. It struck Nicolas that he would never know all there was to know about this man.

No sooner had their coach entered the first courtyard than a page rushed forward to hand a sealed envelope to the Lieutenant General. It was a summons to see Monsieur de Saint Florentin, Minister of the King's Household, without delay. He enjoined Nicolas to wait for him at the entrance to the apartments and hurried off towards the ministers' wing. Nicolas was pacing up and down, idly studying the curious architectural features of the façade, when he felt a tug on the tail of his coat. He was surprised to see his spy Rabouine, a sword at his side, his thin face contorted in a grimace to attract attention.

'What are you doing here, Rabouine? And carrying a sword, what's more!'

'Don't talk to me about that – I had to hire one. They wouldn't let me in without a sword. Apparently around here it makes you look noble. I was furious at having to argue with them, because I didn't want to miss you when I saw you pass with Monsieur de Sartine. Monsieur Bourdeau has sent me with an urgent message. I galloped here as fast as I could on a nag that almost threw me off twenty times!'

Nicolas opened his deputy's note. All it said was: *Rabouine will tell you everything.* He cast a questioning look at the party concerned.

'Strange things have been happening at the Deux Castors, the place you're investigating at the moment,' Rabouine began. 'At the stroke of three this morning, the household was woken by terrible noises – not just the household, the whole neighbour-hood. People gathered outside the Galaine house. They even rang the alarm bell in a nearby chapel. The door of the shop was forced, and those who went in found the family on their knees praying, and the maid, stark naked, dancing a jig and jumping up to the ceiling, with strange lights around her body. The onlookers all fled in terror. Finally, the priest came and calmed the family down, and everyone hailed it as a miracle. It was like the Jansenists of Saint-Médard all over again. The watch dispersed the crowd, and your colleague in the district posted French Guards outside the shop. And that's the story!'

Nicolas thought for a moment, then sat down on a boundary stone and wrote a short note, which he sealed with his signet ring bearing the Ranreuil arms, topped with a marquis's crown.

'Rabouine, go back to Bourdeau and give him this. But have something to eat first.' He tossed him a coin, which the other caught in mid-air. 'I'm staying here with Monsieur de Sartine. I should be back some time this evening. If not, I'll be with Monsieur de La Borde, First Groom of the King's Bedchamber.'

He had barely finished writing down the surprising development in his little black notebook when he was drawn by a crimson-faced Sartine towards 'the Louvre' and the entrance to the apartments. He opened his mouth to speak, but his chief silenced him with a look. He gave up and followed him into the maze of the palace. They climbed a half-spiral staircase and came to a large hall. Sartine, always eager to show off his knowledge of places, from which he drew some pride, but also conscious of his responsibilities as mentor, commented volubly, 'We're going up to the King's private rooms, which used to be Madame Adélaïde's apartments.'⁵ He lowered his voice. 'When Madame du Barry established herself, the King transferred his daughter to the ground floor and took this apartment for himself.'

They walked along narrow corridors, from which windows occasionally allowed vertiginous views of large drawing rooms and small shaded courtyards. They came to a bare room with window seats, which the Lieutenant General indicated as the bathers' room, without going into any further details. On their left, a few steps led to another room, from which came the sounds of swirling water and conversation. They stopped and waited in silence. A page came out, looked at them with a mocking air and disappeared again, without seeing a discreet signal from Sartine. A few moments later Monsieur de La Borde appeared, smiling. He put a finger to his mouth and nodded at them to follow him. They climbed the steps and found themselves enveloped in scented steam. They were in a rectangular room, rounded at one end, which contained two parallel metal bathtubs. Servants in white piqué were bustling around one of the tubs, in which a man, his head wrapped in a knotted madras, was being washed. One of the aides approached with huge towels.[6]

Assuming a solemn air, Monsieur de La Borde cried, 'Gentlemen, the King is leaving his bath!'

Sartine and Nicolas lowered their heads. Louis XV was quickly wrapped in the towels and almost dragged to the second tub.

In a low voice, La Borde explained that His Majesty was to be rinsed in clean water. The King, who had so far not taken any notice of his visitors, now looked up and saw Sartine.

'I'm sorry, Sartine, to have summoned you so early in the morning, but I couldn't wait to see you. Did you follow my instructions? I don't see young Ranreuil.'

'Sire, he's here, behind me. At Your Majesty's orders.'

The King's black eyes peered at Nicolas through the steam. 'Good, good. La Borde, take them where I told you.'

Nicolas always felt the same emotion when he found himself in the King's presence. The strangeness of the place, the rapidity of the scene and the monarch's unusual attire did not allow for lengthy examination. The King was said to have aged: Nicolas promised himself to take a closer look at him. They followed Monsieur de La Borde down a long corridor, then turned right and entered a gilded room, named as Madame Adélaïde's former music room. They then passed a staircase and entered a narrow room lit by a single window. Beyond it was a tiny corridor leading to a wardrobe. Nicolas was immediately struck by the intimacy of the small room. Its lack of light was compensated for by the white, gold-embellished woodwork, the painted pier glasses and a large mirror. The furniture consisted of a writing desk, a *bergère*, some chairs and stools, and a display cabinet filled with *chinoiseries*. There were *layettes*[7] on shelves and in cupboards discreetly built into the walls. They waited in silence. A concealed door opposite them opened and the King appeared to emerge from the wall, wearing a light grey coat and a wig. Nicolas thought he looked very stooped. He had lost that haughty bearing which made him recognisable at a hundred paces: with his stooped back, he now resembled prints of his old adversary, Frederick of Prussia. His features, although still regular, had been encroached upon by the ravages of old age, and there were harsh rings beneath his eyes. He collapsed into the *bergère*. After a moment, he addressed La Borde.

'Make sure no one disturbs us. And I mean no one, not even . . .'

He left the sentence hanging. Who could possibly disturb the King? The Dauphin, so timid and petrified in his grandfather's presence? The mischievous Marie-Antoinette, still such a child? His daughters? They were much too respectful of their father to allow themselves such unseemly behaviour. There remained Madame du Barry, and if this hypothesis was correct, it was a significant piece of information. In spite of her influence over the ageing King, she was not party to certain affairs. Although he could not have said why, Nicolas found this reassuring. To his amazement, the King next addressed him.

'Ranreuil, do you know how to break a rabbit's legs without a knife?'

Nicolas bowed. 'Yes, Sire, by tearing off only the small bones.'

'Sartine, he's as good as Lasmatartes, my first whipper-in.' The King reflected for a moment. 'One day, when I was a child, I wanted to visit the Infanta, but they couldn't find the key to the great gallery. I made representations to the marshal,[8] who had the door broken down. There was much muttering about it. What do you think of that?'

'That we are all under Your Majesty's orders.'

The King seemed to retreat into himself, his head sunk onto his chest. With his right hand, he twisted a button on his left sleeve.

'Let them take my silences for orders! How goes the city, my Lieutenant General of Police?'

His voice still a little hoarse, the King had insisted on the possessive.

'The city,' said Sartine, 'is still coming to terms with its misfortune. It has wept a great deal. It has somewhat shouted down your servant and . . .'

'The wind has turned, as it always does.'

'Yes, Sire, and more quickly than might have been expected. The presence of Monsieur Bignon in his box at the Opéra last night caused a scandal. He was hissed at, and his words condemned him in the eyes of the public.'

'What did he say?'

'That the reason there were so many victims was because there were many spectators, which meant that the festivities were a success.'

'He'll never be any different; his uncle was right! But as far as the causes of the disaster go, I'd like to hear young Ranreuil.'

In the cramped dimensions of the room, Sartine had to move aside to leave Nicolas face to face with the King.

He started speaking without any particular emotion. He had begun his career at court by telling a story, and he felt bound to the King, who had always displayed great benevolence towards him. There had been winks from the monarch at court ceremonies, showing that he had recognized him, regular invitations to the hunt, where his experience of hunting and his skills on horseback were admired, and now access to the King's secret affairs, the symbol of which was his admittance to this remote room. There was also the solicitous friendship of Monsieur de La Borde. Everything combined to make him feel that he was appreciated by a man who, in his private life, liked nothing better than discretion, loyalty, a pleasant manner and the ability to amuse. Without exaggerating, he put the necessary vigour and pace into his narration of the tragic event. He went into detail, but did not insist on apportioning blame. The King, at once fascinated and horrified by the description of the disaster, nevertheless wanted to know more about the real causes. To know more, thought Nicolas, or to confirm what he already suspected about the part that he himself, by his decision to leave the provost free to do as he pleased, might have played in the causes of the catastrophe.

'Sire,' he replied, 'it appears to me, in all good faith, and not-withstanding my position, that the negligence must be attributed to Monsieur Bignon and the aldermen, who claimed that they alone had the right to police the areas adjacent to the centre of the festivities.'

'And why would they make such a claim?'

Sartine threw him an anxious glance, but Nicolas avoided the trap.

'Their argument was that the festivities were being paid for by the city.'

This explanation seemed to satisfy the King.

'Now,' Nicolas went on, 'apart from the fire and the con-gestion in Rue Royale, the City Guards should have been there in greater numbers and under stronger command. Their leaders were playing pontoon in a neighbouring tavern rather than doing their duty and protecting the public. One thousand five hundred *livres* to the colonel of French Guards to deploy one thousand two hundred men accustomed to this kind of gathering would have made all the difference. Finally, the greatest mistake was to let the guests from the ambassadors' mansion drive their carriages into Rue Royale.'

'All that is clear, Monsieur. What is the death toll from that sad day?'

The King had turned to Sartine, who made a sign to Nicolas to continue.

'As Monsieur de Sartine ordered, I tried to establish a precise count of the victims. Officially, a hundred and thirty-two deaths. The Procurator General did the same, and we compared our figures, taking care to collect the death certificates of all those who died as a result of these terrible events. The total is one thousand two hundred.'

'As many as that?' said the King, overcome with emotion.

'We've been able to break it down as follows: five monks, two priests, twenty-two persons of distinction, a hundred and fifty-five bourgeois, four hundred and fifty-four of the common people, and eighty who drowned, plus those who were taken home or to hospital.'

The King, always drawn to macabre details, wanted to know the state of the bodies that had been recovered. Nicolas replied briefly, and Sartine, anxious like him not to plunge the monarch into gloom, hastened to change the subject. He recalled the plan put forward by his office to ensure that, in future, hard stones would be cut and worked on only in quarries, to avoid dangerously cluttering the streets and squares of Paris. 'As the King no doubt knows,' he went on, 'Monseigneur the Dauphin has entrusted to me six thousand *livres* from the sum which Your Majesty allows him for his little pleasures and has asked me to use it for the benefit of the most unfortunate.'

'I'm pleased that he feels such compassion for the fate of my subjects. I know that he has great respect for you – and he's usually extremely sparing of his respect.'

Nicolas had the impression that Sartine was blushing.

'Do you have anything less sad to tell me, Sartine?'

'Sire, the Bishop of Traves managed to get hold of a cab in which there was already a female passenger. Gallant young prelate that he is, he apologised a thousand times on the way to her residence. It was impossible subsequently to conceal from him the fact that the lady in question was La Gourdain, Paris's leading madam.'

The King laughed. 'Ah! I wager some of his colleagues would have recognised the lady! Is that all, Sartine?'

'Nothing else that could interest or amuse Your Majesty.'

The King stretched his legs and rubbed his hands in glee. 'Is that so, Sartine? There is something else happening in your good city. I hear there is agitation abroad, that people are gathering, that emotions are running high. First there was Saint-Médard, now there is Rue Saint-Honoré.'

He was looking intently at Sartine. Nicolas, who was once again behind his chief, took out his little black notebook, opened it and delicately placed it in the Lieutenant General's hand. This gesture did not escape the King's notice.

'Have you forgotten something?'

'No, Sire,' said Sartine coolly. 'I was just checking my notes in case any event that might interest Your Majesty had slipped my mind.'

Nicolas did not quite grasp what was happening.

'Ha, ha!' said the King. 'I've caught you. It seems I have to inform you that there have been some strange manifestations within a family of shopkeepers near the Opéra. People are saying it's a repeat of the scandalous events that occurred over the grave of Deacon Pâris. You know how these things start . . . I can already see the archbishop sticking his nose into the administration and policing of the city, just as he did some time ago when he managed to extract from me a *lettre de cachet*, which you quite rightly considered an extraordinary and unacceptable encroachment on your jurisdiction. Here are my orders. Young Ranreuil, who has again proved his worth and his cool head, will take up temporary residence in the house and investigate the supposed possession. Once he has penetrated its mystery, he will give me a detailed report. He must go at once.'

'Your Majesty's orders will be carried out.'

The King rose. He seemed rejuvenated. 'This interview shall remain between the three of us. You, Sartine, will come to your audience tomorrow, the day of Pentecost, and then you will do me the pleasure of staying to dine with me in my private apartments. As for you, Ranreuil, to horse, tally-ho, tally-ho! Good hunting!'

They bowed. The King bade them farewell with a charming gesture and disappeared in the direction of his apartments. Monsieur de La Borde walked them to the ambassadors' staircase, one floor below. The sunlight in the main courtyard was dazzling. Nicolas opened his mouth to speak, but Sartine forestalled his question.

'I know what you're going to say, Nicolas. Thank you for trying to get me out of a sticky situation. But the King was so pleased to tell me something he thought I didn't know that I had no desire to spoil his pleasure.'

Having delivered this lesson on how to be a courtier and a loyal servant, Sartine, beaming all over his face, left Nicolas and set off to find his crony Saint-Florentin and tell him that his disgrace would not be happening yet awhile.

VI

FEAR

The truth may not always be likely.
Boileau

From Monsieur de La Borde, who wanted to invite him to supper, Nicolas learnt that the King could not stop singing the praises of his visitors, both Sartine and 'young Ranreuil' who 'was a first-class hunter in every field, and a good servant', in his own words. He declined the invitation, informed his friend of the turn of events and the orders he had received, and asked him for help to get back to the capital as quickly as possible. Monsieur de La Borde immediately took him to the Place d'Armes, and from there to the great stable where, after some discussion, a dappled grey horse was brought out. Nicolas would entrust it to police headquarters when he got to Paris, and a messenger would bring it back to Versailles.

It was almost midday. By carriage, it took at least two hours to reach Paris. Going at a decent speed on a good horse, the length of the journey could be reduced. The gelding set off at a fast trot. Nicolas thought about the scene he had just lived through. He was always touched by his encounters with the King. The anecdote of the door to the great gallery being forced open was a transparent apologia for the regrets he must feeling over another decision he now knew to have been unwise. To express such regrets openly was not his custom, but he had suggested enough to dispel any doubts on the subject. The King was not easily fooled, except when he wanted to be. He had his own channels through which to discover things, and this information helped him to reach a balanced judgement. That observation filled Nicolas with joy and reinforced his loyalty to the man whose profile he remembered seeing on coins when he was a child. The King could come down off his pedestal without seeming in any way diminished, quite the contrary. The events of Rue Saint-Honoré, Nicolas thought, could only have been brought to Louis's attention by someone close to him. The Opéra was not far from the Galaines' shop, almost opposite in fact, and there had been a ball that evening. Lost in thought, he almost ran over a little girl who stood at the side of the road, offering bunches of wild flowers she had gathered in the surrounding woods. It was the horse that saved the child by rearing, which almost unseated Nicolas, even though he was a good rider. To gain forgiveness and to calm the terrified girl, he bought her entire stock at ten times the correct price, which was why, when he rode through Porte de la Conférence and entered Paris just before two o'clock, he was laden with flowers.

In Rue Montmartre, Marion and Catherine were stunned by this unexpected harvest. Nicolas brought Monsieur de Noblecourt up to date with the situation, and advised everyone not to worry in any way, as he would only be absent for a few days at the most. He packed a few changes of clothes and his toilet requisites in a portmanteau, as well as a miniature lantern and pistol, masterpieces of precision given him by Bourdeau. Then he led his horse to Rue Saint-Augustin, left it there, and walked to Rue Saint-Honoré by way of Rue d'Antin and Rue Neuve-Saint-Roch.

The church of Saint-Roch reminded him of an intriguing if relatively trivial case he had dealt with recently. It concerned an individual who had found a way to be invited to a wedding feast every day of his life. Good-looking and friendly, he would regularly don his black ceremonial coat and attend weddings in the larger parish churches. He would mingle with the crowd, and after the Mass would follow the guests to the feast. As the guests of the two families were often meeting for the first time, he would pass unnoticed. Distributing compliments and best wishes to all and sundry, he would get a good meal for his pains. Then a friend of Monsieur de Sartine's, a notary, having noticed the man for the fourth time, informed the police. Nicolas accompanied the notary to a big wedding at Saint-Roch. They soon spotted the black coat, and the notary ventured to ask the man 'whose side' he was on. 'On the side of the door,' he replied, and took to his heels. The commissioner intercepted him. Having been severely reprimanded, the man had to promise to mend his ways, and ended up becoming a police spy. His distinguished appearance and his familiarity with society were ideal for the job, especially at Opéra balls.

At the Galaine house, Nicolas found the door closed. Two French Guards were at their posts, dozing. Seven o'clock was a reasonable hour for a bourgeois family in Paris to be having their supper. He knocked at the carriage entrance. After a few moments, he heard shuffling footsteps, and an elderly female servant in an apron appeared, her head held high like the tortoises in the Jardin du Roi. Tufts of dirty yellow hair peeked out from beneath her cap. She had pale eyes, and her sagging face was crisscrossed with deep lines. Her breasts drooped over her large stomach. From the stains on her apron, Nicolas guessed that she was Marie Chaffoureau, the cook. Presumably Miette had not yet recovered enough to come and open the door to visitors.

'What do you want at this hour? If it's charity, we've already given – there are no scraps left in this house!'

He made a mental note of the remark.

'Could you inform your master that Commissioner Le Floch wishes to speak to him?'

The old face creased in a kind of smile. 'Why didn't you say so before, Monsieur? Please come in. I'll tell the master.'

They entered a courtyard that ran alongside the main building. It had seen better days: grass was growing between the uneven paving stones, and old, mildewed crates were in the last stages of decay. The cook noticed his expression.

'It's not like it was before. I mean, in the days of Monsieur's father. There was a horse and carriage then, and all sorts of things . . .'

Marie Chaffoureau took him through an open door, which led to a small corridor, and pointed him in the direction of the office where he had had his first interview with Charles Galaine. She disappeared, muttering something incomprehensible. He did not have long to wait. From somewhere nearby, he could hear voices raised in argument. A door was slammed. Charles Galaine entered the room, clearly in a foul mood.

'Not only do you not respect the fact that we are in mourning, Commissioner, but you present yourself at an hour when any respectable family has gathered for—'

'You're preaching to the converted, Monsieur. But I am not here on the orders of the police, nor at the request of a magistrate.'

'Then—'

'I am here on the personal orders of the King, to pursue my investigations and report on them to His Majesty . . .'

Nicolas did not think he was exceeding his instructions by linking his ongoing criminal investigation with the events of the previous night.

'The King!' said Galaine in astonishment. 'But how does the King know . . . Anyway, it was nothing but a fit of hysterics.'

'The King knows everything that happened in this house last night. He also knows of the scandal and commotion that your maid's fit of madness provoked. Such disorder cannot be allowed in the capital, with the risk of agitating a populace all too ready to be roused for all kinds of spurious reasons. And if it was just hysterics, why were you and your family praying?'

'Monsieur, what do you intend to do?'

'Follow orders and request hospitality for a few days.'

Galaine made a gesture of surprise.

'Oh, don't worry, I shan't expect you to feed me for free. I'll pay for my board and lodgings. Do you think the King is so poor that he cannot pay his servants' expenses? If you wish to discuss it, let's do so. A good hotel is four or five *livres* a day.'

'But all I have is a wretched cubby hole, a maid's room . . .'

'That will do. So, four *livres* for accommodation, plus two *livres* for food, that makes six *livres*. Shall we make it eight? Is that all right with you?'

Galaine's cheeks had turned a little red. 'Your humble servant, Monsieur. Will you share our supper? We were just about to start.'

Nicolas bowed and followed him out of the room.

The private part of the house was behind the shop, to the left of Charles Galaine's office. It was a growing fashion among the Parisian shopkeeping class to set aside one room for meals. The dining room they entered was windowless, apart from a bull's-eye in the wall adjoining the office, which even in the middle of the day probably let in very little light. The only illumination now came from a number of poor-quality candles. The atmosphere in the room was so musty that Nicolas immediately felt a little nauseous. He was rather perfunctorily introduced to the family, and six pairs of eyes turned to him. The master of the house took his place at the head of the table between his sisters, Camille and Charlotte. At the other end sat Madame Galaine, with her stepson Jean on her right and on her left a fair-haired young man who was introduced as Louis Dorsacq, the shop assistant. To the right of her stepbrother, a little girl of seven or eight, with an angular face, was bent over her plate, apparently sulking. An extra place was set, and Nicolas was curtly requested to sit down opposite the child.

After a clear soup, into which they dipped dry bread, a dish of pigeons and broad beans was brought. The birds were so meagre, they seemed to have shrunk in the cooking. To the visible irritation of Monsieur and Madame Galaine, the older of the two sisters, Charlotte, supported by her younger sister's excited chirping, began inveighing against the style of the house in general and this dish in particular. Never, she said, would they have seen such a thing while their father was alive. He had increased the family's holdings and had not risked the business on speculative adventures and the perils of the sea. Oh, it was shameful to have to reiterate such basic precepts in front of a stranger. She threw a vicious glance at Louis Dorsacq and, changing the subject, recalled what the duties of shop assistants were, in both the wholesale and retail sectors, and how they had to behave. A young man in such a position had to be conscientious, sensible, loyal and not given to cheating, for those who did soon brought loss and ruin to merchants. Last but not least, an assistant had to make a constant effort to do his duty and give his employer nothing but satisfaction. The *coup de grâce* was administered by the younger sister, who expressed the opinion that, for a post like this, a fair-haired young dandy was the opposite of a good servant.

Nicolas looked anxiously at the pigeon on his plate, which slid about in its sauce, resisting all attempts to tear it apart. The two sisters were watching him and laughing. Now Charlotte piped up again, but her brother did not even deign to lift his head. As for his wife, she was having a bluestocking conversation with the assistant, comparing the new auditorium at the Opéra with the one at Versailles. Camille's harsh voice again dominated the table. What were these measly pigeons? Surely, examples of those urban birds which so annoyed the people of Paris with their flapping and their droppings. Caught in a net, they were force-fed by men blowing grass from their own mouths down the birds' crops. Then their throats were cut open, and the half-digested grass was taken out and again blown into the birds, which were not killed for another two days. As the police had responsibility for the supervision of food supplies, Nicolas was only too aware of this practice. Absurdly, Charlotte started asking for parrot. Little Geneviève stood up, her hand over her mouth, pushed back her chair, which fell, and ran out of the room. Charles Galaine looked up and pounded on the table with his fist. Two glasses fell, and wine stained the tablecloth and dripped onto the wooden floor, forming a sinister red blotch, like blood.

'That's enough, sisters, that's too much! Go back to your rooms!'

He was a shy man, but formidable in his anger. Everyone stood up: first Camille and Charlotte, looking offended, then Jean Galaine, lost in thought. Charles Galaine bade good night to the commissioner and asked him to forgive his sisters. The cook would show him to his room. Madame Galaine exchanged a few words with the assistant and left the room without so much as a glance at Nicolas. The assistant, who did not sleep in the house but in furnished lodgings nearby, was about to leave when Nicolas held him back.

'Monsieur, I'd like to have a word with you.'

His mouth twisted in an ugly pout. 'Tomorrow if you like, Monsieur. I'm expected somewhere this evening.'

Nicolas took him firmly by the arm, opened the door to the shop and pulled him inside.

'There's time enough for that. You seemed quite forthcoming on the subject of the boxes at the new Opéra. Oh, I agree with you, the auditorium has met with a great deal of criticism. The orchestra sounds dull, you can't hear the voices and the decorations are shabby, poorly coloured and out of proportion to the dimensions of the theatre. And those infamous boxes. Ah, the boxes!'

As Nicolas spoke, he kept prodding the young man until he fell into a chair.

'The first level aren't very high,' Nicolas resumed. 'And, what's more, not very advantageous for women. As for the foyer . . . Ah, the foyer: completely unworthy of the majesty of the place. Don't you think so? With those steep, narrow staircases. No space. As a matter of fact, why don't you tell me your whereabouts on the thirtieth and thirty-first May, more specifically from four in the afternoon on the thirtieth until six in the morning on the thirty-first. It's quite simple, there's no point in complaining. The sooner we're finished, the sooner you'll be able to go.'

'How can I remember that, Monsieur, and, besides, what is it to you?'

'It's a great deal to me. Come on, I'm listening, or would you rather I took you with me to the Grand Châtelet? Let me help you. Just tell me what time you finished work on the thirtieth of May, the day of the festivities in Place Louis XV.'

'That I can tell you. It was six o'clock.'

'Am I to understand that there are other things you are hiding from me?'

His only response was another pout.

'Was that the usual time?'

'No. But Monsieur Galaine gave me permission to leave the shop earlier than usual so that I could see the display.'

'And then?'

'Then I left the shop and joined the crowd.'

'What happened?'

'Nothing. There was such a crush that I decided to leave the square. I reached the boulevards by way of the Feuillants.'

'Before the disaster, then?'

'I suppose so.' The assistant seemed suddenly hesitant.

'Of course,' Nicolas went on, 'you could have reached the Tuileries by way of the turning bridge, which was open.'

It was a crude trick, but the stakes were high enough for it to be worth the risk.

'Yes, in fact I think that's what I did: I took the turning bridge and came out on the Feuillants.'

'What then?' Nicolas continued smoothly. 'Did you take advantage of the food being distributed, thanks to our good provost?'

'Of course, though it was difficult to get to it.'

'I've been told the wine was very tasty, as lively as anyone could wish. Monsieur Bignon certainly didn't thumb his nose at the people of Paris!'

These material details and the meandering conversation were leading the assistant to lower his guard. Nicolas decided to press on.

'Then you went to your rendezvous, I suppose?'

The young man's face turned red. 'I won't say any more.' He hesitated. 'A lady's honour is at stake.'

'Ah, yes, of course,' said Nicolas. 'A man always invokes a woman's honour when he wants to hide something.' He decided to provoke him. 'A position all the easier to maintain because there wasn't in fact anyone there.'

Dorsacq gave him a distraught look, then turned on his heel and slammed the door as he left the shop. Nicolas decided not to run after him. The interview had given him the opportunity to throw an adversary who in any case was not very good at defending himself. But he knew that this appearance might be only a trap. Of the two young men in the house, this one told barefaced lies, while Jean Galaine continued to be vague about what he had been doing on the night of the tragedy. As for Naganda . . . Nicolas went back to the dining room, where the cook was clearing the table. Mechanically, he made a pile of the dirty plates and followed her into the kitchen. There was a basket of bread which tempted him, and he took a hunk and swallowed it down. The old woman was looking at him.

'What an appetite! I'm not saying you should finish the pigeons, mind you. I feel ashamed having to cook those birds. We'd never have treated a guest like that in the days of Monsieur's father, I can tell you!'

Rubbing the small of her back, she walked out into the corridor, listened for sounds in the house, then came back inside, closed the door and drew the bolt.

'There. We'll be quieter. I'll make you an omelette, but first I'm going to have my beer. The heat from the ovens makes you feel dry and thirsty. This bitter drink cut with water is perfect for that.'

She filled a stoneware pot from a small cask on the draining board. Nicolas sat down and watched. Lard was sizzling in the frying pan. Into it she threw some pieces of bacon and small pieces of bread. She beat the eggs with two forks, making the straw-coloured mixture ever lighter and fluffier. She poured it onto the fat, then swirled the frying pan around while lifting the edges with a wooden spoon. A few seconds later, she placed a sweet-smelling omelette in front of Nicolas. He threw himself on it and gobbled it down.

'It's really good!' he said, with his mouth full.

The thick face creased in a smile of satisfaction. 'It does my heart good to see you eat like that!'

'I imagine you've been cooking for the Galaines for a long time.'

'Oh, my good sir, more than forty years! I almost brought up the children. Well, Monsieur Claude and Monsieur Charles. Charlotte and Camille lost their mother, you know; it wasn't always easy.'

'Different characters, I imagine?'

'Oh, yes! The elder of the boys, Claude, was really lively, too much maybe. His father adored him. His preference for him was obvious. I warned him about that. When you want your sons to get along, you treat them the same, otherwise . . .'

'Otherwise?'

'Otherwise, if you give too much to one, the other one resents it, and things turn sour!'

'Wise words.'

She sipped her beer and stared into space. Nicolas had his doubts that the drink was as adulterated as she had said.

'Is that why he left for New France?'

She shuddered. 'That was the day a curse fell on this house. Our Claude wanted to stand on his own two feet. When he did that, he killed his father. With his elder son gone, he started to waste away, lost interest in his shop, stopped caring about anything. Charles, the younger son, took over. But what can you expect? He's always been dominated by his wives. It's just not right! The first wife was thoughtless and extravagant. She died giving birth to Jean. The second . . .'

She slammed her earthenware pot down so hard on the table that it broke, and a stream of amber liquid escaped.

'This one . . . Well, it comes to the same thing. She despises the shop. She always wants more. She thinks her husband's a puppet she can manipulate as she likes. She's the one who ruined the business by encouraging him to do business with the savages of the North. That's how he lost his savings.'

'The savages of the North?'

'Yes, the Muscovites. We don't get hides from New France any more, so he had to look for other suppliers. But he was cheated by a smooth-talking swindler who took all his money and left him with nothing but a single sample, a piece of sable you couldn't even make a handkerchief out of!'

'And the sisters?'

'They lack common sense. Especially Camille, the younger one.'

That made Nicolas sit up: his initial impressions would rather have led him to doubt the elder sister's reason.

'She idolises her brother and bullies her sister. No one finds favour with her. It goes without saying that she hates her sister-in-law, just as much as the first wife, in fact. As for the elder sister, the poor woman finds refuge in dreams to escape her constant obsession.'

Decidedly, thought Nicolas, he had been right to save the cook until last. Things were starting to fall into place. But he remembered that witnesses can often be biased, and that what they say does not always correspond to the truth.

'What about Jean Galaine? He seems quite a melancholy young man.'

'He takes after his uncle. He loves his father, but he'll rebel against him one of these days. Alas, his melancholy is easily explained: he was mad about his cousin! She played with men like a cat with a ball. Hard not to get scratched!'

'So that's what she was like, is it?'

It occurred to him that this was the first time anyone had talked about the victim.

She seemed to retreat into a grumpy silence. 'No,' she muttered. 'It's wrong to speak ill of the dead. Especially now.'

'Why especially now?'

She pushed her stool close to him. 'Because there are strange things happening in this house. And you're making me talk like an old fool. Of course, I know that's what you're here for. Police commissioners don't usually come and stay in private houses, even when there's been a crime. There'd have to be something more serious. It's really true, there's a curse on this house: it makes my flesh creep. It was quite something to see Miette like that. She has the devil in her body. It gives me the shivers to sleep in the room next to hers.' She crossed herself.

'What do you think's happening to the poor girl, in your opinion?'

'Oh, she's been brooding for a while now. I don't know what's going on with her. I was the one who taught her the job, and it's such a shame to see her in that state. I tell you, she's not a bad girl, but there's something in all this I can't get to the bottom of. She's a brave young thing, even though Madame drives her to despair. She's her whipping boy; she takes out her moods on her. Miette just hasn't been herself since Mademoiselle Élodie died. Well, they did use to be thick as thieves, the two of them, always giggling, always playing tricks. They were the same age, after all . . . It makes me feel sick at heart to think about it.' She put her right hand to her cheek, as if life had just given her a slap in the face. 'I can feel terrible things coming, Commissioner! It gives me the creeps. You should have seen Miette on the ceiling, surrounded by the fire of heaven!'

Her chin collapsed into the folds of her neck, a grey lock escaped from her mobcap, and she began to moan softly, then to snore. Nicolas coughed and she woke, wild-eyed.

'Please forgive me,' he said. 'I just wanted to ask you where the assistant fits in to all this?'

'Dorsacq? A rascal, with his tongue out at the first petticoat he sees.'

'That innocent-looking young man?'

'Innocent? That one? He's involved in all sorts of shady business and thinks only of chasing skirts. If you ask me, Commissioner, he spent far too much time sniffing round Mademoiselle Élodie.'

'And what about Madame?'

'Pah! That's all talk. He's just showing off. He's only interested in young girls.'

'Before we go to sleep, could you tell me your whereabouts on the evening of the firework display?'

'That's easy. In the afternoon I'd made dinner for those who were staying at home.'

'Who was that?'

'Charlotte and Camille, little Geneviève, who was poorly and had to stay and be looked after by her aunts, and the . . . savage.'

'Naganda?'

'Yes. Oh, he's not a bad person, but his face scares me. Monsieur has kept him locked in his room since he returned. He's fed twice a day.'

'On what?'

'A little boiled meat with vegetables and bread in sugared milk.'

'What did you do after that?'

'I went out about six to spend the evening with my friends a few doors away. We're too old for crowds. I must have had a hunch something would happen. We played *bouillotte*, drank coffee with cold milk and ate *oublies*.[1] I got back here about ten and went straight to bed. I'm not as strong as I used to be, and the days are long.'

'Did you notice anything unusual?'

'No . . . Or rather, yes, one small thing. I'd made some soup and left it in plates. Only one of them had been touched. I thought that was a bit odd.'

'Is that all?'

'It's quite enough. The next day, everyone was in a panic.'

'Did you see Naganda when you got back that night?'

'No, but I heard him walking up and down in his room.'

'Were you listening at his door?'

'No!' the cook replied, looking shocked. 'His room is just above mine, and the floorboards were creaking.'

'Are you sure it wasn't an owl?' Nicolas was thinking of the eagle owl which had haunted his summer nights at Guérande with its solemn footsteps and sinister calls.

'Commissioner,' said Marie Chaffoureau indignantly, 'I can still tell the difference between a man's footsteps and a bird's.'

'Anyway, you didn't see Élodie that day?'

'Not that day, not the days before that. They said she was poorly. The two sisters were looking after her.'

'Thank you very much for all you've told me,' said Nicolas. 'It's been extremely interesting. Now, would you be so very kind as to show me to my room?'

'It's next to our poor Élodie's. Miette sometimes slept there too.'

She lit a candle and handed it to him. Nicolas noted that it was so small he would not be able to read for very long. He would have to get in his own supply of candles. He followed her as she climbed the stairs one step at a time, puffing, then opened a door to a narrow room, crossed herself again and bade him goodnight.

The room was not as grim as he had imagined, although it was no wider than a passageway and the window was a mere loophole. The bed was on the right. It had a palliasse, a woollen mattress with a check linen cover, a bolster and a brown blanket. The whole thing took up half of the space. The other furnishings consisted of a small table on which stood two brass candelabra, a stool, a toilet mirror in a brass frame, a jug of water and an earthenware washbowl. A commode covered with a red cloth occupied the remaining space by the window. Two thick linen sheets lay on the blanket. As he placed his candlestick on the table, he noticed that there was a door concealed in the woodwork, only its knob visible.

After undressing, he wrapped himself in a sheet like an ancient Roman or an Egyptian mummy. He knew from bitter experience all about the vermin which took up residence in the majority of bedsteads: as soon as it was dark, the bugs would come out of their lairs and attack their recumbent prey. Nicolas's only defence against these hordes was to leave not an inch of his skin uncovered. He blew out the candle, and its foul odour pervaded the room.

Unable to fall asleep, he reflected on the curious situation in the Galaine household. Charles Galaine was a weak man, dominated by women and trapped in an unhappy marriage. His sisters had all the foibles of old maids, and everything about them was vaguely suspicious. Everyone was lying shamelessly: the wife, the son, the shop assistant and Naganda. It struck him that he ought to speak to the little girl. Children often unwittingly revealed hidden truths. What a pity that Miette was not in a state to be questioned! As the closest person to Élodie, she might well know things that others didn't, things that could be very useful to his investigation.

With this thought, he fell asleep.

. . . The condemned man had struggled for a long time before the blue-coated hangman, with the help of his assistants, managed to tie him to the wheel. Why the devil, thought Nicolas, was he wearing that blue coat? It went against the customs of his profession: a blood-red coat was the accepted dress at executions. Sanson seemed different. His mouth was twisted in a terrible grin. He raised his rod, and Nicolas closed his eyes and waited for the horrible noise of bones cracking beneath the skin. There was a kind of dull roll, and then someone knocked loudly, three times, as if in the theatre . . . He opened his eyes, but instead of a crowded Place de Grève, he recognised the dark little room in the Galaine house. He was bathed in sweat, wrapped in his makeshift protective sheet. It took him a few minutes to come to his senses. The dream had been so real, so vivid, he was not sure that this awakening was not still part of it. The insect bites on his ankle convinced him that he had indeed come back to reality. He dreaded to move or light the candle, fearing to see vermin swarming in the palliasse. Again, three distinct knocks were heard, and this time it was clear that someone had struck the concealed door.

Who could possibly be trying to wake him at this hour? He got up, took a lighter from his portmanteau and lit the candle. Smoke rose from it, along with the same acrid smell. He walked to the door and tried to turn the handle, but it resisted: it was well and truly locked. He decided to go back to bed. The sound could have been part of his dream. Or it could have been the house itself: these old houses always creaked, the timber shrinking and dilating with changes in temperature, dampness and dryness. Unless it was a rat. The city was swarming with them, far more than anyone could ever imagine. Whole armies lived in the cellars and came up into the houses at night. Servants were forced to keep their stocks of food and candles well away from their insatiable greed. The arsenic-based rat poison which people put down caused a thousand tragedies. From time to time, one of the fifty thousand skulls on display at the cemetery of Les Innocents started moving, an apparent miracle actually caused by a rat which had lodged inside a skull and was unable to get out. Amused by this image, Nicolas was about to sink unto unconsciousness when three more knocks were heard, this time at the door leading to the landing.

He held his breath and listened, but all was silent. His heart was pounding. He slid out of bed, rushed to the door and pulled it open. Nobody! And yet he was sure he had not dreamt it. He took a few steps out onto the landing, groping along the walls. Then he went back to his room, lit the candle, came out again and examined the next door, that of Élodie's room. He opened it. In the flickering light of the candle, he looked at the flowered wallpaper and immediately spotted the door leading to his cubby hole. As he walked towards it, it was shaken by three more knocks. He ran back into the other room, certain that he would surprise the joker who was making fun of him, but it was empty. The Galaine house was quiet again. The merchant and his wife did not seem to have been disturbed by the knocking, even though their room was not far away.

What was going on? What strange phenomenon had produced these persistent noises? Nicolas was beginning to doubt his own senses. Was his tired mind concocting these apparitions under the influence of the strange events that had already taken place here? For the first time in his life, Nicolas, who had always been guided by reason, was calling that reason into question. He thought for a long time about what was happening to him, but could not find a plausible explanation, let alone an acceptable one. In desperation he went back to bed, his muscles as tense as if he were expecting a blow. What he had just experienced cast doubt on everything he believed in. He tried frantically to find explanations, hidden causes, hypotheses he would not usually have thought of. He recalled his childhood, and the old Celtic stories which Fine would tell him during vigils, as she roasted the chestnuts. He remembered listening with a mixture of horror and delight to detailed descriptions of tortures and the final journeys of the souls of ghosts, imprisoned in the bodies of black dogs and thrown into the *youdic*, the Breton Styx. These stories would be accompanied by the howling of the wind and the crackle of the fire, and, when they were finished, his old nurse loved setting his mind at rest. This memory soothed him and he fell asleep. It seemed to him that only happy childhoods gave you memories like that, full of the faces of people long gone.

Sunday 3 June 1770: Pentecost

At about four in the morning, he was woken by the light of dawn. His mouth was dry and his eyes hurt. Fortunately, in his linen shroud, he was untouched by vermin. No sound reached him from Rue Saint-Honoré, as his room looked out onto the courtyard. He stretched like a cat. His tiredness disappeared as he became aware again of the world about him. He seemed to hear a dull beating in the distance, accompanied by a repetitive chant. He found a little water in the jug and drank it greedily. It did not taste very good, but it refreshed him. He laughed, and sang:

> *The hypocrite has special skills*
> *He knows how to conceal,*
> *He's far too clever to reveal*
> *The gall his mouth distils.*

He hummed as he dressed, and resolved to wash himself at the pump in the yard. The anguish of the night had vanished, giving way to a renewed desire to untangle the mysteries of the case, even those beyond human understanding. He went out onto the landing, careful not to make any noise for fear of waking the Galaines. There, he heard more distinctly the melody whose distant echo had reached him earlier. It was coming from the top of the house. He climbed the stairs, and the higher he climbed, the louder it became. But what struck him from the beginning was a strange, sweet smell that pervaded the attic like a cloud of incense in a shrine. The key was in the lock of Naganda's room. He turned it.

Sitting cross-legged on a mat on the floor, dressed only in his fringed loincloth, the Micmac was swaying back and forth, and beating a kind of tambourine. He seemed to be worshipping the idol whose coarse features had struck Nicolas during his first search. In front of it glowed an earthenware dish filled with hot coals, on which dried herbs were burning. It was a spectacle at once savage and serene. The light of dawn entering the garret gradually lit up the Indian's back, and his skin moved from dark red to bright amber. Nicolas made up his mind to advance, and put his hand on the man's left shoulder. Naganda did not react. Nicolas walked round him. His face was impassive, as if focused on some distant thought, his open eyes pursuing an inaccessible dream.

Such phenomena were not unknown to Nicolas. Sartine had told him about the strange case of a sleeping man who had risen from his bed, taken his sword and swum across the Seine, all without waking up. He had gone to Rue du Bac and killed a man he had threatened with death the previous day. Once the deed was done, he had returned home, still fast asleep, and gone back to bed. The following night, he had repeated the journey and had been seen by the dead man's family, who were in the middle of the wake. He had been tried and found guilty of murder.

Nicolas hesitated to shake the Indian, having heard that it could be dangerous to wake someone from a trance. He was nevertheless about to do so when a shrill cry echoed through the house. There was something inhuman about the cry, and it continued at a pitch high enough to burst the eardrums. Naganda had not even blinked: he continued chanting incomprehensible words, among which Nicolas noticed the repetition of the word *gluskabe*. He retraced his steps, locked the door and quickly descended the stairs from the attic. He almost fell into the arms of Charles Galaine and his son, who were just arriving on the landing in their nightshirts. Marie Chaffoureau was on her knees, pressing her hands into her old cheeks and muttering prayers. The cry had come from the room where Miette slept. They broke down the door.

The scene which greeted them went far beyond anything Nicolas had ever seen before. Miette was on the bed, her shift in disarray, her legs and breasts bare, her body arched in a state of extreme tension. Beneath her, the palliasse was torn, and spilling straw. Her veins and tendons stood out as if on an anatomical specimen: Nicolas was reminded of the terrible wax figures of the 'theatres of corruption' in Monsieur de Noblecourt's cabinet of curiosities.[2] Miette was howling like a wolf in the moonlight. But what struck terror into the witnesses was the sight of the bedstead rising a few inches from the floor and shaking, as if carried on a swell and moved by invisible hands. Nicolas had to get a grip on himself before he could do anything. He ordered the Galaines to help him keep the bed down on the floor. When they laid their hands on it, it felt as if they were touching a boat on the surface of the water. Suddenly, the bed dropped with a dull thud, but then they were astonished to see Miette's taut body gradually rise into the air. Nicolas seized both her feet and the Galaines her hands. Her skin was burning and hard beneath their fingers. They pressed on her with all their weight. As Miette moved, the three men moved with her, undulating like a wave. But, after a while, she stopped howling and fell heavily back onto the bed; her body went limp, and her breathing eased. They were expecting to see the phenomenon recur, but nothing happened. Nicolas asked Marie Chaffoureau to stay with Miette and call them if the girl suffered even the slightest new attack. He continued to call her 'the patient' even though, faced with the increasing number of incomprehensible manifestations in this house, he was starting to have his doubts. Both father and son were too stunned to say a word, and he had to force them to go downstairs. There was one thing he still had to do.

He climbed back up to the attic. Naganda had finished his strange ceremony, and was now sitting with his arms round his legs and his chin on his knees. He looked at Nicolas with an ironic smile.

'Commissioner, I sense that you are wandering on the shores of truth but cannot find it. Am I mistaken?'

'I still have a few questions to ask you.'

'You don't need questions, you need answers.'

Nicolas did not feel in the mood to play this game. 'You may indeed be able to help me find them. First of all, what were you doing a few minutes ago?' He pointed to the dying embers in the earthenware dish.

'So, you were spying on me? Never mind. I was imploring the spirits of my people to welcome Élodie into the great land of the dead.'

'You looked as if you were asleep.'

'That is the power of medicinal plants. Inhaling them plunges a person into a halfway world. His spirit flies away and enters into contact with the gods. My father was not only a chief, but also a shaman, in other words, a priest and healer. A sorcerer, you would call him.'

'I heard you say the word *gluskabe* several times. What's that?'

'*Kluskabe* is a great warrior from the world of the gods, our hero and protector.'

'The statue's very ugly.'

'The statue isn't of Kluskabe, it's the frog monster that stopped the waters of the earth from flowing. When he was defeated, Kluskabe passed into the monster's body. The statue facilitates divination.'

It was now Nicolas's turn to be ironic. 'So you've had revelations, have you?'

'The sacred frog foretold my death. *Only the son of stone can save me.*' He said these words in an even tone, with a melancholy expression on his face.

'Do you by any chance know what kind of stone that would be?'

'Alas, no! Although it would certainly be in my own interest to elucidate this prophecy. My power allows me to receive warnings, but not to decipher them! It's the situation of all Cassandras.'

'Don't worry, the law protects those who tread an honest path. Talking of which, what would you say if I told you that, during the night when you claim you were in a deep sleep, a witness heard footsteps in your room?'

'I would say, Commissioner, that the form of your question implies the answer. There is nothing improbable about it. There must have been a point when someone came in to steal my things.'

He had answered without hesitation, and the explanation seemed plausible. Naganda was holding Nicolas's gaze without the least sign of embarrassment or confusion. He was like a bronze statue.

'I'll leave you to your thoughts,' said Nicolas. 'I'm going to lock you in, not because I don't trust you, but as a protective measure. Be patient, the truth will out. If you are innocent, it can't hurt you.'

As Nicolas was on his way back down to his room, he bumped into a bulky figure charging up the stairs. In the darkness, all he could make out at first was the grey triangle of a hat. Then he recognised Dr Semacgus.

'Guillaume, where are you running so fast? Anyone would think you were attacking a ship!'

'Damn it, man,' replied Semacgus. 'When a friend sends for me, I come running. Bourdeau passed on your message. I left Vaugirard before dawn. In Rue Montmartre, I woke the whole household, but they told me you were here, so here I am.'

'Come in here,' said Nicolas, pushing the surgeon into his room.

Semacgus sat down on the stool, Nicolas on the bed. The commissioner gave an account of the turn his investigation had taken, making no secret of the fact that the highest authorities in the Kingdom were now taking a close interest in the story of the Galaine household. He described the strange events of the night, Naganda's trance and above all Miette's terrible attack.

'If I didn't know you so well,' said Semacgus, 'and didn't know you were a lover of reason and enlightenment, I would fear that the magic spells of your native Brittany had gone to your head.' He shook his head and sighed. 'Mind you . . . What you've told me reminds me of phenomena I've observed when I was serving in the King's navy. At our trading posts in the Indies, and also in Africa, I witnessed a number of intriguing scenes. Remember Awa going into convulsions – you've told me about it dozens of times – and prophesying the death of my loyal Saint-Louis.[3] What can I say? I'd first have to examine this maid. That might tell us a thing or two about this supposed devilry!'

'You have my permission. She's resting in the room above us. The cook's looking after her.'

They went upstairs. Standing flat against the wall, Marie Chaffoureau was saying a rosary, kissing the crucifix after each prayer. Nicolas asked her to leave the room. Semacgus approached the prone body and looked down at it for a long time. Then he took Miette's pulse, lifted one of her eyelids, and parted her legs. Nicolas watched as he lifted her shift. The surgeon stood there for a while, head down, then drew Nicolas outside and asked the cook to resume her watch. Semacgus looked at Nicolas with his large, sanguine face, his eyes sparkling sardonically, and hit his palm with his fist.

'Quite a tall tale, all these virgins of yours! Do you know what's wrong with the poor girl? She's expecting a child!'

Nicolas did not at first react, as if he had not understood.

'Pregnant!' Semacgus almost yelled. 'That's right, pregnant! At least five months pregnant!'

VII

PENTECOST

I shall not speak with you much longer,
For the Prince of this world is coming.
JOHN, XIV: 30

Semacgus was rubbing his hands in glee at Nicolas's stunned expression.

'So both the young girls in the house were impregnated!' said Nicolas. 'One died in mysterious circumstances, and the other, who must either have been concealing her condition or is unaware of it, is now in' – he hesitated over the words to use – 'an indefinable state which has yet to be explained.'

'Don't get carried away,' said the naval surgeon, now serious again. 'It won't help. There are no phenomena which cannot be clarified by reason. So, if this maid of yours is flying, don't take it for a miracle!'

'But the lives of the saints—'

'Ah, there he is, the Breton, the adopted son of a canon! You're not going to convince me with tales told by old women and monks. I look at these apparently unintelligible facts in another way. We doctors of medicine – if I may assume this title, which some dispute[1] – have long observed attacks like this in simple or ill-educated patients, like this girl. To call things by their name, your patient is suffering from hysteria, the manifestations of which used to be considered works of the devil.'

'I'm not unfamiliar with the term,' said Nicolas. 'But you didn't see the bed rising.'

'Come on now, stop wasting your efforts. Over a century ago, Charles Lepois already saw this sickness as originating in the brain. At about the same time, an Englishman named Thomas Sydenham perfected an opium-based remedy called laudanum, which according to him lessened the effects of such attacks. Even before them, Paracelsus defined such attacks of delirium as deviations of the imagination. I agree with them. Man is a world unto himself. His mind deceives his physical nature, not the other way round. Quite apart from the fact that I reject any idea of a malign influence intent on crushing the heart and exciting the body. Mind you, I must admit this house strikes me as unwholesome, and I quite understand that it's turning your head.'

Semacgus's academic little speech left Nicolas perplexed. His friend, who had not known the torments of the night just past, could have no idea how confused and helpless he felt.

'Be that as it may, Guillaume,' he countered, 'everything must be done to throw light on these mysteries. If you have time, you could do me a favour. Go to Rue Montmartre and ask Monsieur de Noblecourt to let me have his dog Cyrus for tomorrow night. If I am tested to the point where I start to see and hear things that aren't there, I assume an innocent animal won't hear or see anything, and that his passivity will confirm your diagnosis. And as I intend to get as much advice as I can from my friends, when you come back I'll leave you to watch over Miette while I pay a visit to Père Grégoire at the monastery of the Discalced

Carmelites. He'll be pleased to see me; I've been neglecting him lately.'

Reading Nicolas's mind, Semacgus raised his arms to heaven. 'After the medicine of the body, the medicine of the soul. You're off to a bad start . . . But, of course, I remain at your disposal. I haven't given up hope of welcoming you back into the legions of nature and truth. And, with that, I must dash off and have something to eat. It seems to me you should do the same.'

'You're right. The only thing I've eaten in the past twenty-four hours was an omelette.'

'That's not very plump, as your friend the good lady of Choisy used to say.[2] May I remind you that an alert mind requires a full stomach. So make sure you get something down you.'

His friend left, and after a last glance at Miette, who was sleeping peacefully, Nicolas went downstairs to the dining room, where Madame Galaine, wearing a *chenille*, was serving coffee to the rest of the family. The two sisters appeared to have calmed down. Charles was not wearing a wig, and his balding head made him look older. After a slight hesitation, he addressed Nicolas.

'Commissioner, I have a request to submit to you. Given our situation, I believe it is imperative that that my family and I attend one of the Pentecost services at the parish church. It will silence the gossips, and the Lord may answer our prayers for peace to be restored to this house.'

Nicolas consented, thinking all the while that peace would only be restored the day the person responsible for the murder of Élodie was discovered. He would stay with Miette, he said, so that everyone, including Marie Chaffoureau, could perform their religious duties on this solemn day.

Once they had all left the room, he tried to drink a cup of coffee with milk, but his stomach rejected it, because of the skin that had formed on the surface of the liquid – something he had found intolerable ever since he was a small child. But the pump in the courtyard was wonderfully refreshing and rejuvenating on this beautiful, late-spring morning. Deep down, he felt Semacgus was right: the well-being of the body depended on peace of mind and nothing else. But how could he be sure? He went back upstairs to dress and brush his hair. On the stroke of nine, the cook put her head round the door and announced that the family were leaving for the church of Saint-Roch. They were all dressed in mourning clothes. He walked with them to the door of the shop, which they locked from the outside. The commissioner decided to follow through an idea that had come to him when he had realised that he would be alone in the house apart from Naganda, who was locked in his garret, and Miette, who was lying unconscious in her bed. There would never be another such opportunity to look for clues. He decided to begin his search with the bedroom of Monsieur and Madame Galaine.

The door was open. The bed, beneath a canopy of dusty Utrecht velvet, was unmade. Rumpled night clothes lay scattered on the counterpane. Two wing chairs upholstered in the same fabric, a worn carpet, a pedestal table on which stood a carafe of water and two silver tumblers, and a wardrobe so tall that it almost touched the ceiling joists were the outmoded and some-what austere furnishings of the room. The only concession to current fashions was a small writing desk of lemon-tree wood, which seemed, in its magnificence, quite out of place in this antiquated environment. Nicolas was always surprised by the interiors of other people's houses. He had made innumerable searches in his ten years as a policeman, and they had given him a complete range of models into which he could classify what he found, but which did not always correspond to the characters and situations he was investigating.

Nicolas got down to work with the methodical determination of a hunter tracking his prey. He first turned his attention to the writing desk. Neither the drawers nor the sliding desk-top were locked. They contained commercial documents, bills and letters, as well as women's jewellery and ornaments, and a man's shoe buckles. Nothing of interest. For a moment Nicolas stood there, thinking and stroking the fine wood. Then he took out one of the drawers and plunged his arm inside the desk. He groped about for a long time until he felt a small, jointed piece of wood beneath his fingers. He moved it carefully, and heard two clicks. Two narrow panels opened at the back of the desk, and two little oblong drawers sprang out. One contained a number of *louis d'or*, the other a letter with a broken seal representing two beavers joined by their tails: the emblem of the family business.

He took it out, his heart pounding. Two feelings struggled within him: the curiosity natural to his profession, and the scruples of an honest man forced to pry into family secrets. Once that border was crossed, there was no turning back, and his innocence could never be recaptured. He sat down in one of the wing chairs and opened the letter. He felt such strong emotion that the characters danced before his eyes and he found it hard to concentrate on the words. The handwriting was small, angular, but determined, and the ink was beginning to fade with time.

Louisbourg, this fifth of December 1750

Brother

The news of our father's death has brought home to me how terrible it is to be separated from one's family and to be forced to rely henceforth on the coldness of a brother whose constant and long-standing hostility towards me is quite unjustified. I hope that time will mitigate a conflict which I have never wanted and which I cannot recall without feeling a genuine sadness.

That being so, I wish to inform you that I am married and have a child, a daughter who bears our mother's second name, Élodie. Whatever the distance between us, I in New France and you so far away and so little concerned with brotherly feeling, I entrust my niece to you in the event of my wife and myself becoming casualties of the war, which is getting worse. A young Indian named Naganda, whom I took in and raised, and in whom I trust completely, has instructions from me to do everything in his power to ensure that our daughter reaches France.

The last years have been profitable and you have had a substantial share in the success of our business. I intend, one way or another, to leave an indication of my final wishes. Our notary will be informed of them in case I die in the coming events.

Embrace our sisters for me. Remember that I am entrusting Élodie to you. Despite everything, your very affectionate

Claude

Nicolas carefully copied this text into his little black notebook, then gently folded the letter and put it back in the secret drawer. He moved the small drawers back behind the panels, replaced the large drawer, and closed the desk. The rest of his search proved fruitless. Élodie's room – curiously devoid of any personal objects – brought no tangible results, nor did Jean's. In Geneviève's little room, Nicolas discovered, hidden among her dolls, a crumpled sheet of paper on which a strange scene had been clumsily drawn. Two men, identically dressed in large cloaks and tall hats, one squeezing a kind of dummy and the other holding a shovel, seemed to be dancing a jig. He put this strange drawing in the pocket of his coat. Was the twice-depicted man Naganda? It seemed very likely.

He finished his inspection in the room shared by the Galaine sisters. Two beds had been pushed together to make one, occupying almost all the space in a room cluttered with devotional objects, two *prie-dieus* and a number of religious paintings. There was also a small chest of drawers and a kind of alcove serving as a bathroom, with cupboards hollowed out of the wall for storing linen and clothes. Here and there, stuffed birds stood frozen in weary poses, adding a grim, fusty note to the rank atmosphere.

Suddenly Nicolas heard floorboards creaking in the corridor. Who could it be? He assumed that Miette had woken and got up, but the footsteps were coming closer and the intervals between the creaks indicated rather that whoever it might be was moving very cautiously. His first reaction was to look for a hiding place. The clothes cupboard? Certainly not: the most obvious refuge was always the riskiest. The fireplace? Much too narrow to hide in. Then, in a flash, he noticed that the faded blue-green cloth that covered the two beds fell all the way to the floor. He quickly slid under the beds and lay flat on his stomach, with his back against the wooden base. In the excitement of the moment, he found it hard to catch his breath, and this was made worse by the fact that his nose was buried in a mass of cloths that lay on the floor. The footsteps had not resumed. The blood pounding in his ears deafened him. A few inches from his face, he discovered a column of tiny ants which seemed to be attracted by the cloths. Quite apart from the rats, vermin and fleas, many houses in the city received visits from these insects in summer.

Now the noise resumed, came closer, very close . . . In the narrow field of vision allowed by the cloths, Nicolas saw two bare brown feet cautiously advancing. It could only be Naganda, and he guessed that the Indian was also searching the room. Would it occur to him to look under the beds? Nicolas trembled as he saw him coming closer on the right-hand side. The cover was lifted, the bedding roughly searched, then light appeared through the cracks in the wood: the mattress had been raised. The Indian stamped around the room a while longer, then finally walked out. Nicolas waited until silence had returned to this floor of the house. Monsieur Galaine kept Naganda locked up, but had forgotten that the Indian had already escaped through the skylight, and that there was nothing to stop him trying again. It would only take a badly closed door or window for him to gain access to the rest of the house. What could he be looking for, if not the famous talisman? After all, he was obsessed with the loss of the necklace on which it had hung, the necklace that had contained the pearl found in the clenched hand of Élodie's corpse.

Nicolas hoped that his own search would lead to something,

even now that Naganda had gone. He forced himself to continue with all the technique of a professional, which the Indian was not. It was as well that he did so, for in passing his hand under one of the drawers in the chest, he found a small piece of paper stuck to the wood with sealing wax. Carefully, he peeled it off. It was a brief note, which read:

No. 8
Received as security, one lot, for the refundable sum of
eighteen livres, five sols and six deniers.
To be redeemed within one month. This thirty-first of May
1770.

Signed Robillard,
Second-hand clothes dealer,
Rue du Faubourg-du-Temple

A pawnbroker? A moneylender? A way for the Galaine sisters to make some additional income? It was not so much the nature of the note which intrigued Nicolas as the date. 31 May was the day after the disaster in Place Louis XV. That pointed to a number of new lines of inquiry. He copied out the receipt, then stuck it back in its place, wetting the little piece of sealing wax with his saliva. At the back of the cupboard he found a soiled pair of women's shoes. There were stains on the soles, which might be coal, or burnt wood, as well as some bits of straw. To which of the two sisters did they belong? Charlotte, the older of the two, or Camille, the younger? For no particular reason, he remembered the ants. He slid under the beds again and pulled out some of the cloths. They were narrow strips of linen, stained with thin trails of something yellowish, along which the insects were still moving. Lifting them to his nose, he retched at the strong smell of sour milk. Why had the sisters kept these soiled cloths? A vague idea came into his mind, and he promised himself to think about it later. He put everything back in its place and left the room.

Miette was still asleep, and had not moved. Nicolas went into Élodie's bedroom and looked down at Rue Saint-Honoré, which was filling with Parisians in their Sunday best. He saw the Galaine family returning. Their mourning clothes looked out of place in the bright sunlight, but the rules, although unwritten, had to be obeyed. Everyone in the shopkeeping classes knew the strict dress code in such circumstances. Whether or not to wear a black muslin bonnet or a dark gauze *fichu* was part of a good upbringing. Only the King wore purple when he was in mourning, and the Queen white. And the Galaines, in the heat of the tragedy and in the absence of a body, which was still at the Basse-Geôle, had not even stopped the clocks, or covered the furniture and mirrors in black.

He soon heard the cook's shuffling footsteps as she came to resume her duties at the maid's bedside. He took advantage of this to escape for a moment. He still had one person to question. He heard her singing to herself in her room, impervious to the sadness around her. Geneviève greeted him with a pout which made her look like her father. She was sitting on a little stool, twisting one of her curls.

'Good morning, Mademoiselle,' said Nicolas.

'I'm not Mademoiselle. Élodie was Mademoiselle. I'm Geneviève. Who are you?'

'I'm Nicolas. I think you were ill, is that right?'

'Oh, yes! But not like Miette.'

'Do you like Miette?'

'Yes, but she cries too much. I don't like Élodie.'

'Your cousin? Why not?'

'She never wants to play with me. Miette is very ill. I think it's because of the monster.'

'The monster?'

She moved closer to him and took his hand. 'Yes, the monster who took her to see the fireworks.'

'How do you know that? You were ill in bed.'

'No, no! I got out of bed and crept across the floor and listened. I know everything. Everything! That's how it is. I saw Miette leave with a monster who had a white face. He had a big black hat, and then the others . . .'

'What others?'

'The same ones.'

'You mean they came back after they'd left?'

She started pounding with her little fists. 'No, no, you don't understand, it was because—'

Madame Galaine appeared at the door. 'What are you doing to my daughter, Monsieur?' she asked curtly. 'Not only do you force yourself on us, you torment our child!'

'I'm not tormenting anyone, Madame. I was merely talking to your daughter – a conversation I will have to resume sooner or later, whether you like it or not.'

Ignoring this argument, Geneviève started humming, hopping from one foot to the other and staring into space.

Nicolas looked at Madame Galaine. Of all the mysteries in this case, this woman was not the least of them. She was still young, but her beauty had already begun to fade, as if clouded over by some inner anxiety. But what was the source of that anxiety? Was it the consequence of an ill-matched marriage, in which her low opinion of her husband nourished frustration in a sensitive soul? What gave her that extremely strong character, which manifested itself in the way she defended her child or in her stubborn refusal to answer questions, even if meant attracting the strongest suspicion? Yes, Nicolas said to himself, only some grave secret could justify such an attitude – the attitude of a hunted animal. He made one last attempt to get through to her.

'Madame, you have nothing to fear from me. You can tell me anything at all; I'll understand and try to help. But please speak if you know anything. At least defend yourself and tell me your whereabouts on the night of the disaster. Otherwise, your silence can only be interpreted as an attempt at concealment.'

She looked at him with an intensity that was almost palpable, and opened her mouth, as if about to say something. Her cheeks turned bright red, she raised both her hands to her flushed face and her expression hardened again. He sensed that she had almost dropped her guard and yielded, but had immediately clammed up again. She clasped her daughter convulsively to her and stepped back, throwing Nicolas a look almost of hate.

In the corridor he ran into Charles Galaine. He assumed that the man had overheard the exchange, but had had no desire to intervene. Without further ado, he asked him for the name of the family's notary. Galaine blinked in surprise and hesitated. At the commissioner's insistence, he finally informed him that it was Master Jame, in Rue Saint-Martin, opposite Rue de l'Ours. At that moment Semacgus reappeared, with a wicker basket over his arm and Cyrus on a leash. The dog seemed rejuvenated, and was quivering all over at this unexpected outing.

'What a pair!' said Nicolas, as Charles Galaine slipped away. 'You're as laden as a mule!'

'Do your friends a good deed and that's how they treat you! On the way back, I dropped into the Hôtel d'Aligre. But let's go downstairs . . .'

In the servants' pantry, he revealed his treasures: a salted capon, tongue from Virezon and a bottle of burgundy. Bread and almond biscuits completed the feast. They immediately sat down to eat. The surgeon tried once again to warn Nicolas against the problems that might result from mentioning in his official report the unusual nature of the phenomena he had witnessed. Damn it, he said, they weren't in deepest Africa or in a trading post in India – that might have been different! To cheer Nicolas, who had grown sombre at these words, he talked about the last 'miracle' that had been seen in Paris, some ten years earlier. During a procession in Faubourg Saint-Antoine, it had apparently been observed that a plaster statue of the Virgin, standing in a niche, had turned her head in greeting as her divine son had passed. The next day, the road was filled with fifty thousand people, placing candles at the feet of the statue. The crowd grew so large that the police were unable to disperse it.

'What happened then?' asked Nicolas, amused.

'Someone noticed that the statue backed onto a grocer's shop, the main trade of which was the sale of candles. In fact, the grocer had very quickly run out of them! In the end, the Virgin was taken away and locked up in a secret place a long way from there.'

'That reminds me,' said Nicolas. 'On the twenty-fifth of April, the night of Good Friday, Monsieur de Sartine sent me to keep an eye on the crowd assembled in Sainte-Chapelle and make sure that nothing unfortunate happened. As you know, according to tradition possessed people go to that church to be touched with relics of the true cross and cured of the devils that torment them. I observed that they stop screaming as soon as their contortions cease, and by the time they leave the shrine they're back to normal. Monsieur de Sartine laughed and told me they're beggars paid to play the part! Hard to believe that respectable priests agree to lend themselves to such obscene play-acting.'

'Priests have done much worse things than that, I can tell you! Besides, who needs to create possessed people? The species is so common, it isn't necessary to create sham ones. One of the holes in your reasoning is to confuse things with their caricatures, and religion with superstition – that's supposing that religion . . .'

They clinked glasses and laughed. Semacgus would have plenty of time to examine the patient while waiting for Nicolas to come back. The commissioner went out to look for a carriage to take him to the monastery of the Discalced Carmelites in Rue de Vaugirard. But as it was a feast day, and people were travelling to other districts of Paris to visit family members, carriages were hard to come by. He had to wait for a while in Place du Palais-Royal, in front of the Château d'Eau, between Rue Fromenteau and Rue Saint-Thomas-du-Louvre, for a coachman to stop for him. He had plenty of time to contemplate this two-storey building, with its monumental oval gate. It was in fact just a façade, a *trompe l'oeil* construction designed as a companion to the Palais-Royal. There was a Parisian joke about sending a domestic, newly arrived from the provinces, to ask for a position with the verger of the Château d'Eau. The real building whose function corresponded to this name was on Boulevard du Temple, opposite Rue des Filles-du-Calvaire. It comprised four pumps, worked by four horses that were relieved every two hours. These pumps filled a tank which, flushed twice a week, on Mondays and Thursdays, cleaning out the great sewer between the Bastille and the west of the city, a place where refuse was discharged downstream in the Seine. Nicolas knew all these facts from the police department in charge of refuse disposal.

By the time he got to Rue de Vaugirard, the main Pentecost service was over. He glanced inside the church, which was cloudy with incense, and remembered the dislocated body of the Comtesse de Ruissec found at the bottom of the well of the dead.[3] Too many of his memories these days were of the faces of dead people. His work consisted of calming the unquiet shades of victims by finding their murderers. As so often before, he headed straight for the dispensary. Père Grégoire was getting older, and these days barely left his laboratory, where he pursued his studies of medicinal plants, except to attend the daily services. By special permission of the prior, he had had a bed put in, and he spent his sleepless nights in prayer and meditation. Nicolas was sure he would find him there, remote from the life of the monastery.

When he entered the vast, vaulted room filled with vapours

and smells, with its strange retorts in which preparations and mixtures slowly simmered, their colours changing from an opalescent white to a deep emerald green, he found his old friend dozing in a large armchair from the time of the last king, covered in a tapestry depicting a forest of ferns. He was struck by how much the monk's face had changed in such a short time. It was as if the effects of illness had scoured his round face, making its surfaces angular, bringing out the pinched nose with its sharp bridge. Of the fat monk he had once known, there remained no trace. The man before Nicolas now was an ascetic. It was if he had been transfigured, and the truth of his character revealed. His diaphanous, ivory-coloured hands were folded over his cowl, like those of a recumbent statue. He was probably praying rather than sleeping. Having sensed a human presence, he opened his eyes. They were still lively, but they softened and misted over when he recognised Nicolas.

'My son, here is the miracle of this day of glory, when the Lord called the Holy Spirit on his disciples. An old man receives your visit!' He raised his left hand and blessed him. 'I don't have much time left to live. Every visit is a joy granted me by God.'

'Have you consulted the Faculty?'

'My son, the Faculty can do nothing for what I have. Each of us must meet his end. The plants I have always loved sustain me, and help me to wait for mine. I pray to the Lord, if he deigns to judge me worthy, to send me his angels to bear my soul to Paradise. But you who are still in the world, how are you?'

He smiled with a kind of delicacy and tapped his fingers on the armrests of his chair.

'You've not only come to say hello; you need my help. Speak.

Don't be afraid of tiring me. The silence weighs on me sometimes, and I have a right to the mercy of words, especially as this encounter will probably be our last, my good Nicolas.'

Nicolas was overcome with emotion. Père Grégoire's subdued voice reminded him of two other revered voices, those of Canon Le Floch and the Marquis de Ranreuil. Of these three men, who had had a major influence on his life, two were now mere shades, while the third was gradually withdrawing from the world of the living.

Nicolas pulled himself together and tried to set out, without too much emotion, the tragedy in Rue Royale, the murder of Élodie, the suspicion that had fallen on the members of the Galaine family and the increasingly strange manifestations occurring in the house. He made no attempt to conceal his doubts and his sense of helplessness, nor the hypotheses to which he had clung in an attempt to shine the light of reason on the incomprehensible. Père Grégoire listened with his eyes closed. On hearing certain details, he tensed his lips until they became white, as if in the grip of an invincible pain. He was silent for a moment, then pointed to a small bottle on a nearby sideboard. He lifted it to his lips, and gradually the colour returned to his face.

'It's a mixture of herbs and snake poison which I concocted,' he said. 'It gives me the illusion of a few moments' respite.' He took a deep breath. 'My son, no counsel is more difficult than the one you are asking of me, nor more dangerous . . . The number of times I've witnessed things that seemed to be the work of the devil, and which in the end proved to be a mere collection of tricks! Evil only exists in relation to good. Any believer who boasts that he has never felt the slightest shudder at the thought of the demon is either a hero or a fool.' He crossed himself. 'The Scriptures are categorical on the subject. It is not for nothing that Saint John warns us that Satan charms the whole world, or that Saint Peter advises us, when faced with this adversary who prowls around us like a roaring lion, to hold firm to our faith. Whether we are bold or blind, we have every reason to dread his lures. It was to struggle against the fallen angel that the son of God came to earth.'

A door slammed loudly in the distance. It seemed to Nicolas as if the liquids in the retorts were bubbling with renewed energy.

'Father, how can I judge the genuineness of these manifestations? How to tell what is incomprehensible but real from mere seduction?'

'First, your soul must be at peace. Only the pure can fight the impure. Then you must learn how to recognise the attacks of the devil. Listen to the age-old word of the Church: the signs of possession are well known, verified and immutable: "Speaking or understanding an incomprehensible language, revealing things which are distant or secret and displaying strength beyond one's age or physical condition." You must bear these three signs constantly in mind. If you encounter them, be on your guard and commend your soul to God, for there can be no doubt that you are in the presence of one possessed.'

'So far, I have seen only the third of these signs with my own eyes and in a way that I cannot doubt.'

'Wait, then, and observe, and if you see them all together, fight.'

'But how?'

'The only lawful way is to call in a priest who is accustomed to dealing with such difficult matters, and who has been authorised by the bishop to do so. Only he can perform an exorcism to chase out the vile beast. When evil has subjugated the victim, has taken over his will and rendered him totally powerless, there is nothing else to do, for the demon is now master of the possessed person's mind and body. It speaks with his tongue and hears with his ears.'

'If the phenomena in the Galaine house get worse, and if the signs leave no room for doubt, who can help me? You, Father?'

'Can't you see the state I'm in?' sighed Père Grégoire, raising his hands. 'Exorcism requires not only spiritual strength – that, at least, God still grants me – but also a physical stamina and a zeal I no longer possess. The only person entitled to deal with this matter is the priest with responsibility for such ceremonies in the diocese of Paris. There have been too many abuses in the past; that's why these precautions are necessary. However, in order for him to intervene, you must obtain authorisation from the Archbishop of Paris, Monseigneur Christophe de Beaumont. You must have met him in the course of your work . . .'

'I've seen him twice at Court. His Majesty keeps him on the sidelines, and has often exiled him.'[4]

'Alas, that's the tragedy of our Church . . . I've known him for years, ever since my time in Blois, where he was vicar general. He's a polite, scrupulous man, but also stubborn, suspicious, opinionated, excessively cautious and too inclined to listen to the advice of his entourage. His delicacy consists in not having any, which means that his bluntness all too often verges on tactlessness. The court is a foreign country in which he cannot help but fail.'

'What else can you tell me about him?'

'He never wanted his elevation. He was perfectly happy being the Archbishop of Vienna. He led a pious, well-ordered life, and was on good terms with his canons. When his predecessor died, no one even thought he was in the running for Paris. His friends were amazed when he was appointed.'

'So he overcame his misgivings?'

'His Majesty intervened personally and wrote him a letter in his own hand, after which there was no way he could back out. He was not used to the ways of the world, and when he took his vow at Versailles, he made rather a ridiculous show of himself. According to tradition, he had to greet the King's daughters and kiss their hands, but he was so shy and embarrassed that as they walked towards him, he backed away.'

'If memory serves, he has difficulty moving.'

'His health is not much more satisfactory than mine,' said Père Grégoire, with a weak smile. 'He's suffered from kidney stones, gallstones and diurnal fevers since his elevation. Little by little, the struggle with the Jansenists and the expulsion of the Jesuits have sapped his strength. In his isolation, he's prone to fantasies, such as his claim to be descended from an illustrious line. I can intercede with him, but before you have your audience it would be wise to obtain a *nihil obstat* from Monsieur de Sartine, in other words, from the King. Of course, as a defender of the Jesuits, he should be impressed by the fact that you were educated by them.'

'And who is currently the exorcist of the diocese?' asked Nicolas.

'Père Guy Raccard,' murmured the Carmelite, shaking his head. 'A strange but very scholarly colleague,'

They had said all they could. Nicolas's uncertainties had not been dispelled by this interview, but he had been shown a course to follow. He would just have to wait and see what happened next. He took effusive leave of Père Grégoire, who remembered as they bade each other farewell that he had a letter for him from Pierre Pigneau de Behaigne,[5] who was working as an apostolic missionary in Cochin-China. A native of Thiérache, who had pursued his studies at the Seminary of the Thirty-Three in Paris, he had been friends with Nicolas in the old days. They had attended concerts of sacred music at the Louvre together, and had both savoured the delights of the Stohrer pastry shop in Rue Montorgeuil.

Nicolas decided to return on foot: he needed to think, and being in the open air helped him to do so. Père Grégoire's words may have traced a path for him, but they had not lessened his sense of dread – in fact, the monk's physical condition had increased it. He realised that the generation which had surrounded him in his youth was on the verge of dying out. His closest friends, he thought with regret, were also the oldest. Even Inspector Bourdeau was old enough to be his father. The only exceptions were Monsieur de Sartine, who was younger than generally supposed, La Borde, who was not much older than he was, and dear Pigneau, now a long way from France. He unsealed the letter, all stained and yellowed by its journey, and read it as he walked:

Hon-dat, this fifth of January 1769

My dear Nicolas

You must have been surprised by my mysterious departure in September 1765. Called to the hard but fertile labour of the apostolate, I told neither family nor friends (in the first rank of whom I place you), being aware of both my weakness and their friendship. It cost me a great deal to make that decision without telling you.

I embarked at Lorient on one of those ships belonging to the Company of the Indies. I arrived at Hon-dat, a small island in the gulf of Siam, after many adventures which I hope to tell you about one day. At the beginning of January 1768, the Siamese invaded and I had the joy of spending the holy time of Lent in prison, condemned to the cangue, *that is, carrying a six-foot ladder around my neck. I caught a fever and was sick for four months, but I am cured now.*

I pray the Lord to grant me the honour of going back to prison soon, there to suffer and die for his holy name. Remember me, I have not forgotten you.

Pierre Pigneau
miss. apost.

What were his own torments compared with such faith, such sublime self-denial? Nicolas suddenly realised how much he missed this friend of his youth. He hailed a two-wheeled sedan chair. He had decided to go to the Grand Châtelet. Semacgus could wait until his return. He needed to speak to Bourdeau and entrust him with various missions designed to verify the findings he had made in the course of his search of the Galaine house. But the inspector was nowhere to be found. Old Marie, surprised by his presence, pointed out that it was Sunday, and Pentecost, and that on this major feast day Bourdeau devoted himself to his large family. Disappointed, Nicolas was just setting off back to Rue Saint-Honoré when he felt someone tugging at the sleeve of his coat. It was Tirepot.

'Don't go, Nicolas! You're going to like this. I've been working for you, like you asked. Bourdeau described your savage to me. I know him well. Not difficult to spot in that bizarre get-up. He was always hanging around the area.'

'Before the day of the festivities on Place Louis XV?'

'Well before that! Months even. A big gangling fellow like that, you can't really miss him. On the night of the disaster, I saw him twice.'

'Twice?'

'Twice, yes, and not in the same place.'

'There's nothing remarkable about that.'

'Really? So if I see you on the banks of the Seine, standing motionless near the parapet, and then in town, three hundred yards away, I see you walking towards me, I can take it you're a ghost playing hide and seek, can I, or that there are two of you? If you think that's normal, I bow down to your superior judgement.'

He bowed, and the two pails he was carrying rang on the stones.

'All right, then. Was he alone?'

'No, the first time he was with a girl in rags, and the second time with a girl in yellow. And that's not all. The same evening, I heard a couple of French Guards who were using my services – they'd been knocking them back a bit too much, if you ask me – anyway, I heard them chatting away merrily and they described the savage, in his hat, leading this girl in a pale yellow dress into a hay barn near the gardens of the convent of the Conception. Yelling her head off, she was. They were laughing about it, saying he must have tipped the girl in the straw and had his way with her.'

'Yelling, you say? What do you mean?'

'Seems she was struggling and kept shouting insults.'

Nicolas's head was buzzing with ideas. Surely this was it, he thought, the Ariadne's thread which might lead him out of the maze of assumptions and towards real evidence. Geneviève's remarks, as well as her apparently meaningless drawing, suddenly took on a whole new significance. Now it was a question of reducing what he knew to a logical sequence of facts, then confirming those facts and comparing one with another until he discovered the truth.

'Jean,' Nicolas resumed, 'when was the first of these appearances?'

'I'm not too sure, but certainly before the firework display. And, as I sense you're going to ask me about the second one, too, I'd say that was a few minutes later.'

'And you're sure it wasn't the same person?'

'Absolutely! The first savage was shorter than the second one.'

'Let's see if I've got this right. You saw two individuals resembling the savage, accompanied by two girls who were dressed differently, and you're certain they couldn't have been the same. What about the French Guards? When was it they needed your services?'

'After the display. There were already rumours that things hadn't gone too well in the square. But this thing they mentioned, about the savage and the girl, I got the impression that had happened quite a while before. When they came to me, it was two hours to midnight, at the latest.'

'Thank you, Jean. You've been a great help.'

Shaking his hand, he slipped him a five-*livre ecu*. Tirepot grinned with pleasure. Nicolas continued on his way. How unfortunate, he thought, that Miette had not regained consciousness and it was still impossible to question her! He had been told very explicitly that she had accompanied her young mistress to the festivities. What had happened? And what was behind this absurd double appearance of Naganda when the man himself lay drugged in his attic and his clothes had been stolen?

Nicolas decided to take his time getting back to the Deux Castors. He needed to clear his mind in order to try to make sense of all the confused and contradictory elements this investigation kept throwing up.

By the time he arrived in Rue Saint-Honoré, the Galaine family were getting ready to have dinner. He declined Charles Galaine's invitation to join them, but reassured him that he would continue to pay his board and lodgings. He found Semacgus in Miette's room, puzzling over the nature of the girl's drowsiness, which he could do nothing to dispel. He entrusted Cyrus to Nicolas and informed him in a sardonic tone that he planned to spend the evening, and probably also the night, at the Dauphin Couronné. In other words, he would not be far away and would come running immediately if Nicolas sent for him.

Back in his room, Nicolas contemplated what was left of the food Semacgus had brought. He was not hungry, so he let Cyrus have it, and also poured a little water into a bowl for him. Fortunately, his friend had brought him some candles made of good-quality wax. As soon as it started to get dark, he lit them, undressed and lay down on the bed, intending to catch up with his reading. Monsieur de Sartine had authorised him to borrow books from the library at the Hôtel de Gramont, a particular privilege as he collected banned or confiscated works. He plunged into d'Alembert's *Essai sur les gens de lettres et sur les grands*. In it, the philosopher contrasted the vain pretensions of the aristocracy with the virtues of talent and equality, and argued that society should be organised around the progress of science and trade. Soon, the book fell from his hands. He heard the members of the Galaine family return to their respective rooms. He thought back over his day and, remembering the ravaged face of Père Grégoire, his tired mind suddenly superimposed on it that of the King. He, too, had aged a lot, and was going through an unhappy time. His daughter Louise's piety had led her to envisage becoming a Carmelite nun. In April that year, she had finally yielded to her vocation and, with her father's agreement, had entered the convent of Saint-Denis, cutting herself off from everything pertaining to society and the dignity of her rank. According to La Borde, the King had not yet recovered from this blow. Only the celebrations for his grandson's marriage had somewhat lightened his mood, but there was a strong possibility that the disaster of 30 May would plunge him back into depression.

Cyrus had heaved himself up onto the mattress and was sleeping trustfully, one paw on his friend's leg: Nicolas gently moved it away. Before falling asleep, he had one last thing to do.

He took a bottle of wig powder from his toiletry bag, tiptoed to the door and out into the corridor, and spread a semi-circle of the substance all around the entrance. If anyone tried to play a trick on him, he or she would leave footprints. Then he went back to his bed, observing the same precautions against creepy-crawlies as he had the previous night. Lulled by Cyrus's calm breathing, he fell asleep immediately, although not without first saying the prayers he had learnt from the lips of Canon Le Floch and his nurse when he was a child. Never forget them, his nurse had advised him, for fear of rousing the demon.

Monday 4 June 1770, three in the morning
Someone was knocking loudly at the door. He sat up, breathing heavily and bathed in sweat, and listened. But all was silent again; nothing moved. There was no doubt, though, that the noise had been real: poor Cyrus had also woken, and was trembling with fear and whining plaintively. Just as Nicolas was starting to get a grip on himself, the knocking came again, as loudly as before. This was followed by a series of unconnected sounds – banging, whistling and scraping – which suddenly gave way to a muffled cry, itself then transformed into a mocking laugh. Nicolas took a lighter and lit his candle, then walked resolutely to the door and opened it. Nobody. He crouched to light the entrance: the layer of powder was undisturbed. Once again, he heard what sounded like a storm inside the room, and felt poor Cyrus against his legs. The dog, mad with terror and desperate to leave, now lay down on the floor and relieved himself. Then Nicolas felt a kind of emptiness: the presences responsible for the din had gone. The outside world

gained the upper hand again, and in the neighbouring garden a night bird gave a call that echoed like a cry of liberation. Should he send for Semacgus? He did not think that the surgeon would be any more convinced by these new phenomena than he had been by the previous ones. He would merely take Nicolas to task again, and deliver platitudes on the weakness of the human mind and the light of reason.

Nicolas went back to bed, but could not sleep. At about five, a wild cry rang through the house. He quickly dressed and rushed to Miette's room. The men of the house had also come running. They found Marie Chaffoureau lying on the floor outside the door, unconscious. In the room itself, Miette, almost naked, her palliasse floating a few inches from the floor, seemed to be suffering unbearable tortures. Completely silent, her mouth wide open, her lips flecked with foam, she was tearing at herself with her nails, as if struggling with incredible strength against an invisible adversary. Nicolas, Charles Galaine and his son ran to her. For a long time, at the risk of having their own eyes poked out, they fought to stop the girl from wounding herself in the face or chest. Every time one of them seized a limb, it immediately became as stiff and as hard as a bar of iron, but no sooner was it released than it relaxed again. Finally, however, she regained her former immobility. Nicolas noted with astonishment that the sweat and foam with which she was covered receded like the waves of the sea at ebb tide, or like water evaporating from a white-hot plate. He placed his hand on one of her arms and immediately recoiled: it was an inferno. The sensation was that of a burning coldness, the kind you feel in winter when you leave your hand for too long on the iced-over surface of a pond.

Miette's breathing, almost choked at the height of the attack, recovered its normal rhythm.

Exhausted, the men stood catching their breath. Jean Galaine seemed to Nicolas to have the air of a hunted animal: he kept looking about him, as if fearing that someone or something were about to attack him. Nicolas was getting ready to make new arrangements, judging that, now the morning attack was over, nothing more would happen immediately, and that Miette would wait, prostrate, for the dawn of the following day to exhibit further symptoms – if, that is, her condition showed no improvement. Such was often the way with certain fevers or agues which recurred at regular intervals.

He was about to go and attend to the cook, who was still unconscious, when Miette sat up, her arms stretched before her, until the top part of her body was at right angles to her legs. Her eyes slowly opened, like those of one of Monsieur de Vaucanson's automata. Her head swivelled to the side, jerkily, as if driven by an invisible inner mechanism. Her dilated pupils seemed to Nicolas to have changed colour – the dull blue-grey he remembered had assumed a deep, bronze-green tinge, like the liquid in Père Grégoire's retorts – and there were disquieting purple specks in them. Her head suddenly stopped moving, and her frighteningly intense gaze came to rest on Nicolas. As the three men looked on in astonishment, the girl's tongue emerged in a snake-like movement, grew inordinately long, then slid sinuously back inside her mouth. Nicolas remembered another face, other eyes, and as if the memory had set something irresistible in motion, he heard Miette utter, in a man's voice, words that made him freeze with terror.

'So, my Breton friend, I see you've recognised me! No, you're not dreaming, these are my beautiful green eyes, my snake's eyes, as you thought nine years ago, on the staircase of the Châtelet. Yes, you may well tremble, for it was indeed me you ran through with your sword.'[6]

Nicolas resisted the desire to run out of the room with his hands over his ears to blot out that mocking voice from beyond the grave. It was the voice of Mauval, Commissioner Camusot's angel-faced henchman, whom Nicolas had killed in self defence in the drawing room of the Dauphin Couronné. He somehow found the strength to cry out, 'Who are you?'

'Ah! Ah! *Antichristos*, the counterfeit of the lamb! He who was foretold by Irenaeus, Hippolytus, Lactantius and Augustine.'

'Are you a demon?'

'*In Ja und Nein bestehen alle Dinge!*'

'I don't understand that language,' said Nicolas.

'It's German,' said Charles Galaine, in a faint voice. 'It means "all things consist of yes and no".'

'In the name of Our Lord,' said Nicolas, crossing himself, 'be off with you!'

Rather belatedly, he remembered Père Grégoire's advice about the caution that needed to be observed with such entities. It was clear now that whatever it was that was speaking through Miette was a loathsome thing, a demon. Miette swayed like a statue being rocked on its pedestal and spat out a long jet of slime. Nicolas, fascinated despite all that he was feeling, realised that the 'thing' was changing, that the maid's poor envelope was about to be used, like a garment sold to a second-hand clothes dealer continuing its existence on other backs, to house another deceptive presence.

'You're threatening me,' uttered another man's voice, 'as you one day defied me, you who tried to seduce my daughter, your own sister.'

Nicolas felt weak at the knees: Miette was now speaking with the voice of his father, the Marquis de Ranreuil.

'Yes, your father,' the pitiless voice went on. 'And I see the man who lent you his dog struck down instead of you.'

After this last taunt, Miette fell back on the bed. For a long time the three men stood there motionless, unable to look at each other or say a word. Nicolas kept asking himself why this 'thing' – he could find no other name for it – was attacking him, revealing secrets of his past life that he alone knew, secrets he kept buried deep in his heart like ever-open wounds. He sensed vaguely that this frenzy must be connected with the visit he had paid Père Grégoire, that the creature expressing itself through Miette's body had recognised him as its principal adversary, the man through whom would be delivered the lightning stroke destined to thrust it back into outer darkness. He shuddered at the curse uttered against his friend and host in Rue Montmartre, Monsieur de Noblecourt.

The sound of voices and hurried steps came from the staircase. Everyone rushed out to the landing. An old man was climbing the stairs, followed by Madame Galaine. It was Poitevin, Monsieur de Noblecourt's old servant, with his white hair dishevelled, his livery in disorder, his breath coming in gasps. He fell into Nicolas's arms.

'Oh, Monsieur Nicolas, God be praised, I've found you! Monsieur de Noblecourt has been murdered!'

VIII

CHRISTOPHE DE BEAUMONT

Mar quirit pidi evidomp
Birniquen collet ne veʒomp.

As long as you pray for us
We will never die.
ANON. (BRETON)

Nicolas made an effort to control the emotions that swept over him. Although he could be fearful when contemplating future events and their possible consequences, whenever something unpleasant happened he had a remarkable ability to stay calm and make the kind of quick decisions needed in such circumstances. He let Poitevin catch his breath, then questioned him about what had happened. Monsieur de Noblecourt had gone out very early for his daily walk. No sooner had he walked through the carriage entrance than several individuals – the details of the attack had been reported by the baker's boy from the shop on the ground floor – had set upon him and given him a sound thrashing. Monsieur de Noblecourt had collapsed to the ground and his head had struck a milestone. The baker's boy had raised the alarm. They had carried the former magistrate to his room and called a local doctor. Catherine had asked Poitevin to take a carriage and fetch Nicolas from Rue Saint-Honoré. He was unable to give any further details of his master's condition, and begged Monsieur Nicolas to rush to his bedside.

'He'll be right there!' cried a loud voice.

Semacgus had just come in. He bowed to Madame Galaine, who was looking at him in annoyance.

'A thousand pardons, Madame. The door was open so I took the liberty of coming in.' He turned to Nicolas. 'After the diverting night I had, I thought I'd come and see if yours had been as satisfying.'

Nicolas drew him aside. 'Guillaume, last night went far beyond anything I told you about yesterday. I heard noises in my room, and Miette had a terrible attack. She spoke with the voices of the dead.'

'With what? What on earth are you talking about?'

'I don't really have time to go into the details. All you need to know is that Mauval – do you remember him? – and my father, the Marquis de Ranreuil, spoke to me through the maid! And, what's more, these voices revealed secrets only I could know.'

'Good Lord!' said Semacgus. 'They've really got you under their spell! And what about Cyrus?'

'He was terrified. I don't have time to discuss it. I have to go to Rue Montmartre. Could you stay here? I think the first thing to do is to take a look at the cook. We found her unconscious. As for Miette, she seems calm during the day, as usual. To think we can even talk about what's usual!'

'You can depend on me,' said Semacgus. 'Run to our friend, I'm just as impatient as you to know how he is.'

Nicolas told the Galaines that he would be absent for a short time and advised them to refer to Dr Semacgus for anything concerning Miette's condition. Charles Galaine seemed to be about to speak to him, but then changed his mind. At the foot of the stairs, Nicolas found little Geneviève sitting on the bottom step in her long nightdress.

'Miette is really naughty,' she said. 'She woke me up with her shouting. I was very afraid.'

'You really hear everything in this house!'

'It would be hard not to hear her.'

'You're a very interesting little girl, but I have to leave you.'

'You shouldn't. I know things, and you'll never find out!'

Nicolas hesitated, torn between the urgency of the hour and the risk of missing useful information.

'Listen, if you know things, tell me. It'll just be between the two of us.'

It was a clever move on Nicolas's part, although the deception left a bitter taste in his mouth.

The little girl got to her feet, stood on tiptoe and whispered in Nicolas's ear, 'I heard . . . I heard Miette tell Élodie she didn't want to be burdened with something that would get her thrown out of the house if anyone found out about it.'

'And what did Élodie say to that?'

'That there was a way to deal with it and she'd help her.'

'And then?'

'That's all. Someone came and I ran away.'

'And you didn't tell anyone about it? . . . Your parents?'

'No . . . no.'

He sensed hesitation. 'I understand, but you have to tell me everything.'

'I told Aunt Camille and Papa,' she said, apparently contrite at having confessed this.

'That's quite natural,' Nicolas said reassuringly. 'Is there anything else?'

'Élodie was always eating. She took food into her room, even though it attracted mice. She got very, very fat. I saw her one day in her petticoats. She hit me and threatened me if I told anyone.'

'And did you tell anyone?'

'Yes, Papa.'

'And what about the shovel?' asked Nicolas, who always knew the right moment to take a witness by surprise.

Alarmed, the girl blushed to the roots of her hair. 'You were the one who took my drawing. You're naughty, you are!'

'Never mind that. You draw very well. What does that figure with the shovel mean?'

She hesitated for a moment, then took the plunge. 'It's the savage. I prefer him without his uniform, you know, without his cloak and his hat. When he wears those you can't see his face, and that scares me. One night, I heard the wood creaking.'

'The wood?'

'The floorboards. I opened the door and slipped out to have a look. The savage was going downstairs in his cloak and hat, carrying a packet and a big shovel.'

'How could you see that in the dark?'

'There was moonlight on the stairs.'

'Did you follow him?'

'Oh, no, I was too scared. I went straight back to my room. I'd already heard him breathing with Élodie. I was sure he was hurting her, she was moaning.'

'When was that?'

'One afternoon. They were both breathing very hard.'

Nicolas did not persist with that, but there was one detail he needed to clarify. 'The night you saw him with the shovel, when was that?'

'At night.'

'Yes, I know, but how long ago? Two days, a week, two weeks?'

'I think . . . I think at least a week.'

'Thank you, Geneviève,' said Nicolas. 'You've been a great help, but you must promise never to tell anyone about our conversation.'

'Not even Aunt Camille and Papa?'

'Not even them. Nobody at all. I wouldn't want anyone else to listen to you the way you listen to things sometimes. Do you understand? It's very dangerous.'

She sniffled, and slowly nodded her head. The child's innocence, Nicolas thought, was already quite compromised, but had she ever really been innocent? The house was so filled with madness and pretence that anything was possible. At the door, Poitevin was stamping his feet with impatience. As they climbed into the carriage, Nicolas observed that the two French Guards had not been replaced. Was it because such protection was judged to be more dangerous than the lack of it, by attracting the attention of the common people? Last night's events seemed not to have gone beyond the borders of the domestic this time. The district was still peaceful, and was waking up without doubts or questions. But Nicolas was under no illusions: whatever had been silenced or concealed would eventually penetrate beyond the walls of the house, and before long rumour would lead to increased fear and then to anger at the unknown forces threatening the district. Nothing could ever remain secret in the capital of the Kingdom. He knew that anything hidden within a house, however intimate, would soon become known to the outside world. There were no clearly defined limits between private and public.

He recalled Geneviève's revelations. They were surprising indeed, and, if correct, they opened new lines of inquiry. But nothing yet pointed to an obvious culprit. The members of the family – and that included the shop assistant and Naganda, even though they were not part of it – were all, without exception, still under suspicion. From his conversation with the child, he concluded that Naganda and Élodie had probably been lovers, and that the Micmac had played a central role in the tragedy of Rue Saint-Honoré.

His head was starting to ache. He had to let all these things settle, like leaven in dough. He took a deep breath, and Poitevin, aware of his unease, squeezed his arm in a friendly gesture. He seemed to think that Nicolas's mere presence would settle matters, that his master's health depended on it. Nicolas knocked on the window to hurry up the coachman. The area around the central market was beginning to fill with people. They turned so suddenly at the corner of Rue des Prouvaires that the box lifted and the old servant was thrown against Nicolas.

When they got to Rue Montmartre, Nicolas leapt from the cab, leaving Poitevin to pay the fare. He was received like a saviour by

Marion and Catherine, both of them in tears, and neither daring to go up to Monsieur de Noblecourt's room. Dr Dienert was there, having been fetched from Rue Montorgueil. He was regent of the Faculty of Medicine at the University of Paris, and one of the most reputable doctors in the city. But titles meant nothing to Nicolas: his experience of the medical profession always made him fear the worst. It was with apprehension that he approached the bedroom. What he saw as he entered reassured him immediately. Monsieur de Noblecourt was sitting in his favourite armchair, bareheaded apart from a bloodstained strip of cloth tied around his skull. Beaming all over his face, he was drinking from a glass which, at the sight of the bottle, Nicolas knew to be Malaga, in the company of a potbellied, red-faced, good-natured person. When he saw Nicolas, the old procurator pointed at him.

'Here's Commissioner Le Floch, I'm saved! As you see, Nicolas, all this is nothing but a bad joke. First my feet, then my head. I'm going gradually, drop by drop.'

'Don't worry, he's not going yet,' said another voice, that of a man in the background whom Nicolas had not noticed and whom he recognised as his colleague Fontaine, one of the local commissioners.

'Come on, Nicolas,' said Noblecourt, 'don't make that face. My mind's not wandering beneath this turban. I know I had a close shave; I'm perfectly well aware of that.'

'You seem to be taking it very lightly.'

'What should I do, take it heavily? I've always dreamt of leading an adventurous life, being a soldier, a pirate, a police commissioner, but alas I've never attacked anything but files and never cut anything but legs of lamb. At last something's happened! At my age! I think a few drops of my blood are an acceptable price to pay.'

'This potion will help you recover,' said the doctor, 'and applying camphorated castor will heal your bruises.' The doctor offered a glass to Nicolas. 'You should drink this, too, Commissioner. By my faith, you're even paler than the procurator, and you haven't been beaten up!'

'It's a sign of his affection for me,' said Noblecourt with a laugh. 'It's quite nice to almost die; you find out who your friends are. My dear Nicolas, I promise to inform you when the time comes.'

'We shan't tire you. You need quiet and rest to savour your . . . medicine. I have to go. I'd like to have a few words with you, Fontaine, if you don't mind. Doctor, I bid you farewell. Take good care of our friend.'

Monsieur de Noblecourt waved gaily at Nicolas and held out his empty glass to Dr Dienert. He was delighted: thanks to this business, he was now authorised, with the blessing of the Faculty, to eat and drink the kinds of things his gout had forbidden him.

Beneath the entrance arch, Nicolas informed the commissioner of what Poitevin had told him. Then he went and knocked at the door of the bakery and returned with a barefoot baker's boy of about twelve, covered in flour, and embarrassed because his hands were coated with dough.

'Jean-Baptiste,' Nicolas said, 'Poitevin told me you witnessed the attack on Monsieur de Noblecourt. Can you tell us about it?'

'I was waiting for Pierre, who was late. He's the baker's apprentice . . .' The boy stopped and looked behind him to make sure that no one was listening. 'He always arrives drunk in the morning, and I take him to the pump to wake him up. Anyway, I was waiting when I heard the door to the staircase open. At that hour of the morning, I thought it was you, Monsieur Nicolas, going out. But it was the old gentleman, singing under his breath. Just then, three men jumped out of the shadows and started beating him with their canes. The old gentleman clung to them. They pushed him away and he fell on that milestone.' He pointed at it. 'I thought he was dead. The one who was the leader, who had a uniform, said, "Good God, it's the wrong man! It's not the commissioner!" '

With one hand in his pocket, Nicolas searched the area around the entrance. Suddenly, he bent and picked up something from the ground. He held out a small, shiny object to Commissioner Fontaine.

'This may well belong to one of the attackers. Noblecourt must have grabbed it and torn it off when he fell.'

'Curious. Any idea what it might be?'

'Oh, some kind of ornament . . . Jean-Baptiste mentioned a uniform.'

Fontaine handed the object back to Nicolas. 'I assume, my dear colleague, that you'll be pursuing this matter? It concerns you in more ways than one. It was a case of mistaken identity. You were clearly the target.'

'You're most kind, I thank you. I'll keep you informed.'

'Likewise. Give my regards to Monsieur de Sartine.'

Nicolas smiled. Everyone attributed influence to him, but it was one he never used, either for the benefit of his colleagues or to their detriment. He got back into the cab, which had waited, and asked to be driven to police headquarters in Rue Neuve-

Saint-Augustin. Reassured about Monsieur de Noblecourt's condition, he now had to see the Lieutenant General of Police, to explain the situation and convince him to obtain the support of the King, so that the matter could be referred to the Archbishop of Paris and the process set in motion which would result in the Church deciding on the ritual measures to be taken now that a case of possession had been established. The very oddity of this thought struck him: it was as if the century in which he lived, the century of Voltaire and the Encyclopaedists, had been revealed as an illusion, and the city and its inhabitants were being thrown back into the past. And yet, what had happened in Rue Saint-Honoré had not been a dream. His muscles still hurt from the efforts he had made to hold Miette down on her floating palliasse.

He went back over the attack on the former procurator. The culprit was obvious: Major Langlumé harboured a grudge against him, doubtless exacerbated by the first results of the inquiry into the disaster in Place Louis XV, and had decided to take his revenge. Nicolas had pretended to find the major's brass tag on the ground, but it was in fact the one which had blocked the lock of the attic door at the ambassadors' mansion. It was because he was so angry at the thought that Noblecourt, who had harmed no one, had got caught up in this business and almost died, that he had resorted to such a trick. Morally reprehensible as it might be, it was justified, being the only way to confound Langlumé. There was no point in feeling remorse: if Monsieur de Noblecourt's head had hit the milestone any harder, the major would have been guilty of murder.

Everything went very quickly. At police headquarters, Nicolas discovered that Sartine was away and would not be back in Paris until the following day. Nicolas retrieved the gelding lent by the great stable in Versailles: there had not been anyone available to take it back yet. Before setting off, he wrote a short note to Bourdeau, entrusting him with various missions. He then crossed the Seine to the monastery of the Discalced Carmelites, where he told a horrified Père Grégoire all about the events of the previous night. Convinced by his story, the monk wrote a letter addressed to the Archbishop of Paris, recommending Nicolas and vouching for the genuineness of his words. He again blessed Nicolas and turned to pray to the white marble Virgin, the pride of the sanctuary.

Nicolas rode through the woods, reaching the road to Versailles by way of Meudon and Chaville. By the stroke of one, he was in the Place d'Armes. He was as exhausted as his foam-flecked mount, which neighed with pleasure to be back in its stable. He entrusted it to a groom, and immediately headed for the ministers' wing, certain that he would find Monsieur de Sartine there with Monsieur de Saint-Florentin, the Minister of the King's Household. He was not mistaken, as was confirmed to him by a secretary surrounded by a crowd of supplicants hoping for an audience, or even a brief word in the corridor. Since Nicolas was known to be in the minister's favour, no obstacles were put in his way. After a short wait, he was admitted. Monsieur de Saint-Florentin and the Lieutenant General of Police were together at a small gaming table, examining a pile of documents, which Nicolas recognised as police reports on foreigners staying in Paris.

'Why, here's our good Monsieur Le Floch!' said Monsieur de

Saint-Florentin. 'I assume you haven't made this journey for nothing. What ill wind brings you here?'

Nicolas summed things up clearly and concisely. The minister listened to him, his eyes staring into space and his chin on his fist. Sartine, although apparently impassive, was unable to stop his right foot from moving up and down.

'Therefore,' concluded Nicolas, 'I would like to have permission and authorisation to refer this exceptional case to the Archbishop of Paris. If you'll allow me . . .'

'Go on.'

'If we don't do it, and the case comes out into the open, there's a risk the Church will assume the right to deal with it independently of us . . .'

'Well put, very well put. What do you think, Sartine?'

'I tend to the opinion that Monsieur Le Floch is trying once again to pull the wool over our eyes, but since, as usual, everything is contriving to prove him right, I am inclined to give him *carte blanche* in this case, if the King agrees to it. In addition,' he added with a meaningful gesture, 'if things turn out badly, we won't have the archbishop against us, because he'll be forced to form a united front with us. That reason alone convinces me, because, to be quite honest, I don't believe in the devil and all that nonsense. Still, if a bit of holy water can get rid of him, why deny ourselves the pleasure? All the same, I don't trust the archbishop. Remember the affair of the *Gazette ecclesiastique*?'

'I don't remember it, but remind us of the facts, for the edification – if that's the word – of our commissioner.'

Nicolas carefully neglected to mention that he had already heard his chief tell the story many times.

'The thing is,' Sartine said, 'I'd managed to get a writer for that periodical in my pay. He'd bring me proofs from the printing shop and delete passages that were too satirical. Monseigneur de Beaumont managed to intercept one of these proofs and unmasked my man. He asked the King to have the man arrested. A *lettre de cachet* was immediately issued, and he had it delivered by one of his own bailiffs. As soon as I found out, I ran to the King and protested. I pointed out that it was only the actions of my man that had prevented the *Gazette ecclésiastique* from becoming a channel for religious dissent, among both the Jansenists and the Jesuits. I also told him that I thought there was a great risk in having anyone other than the Lieutenant General of Police deliver *lettres de cachet* in Paris.'

'I remember the King sending for me,' Saint Florentin cut in, 'and ordering me to deliver another *lettre de cachet* freeing the prisoner. He asked me to make sure that in future his orders were carried out strictly according to the rules. As for this present case, I think we've made the right decision. We still have to find the King. He went hunting this morning in the great park. I have a whole chain of scouts along the route to inform me when he's about to return.'

He rang a little bell and a servant appeared, to whom he gave instructions. Turned away from Nicolas, he went back to examining the documents that Sartine handed him. As he did so, he made a few brief comments, which the Lieutenant General took down in writing. It was the whole secret life of the capital they were reviewing, in particular the presence in hotels and furnished lodgings of foreigners, all suspected of being hand in glove with foreign powers. The servant returned and whispered a few words in the minister's ear.

'Good, good. His Majesty has just passed the gate of the reservoirs.' He rose. 'I think we can get a note to him.'

At the foot of the stairs was a throng of supplicants and a stiff-looking usher trying to push them aside with his rod. Monsieur de Saint-Florentin's head disappeared for a moment beneath a wave of petitions that encircled his wig like a flight of white butterflies. Once past the Marble Courtyard, they entered the great apartments. On his first visit to Versailles in 1761, Nicolas had taken the same, almost initiatory route. He had passed this flight of steps, that hall, these long corridors, that maze of shorter corridors, and finally come out, as he did now, into a room of vast dimensions looking out on the park. It was gradually filling with courtiers and pages, and valets carrying towels in wicker baskets. Monsieur de La Borde greeted the three men. The King was coming, and a cacophony of footsteps, cries and solemn announcements rose like a tide and echoed through the palace. La Borde enquired as to the reason for the unexpected appearance of Monsieur de Saint-Florentin and his companions. Nicolas explained the situation briefly. La Borde grimaced: Madame du Barry was waiting for her master in the little study. He reminded his friend that the new concubine was of a different calibre from La Pompadour: young, beautiful and more temperamental than the marquise. The kind of attention she expected from the King was more likely to follow the excitement of the hunt than the dissipation of a midnight meal. Not surprising, therefore, that the King did not like to be disturbed at this intimate hour. The pleasant conversation and refreshments of the old days had given way to other games. At last the monarch appeared, wearing a blue coat trimmed with gold braid and beating his thigh with the handle of his whip. He was smiling: the hunt had obviously gone well. But once again Nicolas noted how stooped he was. The King looked all of his seventy years, and his associates were worried at the excesses which his young mistress's ardour was imposing on a weary organism.

As calm returned, the usual ceremonial began. Louis XV made a sign to Saint-Florentin, who approached. As he was short, he got up on tiptoe and talked at length in the King's ear. The King blinked and looked first at Sartine and then at Nicolas, to whom he addressed a gracious gesture, the kind he had given young Ranreuil, recognising him in the Hall of Mirrors as the royal family walked in procession to the Saint-Louis chapel. The minister finished his aside. The King raised his hand and La Borde approached to receive his orders.

'His Majesty wishes to be alone,' announced La Borde, pointing to the minister and his two companions.

The crowd of courtiers hesitated. A dull murmur rose from the disconcerted audience. The King frowned imperiously, and the stream of people withdrew, casting curious or hostile glances at the privileged few because of whom the usual protocol had been disrupted.

'You, stay,' said the King to a short old man wearing make-up and perched on red heels, whom Nicolas recognised immediately as the Duc de Richelieu. 'Where there is devilry, you have your place reserved!'

'Sire, the Bourbons have always been afraid of the devil; it's well known.'

'That's as may be,' retorted the King, 'but only because they've never seen him, unlike you!'

The old man laughed and bowed.

'Yes, gentlemen, when he was ambassador in Vienna, my cousin here,[2] who was supposed to be representing me, got it into his head to be initiated into a society of necromancers who promised to show him Beelzebub.' The King lowered his voice and crossed himself.

'Sire, to name him is to invoke him.'

'Quiet, libertine! Anyway, gentlemen, he pursued this illusion. The meeting took place at night, but some of those present spoke up afterwards. The affair became public, and all Vienna took sides in the scandal. Now, Richelieu, young Ranreuil here . . .'

'Whom I know,' said the marshal with a smile, revealing his false teeth.

'. . . has seen strange manifestations and incidents of possession with his own eyes. He's asking me to give authorisation for the Archbishop of Paris to order an exorcism. What do you say to that, Richelieu?'

'I say that between leaving an established case of possession unattended to and letting the Church make a legal and authorised attempt to deal with it, it is better to choose the second way, however uncertain the outcome. Otherwise, the archbishop will bide his time and do all he can to get the better of us. I had to deal with a similar problem when I was governor of Aquitaine. I nipped it in the bud with the aid of holy water and candles, and prevented unrest among the people.'

The King was still beating his whip against his thigh,

seemingly in the grip of opposing thoughts. 'Ranreuil, did you really see him?'

'Sire, I beg Your Majesty's pardon, whom?'

'The . . . well, that palliasse didn't move all by itself!'

'I can state that it was shaking violently, that it was so far above the floor that you could have put four hands beneath it, that the girl was speaking German and Latin and that . . .'

'Yes?'

'And that your late servant, the Marquis de Ranreuil, spoke through her mouth, referring to matters known only to myself.'

'Very well!' said the King. 'If that's what we have to do, I authorise you to approach the archbishop. Saint-Florentin, do what you have to do: you have enough blank signed letters. Let Commissioner Le Floch have free access to the archbishop. But, Ranreuil, you owe me a detailed report – you're such a good storyteller.'

With these friendly words, the King turned his back on them and gave himself up to his valets. Nicolas, Sartine and Saint-Florentin went back to the ministers' wing. Monsieur de Saint-Florentin wrote a few words on a blank document, sealed it and carefully wrote the address. As soon as the wax was dry, he handed over the missive without a word. Nicolas was about to leave the courtyard when a breathless Sartine caught up with him, told him that he wished to be kept up to date with the case and advised him to make sure of the wisdom of his decisions in such a delicate situation. Obviously, for Sartine, collusion with the Church could well have unfortunate consequences, even if started in a rare spirit of agreement between the temporal and spiritual powers. He also enjoined him not to forget, however compelling this crisis, that he was also supposed to be investigating the disaster in Place Louis XV. Nicolas used this opportunity to inform his chief of the attack on Monsieur de Noblecourt. Sartine was so shocked that Nicolas felt emboldened to reveal to him the trick he had played with the brass tag. The Lieutenant General said nothing, but gave his deputy a curious look. Nicolas added that he was aware that he had overstepped the mark, by forgetting the principle which Monsieur de Sartine had inculcated in him on his entry into the police force, 'that on his rigour would depend the life and honour of men who, however lowly their station, should be treated according to the rules'. Aware that he had done wrong, he was consequently placing his position at the King's disposal, once the investigation on which he was engaged had been concluded.

Sartine smiled. Of course he understood Nicolas's scruples – indeed, they increased the respect he bore him – but this was all nonsense. Why should one treat equitably a man responsible for the incompetence of the municipality and the deaths of so many innocent people, a man who had escaped being the murderer of an old man by pure luck? Was there a way to confound him, yes or no? If there was, then it had to be used. Justice must be done, whatever the cost, and he, the Lieutenant General of Police, took full responsibility, relieving Nicolas of any blame and any remorse. Major Langlumé had to be arrested, he insisted. The brass tag would certainly help to prove his guilt, at least in the eyes of the judges.

And so it was with a light heart that Nicolas set off back to Paris, after the great stable had again provided him with a horse – a sturdy, frisky light-tan mare. The journey passed uneventfully, and Nicolas no longer felt tired or hungry. By five he had passed Porte de la Conference. By five thirty he had abandoned his mount to the good graces of the duty groom at the Châtelet. He immediately left the houses of Pont au Change on his right, and set off along the Quai de Gesvres. This embankment above the river, which went under an arch before joining up with Pont Notre Dame, was a terrible cesspool where four sewers emptied their muck, where blood from the slaughterhouses ended up and into which all the latrines of Paris unloaded their refuse. Nicolas had to cover his nose with a handkerchief to protect it from the foul stench. The heat of summer was beginning, and the river, relieved of the spring floods, no longer lapped at the fetid arches of this bridge. He stepped onto the Cité, a district that still remained, much to the displeasure of Monsieur de Sartine, 'an unplanned meeting of a great number of houses . . .' They were all at odd angles to each other, creating all sorts of diversions and bottle-necks for the carriages, which found the streets extremely difficult to negotiate. Nicolas crossed the narrow square in front of Notre Dame and knocked at a door reinforced with nails and iron bars, which gave access to the archbishopric, a medieval house with its own turret situated on the south side of the cathedral.

A liveried valet opened the door and asked him the purpose of his visit. He gave a start when Nicolas told him that he wished to see his master immediately. He was clearly about to send him away when a thin man in the short coat of a cleric emerged from the gloom of the entrance hall. He was one of the prelate's secretaries, and Nicolas did not see any reason to conceal his own rank or in whose name he was venturing to disturb the arch-bishop's peace of mind.

'Do you have some sign or proof of your mission?' asked the secretary.

'I have two letters for the archbishop.'

The man held out his hand with the feigned innocence of someone taking a chance without really believing in it.

'Monsieur,' said Nicolas coldly, 'they can only be delivered into the hands of the person to whom they are addressed. But I consent to you looking at the seal of one of them.'

He showed him the letter from the King, sealed with the three *fleur de lis* of the French coat of arms.

'Monsieur,' the secretary said, 'it's very late, you've come unannounced and Monseigneur is very tired after the Pentecost ceremonies. I would therefore urge you to leave your letters with me. I shall give them to him tomorrow, and then we can decide on the best thing to do.'

'Monsieur, I'm extremely sorry, but I have to see the archbishop. It's an order of the King.'

The man went red in the face. Nicolas could see what was going through his mind, as if it were an open book. Monseigneur de Beaumont had already been exiled three times, so it was natural to fear the worst.

'Surely, Monsieur—'

Nicolas did not let him finish. 'Do not worry, Monsieur. I've only come here to discuss an affair which falls within the province of your master's spiritual magisterium. He isn't threatened in any way, if that's what you were thinking.'

'God be praised! All right, I'll go and see if Monseigneur can receive you. He was about to dine with a visitor.'

The cleric withdrew, leaving Nicolas facing a gloomy,

suspicious valet. He did not have long to wait. Without a word, he was invited to climb a large, dark, wooden staircase. On the first floor, a vast antechamber – its walls decorated with portraits of cardinals and archbishops, whom he supposed to be the present incumbent's predecessors – served as a waiting room. The secretary knocked at a door, opened it, murmured a few words and moved aside to let Nicolas into the room.

Nicolas was struck by the mixture of austerity and sumptuousness in the sparsely furnished room. The ceiling with its emblazoned beams was lost in shadow. An unseasonable fire blazed in the Renaissance fireplace. A huge chiaroscuro *Descent from the Cross* which Nicolas, as a lover of paintings and a tireless visitor of churches, judged as dating from the previous century, glowered over the room. The floor was covered with an oriental carpet in reddish shades.

The archbishop was sitting in a vast armchair to one side of the fire, next to a table on which stood a large silver candlestick with all the candles lit. There was another armchair facing him. To Nicolas, the prelate's pose seemed somewhat theatrical. He was wearing a purple cassock with a flapped cravat, the top half of his body covered in a clerical overcoat, and sat staring at the fire, his chin on his left hand, and his right hand caressing the cross of the Order of the Holy Spirit, which hung round his neck on a large blue moiré sash that passed beneath the two flaps of the cravat, and which he wore as if it were a pectoral cross. He turned his pale face and bloodshot eyes to Nicolas. His well-drawn mouth was framed by two deep, bitter folds. His chin was dimpled and somewhat weak, making a strong contrast with his high forehead and almost white hair, combed with little affectation. He held out his hand to Nicolas, who bowed and kissed it.

'I'm told that you have orders for me from the King.'

This was said in an ironic tone, which implied that it was an obvious fact.

'Monseigneur, all I have for you is two letters. One is from His Majesty, the other is from Père Grégoire, of the Discalced Carmelites in Rue Vaugirard. I won't conceal from you the fact that they both concern the same disturbing case.'

He handed them to the prelate, who searched in his sleeve for a pair of spectacles and opened the two letters, beginning with the King's, which he immediately refolded and placed in his sleeve. Père Grégoire's letter was read very quickly and thrown on the fire.

'Père Grégoire's letter would have sufficed,' said the archbishop. 'I have the greatest respect for him, and he often provides me with effective remedies for my ailments. Much more effective, I must say, than those with which the gentlemen of the Faculty deluge me. Commissioner – or should I say Marquis? – I take it as a sign of friendship that His Majesty has sent you.'

Nicolas refrained from answering, knowing the archbishop's aristocratic obsession and his pride in the ancient origins of his family – the Beaumont de Repaires – which he traced back, some joked, as far as the Flood.

'But does His Majesty really think,' the archbishop went on, 'that I am unaware of this affair? The parish priest of Saint-Roch brought it to the attention of my men. If the King had not decided to act in order to preserve order in his city, I would have done so myself to ensure the tranquillity of my flock.' He added, as if speaking to himself, 'A century of decline, in which this poor lost people, led astray by so many reprehensible examples, searches for the way without finding it and ignores the good shepherd! Alas, charity abates and the Church is riven with dissension. Where is the truth hiding? And as for obedience . . . When the State is threatened, the good side is always the King's; when the Church and its doctrine are called into question, the good side is always that of the body of bishops.'

He had been staring into the dancing flames. Now he again turned to look at Nicolas.

'Let us go through this point by point. And the better to clarify this matter, I need to know more about you. You had a good education at a reputable school in Vannes.'

Nicolas did not take this as a question.

'Do you believe in the devil, my son?'

'I believe in the teachings of the Holy Church. In my work, I often encounter evil. But what happened in Rue Saint-Honoré turns all my certainties upside down and goes beyond human understanding.'

The archbishop's hand tightened on the dove of the Holy Spirit. 'God sometimes makes use of that which is lowest, most despicable in the universe, and even of things which are not, in order to destroy those which are.'[2]

He stood up. Nicolas had never imagined he was so tall. He cut an impressive figure in his Episcopal garments. But his neck and the top part of his body were at a curious angle to the rest – a strange impression caused by the prelate's fruitless efforts to stand straighter – and it was obvious that he was in pain. He hung, rather than pulled, on a long strip of tapestry. A distant bell jingled. Monseigneur de Beaumont sat down again with a sigh of relief.

'I'd already formed an opinion on this matter before you arrived. I simply wanted to know if the King would decide that his people should intervene, and who would be appointed to do so.'

Behind these words, Nicolas sensed the power of the Church, as if his own life in the police had been observed, weighed in the balance and judged.

'Père Grégoire vouches for your . . . honesty, to use a worldly term. He assures me that in tackling this grave and troubling affair you will combine your sense of reason with obedience to the precepts of our Holy Church. I wasn't expecting you this evening, but I know you managed to speak to the King after his day's hunting.'

Nicolas savoured the subtlety of this statement. What better way to inform him that the archbishop had eyes and ears everywhere, even at Court, even within the monarch's immediate entourage?

'So I made the first move,' the archbishop went on. 'When my secretary told me you were here, I was about to dine with Père Raccard, my military arm in the shadowy regions, the diocese exorcist.'

At that moment, the secretary emerged through another door concealed by a tapestry, which he then held up to admit a tall man who seemed to be a veritable force of nature. Nicolas estimated that the man was approaching fifty. His greying hair was pulled back to reveal a face that was more military than ecclesiastical. It was clear that Père Raccard was little concerned with outward appearance: his cassock was so worn, so often washed and ironed that it shone with a greenish hue and in places the cord showed through at the edges. The short sleeves allowed a glimpse of the remains of torn, yellowish lace cuffs, which drew attention to his thick hands, the phalanxes covered in tufts of brown hair. The man reminded Nicolas of a woodcutter who worked in the grounds of the Château de Ranreuil, and who had terrified him every time he saw him. But the exorcist's brown eyes were gentle, and the smile he addressed to Nicolas attenuated the shock of his appearance.

The archbishop made the introductions. He seemed to be in increasing pain and collapsed back into his armchair, thus proving that his hieratic attitude was the result of a painful effort of will.

'My sons, I am going to leave you to prepare your battle. It demands a clear soul, but also the simple force of truth. You have my blessing.'

He raised his right hand and uttered the sacramental words in a genuinely majestic voice. Raccard took Nicolas by the shoulder and drew him to the door. The archbishop seemed to have fallen asleep, but the tension in his features indicated that he was having a painful attack. Ignoring the visitors, the secretary hurried to him. Raccard and Nicolas soon found themselves back outside on the square in front of Notre Dame, which was already in darkness.

'Shall we go straight to Rue Saint-Honoré?' said Nicolas. 'I can tell you my observations as we walk.'

'No, you deprived me of the archbishop's dinner! Not that I missed much. Because of his health, he only eats roots and greens.

The task awaiting us demands that we do not mistreat our bodies. Exorcism – which incidentally we practice only rarely, since extreme cases are the exception – requires physical strength and an ability to withstand anything. Here's what I suggest. I live very near here. I'll cook something up for us. Though you'll have to turn a blind eye to my untidiness, my dear Commissioner.'

Père Raccard led Nicolas to Rue aux Fèves, where they entered a house that was all askew. The treads creaked on the unlit stairs – unlit because of the fear of fire in these old houses, which were as inflammable as tow. Nicolas heard a key squeak in a lock. The priest lit a match and carried the fragile flame across a room until it reached a candle. The sight which met the commissioner's eyes took his breath away. They were in a bedroom as narrow and crooked as the gangway of a ship and monstrously untidy. The ceiling, its beams warped with age, was sagging, and none of the lines was parallel or perpendicular. It was like the interior of a cave. The walls were covered in shelves filled with countless books, some of which appeared to be very old. On a table with elaborately carved legs, covered in manuscripts and papers, a black cat kept guard. Its green eyes stared at Nicolas with placid indifference. Père Raccard bustled about to light his stove. As his guest looked on, he melted a cheese from Piedmont, which a Dominican friend in Turin sent him regularly by mail coach. He added butter and ground pepper to the mixture and spread it on some large slices of bread. He then ran to one of the shelves and cleared the books to reveal a number of dusty bottles. He went back into the alcove where the stove was and warmed up a soup for the commissioner's enjoyment, composed of boiled vegetables mixed with a confit of duck from his province, to which he added a touch of old plum brandy to give it, he said, body and accent.

The dinner proved to be much more delicious than Nicolas would have expected in such a strange place. The well-aged wine helped a lot, a hearty Burgundy from the hospices of Beaune. Nicolas suggested to Père Raccard that he rest tonight, and they would meet the next day in Rue Saint-Honoré. The exorcist dismissed this suggestion: the demon, if it was indeed he, would not wait. The sooner battle was joined, the greater the chances of limiting the infestation. In addition, the archbishop wanted the affair to be dealt with as soon as possible before it sowed confusion in the faithful, with the disastrous consequences that such manifestations always entailed. They had to tackle the enemy head-on, and since the attacks happened at night and early in the morning, he wanted to be in place already in the evening. From a cupboard he took a portmanteau, into which he piled a thick breviary, his stole, a bottle of holy water, a crucifix and a small silver box, as well as a branch of boxwood and some candles.

'All these things are necessary, but not sufficient,' he declared. 'Everything is here.' He pointed to his head and his heart. 'Are you in a position to confront the demon? Does he have ways to surprise you, to throw you, to make you lose your composure by revealing buried facts or forgotten actions?'

'That has already happened, Father,' replied Nicolas. 'It convinced me of his power, but not of his influence over me.'

'Good, but you must guard against pride. He insinuates himself into us through all our failings and even our virtues. If you don't feel strong enough, abandon the fight now, or, like Ulysses, stop your ears with wax! Not that that would help. The demon is quite capable of speaking within us. Reciting one's prayers is still the best protection.'

They plunged back into the night, walking quite quickly. They were unable to find a carriage, but hired the services of a lantern carrier to light their way. Nicolas could not resist telling his companion, with a certain self-satisfaction, that it was on his initiative that in 1768 Monsieur de Sartine had created a service of umbrella and lantern carriers, available day and night. The unskilled men who performed this function carried numbered lanterns. Naturally, they were registered with the authorities, and the commissioner made no secret of the fact that they were of great help to the police. On the Quai de la Mégisserie, they were followed for a time by two or three robbers, but the priest's height and Nicolas's sword – not to mention the arrival of a watch patrol – dissuaded them from taking the risk. When they reached Rue Saint-Honoré, Semacgus opened the door to them, his complexion even ruddier than usual.

'You've come just at the right time!' he cried. 'I was resting a little in your room when I heard a strange noise. Soon after, Miette started one of her attacks.' The surgeon, who seemed to have aged, looked at him wild-eyed. 'She spoke with the voice of Madame Lardin!³ We had to strap her to the bed.'

IX

EXORCISM

'In that combat, Christ does not remain in the middle. He is wholly ours. When we entered the lists, He anointed us and put the other in chains.'

Saint John Chrysostom

Semacgus described what had occurred so far that night, corroborating Nicolas's previous accounts. The surgeon was so distressed by what he had seen that he almost doubted his own sanity and spoke of consulting a colleague to check the state of his health. He lost himself in conjectures, each more unlikely than the last, trying to find an explanation to assuage his doubts and anxieties. Nicolas refrained from exulting at this turnaround, but he was pleased and reassured that his friend could now share the burden of his confusion. As for Père Raccard, he was rubbing his hands with a kind of glee, like an old soldier preparing to mount an attack on a redoubt. His good humour acted as a stimulant on Semacgus, dispelling his low spirits. Meanwhile Nicolas, his senses ever alert, had been aware, ever since entering the house, of the distant sound of Naganda's drum. For a moment – although he did not linger on it – the idea struck him that there might be some connection between these savage practices and the drama unfolding once again in Miette's room, the

231

obscure, threatening force tormenting the maid's body and mind.

Cries suddenly reached them from the second floor. Almost immediately, Jean Galaine, bathed in sweat, his hair matted and his shirt torn, came hurtling down the stairs, screaming more than speaking. Miette had got free! An unknown force had broken the straps holding her to the bed. Père Raccard calmed everyone down. He opened his portmanteau, took out his stole, which he kissed and put round his neck, then the bottle of holy water and the other liturgical objects. He lit the candles and distributed them. They had been joined by the other members of the family, apart from Charles Galaine who had stayed with Marie Chaffoureau outside the door of Miette's room, which no one dared enter. The exorcist asked for a plate, into which he poured a little holy water. He prayed, then dipped the branch of box-wood into the water, and sprinkled it at the four cardinal points. He ordered everyone to kneel. In a loud and determined voice, he uttered a first admonition.

'I implore you, ancient serpent, in the name of the judge of the living and the dead, the creator of the world who has the power to cast you down into Gehenna, to leave this house at once. Cursed demon, He commands it. He who is obeyed by the winds, the sea and the tempest commands it. He who, from the heights of heaven, flung you down into the bowels of the earth commands it. He who has the power to make you draw back commands it. Listen, Satan, and tremble. Be gone from here, crawl away defeated. I implore you in the name of Our Lord Jesus Christ who will come to judge the living and the dead. Amen.'

He continued sprinkling holy water and made everyone recite the Pater Noster. The dull murmur of the prayer was punctuated by dreadful screams. Now Charles Galaine and the cook, both terrified, came down and joined the group. The priest asked for coals. They were brought from the stove in the servants' pantry on a small terracotta plate-warmer. From the little silver box he took the incense and placed it, in the shape of a cross, on the coals. The ground floor filled with smoke.

'Do you perform exorcisms from a distance?' asked Semacgus.

'Not at all. First I must try to cleanse the house. Then we will deal with the patient.' He put his hands together and resumed, 'I implore you, demon, to leave this place, to cease frightening those who live here and not to place any curse on it. May God Almighty, creator of all things, sanctify this house and all its dependencies, may all phantoms disappear from it, all mean actions, all clever ways, all diabolical tricks and all unclean spirits.'

He began again to bless the house.

'By this sign, we command him to cease this instant and forever all his vexations, that his spells and illusions may disappear and the terror of this poisonous serpent vanish forever. Through the Lord who will come to judge the living and the dead and will purify the world in fire. Amen.'

The sounds from upstairs suggested that furniture was flying and smashing against the walls. Loud thuds shook the house.

Père Raccard rubbed his hands: 'He's reacting, the rascal! That's a good start. All of you, go back to your rooms. I shall officiate upstairs in the presence of the Commissioner and Monsieur . . .?'

He pointed to Semacgus. Nicolas made the introductions.

'The Faculty,' said Raccard, 'will not be out of place in our battle with the unnameable. Monsieur Le Floch has told me of your scepticism. Be our reason and our conscience, now that you are convinced of the reality of these phenomena.'

'You can count on me, Father,' said Semacgus, resolutely.

Nicolas was pleased to see these two men, one a friend of long standing, the other a more recent acquaintance, forming such an effortless bond.

Looking more relaxed now, Dr Semacgus added, with a laugh, 'It's always better to hunt a wolf in packs.'

'If only we were dealing merely with a wolf! The devil is a sinister joker, filled with hate. He loves mocking poor humans, ingratiating himself and playing the fool, the better to lead his victims astray. He is the father of lies, and his name is legion. He will be sure to lay traps to try and put us off the scent! But I promise you, we will see this through.'

He gathered his tools, entrusting the plate-warmer to Semacgus.

The three of them climbed the stairs and found the cook pinned to the wall on the landing, staring in astonishment at Miette, who was sitting in the air above her bed, looking at them with bright, bloodshot eyes and a wicked smile on her lips.

'The hussy!' said Père Riccard. 'I'll wipe that smile off her face, you wait and see!'

He approached Miette, and her head turned like a dummy's, following his movements with her stony gaze. He placed his hand on her head. Her body swayed like a soap bubble caught between two currents of air. She began to moan dully, like an animal containing its rage.

'Yes, yes, prepare to recognise your master and obey him.'

Miette opened her mouth and spat at him. Without showing any emotion, the priest wiped himself with the back of his sleeve. Now a man's voice emerged from the tortured little body.

'Monk, you make me laugh! You have no power over me, remember that.'

Imperturbably, the father arranged the contents of his portmanteau on a little table. Semacgus placed the plate-warmer with the coals beside them. The sacred odour of incense filled the room. Miette's growls rose in volume and pitch until they were deafening, and her head went back until it was almost at right angles to her body. She was howling like a wolf baying at the moon, as if struggling against the heady perfume.

'It isn't possible!' said Semacgus. 'Look how distended the muscles and skin are!'

'Oh, I've seen worse than that!' growled Raccard. 'I've seen possessed people stretch so much they added a quarter to their length.'

'Is that an illusion, a sham? Is someone pulling the wool over our eyes?'

'Oh, no, these phenomena are dramatic and disturbing, but very real. We must keep a cool head.'

He took his stole and moved it over Miette's face. The girl tried to grab it with her claw-like hands, and in doing so her nails scraped the silk fabric, scratching in passing the silver cross embroidered on it. She fell back heavily on the bed.

'That has an effect on you, does it, strumpet?' said the exorcist. 'Have no fear, we're going to free you of your visitor.'

Nicolas admired Père Raccard for retaining his composure, humour and courage even in these hallucinatory circumstances.

But the priest's mobile, piercing eyes remained constantly alert, like those of a hunter tracking a dangerous prey, anticipating its every move.

'You two, hold her firmly, and press down on her with all your weight. It doesn't matter if she struggles, and don't worry about crushing her. The most important thing is to stop her getting away from you.'

Semacgus and Nicolas took up position on either side of Miette. Nicolas had assumed that she would be hot and feverish, but when he touched her, he found that her skin was freezing cold. She was moaning softly. The father put his stole back on and resumed the ritual. After several minutes of silent prayer, he spoke again.

'Lord God of virtue, receive the prayers we offer you, unworthy as we are, for your servant Ermeline. Deign to grant her forgiveness for her sins and rescue her from the demon that torments her. Holy God, Eternal Father, cast a favourable glance upon your servant, who is in the grip of a painful affliction . . .'

A deep groan came from inside Miette. In some strange way, it merged for a moment with the moaning, then swelled and rose above it in volume. To the alarm of those present, the girl's body produced two different cries at the same time, one low, the other shrill. Père Raccard could see that his companions were on the verge of panic. Again he sprinkled holy water.

'Back, back, foul beast, return to your lair. Back, back, back!'

He looked at Nicolas and Semacgus.

'Do not be disturbed, these are just some of the preliminary tricks used to batter our defences, wear down our will and deceive our faith. Remember that the kingdom, the power and the glory are within us!'

Miette had fallen silent now, but a kind of slime – which reminded Nicolas, somewhat incongruously, of snails plunged into nettles by Catherine in her kitchen in Rue Montmartre – was flowing in an uninterrupted stream from her mouth, gradually covering her poor chest.

'I implore you, demon,' Raccard resumed, 'in the name of Our Lord who rose again on the third day, to flee the body of this servant of God, with all your iniquities, your evil spells, your incantations, your ligatures and all your acts. Do not remain here, foul spirit. The day of everlasting judgement is at hand and you and your apostate angels will be flung into a raging inferno for all eternity.'

Suddenly, the two friends were thrown back against the walls of the room. Miette's thin arms, having turned as stiff as steel, had swollen beneath their fingers, and they had felt an incredible force push them away.

'He's resisting,' screamed Raccard, 'he's resisting!'

Nicolas had lived through many dramas and seen many horrible sights in his time, but the scene that followed would lodge itself in his memory and would stay with him until the day he died. Père Raccard was breathing as heavily as a woodcutter trying to fell a great tree, as he mustered all his strength to overcome and chase away the demon possessing Miette. It seemed as though the muscles and tendons were multiplying over the servant's body, hardening it to an extraordinary extent. The priest's face was scarlet, sweat was pouring into his eyes, and the veins on his forehead and temples were swollen and bluish, ready, it seemed, to burst. And all through this combat, the thing poured out, in a grating voice, a stream of obscenities which left Raccard impassive, but which horrified Nicolas and Semacgus. Now the priest was shouting to drown out the voice of the demon.

'Whoever you are, proud and cursed creature, who, despite the invocation of the Divine Name, continue your vexations against this child and spew forth filth, do not think you are safe from the wrath of the Almighty, for fire, hail, snow, ice and the spirit of the storms will be your portion!'

Miette was breathing heavily now, like an animal at bay. Père Raccard redoubled his efforts. He held out the crucifix. As the sacred object came close to her face, the girl sank into the bed, whistling and spitting like a cat and giving off a foul smell.

'I exorcise you, vile spirit! Leave the body of this creature of God! It is not I, a sinner, who commands you, but the immaculate lamb. The archangels and the angels, the apostles, the martyrs, the confessors and the virgins are coming to vanquish you. Your diabolical forces are collapsing. Restore to your victim the strength of her limbs and the unity of her senses. Do not appear to her either when she is awake or when she is asleep, and do not trouble her in her search for everlasting life. Cursed Satan, accept your sentence. I cast you out and uproot you from the body of this servant. God Almighty, through your mercy, may this tormented body be entirely delivered from the devil's wiles. Through Jesus Christ Our Lord, who will judge the living and the dead and the century with fire. Amen.'

Exhausted, Père Raccard fell back against the wall. The others felt a strange sensation, as though a hot, fetid breath were passing by them. The pane in the little window shattered, and silence fell once more on the room. Miette lay there calmly, apparently freed from the oppression that had held her in its grip for days. The excreta with which she had been covered at the height of her attack disappeared, as if they had evaporated. Nicolas noticed that Naganda's drum had ceased its obsessive rhythm. Miette began to move suddenly, with her eyes closed. She rose stiffly and, without looking at the three men, opened the door, went out on the landing and descended the stairs. Nicolas seized a candle and rushed after her, motioning to the others to come with him but putting a finger to his lips to indicate that they should observe complete silence. He wanted to avoid disturbing what seemed to be an attack of somnambulism, doubtless a result of the possession or of whatever had taken its place.

They did not encounter any members of the family, who were all still shut away in their rooms. On reaching the ground floor, the maid entered the servants' pantry and opened a half-arched, latticed wooden door leading to a steep staircase. At the bottom, they found themselves in a rather large cellar, filled with bundles of hessian, which, to judge from the animal smell that pervaded the room, probably contained the hides used in the Galaines' business. Miette stopped in front of one of the bundles, fell to her knees and began weeping and putting her hands together as if in prayer, then suddenly collapsed lifeless on the floor. The priest and Semacgus ran to help her. Nicolas pushed aside the bundle: beneath it, the beaten earth showed signs of having been recently disturbed, as if a hole had been dug and then smoothed over. He looked for a tool, but found only his pocket knife. He scratched at the earth, which was still quite loose at this spot, and dug up a few bushels of it with his hands. Soon, his fingers touched a piece of cloth. The smell of decomposition rose to his nostrils, overcoming the acrid odour of the hides. Carefully, he continued working away at the earth and at last brought out a small, light, oblong mass wrapped in cloth: the already rotting body of a baby in its swaddling clothes.

Miette had regained consciousness, but, according to Semacgus, she had lost her mind. She was unable to speak, let alone answer any questions. It was necessary to decide what to do next, and Nicolas was never more at his ease than at these moments when a semblance of order had to be re-established in a disturbed universe. First, Père Raccard would take Miette back up to her room, as there was nothing that could be done for her at the moment. The exorcism had succeeded, but now the sick girl had to be allowed to rest: only the Lord's tender mercies could help her now. Perhaps her reason would return. Semacgus would examine the corpse of the child, then it would be taken to the Basse-Geôle, where Sanson would perform an autopsy. They were the only ones aware of this discovery. Two suspicious deaths in one house were too much: the whole household had to be arrested and placed in solitary confinement in the Châtelet prison, all separated from each other. Only the cook and Geneviève, the little girl, would be allowed to stay in the house. Dorsacq, the shop assistant, would be arrested as soon as day broke.

Suddenly, through the basement window that looked out on Rue Saint-Honoré, Nicolas heard a voice calling him and recognised Bourdeau. The inspector had the precious and almost magical quality of always appearing at the very moment when his presence was most needed. Nicolas went back upstairs and ran to greet him. Bourdeau seemed to be in a hurry to tell him various pieces of news, but Nicolas interrupted him and briefly brought him up to date with the extraordinary events that had taken place in the house. Bourdeau screwed up his eyes mockingly, which somewhat irritated Nicolas. There was no time to lose, and he quickly ordered him to call the watch, to establish a cordon around the house, and to fetch carriages to take the Galaines to the Châtelet. Dorsacq had to be seized as soon as he got out of bed, and taken to join the others immediately. Everything else could wait until later. And anyone who had not seen what he had seen, added Nicolas, would do well not to mock. Nor did he want anyone to come and tell him, all shamefaced, that on top of everything else, one or other of the suspects had committed suicide. They all had to be watched closely. Bourdeau, laughing up his sleeve, remarked with an ingratiating air that some deputies were increasingly adopting the tone of their chief, and that Commissioner Le Floch was starting to *Sartinise* with the greatest ease and pleasure. That had the effect of lightening the mood, and Nicolas was unable to suppress a nervous giggle – much to the alarm of Semacgus, who at that moment walked up to them carrying the little corpse in his arms.

Bourdeau left to carry out his orders. The body of the baby had been entrusted to him for transfer to the Basse-Geôle. Nicolas again thought of Naganda, and felt a gnawing sense of foreboding. Why had the drumming stopped? An inner voice told him not to worry, that it had ceased simply because the ritual which the Indian was performing had come to an end. But he wanted to set his mind at rest, and he gestured to Semacgus to follow him. They went back upstairs to the attic. The key was still in the lock. Nicolas opened the door and lifted the candle he was carrying. Naganda's inanimate body lay on the floor, a knife in his back. Semacgus rushed to him, knelt and felt his pulse. He looked up, smiling.

'He's still alive! He's breathing. Let's get him out of here. The weapon doesn't seem to have touched any vital organ. It's been inserted quite clumsily, at an angle. The only danger might be if the tip has punctured the left lung. The resulting loss of blood might lead to asphyxia. Will you help me, Nicolas?'

They lifted the Indian's large body and laid it on the palliasse. Semacgus was transformed. He took off his coat and waistcoat. 'Find me a piece of cloth, and some wine or vinegar.'

Nicolas went back downstairs to his room and came back immediately, holding one of the small phials of Carmelite water with which Père Grégoire supplied him with touching regularity. Semacgus washed his hands.

'We'll never know exactly how many of our soldiers and sailors have died from being touched by dirty hands. No one can explain it, but there it is.'

The important thing was to remove the weapon without aggravating any possible lesions, and without provoking a haemorrhage that would flood the victim's lung. By the light of the candle, the operation was performed without difficulty, made easier by the fact that Naganda was unconscious. The blade had gone through a muscle, then hit a rib. One of Nicholas's clean shirts was torn to make a reasonable temporary bandage. The wound had stopped bleeding. Cradling him in their arms, they turned him over. He was starting to come to his senses. Semacgus poured a few drops of Carmelite water on his lips. He grimaced and woke completely.

'I . . .' he said, stifling a cry. 'What happened?'

'We should be asking you that,' said Nicolas.

'I remember feeling a strong pain in my back, and then everything went black.'

'Someone planted a knife between your shoulder blades. You must have been in the middle of one of your strange ceremonies. I heard you stop drumming, which I thought was odd. It was like an intuition . . .'

'It was written that you would be the hand of destiny, and that you would save my life. The sacred frog predicted it. I am sure that, although you not aware of it, you are *the son of stone*.'

'*Here* is your saviour. Dr Semacgus.'

'I think, Nicolas,' said the party concerned, 'that you are underestimating your ability to foresee events. If we hadn't intervened, Monsieur here would have died. And *the son of stone* fits you like a glove.'

'In what way?'

'Didn't you tell me that Canon Le Floch, your guardian and adoptive father, found you on the tombstone of the lords of Carne, in the collegiate church of Guérande? That's one mystery neatly solved. We really are living through some inexplicable events. And, what's worse, we're getting used to it!'

'Naganda, do you suspect anyone in particular?' asked Nicolas.

'I've never met with anything but hostility and threats in this house,' the Indian replied.

'Don't you have anything to add to what you've already told me?'

'No, nothing.'

'It's vital that you tell me everything. If you remember any significant facts, don't hesitate to send for me. By the way, do you still claim that for nearly a day you were drugged and asleep?'

'Indeed I do.'

'Very well. I'm sorry to have to tell you – and this has no connection with our conversation – that the occupants of this house are to be placed in solitary confinement in a State prison.'

Semacgus pointed to the wound and shook his head.

'Taking your wound into account,' Nicolas went on, 'you will be taken to the Hôtel-Dieu hospital to receive the care you require. Very soon, the truth will out. Do you have a shovel?'

Naganda looked him in the eyes. 'I don't have one, but you'll find one in the lean-to in the courtyard, along with the garden tools and a wheelbarrow used for transporting the bundles of hides when they arrive.'

Nicolas left the Indian in Semacgus's care, and went back downstairs to the shop to think and to wait for Bourdeau, the men of the watch, the police officers and the carriages. It was his first chance to take stock of the night's events. He had not yet recovered from the shock of what he had seen and, the more he thought about it, the more insane it seemed. He no longer knew what to make of the physical manifestation of Miette's possession. As the heat of the attack faded, reason came back to him, and with it logic and a degree of scepticism. He had definitely not been dreaming, and nor had his companions, but he had to get back on to firm ground, to a world of facts, evidence and normal life.

The fact remained that Miette's attack, whatever its cause, had led his investigation in a new direction by revealing what certainly appeared to be an infanticide. It was quite likely that the attacks had their origin in the uneasy conscience of a young girl in a difficult situation, who may have been an accomplice in the murder of a baby. It was certainly an explanation, and Nicolas was quite prepared to believe that complicity in such a barbaric act could lead to a decay of the soul and that the strange manifestations were its consequence. Of course, it still had to be established that the baby was the victim of foul play. Only the opening of the corpse could tell them that. But what seemed certain was that Élodie, a girl of easy virtue, surrounded by many suitors, had reaped the fruit of her wandering ways. Had she decided on the crime herself, or had it been committed without her knowledge? Who could have been the instigators and the accomplices?

Tuesday 5 June 1770

Nicolas had dozed off in an armchair in the shop, and was woken an hour later by Bourdeau knocking at the window. The house immediately came to life. Two stretchers were brought, one for Naganda and the other for Miette: Nicolas did not want to leave her behind, and still hoped that she would recover her senses and be able to give testimony. For that to happen, they would have to keep a close watch on her and make sure she had no contact with anyone except the police. The members of the Galaine family, who had all gone to earth in their lairs, were gathered together. A police officer soon arrived with Dorsacq, hastily dressed and with his hair dishevelled. Nicolas gave a little speech without mentioning either the results of the exorcism or the macabre discovery in the cellar. At this stage of his inquiries, he told them, he considered it vital to their discovery of the truth that they should be separated from one another and placed in solitary confinement in a prison until his investigations were complete. Those who were innocent of any wrongdoing had simply to accept a measure designed to bring the case to a speedy conclusion. As for the others . . . Since her husband seemed unable to say anything, Madame Galaine made herself the family's advocate. This was a denial of justice, she cried. The commissioner, whose bias was clear to everyone involved in the case, was acting in a heavy-handed and arbitrary manner. The magistrates would be on their side, she said, and she urged her family not to give in and to resist being removed from their house. But the police, it was pointed out to her, had the power to do what they liked with them: what she called arbitrariness was simply the will of the King, acting through his commissioner, therefore any argument would amount to sedition.

Their departure took place amid noisy protests. A long file of cabs, along with two police wagons carrying the sick and injured, set off for the Châtelet and the Hôtel-Dieu respectively. Before he, too, left Rue Saint-Honoré, Nicolas went to have a quick word with the cook to ask her to look after Geneviève. She assured him that she was perfectly capable of doing so: after all, she had already brought up the girl's father and aunts. But she was afraid of staying in a house where the devil had been causing mischief for the past few days. Nicolas, however, managed to convince her that all danger was past, and that one of his men would be on duty close by to deal with any eventuality. She was so anxious to give vent to her feelings and to delay Nicolas's departure that he let her ramble on about the past without even dreaming of interrupting her. These reminiscences eventually included a few anecdotes about the early lives of Camille and Charlotte. In their youth, she informed him, there had been a serious conflict between them. They had been rivals in love, and their quarrel had been so fierce that they had ended up frightening off their mutual suitor.

Nicolas then went upstairs to see Geneviève, who was not asleep but sitting up in bed, clasping a rag doll to her breast, tears streaming down her face. He tried to console her, explaining the situation in simple words, without going into details. He tucked her in and she fell asleep almost immediately. Cyrus, who had followed the commissioner, was playing languidly with a screwed-up piece of paper, chewing on it with his aged teeth. Intrigued, Nicolas took it out of the dog's mouth, unfolded it and moved it closer to the candle. To his surprise, and a kind of glee, he recognised the handwriting: it was that of Élodie's father, Claude Galaine, who had died in New France. These were his last wishes, written on a small parchment, then folded and refolded. They clearly stated that his entire fortune, listed at the bottom of the document and consisting of a considerable number of investments and properties, was to go to his only child, Élodie. However, she would only have use of it until such time as she gave birth to a male child, who would then become the heir. If she were to die childless, the inheritance would revert to the first male child of Charles Galaine. This opened up some interesting lines of inquiry. The essential thing for the moment was to find out who had possessed this document, and who else knew of it. Nicolas searched among the little girl's toys and found a necklace of black pearls identical to the pearl found in Élodie's hand. There could be no doubt about it: the pearls had come from the necklace that had been stolen from Naganda. Geneviève, delighted with these pearls, must have rethreaded them to form a new necklace.

Nicolas was truly sorry to have to wake the little girl. She made a sullen face and stretched. When he questioned her, she first said nothing, then started crying. Yes, she had found the piece of paper and the pearls in her aunts' work-box. The box contained a mahogany darning egg, which she loved because it was hollow and you could unscrew it. Usually, her aunts put pins and needles in it. The last time she had opened it, she had found a much-folded piece of paper and some black pearls. Nicolas asked her when this had been. In the last day or two – the girl was no longer very sure. Nicolas was intrigued by one thing: when he had searched the sisters' room, he had not found the box. After digging a little deeper, he learnt that it was not always kept in the bedroom, but was moved about from room to room, wherever Charlotte and Camille happened to be sewing. He calmed the child down, and did not leave her until she was asleep.

Nicolas went back up to his room to get his portmanteau. Semacgus and Père Raccard were nowhere to be found: they must have left with their patients. Bourdeau, far-sighted as ever, had reserved a carriage for him. Nicolas ordered the coachman to drive him to Rue Montmartre. He wanted to take Cyrus home – the old dog, although quite playful and spry, deserved a good meal and a rest – and to wash and change and find out how Monsieur de Noblecourt was faring. By the time he reached the entrance archway of the old mansion, the baker's shop was giving off the comforting aroma of the first batch of bread. He asked the coachman to wait for him, and walked in through the carriage entrance. As he did so, he heard a timid voice hailing him. It was the baker's boy.

'Monsieur Nicolas, I need to tell you something. When I was sweeping up this morning, I found this metal thing, just like the one you picked up. I kept it because I thought you'd be interested.'

He held out a little brass tag identical to the one found in the lock of the attic door in the ambassadors' mansion.

'You couldn't have pleased me more!' cried Nicolas. He searched in his pocket, pulled out a handful of coins and handed them to the boy, who blushed as he took them. 'Have you already taken the soft rolls up to Monsieur de Noblecourt?'

'Not yet. I was just about to, but I was waiting for you to come back.'

'Will you make me even happier? Add some croissants and brioches to the rolls. Right now, I'd quite happily eat the whole shop, and the baker's boy with it!'

The boy laughed and ran off. Dawn was bathing the old courtyard in a hazy light. The square of sky turned from blue-black to pearl-grey. Birds were chirping and shaking themselves beside a puddle. A new day was replacing the horrors of the night. Would it reveal the truth? Would it allow him to make the connection between the various elements laboriously assembled in the course of the investigation, and confound the guilty? Would some fleeting, irrational vision help him to put the pieces together in a new order and reveal the solution, like dice being shaken in a bag then thrown onto a table? With the discovery of a second brass tag, the scruples Nicolas had had now vanished.

Despite Monsieur de Sartine's *nihil obstat* and his official absolution, he had not been convinced so far that the act intended to confound Langlumé was not the kind that stays with you as a bitter memory all your life. Providence, that immanent justice, had decided otherwise. The law would punish, not simply an attack on an old man, but also an insult to a magistrate, that is, a representative of the King's authority.

The Noblecourt household was already bubbling with excitement. After a good night's sleep, the former magistrate had woken at dawn, still slightly bruised from the previous day's attack, but cheered by the possibility of a respite, authorised by the Faculty, from his usual austere regime. He had ordered his chocolate and was waiting for his soft rolls. When Nicolas entered his bedroom, the old man, dressed in a reddish-purple robe and with his head wrapped in a madras to hide his bandages, was watching impatiently as Marion and Catherine bustled about – Marion with her small steps and Catherine with her long strides – setting the table close to the window that looked out on the street. Yapping and whining, Cyrus rushed to his master's feet.

'Ah, my old companion,' said Noblecourt, half ironically, half moved, 'you must have been through some terrible adventures with Nicolas! You run off without a second glance, but now you're happy to be back!' He turned to Nicolas, and made a theatrical gesture towards his clothes. 'Don't I look like a Mamamouchi? *Quid novi*, my good friend? You look tired. Sit down and tell me everything.'

Catherine put down a large tray containing the chocolate, the cups, the rolls, the croissants and brioches, and three pots of jam.

'I think we must first ask Catherine to prepare a good meal for Cyrus, who didn't eat well in Rue Saint-Honoré.'

At these words, the dog stirred and ran off on his old paws towards the servants' pantry.

'And what's more, you starved him! But what's this I see? Croissants and brioches!'

'It's for Nicolas, Monsieur,' Catherine muttered, 'not for you. Be reasonable. The little rolls are enough.'

'All right, all right. You can go now.'

Grumpily, he chased her away as if swatting a fly. No sooner was her back turned than his hand closed around a brioche, which he opened and filled with a large spoonful of cherry jam while Nicolas looked on sternly. The commissioner began telling his story. When he fell silent, the former magistrate, having eaten his fill, sat back in his armchair, glanced out at Rue Montmartre, and put his hands together.

'If anyone other than you had told me this,' he said, 'I would never have believed it. Of course, our faith asks us to give credence to a thousand stories from the lives of the saints. Can it be that there exists another side of the coin, a dark mirror image of our own existence? The Church certainly encourages us to believe so, and I'm pleased to learn that the exorcist, this Père Raccard, is evidently a reasonable man and not one of those petty, narrow-minded people who miss the Inquisition and wish they could still burn the poor, deranged victims at the stake. You'll have to introduce us. I'll invite the Duc de Richelieu and a few fine minds, and we can debate it over some good bottles of wine. What an evening in prospect!'

As he talked, he was slyly twisting the end off a croissant.

'Have you asked yourself all the right questions?' he resumed. 'Either the girl really was possessed, in which case why? Or else she was sick, as our friend Semacgus originally thought, and if that's true, what does her "attack" contribute to your investigation? In the first case, why would the devil be interested in a poor maidservant? From the point of view of the Church, it must have been because she gave the demon an opportunity to seize her soul. And if such is the case, draw what conclusions you will. This Miette is at the centre of your investigation. In the second case, that of the poor girl being sick, we are drawn to the same conclusions. Did some terrible acts weigh on her conscience, acts for which she was responsible or in which she was complicit, which led her to this state of mental decay? For me, that's the crux of the whole thing. You must get her to talk.'

Nicolas sighed. 'Alas, she's lost her reason and there's nothing to indicate that she will recover it. You've put your finger on the one thing we're unable to do. Once I've accumulated a certain number of facts, I'm obliged, despite everything, to continue my inquiries in different directions and pursue all the suspects. There are still many elements missing, but for the moment suspicion falls on all of them. None of them has an alibi for the time of Élodie's death. As for the infanticide, if that's what is, it's not going to be easy to find out who's responsible.'

'And what about that curious native from New France? He seems to be out of the running. After all, they tried to murder him. You're surely not going to tell me he's still on the list of suspects?'

'Oh, yes! His wound proves nothing. It was a very clumsy blow, which barely touched him! Don't you find that strange?

The attempt on his life may have been genuine, but it proves everything and nothing. It's possible that an accomplice of his wanted to get rid of him. I'm starting to have my doubts about Naganda's alibi. He had reasons to want Élodie out of the way, too.'

'Don't let yourself get too tangled up. I wouldn't want my questions to make you even more confused. There are already too many hypotheses in this case. Any crime, as I know from experience, is a complex machine with three or four centres. Don't rule anything out, but keep things simple, and look at the facts. Who stands to benefit from the crime? What are the usual motives? Passion and financial gain, of course. Dismantle your suspects as you would a watch, and the missing piece will easily be found.'

'You're right,' said Nicolas. 'The more we talk about a case, the more we confuse it, and the more inextricable it becomes.'

'That's it! If you shake the torch of truth too much, it goes out. Look at what you know, and draw up a battle plan. Listen to your intuition. Years of observation have taught me that intuition guides us more than it leads us astray. Let your heart be moved, and only then let your mind reflect.'

The other end of the croissant disappeared into his mouth, and was quickly swallowed. The rest was about to follow when Cyrus, who had come back, seized it, much to his master's annoyance.

Nicolas burst out laughing. 'Oh, the rascal! He's so concerned about his master's health that he's prepared to risk your anger. I'm going to do the same and let you rest.'

He stood up, wished Monsieur de Noblecourt a prompt recovery – the former procurator waved his fist at him threateningly by way of farewell – took what remained of the croissants and brioches and went back to his apartment. A few moments later, just as he was about to leave, Bourdeau knocked at the door and put his ruddy, cheerful face inside the room. Nicolas often thought that there was nothing in his deputy's appearance that really indicated the depth and subtlety of the man. The inspector rarely dropped his guard and preferred to keep his own counsel. There had only been a few rare but precious moments when he had revealed to Nicolas the hidden aspects of his attractive, complex personality.

'It's all done,' he said. 'Every member of the Galaine family is in solitary confinement. It wasn't all that easy to find six secure cells.'

'Do they have special privileges?'

'Oh, no. That would mean constant comings and goings. They're in strict solitary, but there shouldn't be any problems; you'll be finished well before.'

'Thank you for your confidence! Our prison system is intolerable, and doesn't help us to get at the truth. The real masters there are the caretaker, the gaolers and their servants, and the counter clerks with whom the prisoners are in daily contact. I'm not talking about the commissioners who go in and out. I've put a few thoughts about this down on paper for Monsieur de Sartine. One of these days, I'll submit them to him. What about Miette and Naganda?'

'The Indian's at the Hôtel-Dieu. But I had to make a fuss. The sick are four to a bed there, passing their vermin to each other. I had to leave a few *écus* to get Naganda a truly horrible room. I left a police officer with him. It's all going to cost money . . .'

He waved a paper.

'Make out a memorandum, and I'll sign it. You know how pernickety the Duvals, those harpies on Monsieur de Sartine's staff, are about these things, father and son both.'

'Paperwork will be the death of France!'

'And Miette?'

'Impossible to get her into the Hôtel-Dieu, and Charenton and Bicêtre are much too far. I had her taken to the convent of the Lazarists in Rue du Faubourg-Saint-Denis, with precise instructions. That'll be expensive, too – there's a nun looking after her.'

'It's only temporary. At least I hope so. We're nearly at the end of the investigation.'

'I have some other important things to tell you, but you jumped down my throat back there in Rue Saint-Honoré.'

'The urgency of the moment, my dear fellow! I did notice you wanted to speak to me, and now I'm all ears.'

'Rabouine did as he was told when he got back from Versailles. I took the note you put with your instructions and went to see Robillard, the second-hand clothes dealer in Rue du Faubourg-du-Temple. The vilest, seediest dump you can imagine. All the unwanted clothes from all the rented lodgings in Paris end up there. I had to shake him up a bit, but he finally showed me the items that corresponded to the note. A strange batch of things, which I'm sure will interest you.'

'I'm listening – don't keep me waiting.'

'You'll see it was worth the wait,' said Bourdeau with a laugh. 'He showed me two dark cloaks, two hats and two white papier mâché masks. Oh, I was forgetting, an apothecary's glass bottle as well. This odd collection had been brought in to him in great

255

haste early on the morning of the thirty-first of May. In other words, the morning after the disaster in Place Louis XV.'

'And who brought it to him?'

'A young man.'

'Nothing more precise than that?'

'No. You seem disappointed.'

'Not at all. But it does complicate things. Did you manage to get any kind of description?'

'Nothing specific. The interior's dark, there's not much light in the morning and Robillard didn't see anything. And, anyway, people tend to be discreet in that line of work. It's not much of a step from a second-hand clothes dealer to a fence. Plus, it all happened very quickly. What was surprising to him was that this was a better class of customer than he was used to dealing with, and that the clothes he brought in were of good quality, but he didn't even haggle over the price, even though they were worth a lot more than he was offered.'

'So it was a man . . .' said Nicolas, pensively. 'Well, why not? Or else a woman disguised as a man. Anything's possible.'

'I'm really sorry,' said Bourdeau, 'not to have more enlightening news for you.'

'Not at all, Pierre, it's not your fault. The suspect I had in mind doesn't quite fit the facts any more, that's all. We mustn't forget to have that bottle examined. It must have had something in it. Semacgus should be able to help us with that. As for the other pieces of evidence, make sure they're kept locked in our duty office at the Châtelet. Anything else?'

'Coming out of the Deux Castors last night, I bumped into Monsieur Nicolas, who was watching the house.'

'Monsieur Nicolas? Since when do you call me Monsieur Nicolas?'

'No, not you, of course. You know who I mean, the printer and writer, the one who's always defying the censors.'

'Ah! Restif, Restif de la Bretonne! The vice division have long had their eyes on him. He's a licentious rogue, totally insatiable.'

'You know he can't refuse us anything, and has been a very useful informant at times. We turn a blind eye to a lot of things . . . I asked him what he was doing there, and he seemed embarrassed. He pointed at the shop, laughed and ran off. I didn't have time to chase after him, I had a whole caravan of carriages to see on their way, after all. But I'm convinced there's something going on. I suspect he's having an affair with a woman in the Galaine house.'

'Given the man's reputation, that does indeed seem likely. Pierre, get me his address. Unless I'm mistaken, he lives somewhere not far from Rue de Bievre. We can nab him at home during the day; he only goes out at night. Is that all?'

'Oh, no! I consulted Galaine's notary. He also shut up like a clam. But these pen-pushers always wilt under pressure!'

'Inspector,' said Nicolas in a dignified tone, 'you forget yourself. Don't you know you're talking to a former notary's clerk?'

'Thank God you got out of it! Anyway, the man spoke up in the end. There's no will, but he does have a letter from Claude Galaine saying that his last wishes will be found in the innocent hands – he insisted on that word – of an Indian of the Algonquin tribe who has the responsibility of making them public when the time comes.'

Nicolas rubbed his hands. Much to Bourdeau's surprise, he

took a small folded piece of paper from his pocket and waved it victoriously.

'Here's the will! It was in the egg, and before that round Naganda's neck!'

He did a pirouette, took the inspector by the shoulder and led him downstairs.

X

LIGHT AND TRUTH

And lastly, to make calculations so complete, and studies so general,
that I would be certain I had omitted nothing.

DESCARTES

Balancing on the running board of the cab in Rue Montmartre,
Nicolas explained his battle plan to Bourdeau. First he had to go
to see the Criminal Lieutenant to head off any criticism of such
an unusual investigation. He did not suppose he would be able to
see Monsieur de Sartine, who had spent the night in Versailles and
was only now on his way back. When that was done, he next had
go to the convent of the Conception, where the two French
Guards had witnessed a scene between a girl in yellow satin and a
man who might have been Naganda. With a little luck, he might
be able to find some clue, however small, which would help
advance matters.

In the meantime, Bourdeau would try to find Semacgus.
Curious as he, too, was to know the outcome of the investigation,
he would not have been far away. He would also have to summon
Sanson to the Basse-Geôle for the autopsy on the baby, at which
Semacgus would be welcome as well. As Sanson had an execution
to carry out in Place de Grève that very morning, they would not
be able to start until mid-afternoon. Nicolas would still have to

report to Sartine when he got back from Versailles and, some time before nightfall, he needed to speak to Restif de la Bretonne who, according to the inspector, was living in furnished lodgings in Rue de la Vieille-Boucherie, on the left bank. His one regret was that there was no time in all of this to arrest Major Langlumé of the City Guards.

Nicolas had himself driven to the Grand Châtelet. He was admitted to the office of the Criminal Lieutenant, who was putting on his dress uniform. It was, as it happened, one of this magistrate's duties to attend executions. His mood reflected this prospect, and he received Nicolas with a grim look on his face, which made him rise in the commissioner's estimation: a person who was upset by another man's death could not be wholly bad. He did not seem shocked by Nicolas's explanations. His one comment was that the King's will prevailed over rules and customs which, in any case, everyone interpreted in his own fashion, that the normal order of things had been disrupted and that he was past having anything to say about a procedure so extraordinary that he had never known anything like it in his life.

Gradually becoming heated, he made a few unfriendly comments, but, immediately remembering that he was addressing someone who had the confidence of the King, he cut short his exordium and adopted a softer tone, putting his irritation down to a momentary feeling of exhaustion. Before long, he had given his consent to everything that Nicolas proposed concerning both the case of the Galaine family and that of Major Langlumé – including a hearing in Monsieur de Sartine's courtroom, the date of which had still to be fixed, to which all the members of the Galaine household would be summoned, and in the course of which, he guaranteed, the culprits would be identified and formally charged. Given the particular nature of the investigation and the act of exorcism authorised by His Majesty and by the Archbishop of Paris, the intention was to hold this hearing *in camera*, to avoid any information which might disturb the populace and threaten public order filtering out.

Agreeing to this proposal, Monsieur Testard du Lys recalled with a learned air, as if to justify himself in his own eyes, that at the end of the previous century, a terrible wave of poisonings had shaken the city and the present King's grandfather had created a special court, the *Chambre ardente*, to hear these cases, as well as – and here he lowered his voice – to consider the terrible accusations against the King's mistress, who was suspected of having participated in black masses. Nicolas let him ramble on: in his own opinion, the two situations had nothing in common except the desire to shroud in secrecy certain proceedings that touched on scandalous matters.

By the end, the Criminal Lieutenant had tempered his original attitude to such an extent that he proclaimed himself quite touched by the fact that there existed, among the staff of the Lieutenant General of Police, magistrates who were conscientious enough to come to him for advice. He recommended Nicolas to persevere in his course of action and added that in doing so he would always have his ear and be assured of his benevolence. They parted, well pleased with each other.

As Nicolas was leaving the office, Old Marie came up to him, out of breath, and informed him that Monsieur de Sartine, who had arrived suddenly during the night, wished to see him at once. He ordered the coachman to take him to police headquarters where, as soon as he arrived, a nervous footman told him that his master was in a particularly foul mood. He was reassured to find his chief sitting behind his desk looking through his wigs – always a good sign. This propitiatory exercise often foretold the dominant characteristic of the day. At the moment, he had a grey wig with darker highlights in his hands, and was rolling one of the curls round his fingers. Each time he stretched it, it fell back into shape, like a well-coiled spring.

'Look at this extraordinary model, my dear Nicolas. I got it from Palermo. It was made by an ex-Jesuit expelled from Portugal. It remains to be seen if it lasts the course and retains its quality after constant use and daily brushing.' Sartine put the object down and turned to Nicolas. 'Now then, Commissioner, where have you got to with the archbishop and the grotesque ceremonies you asked permission to organise? It's all dragging on, and His Majesty, whom I've just left . . .'

He sighed as if this observation saddened him, suggesting as it did that the King had been feasting until late into the night.

'Anyway, the King advised me once again to hurry things along. The interests of the State are involved, and we must make sure that the Church doesn't exceed the limits we have set. He also impressed on me how important it is to keep this matter absolutely secret. Let one journalist with a nose for scandal get hold of it, and immediately every clandestine printing works in France, Navarre, and especially London and the Hague,[1] will start putting out lampoons and ballads.'

An idea occurred to Nicolas as his chief spoke: a way to get what he wanted while leaving Monsieur de Sartine with the impression that he had thought of it himself and, even better, that he was imposing it on his narrow-minded subordinates who did not really see the need for it.

'Monsieur, I have the satisfaction of informing you that the exorcism was performed. Successfully, I believe. It led to the discovery of the body of a new-born baby in the cellar of the Galaine house. We have presumed infanticide and I am currently in the final stages of my investigation. I fully hope to finish today and, in your presence and that of the Criminal Lieutenant, to publicly confront the suspects with my conclusions.'

The word 'publicly', so casually tossed off, was like a spark in a powder keg.

'What do you mean, "publicly"? Are you out of your mind, Monsieur? Didn't you hear what I just said? Do I have to dot the i's and cross the t's – to you of all people, with your many years of navigating the choppy waters of crime? Don't you consult the compass or work the tiller any longer in such delicate cases?'

'I understand, Monsieur. You'd prefer a session behind closed doors. Given the number of suspects, I think we'd need your courtroom at the Châtelet. And perhaps it would be advisable not to inform the Criminal Lieutenant . . .'

'He's doing it again! Not inviting Monsieur Testard du Lys would be to violate the rules of a procedure which he himself . . . er . . . he himself . . . authorised us to use with great freedom.'

Suddenly his stern face lit up and he burst out laughing, sending the curls of the grey wig flying.

'By God, you had me worried for a minute! You don't usually talk such nonsense! You're a sly one, but I see we're in agreement. A hearing *in camera* in my courtroom with the Criminal

Lieutenant who will, I hope, spare us lengthy commentaries and be content to watch.'

'It was all in a good cause,' said Nicolas, also laughing.

'Commissioner, I don't hold it against you. The truths we least like hearing are those we most need to hear. To return to the matter in hand, I don't have time to discuss it with you at the moment. You assure me that we will finish tomorrow and that the demon – or whatever took its place – will no longer have a part to play. Let's see what happens in my courtroom, behind closed doors!'

'Monsieur, only the ignorant can be totally assured of anything. But I do hope to be in a position to bring things to a satisfactory conclusion.'

'Well said, Monsieur. And where are you off to now?'

'To a barn, and then to the Basse-Geôle where we will verify if there was indeed an infanticide.'

'Monsieur Sanson will be lending a hand, I assume? He's at an execution right now.'

'We'll fetch him from the foot of the scaffold if need be!'

'Until tomorrow then, at five o'clock in the afternoon. Be on time and take all necessary measures. Then, if everything goes as you hope, the King is expecting a detailed report, from your own mouth. That's something you're good at.'

Monsieur de Sartine's good humour was very obvious now. Nicolas assumed that the previous night's supper with the King had a lot to do with it. Turning away from him, the Lieutenant General hastened to open an oblong box and carefully took out an object wrapped in silk paper. It was a head of lilac-coloured velvet on which sat a magnificent tawny wig. Carried away with enthusiasm, he showed the wig to Nicolas.

'Splendid, isn't it? It's a speciality wig by Friedrich Strubb, a master from Heidelberg. So brilliant! So light! So sensual! Good hunting, Nicolas.'

The commissioner withdrew, pleased to have obtained everything he wanted. He left police headquarters whistling a melody from an opera by old Rameau and set off on foot, with his carriage following behind. It looked like it would be a beautiful day, and this well-to-do district of Paris, with its abundant greenery, exuded an air of youth and light-heartedness, enhanced by the colours of the flower girls. The scent of the flowers struggled with the ever-present odours of the city. In the distance, the morning sounds of the more animated districts could be heard. It was too early to go to the Basse-Geôle. The most sensible thing to do would be to take a short cut to the Rue Royale area, where the vast quadrilateral convent of the Conception was situated. He idled a while longer amid the new mansions, then got back in his carriage.

The high perimeter wall of the convent came into view. Nicolas drove all the way round it, looking at the old houses built into the wall at the ends of little dead-end streets. At last, at the end of a narrow dirt track lined with flowering lilacs, he saw a half-collapsed old barn, leaning up against an even more ancient building. A wooden fence led to a vegetable garden, bordered by a clump of trees. This rural spot, miraculously preserved in the heart of the city, was filled with birdsong. The wooden barn door creaked open. Inside, there were gardening tools, an old cart and the remains of a pile of hay from the previous season. The noonday heat and the silence of the place evoked no images of blood and death. Nicolas sat down on a block of wood, picked up a twig, and began drawing geometric shapes on the ground. He let his mind wander. Suddenly, the end of the twig snagged something on the hay-strewn ground. It was a stained piece of cloth. He carefully picked it up and looked at it. It seemed to be a fine percale handkerchief. Nicolas shook it to get the earth and vegetable matter off. Beneath his fingers, he could feel something finely embroidered into the material. It was two intertwined initials: a C and a G. Could the handkerchief have belonged to the Galaine family? Several of its members had the same initials: Claude, who had died in New France (in which case the handkerchief might have belonged to Élodie, his daughter), Charles Galaine the furrier, and the victim's two aunts, Camille and Charlotte . . .

Finding this clue where vague but credible testimony had placed an incident involving an angry Élodie being dragged inside by a person who might have been Naganda had to be significant. Nicolas carefully put it in his pocket, and then got down on his knees and went over the ground with a fine-tooth comb. Although he examined every inch of the barn, he found nothing else. He looked at his watch. It was high time he got back to the Châtelet for the autopsy on the baby, which he hoped would tell him a lot. He found his coachman fast asleep in the hot June sun. The horse had moved away from the path towards the ditch, taking the carriage with him, and was now decapitating a bank of budding dandelions with relish.

At the Basse-Geôle, Nicolas found Bourdeau and Semacgus conversing in low voices. He was not at all surprised to hear them discussing a nice little wine from the slopes of Suresnes, a speciality of an open-air tavern near the Vaugirard tollgate. On the autopsy table, the meagre remains found in the cellar in Rue Saint-Honoré lay beneath a small piece of cloth. Bourdeau announced that Sanson would not be much longer: informed that they required his services, he had promised to cut short – the phrase made Semacgus laugh – the formalities that always followed an execution, and to join them without delay.

No sooner had the inspector finished speaking than Sanson appeared. Nicolas had the impression, or the illusion, that he had become a different man. Was he still under the influence of what he had recently found out about his friend? Perhaps it had something to do with the fact that he was dressed in the traditional costume of his profession – the red jacket embroidered with a black ladder and gallows, the blue breeches, the crimson bicorn – and carried a sword at his side. His face, pale at the best of times, seemed ashen and cold, an impression reinforced by his eyes, which stared unseeing into space. Becoming aware of their presence, he shook himself, as if emerging from a nightmare, and greeted them all in his usual ceremonious tone.

Nicolas, as usual, held out his hand as usual, but was brought up short by Sanson's gaze, at once imperious and pitiful, in which he read a kind of supplication. The three of them watched with a pang in their hearts as Sanson washed his hands at length at a brass fountain. Serene again, he turned to them with a weak smile.

'Forgive my reserve, it's been an unusual day . . .'

'Which makes us all the more grateful,' Nicolas said, 'that you have agreed to devote your talents to this task.'

Sanson waved his hand as if swatting a troublesome fly. Nicolas immediately regretted using the word he had.

'My talents! If God had only granted me the possibility to devote myself entirely to my talents . . . But let's get down to this case of yours.'

'A new-born child, or a still-born foetus, found in a cellar, wrapped in cloth and buried. Probably several days ago, let's say between four and eight.'

'I see. The object of this autopsy is, I assume, to determine if there was infanticide.'

'That is indeed our purpose, yes.'

'The first thing we have to do,' said Sanson, 'is to ascertain whether the foetus was alive after delivery. I don't think I need to impress upon you the importance of this question.'

'Of course not, my dear colleague,' Semacgus cut in. 'How, after all, could we suspect that a crime has been committed after birth if it is proved that the child never lived? In such a case, breathing and living are one and the same thing. We therefore have to establish whether or not the foetus ever drew breath.'

'Otherwise,' said Bourdeau, in a sententious tone, 'there's always the possibility that an abortion was carried out just before term.'

'Gentlemen,' resumed Sanson in his gentle voice, 'the solution to these two pertinent questions rests entirely on an examination of the thorax and the lungs and, if need be, the heart, the arteries and veins, as well as the condition of the umbilical cord and the diaphragm.'

'Gentlemen, gentlemen,' cried Nicolas, 'your words are wise, but your knowledge is greater than mine! Please keep things simple, I beg you, so that I can follow you.'

'You see, Nicolas,' said Semacgus, 'the lungs increase in

volume as they breath. They change position and colour and push up the diaphragm. Their weight increases with the blood that goes through them, but their specific weight decreases when they are dilated by air. I'll skip over the details and the advanced aspects of the phenomenon. Let's proceed. As my instrument case is at Vaugirard, the Châtelet surgeon has lent me his – the mere mention of Commissioner Le Floch having worked wonders!'

He pointed to a leather case, which, when opened, glittered in the torchlight. From a black bag, he took a measuring glass. Then he took off his coat, while Sanson removed his bicorn and his ceremonial jacket and Bourdeau lit his pipe. Almost instinctively, Nicolas took a small tobacco pouch from his pocket and watched with horror as the autopsy got under way. An observer could not have failed to see how strongly affected he was by what was happening. These two men, whom he knew all too well, with their qualities, their failings, even their vices, were bustling about in the middle of this squalid cavern, bent over a poor rotting thing, muttering incomprehensible words. He closed his eyes as the tiny organs were extracted, weighed, dissected and examined. At last, after what seemed like an interminable time, the baby's lungs were placed inside the measuring glass, which was now filled with water. The two men washed their hands, exchanged a few more remarks in low voices, and turned to the commissioner.

'So, gentlemen,' said Nicolas, 'what do you conclude, if there is indeed a conclusion to be drawn from this examination?'

'The foetus breathed,' Semacgus replied. 'We can be sure of that.'

269

'And we can rule out the possibility that it was still-born,' said Sanson.

'The lungs overall are light red in colour, but weigh less than water.'

'I understand what you're saying. But if everything points to the fact that the foetus was alive after its mother gave birth, can you determine if the death was natural, or if it can be ascribed to an act of violence and, if so, what kind of act?'

After a long silence, Sanson folded his hands. 'We've ruled out malformation, which is a common cause of death. The child was normal, and even well formed. We don't know if the labour was easy or difficult, but there are no signs of imperfection on the body. Nor can we assume asphyxia.'

'What can we assume, then?'

'An umbilical haemorrhage. That happens when the cord is not tied immediately. In law, that constitutes infanticide. We think the murderer tied the cord only after letting the blood flow back, to allay suspicion. That would explain why you didn't find any bloodstained cloths or any traces of blood in the earth where you found the corpse.'

'That's horrible,' said Nicolas.

Semacgus nodded. 'Yes, it is. But, to a deranged mind, there's nothing guilty about draining a baby of its blood. The criminal feels that he is letting nature take its course rather than performing a terrible act. For our part, we do indeed consider that infanticide was committed on a baby that had breathed.'

'Gentlemen, I thank you once again. Before we part, one last service. Bourdeau, did you bring the apothecary's bottle that was found at the clothes dealer's?'

The inspector rummaged in his coat pocket and took out the bottle.

'Would it be possible,' asked Nicolas, 'to tell me what it might have contained?'

Semacgus took the bottle, removed the glass stopper and lifted it to his nostrils. He wrinkled his large nose as he breathed in, then handed the bottle to Sanson, who did the same.

'It's obvious,' murmured the hangman.

'There are still some tiny crystals. With a little water, perhaps . . .'

Semacgus walked to the fountain and held his finger under the water. Then he let a few drops of it trickle down the inside of the bottle, which he shook and closed again. He asked Bourdeau to light his pipe. When the tobacco glowed red, he placed the bottom of the bottle over it for a few moments.

'That will help us to extract it.'

He reopened the bottle, breathed in the contents and passed it to Sanson, who nodded.

'Laudanum.'

'The sap of the white poppy, a narcotic and a soporific,' Semacgus explained.

'Is it dangerous?' asked Nicolas.

'It can be. It causes deep sleep, varying in length depending on the quantity absorbed. An excessive amount can be fatal. Repeated misuse can induce a mindless state.'

Semacgus looked at Sanson, who nodded.

'Obviously,' Semacgus continued, 'everything depends on the age and state of health of the person who uses it.'

'You've been very clear, my friends. Your conclusions and

explanations have been most enlightening. I'm going to have to leave you now; my continuing investigation calls me elsewhere. Bourdeau, tomorrow at five o'clock in the afternoon, a hearing will be held *in camera* in Monsieur de Sartine's courtroom in the presence of the Criminal Lieutenant. I want you to make sure Naganda and Miette are there. It would be good if Marie Chaffoureau, the cook, could also attend.'

'Nicolas,' said Semacgus, 'what would you say to a meal at one of those cheap eating houses Bourdeau is so fond of?'

'Cheap perhaps,' replied Bourdeau, offended, 'but the food is good. As you yourself should know from experience, Doctor.'

'Of course. Don't take my words in the wrong way. I am grateful to you, and so is my stomach. Well, Nicolas?'

'A nice thought, Semacgus, but time is short. There's someone I have to track down before it gets dark. If I leave it any later, it'll be the devil's own job to find him before dawn.'

Nicolas held out his hand to Sanson, who this time shook it without hesitation. In the doorway, he turned and reminded Semacgus and Bourdeau that he was counting on them to be present at the hearing the following day. It was only with difficulty that he found his coachman, who had gone to have something to eat and then, exhausted, had fallen asleep with his face in his plate. An errand boy was sent to fetch him, and took advantage of the opportunity to scold him, to which the coachman responded by threatening him with the lash as punishment for his insolence. Nicolas's composed presence restored calm. The carriage set off for Rue Saint-Honoré.

Nicolas needed to check something with the Galaines' cook. He was not especially surprised that infanticide had been confirmed. As for the bottle, which he could feel in his pocket, the fact that it had been taken away and left with the clothes dealer was obviously significant. It was as plain as the nose on his face that there was a connection between the contents of the bottle and the strange state of which Naganda had complained. On the other hand, what credence could be given to a witness who it was now clear had been lying, concealing facts and misrepresenting his own actions, without giving a detailed account of his whereabouts on the night of the murder? The Deux Castors soon came within sight. The cook opened the door to him and, doubtless deprived of anyone to talk to since dawn, was soon chatting away freely.

It was not easy, she explained, to look after a little girl who was so advanced for her age, who did not answer the questions you asked her, but fired off others of her own that were a lot more annoying. She reminded the cook of her aunts at that age. Of course, Camille and Charlotte were not as clever and one of them had taken years to learn how to tie a knot, in fact she still couldn't do it except by tying it upside down. Nicolas let her talk, without showing the slightest sign of impatience. He only interrupted her when she mentioned that, early in the morning, when the child was finding it impossible to sleep after that dreadful night, the thought of which still terrified her, she'd had to serve her a little sugared milk with a good spoonful of orange-blossom water. It was the perfect remedy for calming you down and putting you to sleep, a remedy used by her aunts, who got their supplies from a neighbourhood apothecary. He asked to see the bottle. It was in every way identical to the one found at the second-hand clothes dealer's. As it did not have a label, though, there was nothing to

273

indicate that it had not been bought from another source. He asked which of the two sisters in particular used this medication. Marie Chaffoureau assured him it was Camille, the younger. He recorded this fact in his little notebook, having observed that such apparently insignificant details were easily forgotten. Nicolas thanked the cook and asked her to be present at the Grand Châtelet the following day. This seemed to upset her. She was worried about leaving Geneviève alone in the house. It wasn't really a problem, he said – in fact, all things considered, it might be useful for the child to be there, too. He promised to send a carriage, and once again thanked the cook for the omelette the previous Saturday.

Thanks to the directions he had been given, he had no difficulty in finding the apothecary's shop patronised by the Galaine family. It was only a short distance away, at the corner of Rue de la Sourdière and Rue Saint-Honoré. When he opened the door, a distant bell rang. The shop seemed huge. In the middle stood a monumental counter of carved wood. Shelves covered the walls all the way up to the ceiling, supporting rows of containers, in particular a number of richly decorated porcelain vases bearing inscriptions in Latin. There were other vases in ivory, marble, jasper, alabaster and coloured glass. After some minutes, a short man in his fifties appeared, dressed in black silk serge and wearing a powdered grey wig. Beneath thick eyebrows dyed black, his little blue eyes stared at Nicolas without expression.

'What can I do for you, Monsieur? I'm sorry I kept you waiting, I was supervising an assistant who was gilding the pills.[2] It's a delicate operation that demands all my attention.'

274

'That's quite all right. Nicolas Le Floch, police commissioner at the Châtelet. I wonder if you'd be so kind as to provide me with some information that could be useful in an investigation I am conducting.'

The man's eyes lit up. 'Clerambourg, master apothecary, at your service. I did hear of some problems in the house of one of my neighbours, a master furrier named . . .' His tone suggested that this was an observation he would rather not have had to make. 'But you're not in your robes?'

'Oh, no, you're not a suspect. We're just having a friendly conversation. There's something I'd like to check.'

'And what is that, Monsieur?'

Nicolas took the bottle from his pocket and handed it to the apothecary, who held it between two fingers, as if it were a poisonous animal. 'Well, Commissioner?'

'Well, does this bottle come from your shop?'

'I assume someone has told you it does.'

Nicolas made no reply to this.

The apothecary turned the bottle over. 'I think it is one of ours.'

'Could you be more precise?'

'Of course. It's one of a series of bottles that are specially blown for me. They have a little bulge in the glass. They're unmistakable; you won't find them among any of my competitors.'

'And what's the point of this little bulge?'

'That's the thing, Commissioner . . . I use this kind of bottle for delicate products which can be dangerous when used internally.'

'But aren't such products only used after a detailed

consultation between the doctor and the apothecary, resulting in a prescription, after which the medicine is made up and delivered to the patient by one of your assistants?'

'That is the way it's usually done, yes. However, the patients often demand these dangerous products themselves . . . and business is business. And, what's more, we're not the only ones to supply them. The grocers' – his tone had become sharp and acrimonious – 'also claim the right to deal in our preparations. They sell products that are just as dangerous, even deadly. We've been pursuing them through the royal courts for years.'

Nicolas interrupted him. 'I understand. As for this bottle, what did it contain and who bought it from you, if your memory can stretch that far?'

'The last purchase made by the Galaine family – I assume that's who we're talking about – was a product which is of no particular danger when used sensibly and in moderation.'

'What substance was it?'

The apothecary hesitated for a moment. 'A new substance called laudanum, extracted from the sap of the white poppy. It soothes pain and calms the patient.'

'Can it send him into a deep, prolonged sleep?'

'Of course, if the prescribed dose is exceeded.'

'To get back to my original question, who bought it from you?'

From under the counter, the apothecary produced a large register bound in calfskin, which he looked through, wetting his finger every time he turned a page.

'Ah, here we are! Twenty-seven May this year. When it comes to these delicate products, we write everything down. Twenty-seven May, Monsieur Jean Galaine, one bottle of laudanum. I remember it well. The young man told me he needed it for a toothache. They're neighbours, and Charles Galaine is an honourable tradesman, highly regarded in the little world of the trade guilds, although there have been rumours about his financial difficulties, which I'm sure are only temporary. I hope that answers your questions, Commissioner. No one more is concerned than I about the maintenance of order in our city.'

'I'm most grateful. You've been a great help.'

As his carriage drove along the *quais* towards Pont Neuf, Nicolas thought about this new element that clearly pointed to one of the suspects. So it was Jean Galaine, whose attitude had been evasive from the start, whose relationship with his cousin was still shrouded in mystery and who hadn't been able to account for his whereabouts on the night of the murder, who had bought the product intended to drug Naganda. It suddenly occurred to him that perhaps all these Galaines were in cahoots, that perhaps they had committed the crime together and woven a tissue of untruths and false leads to conceal their guilt. What could Restif de la Bretonne possibly tell him? He was convinced that the man's presence outside the Deux Castors was not merely fortuitous.

When they reached Place du Pont Saint-Michel, Nicolas ordered the coachman to turn left into Rue de la Huchette. He remembered Semacgus's suggestion and suddenly felt hungry – a hunger that was all the stronger for being held back until now. As a great connoisseur of the capital, Nicolas was not unaware that, at any hour of the day or night, cooked food could be bought in this street. Roasting spits turned constantly, like the damned stoking the fires of hell, and smoke only stopped rising from the chimneys during Lent. Monsieur de Sartine, concerned as ever about risk and the ways to minimise it, often prophesied that, if a fire broke out in this narrow street, which was made all the more dangerous by its old wooden houses, it would be impossible to extinguish. The members of the last diplomatic mission from the Ottoman Empire had been delighted with this street because of the wonderful smells that pervaded it.

Nicolas ordered the coachman to stop, lowered the window, called to a young kitchen boy who was admiring his horses and ordered half a chicken, which was immediately brought to him on an oil-paper with a little coarse salt and a new onion. He devoured it with enormous pleasure and, remembering his chief's tastes, ascertained that the wings of the chicken, perfectly roasted, were indeed a dish fit for a king. He next stopped at a fountain on the corner of Rue du Petit-Pont to quench his thirst and wipe the grease from his mouth.

Rue de la Vieille-Boucherie, however, was impossible to find in this maze of alleys, colleges and impasses. Nicolas abandoned his carriage and continued his search on foot. He lost his way, was sent off on wild goose chases and was eventually directed to a shabby-looking house where a slovenly woman told him that the good-for-nothing he sought was now living in Collège de Presles, a few streets away in the Écoles district. At last he came to an almost ruined building. In its courtyard, he approached an old man who was picking up litter with a spike and asked him which floor 'Monsieur Nicolas' lived on. The man held up all five fingers of his left hand. Climbing the rickety, rubbish-strewn stairs left the commissioner breathless. Through an open door, he saw a room furnished only with a trestle bed, a table and a straw-bottomed chair. A young girl in a *chenille*, not much more than a child, was washing her legs in a chipped washbowl. She threw him a mischievous, questioning look.

'Are you looking for Papa Nicolas?'

'Yes, I am, Mademoiselle. Are you his daughter?'

She burst out laughing. 'Yes and no, and many other things besides.'

This, he thought, tallied with certain malevolent rumours that had reached the ears of the police, especially the inspector from the morals division.

'You won't find him here; he's already gone.'

'Where could I find him, then? Would you be so kind as to tell me?'

'Why not, as you're asking so nicely? He's been invited by Mademoiselle Guimard, who's giving a big party tonight at Chaussée d'Antin. But he won't be there before ten – he had a lot of things to do in town first.'

'Would I be taking advantage of your kindness if I asked you whether or not he's planning to come back tonight?'

'Go ahead, take advantage, I'm used to it . . . No, I don't think so . . . In fact, I'm sure he won't.' She laughed mischievously. 'He's bound to find another dainty little pair of feet . . .'

'Would you mind explaining that?' said Nicolas.

'You know what I mean. He never gets home before dawn. We could wait for him together . . .'

It was said casually, with a wink and an engaging sway of the hips.

'Alas, my business is much too urgent,' said Nicolas, 'but I'm grateful for the offer.'

She gave a little curtsey, like an actress acknowledging applause at the end of a play, and without a word went back to her washing.

Nicolas retraced his steps through the warren of alleys until he found his carriage. Half past four had just sounded, and trying to find Restif now was to attempt the impossible. But if he had announced that he was going to see Mademoiselle Guimard, the most famous dancer at the Opéra, Nicolas was convinced that he would indeed respond to an invitation from such a goddess, who was always surrounded by a court of admirers. He recalled the lady's file, which he had consulted quite recently, out of simple curiosity, after learning from a report that his friend La Borde was protecting her – not surprisingly, as the First Groom of the King's Bedchamber had long had a taste for pretty young dancers. Marie-Madeleine Guimard had begun as a member of the *corps de ballet* and for the past ten years or so had been one of the leading attractions of the Opéra. A number of powerful men, such as the Bishop of Orleans and the Maréchal de Soubise, had ruined themselves over her. It was said that she had commissioned the architect Ledoux to draw up plans for a house and a private theatre on a long, narrow site looking out on Chaussée d'Antin, where there was to be a frieze depicting the coronation of Terpsichore, the muse of the dance, riding in a procession on a chariot pulled by cupids, bacchantes, graces and fauns. As permission had not so far been granted and construction was yet to begin, Nicolas assumed that Mademoiselle Guimard was giving a reception on the site she had chosen for her mansion.

After much thought, he decided to go back to Rue Montmartre and change before going on to Chaussée d'Antin, where the likely presence of Monsieur de La Borde would gain him admission. For a moment, he was tempted to use this time to arrest Major Langlumé, but there was no reason to suppose that he would find him at home and he suspected himself of merely wanting to satisfy a personal grudge.

In Rue Montmartre, he was told that a weary Monsieur de Noblecourt had agreed to respond to the combined entreaties of Marion and Catherine and drink a good purgative herb tea to counter the consequences of the extreme diet authorised by a doctor whom the two women could not condemn strongly enough. They were taking advantage of this lull to make cherry jam, and the sour smell of it wafted through the house. Nicolas, remembering how, as a child, he had loved cleaning out the preserving pans, regretted that he no longer had the time. He told them that he was going to have a thorough wash, naked, at the large fountain in the courtyard. They protested: not only would he be offending against modesty with such an insane practice, but he would catch *malmort*.[2] Only Poitevin, who was usually silent, spoke up in his defence, observing that what was good for horses could not be bad for human beings. They laughed a lot at this sally, and Nicolas left the kitchen, chased out by the two half-delighted, half-furious women.

After washing, he went back upstairs to dress, and stopped for a moment to look at himself in the mirror. His body had broadened out since his youth, and his face had grown harder without becoming fleshy. The scars he had had since his adolescence, as well as other more recent ones, emphasised the seriousness of an affable countenance on which lines were beginning to form. Reaching thirty had not modified his youthful appearance: he looked like a man who had barely been touched by the trials he had been through, which made his one white hair seem quite incongruous. He selected a plum-coloured satin coat and a cravat of Bruges lace, letting it flow through his hands and appreciating its lightness. He tied his hair with a ribbon that matched the colour of his coat and adorned his shoes with shiny silver buckles. After all, he had not been invited, and there was no point appearing in a costume that would not argue in his favour. The presence of La Borde justified the extra care he was taking: he did not want to shame a friend who was the arbiter of elegance in Paris and Versailles.

At ten o'clock, Nicolas went to find his coachman, who had taken a rest and changed horses. Chaussée d'Antin was not far from the Comédie-Italienne, where a case had taken him a few years earlier. The area towards Les Porcherons, to the south of the Butte Montmartre, was still rural, and Chaussée d'Antin had just started to expand as a result of the sale of property belonging to various religious orders. For the moment, it was still nothing but a vast space filled with gardens and marshes, with a few scattered houses. But it was beginning to attract the wealthy, who saw it as a place to build sumptuous mansions.

They rode around for quite a long time before seeing a multitude of carriages, and footmen carrying torches. Parallel to the road, in the middle of an orchard, a long wooden building with *trompe l'oeil* decorations had been erected. Beneath the antique-style archway, black men in ribbons lit the way for guests. A silent crowd, held at a distance by the valets, gaped in awe at this display of riches. Nicolas got out of his carriage and approached. A major-domo was collecting the invitations, which were tied with bronze-coloured ribbons. He looked Nicolas up and down. The commissioner, preferring not to rely on his rank, asked him if Monsieur de La Borde was present. This request, reinforced by the elegance of his costume, seemed to do the trick, and he was admitted. The pavilion comprised several large rooms, richly furnished and bedecked with flowers. They were arranged in two semi-circles, leading to a vast reception room that looked out on the garden, the doors to which were open thanks to the clement weather on this June night. Buffet tables offered a sumptuous spread of dishes and pyramids of fruit. An army of valets was opening bottles of champagne and Romanée wine, and holding out flutes and glasses to the guests pressing around them. Walking through this noisy, laughing crowd, Nicolas finally spotted a group forming a deferential circle around a deity in a diaphanous silk gown studded with gold. He recognised Mademoiselle Guimard. In the front row of her courtiers was Monsieur de La Borde, playing the host. As soon as he saw Nicolas, he let out a cry of joy.

'Dear Nicolas, I must be dreaming! Madeleine didn't tell me you were coming! What a pleasant surprise!'

'Alas, my dear fellow, I haven't been invited, and I was only admitted because I was well dressed and mentioned your name. I'm looking for someone I need to question. A strange man, a writer, a printer, an unrepentant skirt-chaser and many other things besides.'

'I know him well! You're talking about Restif. He's been invited this evening to add spice to the party, being such a great talker, indeed much more interesting in his conversation than in his appearance.'

The hostess approached, giving a half-amused, half-serious pout. 'Darling, you're neglecting me.' She greeted Nicolas. 'Good evening, Monsieur. Is it thanks to you that I've been abandoned?'

'Beloved, let me introduce Monsieur de Sartine's right-hand man, Nicolas Le Floch. The King is mad about him.'

'But of course! I know Monsieur by reputation. The Maréchal de Soubise . . .'

La Borde made a face.

'. . . who knew his father, the Marquis de Ranreuil, used to speak very highly of him. It's said he performed some signal services for the late Madame de Pompadour.'

Nicolas bowed. 'Madame, you are too indulgent . . .'

'I invited him,' said La Borde. 'He's not a man to be neglected.'

'In that case, I wish I'd invited him myself! You are most welcome, Monsieur.'

'Thank you, Mademoiselle. May I be so bold as to confess that I have long been an admirer of yours? Your charm both onstage and off and the perfect taste of your performances are inimitable.'

She smiled and held out both her hands, which he kissed. Monsieur de La Borde thanked him with a look, asked to be excused and followed her out.

Time passed quickly as Nicolas circulated among the groups, catching snatches of conversation and spotting a number of illustrious guests. A young girl took hold of his arm. She was a younger friend of Mademoiselle Guimard, and admitted quite openly that she was looking for a protector, rich of course, but also young and good-looking. He was forced to disappoint her. He stayed as close as he could to the room nearest the entrance. At about half past eleven, he saw a curious character answering to the description he had been given of 'Monsieur Nicolas' come in. He was slightly hunchbacked, and moved in such an awkward, tightly wound way as to appear like a savage. Neither fat nor thin, he had lively eyes beneath unattractively thick eyebrows, a long face, a slightly hooked nose, a ruby-red mouth and a bushy grey beard, all of which made for a very disparate overall impression. As for his attire, it was neither clean nor dirty, and between grey and black in colour. What he looked like, it struck Nicolas, was the foreman of a workshop in Faubourg Saint-Antoine. He went up to him, and the man drew back in alarm.

'Please, Monsieur, no scandal,' he said. 'I'll pay; I'm sure we can come to some arrangement.'

'This isn't about that. Are you Monsieur Nicolas Restif de La Bretonne? I'm a police commissioner at the Châtelet, and I need to ask you some questions.'

Restif sighed. The reference to Nicolas's position seemed to have reassured him. He drew Nicolas towards two gilded *bergères* in grey damask.

'You know perfectly well I can never refuse the police.'

'Yes, we do know that. That's why we expect a lot from you. Inspector Bourdeau caught sight of you outside a furrier's shop in Rue Saint-Honoré this morning. You left quite abruptly. We're curious to know why.'

'May I be completely open with you?'

'I ask for nothing less.'

'Very well. I'm extremely fond of women, as you know.' He

seemed lost in thought, as if talking to himself. 'What is more charming than a woman's little foot in its slipper? Yes, in its slipper. She had such pretty feet and was so yielding. I wanted to see her again – that's why I was waiting outside her house. There you are, Monsieur. That's all it was.'

'I see. But who are you talking about?'

'Why, the shopkeeper's wife, of course, Madame Galaine. She tried to conceal her name, but I followed her and found it out. When we met again, I told her I knew who she was.'

'So you admit you had an affair with this woman?'

'Of course. I not only had an affair with her, I'm still having it! In fact, I'm having her in every sense of the word. At least for the past few months, since I recovered from a sickness that took me away from the scene of my pleasures for a while. And I'm not the only one, either. She has many patrons.'

'What do you mean by that, Monsieur? That you paid for Madame Galaine's . . . services?'

'Commissioner, I don't think I have to teach you about life.'

'Would you say that she . . . sacrificed herself to you because she enjoyed it, or for money?'

'Why, for money, of course! Or rather, as she confessed to me one day in floods of tears, because of her wish to amass as much money as possible for her little daughter, since her husband is heading for certain ruin. I'm not demanding, and she overlooks my funny little ways. She has other customers, though, which means she's been gradually feathering her nest. What an angel! What devotion!'

Nicolas had certainly not been expecting this. 'I have one important question,' he resumed, after a silence. 'On the evening of the disaster in Place Louis XV, where were you?'

'With her, in my garret in Collège de Presles. We ate first in a restaurant, then went back to my place. Afterwards . . . she fell asleep. When she left me it was very late, or rather, it was very early the next morning.'

'From what time to what time?'

'Between half past six and three o'clock in the morning.'

'One last question, Monsieur. You don't seem to be rolling in money. How have you been able to help this woman?'

'That's precisely why I'm so poor, Monsieur! I only spend money on my pleasures.'

They were interrupted by cries and cheers, and were swept up in a movement of the crowd that carried them into the reception room. There, Monsieur de La Borde was standing on a table in his shirtsleeves, with a glass in his hand, and reading aloud a poem of his own composition in honour of Mademoiselle Guimard:

> *As Aesop rightly said,*
> *A bow we stretch too tight*
> *Will doubtless always break.*
> *If we put ours to bed,*
> *And let it rest one night,*
> *We do it for your sake.*
> *For, ladies, it is said,*
> *And surely this is right,*
> *This rest we all must take.*
> *To rest our bow a while*
> *Will give it added might*
> *To go that extra mile.*

The poem was greeted with thunderous applause, and the party became even livelier, taking here and there a distinctly indecent turn.

'You see, Commissioner?' said Restif, pointing to the assembled throng. 'You see what makes the world go round? May I join that beauty over there?'

'You are free, Monsieur. Go and enjoy yourself.'

Nicolas fled, having no desire to see or hear more. He found himself back out in the street, where onlookers still stood gazing in awe at the festivities. He felt tired, and this tiredness coloured his thoughts. There was good reason, it seemed to him, for the present time to be condemned. It was a time in which there was no interest that was not despised, no honour that was not trampled, no dignity that was not sacrificed, no duty that was not tarnished for the sake of passion. The headlong rush to pleasure brought dishonour to even the best of men. And it was those above who set the example. But who was he to judge others, when his own destiny had led him into the arms of a courtesan who was now on her way to becoming a madam, the glorious successor to La Paulet? Yes, who did he think he was, and what gave him the right to throw stones at other human beings for their erring ways?

XI

THE HEARING

It is only in the person of His Majesty that the plenitude of Justice resides, and only thanks to him that the magistrates hold their position and the power to give Justice to his subjects.

MAUPEOU

Wednesday 6 June 1770

Nicolas rose early. He wanted to be alone for a while to write a short explanatory memorandum. He would make two copies and send one to the Lieutenant General of Police, the other to the Criminal Lieutenant. He spent most of the morning in Monsieur de Noblecourt's library, and at about eleven, when the task was completed, he decided to get some fresh air in order to reflect on that evening's decisive hearing. Walking always set his mind racing intensely in a way that was at once passionate and unconscious, the results of which were not to be used immediately, but deliberately stored, ready to be brought out at the least command, like reserves of ammunition held ready in case of emergency. He set off at a brisk stride towards the Tuileries, giving free rein to his imagination, helped in this by the spectacle of the streets.

The gardens were very pleasant on this beautiful June day. The great avenue was lined with two rows of young women in light dresses, while here and there children chased one another.

For some time now, the officers of the vice division had been observing the prostitutes who occupied strategic positions on their hired chairs. From there, they would solicit passers-by with glances that made even the boldest lower their eyes, let alone the straight-laced. They would wait all morning for someone to offer to buy them a meal, and they rarely failed. The district commissioner had opened his heart about it to Nicolas, although he had to admit that the Tuileries were an enclave outside his jurisdiction, since responsibility for the royal gardens lay with the Hôtel de Ville. But the agents of this institution were infinitely less strict than the police. It was in fact rumoured that they were easily corrupted, and were perfectly happy to levy a tribute in the form of free pleasures in return for agreeing to turn a blind eye to the evil trade of the maidservants of Venus.

These reflections reminded him of his conversation with Restif de La Bretonne, and his surprising confession. So even Madame Galaine had taken up that profession! The respectable wife of a master furrier had seen it as the only way to ensure her child's future after the imminent ruin of her household. Nicolas found it hard to believe, although his informant, who had such close ties to the police, had proved, thanks to his own habits and vices, an absolutely reliable witness. Nicolas suspected that he had been misled by his own innate naivety: he was still a little bit of an innocent in some matters, even though his innocence had been battered repeatedly over the years by contact with real life. The fact was that Madame Galaine, who was still young, might have given pleasure to a whole host of respectable bourgeois repelled by the vulgarity of her fellow practitioners. She could well have built up a regular clientele in this way and, week after week, happily accumulated her nest egg. The Galaines' marriage had clearly disintegrated. The husband paid hardly any attention to his wife's frequent absences. Excursions to the theatre or the Opéra, the expense of which did not worry him because he was not asked to contribute, were a good pretext for his wife's nocturnal absences. As for Dorsacq, the shop assistant, whose part in all this still had to be clarified, at best he played the thankless role of an escort, at worst that of a pimp, soliciting for the woman in return for financial rewards and perhaps a few little favours. The outcome of this surprising piece of information was that Madame Galaine, as one of the suspects, now had an alibi – not that this necessarily meant that she was entirely innocent of the crimes committed in Rue Saint-Honoré. Sometimes, being an accomplice was worse than being a perpetrator.

Nicolas's thoughts continued to wander, drawn to the little white clouds that sped towards the boulevards above Place Louis XV, where the vestiges of the fire had almost disappeared. A thinner cloud than the others reminded him of the attack on Naganda. He saw again the weapon being carefully withdrawn by Semacgus from the Indian's back. It was a kitchen knife with a wooden handle and one rivet – the kind that were sold in their hundreds in the area around the central market. He regretted now that, in the chaos of that mad night, he had not investigated further an act which, although it had not cost Naganda his life, nevertheless constituted a crime, one of a succession of criminal acts committed in the Galaine household since the disappearance of Élodie.

Thinking about it, Nicolas came to the conclusion, which

would still have to be confirmed, that the attempted murder must have coincided with the abrupt end of the drumming that accompanied the Micmac's curious rituals. But he was unable to determine where everybody had been at that moment. After the first exorcism on the ground floor, Père Raccard had advised everyone to go back to their rooms. This meant that, once more, all the members of the Galaine family came under suspicion: while he himself, Semacgus and the exorcist were with the possessed girl, any one of them could have stabbed Naganda. Since the weapon must have come from the kitchen, he would have to question Marie Chaffoureau about that.

He was anxious about the hearing at the Grand Châtelet. It was not enough to summon the suspects: he also had to think about how best to present the evidence. That would require a certain amount of organisation, and he would need to enlist the help of Old Marie, the usher, and Bourdeau. Nicolas ran through the exhibits that needed to be included in this judicial high mass, and displayed in such a way as to have the maximum effect on those present. First of all, Élodie Galaine's effects: her yellow satin dress with the floating back, her straw-coloured bodice, her two petticoats, her stockings of grey yarn, as well as the black pearl found in her hand and the pieces of hay. Then the two sets of clothes Naganda wore when he went out, the apothecary's bottle, the strips of material found under the bed in the Galaine sisters' room, the handkerchief with the initials CG found in the barn of the Daughters of the Conception, Claude Galaine's letter to his brother, the will, the rethreaded necklace of black pearls and finally the kitchen knife used to wound Naganda. One or two dressmaker's dummies, he thought, would add a nice touch: dress them in the clothes of Élodie and Naganda, and even the strongest characters might be thrown.

For the first time since the exorcism, he remembered the extraordinary phenomena he had witnessed. He had been trying to repress them, to act as if they did not belong to the real world. Part of him had rejected them for fear that the mere thought of them would reawaken his terror. What guarantee was there that Miette would not revert to that same state? What was the nature of the force or influence he had confronted? What he had felt in his room in Rue Saint-Honoré seemed to be a kind of sign, an encouragement to pursue his investigation, whereas the manifestations connected with Miette's possession had simply revealed the presence of evil, and did not contribute in any way towards a resolution of the mystery. The proof of this was that, once the exorcism was over, it was a calmer, liberated Miette, although a somnambulistic one – a strange state, certainly, but not unnatural – who had led them to the cellar and the place where the murdered baby had been hidden.

Gradually, the June sun penetrated Nicolas's body. He had sat down on the Terrasse des Feuillants, and a plump woman had come to him and demanded two *sols* for the hire of the chair. Now, with his eyes closed, the cooing of the pigeons in the big chestnut trees and the shrill cries of children drowning out the distant noise of horses and carriages trotting across Place Louis XV, he felt pleasantly lethargic. This state, brought about by the accumulated fatigue of relentless days and sleepless nights, lasted until well after midday. Then he walked back across the gardens to the *quais*, and from there to the Grand Châtelet.

He found Old Marie in his room under the staircase of the

medieval palace, dining alone on a piece of veal and a steaming stew of eggs and bacon spread on thick slices of fresh bread. The usher invited the commissioner to share his meal, adding, to entice him, that it would be washed down with a new beer from a local tavern. Nicolas did not need to be asked twice. As he ate, he listened in amusement to his host's complaints that the meat, which he had taken that very morning in its earthenware dish to the oven in the neighbouring bakery, had come back reduced in both weight and quality – a clear case of fraud, in his opinion. Nicolas reassured him, recalling that, back in Guérande, his nurse, Fine, used to say the same thing every time she took her famous dish of duck with apples to be baked. He pointed out that, for such rustic dishes, there was nothing to equal the intense heat of a baker's oven, and that the results were well worth the few disadvantages, which in any case were largely imaginary. They talked about their native Brittany, and Old Marie said that they absolutely must drink some of his lambic beer, which was very strong, inflamed the entrails and woke the dead. Nicolas had no choice but to accept, for fear of upsetting him, although he did manage to surreptitiously pour some of it on a slice of bread. They then discussed the arrangement of the exhibits, currently being kept in a cupboard in the duty office. Old Marie knew a little dressmakers' workshop that, for an honest remuneration, could lend them two dummies.

Bourdeau suddenly appeared. Nicolas informed him of the latest elements in the investigation and asked him to go and fetch the second-hand clothes dealer in whose shop some of the exhibits had been pawned. Then, with his little black notebook in his hand, he went to the Lieutenant General's courtroom to think in peace. He needed to reflect on the best way to handle the hearing and obtain a result. His belief in reason made him feel certain that the key to the case would emerge from a clear demonstration of the results of the investigation. He was aware, though, that the narrow framework of a police inquiry could not express all the subtleties of living people and the human condition. Only intuition – his own personal, private feelings about the suspects, including even sympathy and understanding – could bring the truth to light.

At about four thirty, the torches were lit in the great Gothic room, into which the light from outside barely penetrated through narrow windows. There was a worn old wall tapestry with the arms of France and, on a dais, two chairs awaited the magistrates. Guarded by police officers, the suspects would take their places on the left-hand side. Nicolas, in his black robe and his wig, would be opposite them, at a table bearing the exhibits, flanked by two dummies wearing the clothes of Naganda and Élodie. In the flickering torchlight, the shadows cast by these figures would create a disturbing image.

The prisoners entered in grim silence. Only the two sisters seemed indignant at being there and looked about them with an air of self-importance. Once seated, they kept looking Nicolas up and down and holding forth in low voices, as if trying to provoke him. Madame Galaine looked as indifferent as ever, as grave as a worshipper listening to a boring sermon. Charles and Jean Galaine both had their heads lowered in dejection. Miette, looking almost beautiful, and moving unaided now, was smiling like a seraph, her face restored to its former simplicity, the stamp of evil completely gone. Naganda, who had also recovered, although he was a little unsteady on his feet, was observing the scene with the curiosity of a traveller discovering incomprehensible foreign customs. Marie Chaffoureau was wringing her hands in anguish, her little eyes darting to every corner of the room without coming to rest in any one place. Dorsacq was trying to get as far as possible from the Galaines, as if he wanted to dissociate himself from the family. Bourdeau and Semacgus stood at the back of the room, where they were soon joined by Père Raccard.

Just before five o'clock, the doors of the room were closed. Old Marie, in his black usher's uniform, announced the magistrates, who took their seats. They both wore robes trimmed with bands of ermine that, Nicolas recalled, symbolised the coronation mantle, in other words, the authority of the King. After a glance at the commissioner, Monsieur de Sartine spoke.

'In the name of the King, I hereby declare this hearing, summoned before my court, in the presence of the Criminal Lieutenant of the viscountcy and generality of Paris, to be open. This exceptional procedure has been requested and ordered by His Majesty, taking into account the somewhat extraordinary circumstances of this delicate affair, involving, may I recall, both a murder and an attempted murder. Commissioner Le Floch, secretary to the King in his counsels, the floor is yours.'

Sartine had carefully avoided mentioning the infanticide, news of which had not been spread. All eyes were turning to Nicolas when Charles Galaine suddenly stood up and began speaking in a shrill tone.

'Lieutenant General, I wish to make a solemn protest to the court, on behalf of myself and my nearest and dearest, at these absurd proceedings to which my family, incarcerated for no reason, are now summoned, without knowing or understanding what they are accused of, and without being given the right to be represented by counsel. I appeal to the King's justice!'

In these words, it was easy to recognise a representative of one of the great Parisian trade guilds, a man used to debates and court proceedings, as well as a supporter of the faction that had once revolted against royal power. Now the two sisters also rose and started shouting, both at the same time, so that it was impossible to understand what they were saying. Monsieur de Sartine struck the armrest of his chair with the flat of his hand. His usually pale face had turned red.

'Monsieur,' he replied in an even tone, 'your protest is not admissible. The King acts through us; we are answerable to him and carry out his orders. The rights you demand will be granted to you and to those who are charged with the crimes in question only when we are certain of the guilt of one or other of you, or when your innocence has been proved. My presence and that of the Criminal Lieutenant should be proof enough of the seriousness and fairness of this preliminary hearing. Normal proceedings will resume at the end of this hearing, and will take account of its results.'

The two Galaine sisters were still yelling.

'I beg you, Monsieur,' Sartine went on, 'please calm your sisters before I take further measures to restore dignity to this courtroom.'

'But—'

'That's enough, Monsieur Galaine. Commissioner Le Floch has the floor. May the proceedings of this court throw light on this murky affair.'

Nicolas folded his hands, took a deep breath and turned to look at the two magistrates. 'We are here today,' he began, 'to write the last act of a domestic tragedy with links to the disaster in Place Louis XV. Among the many innocent victims of incompetence and fate who perished on the night of thirtieth to thirty-first May 1770, the body of Élodie Galaine was discovered. Her presence there was evidently intended to conceal a crime. Identified by her uncle, Charles Galaine, and by her first cousin, Jean Galaine, her body was transported on my orders to the Basse-Geôle, where experienced practitioners ascertained that she had been strangled, and in addition that she had recently given birth to a child. Immediately, on the orders of the Lieutenant General of Police, an investigation was begun at her home in Rue Saint-Honoré, where her uncle owns a shop selling furs. From the start, none of the occupants of the house, whether relatives or friends, seemed to be able to account for his or her whereabouts at the estimated time of the murder. That means that any of them could have been in a position to take Élodie Galaine's life.'

Once again, Charles Galaine rose. 'I protest again. Commissioner Le Floch himself admits that it is not possible to state the exact time of my late niece's supposed murder. If that is the case, how can this hearing, held outside common law, lead to the truth and preserve my family's rights?'

'Monsieur,' said Sartine, 'you will have every opportunity to speak, to question and to be questioned, to prove and to disprove, to attack and to counter-attack. For the moment, I order you to let Commissioner Le Floch demonstrate to this court the elements of what has been a delicate case and a difficult investigation.'

Nicolas continued, detailing the results of his inquiries.

Without making any comment on the things he had observed and recorded, he listed them in a steady tone, like a sad inventory of human turpitude. The information that Élodie had recently given birth and that Miette would soon be doing the same provoked no reaction in those present. The Galaine sisters had calmed down and their brother, after his initial outbursts, had resumed his original demeanour. Everyone was listening attentively to this long introduction in such silence that, whenever Nicolas paused, it was possible to hear the sputtering of the torches and candles, the blackish smoke from which rose in wreaths to the vaulted ceiling. Nicolas took care not to mention Miette's possession, as any reference to it might well disturb the logical progression of the hearing and divert it from the paths of reason.

'Gentlemen,' he concluded in a louder voice, 'with your permission, I should like to question the witnesses and suspects one last time.'

'Proceed, Commissioner,' replied Sartine, after a courtesy glance at the Criminal Lieutenant.

'I shall naturally begin with Charles Galaine, head of the family and guardian to Élodie, the daughter of his elder brother Claude who died in New France. Monsieur, do you have any further statement to make concerning your whereabouts on the night of thirtieth to thirty-first May?'

Charles Galaine got heavily to his feet. 'I have nothing to add to my statements, nor to retract from them. I continue to protest at being forced to take part in these proceedings.'

'As you wish. Do you admit that you were aware of the arrangements your brother made for his succession, as laid out in the letter now among the exhibits in this courtroom?'

'It was a private letter.'

'I note, then, that you *were* aware of them. Have you read your brother's will and, if so, when and by whom were you informed of it?'

Galaine glanced at his wife and sisters. 'No.'

'Did you know that your niece was pregnant?'

'I had no idea.'

'How is that possible?'

'Girls these days are capable of many things. They are set plenty of bad examples. Clothes may, I suppose, conceal what might otherwise be obvious.'

'And were you aware of your maid's condition?'

'I had no idea about that either.'

'How do you account for their situation?'

'In my niece's case, her negligent upbringing in a half-savage country where she was probably given nothing but bad examples and fell under the most pernicious influences.'

'Really? I thought she was raised by nuns in Quebec?'

The merchant did not reply.

'And Miette?' Nicolas went on.

'She won't be the first maidservant to have lost her virtue. Sadly, it's an all too common occurrence these days.'

'You stated that your sisters accompanied Élodie to the festivities. Do you still maintain that?'

'Of course.'

'And yet they deny it.'

'I put that down to emotion. Their niece's death really upset them.'

'So, Monsieur, you have no alibi. A night when not a single

person can testify in your favour, a night shrouded in mystery, during which you met no one, but had plenty of time to murder your niece and abandon her body amid the chaos of the disaster, then go about innocently enquiring after her. Monsieur, you are a suspect in more ways than one. You, the unloved son, who suffered from your father's preference for your more brilliant, more enterprising, more attractive older brother. You, a shy man prone to outbursts of violence, always dominated by the women around you: your mother, your nurse, both your wives. You who concealed from me that letter from your brother, the brother you hated. You who knew, or sensed, that the pouch Naganda wore round his neck contained something important. You to whom your daughter Geneviève, the circulating spirit of the household, the innocent instrument of corruption, always repeated what she saw and heard. Yes, truly, everything points to you, Monsieur!'

'I protest! What motive would I have had to murder my niece?'

'Why, financial gain, Monsieur, financial gain! Here we have a reputable merchant from one of the great guilds, highly respected in his trade, who, as a result of risky speculations in Muscovy, is on the verge of ruin and of bringing his house and family down with him.'

Charles Galaine tried to protest.

'Be quiet, Monsieur! Informed that your brother left a large fortune in France, which has been yielding a profit, and that the only obstacle standing between you and that money is a poor young girl, can you resist the temptation? She has no one to turn to, no one to lean on; she is practically in your hands. Isn't that sufficient motive? We know from the will that her first-born male child was to be Claude Galaine's heir.'

'But if I'd had my eyes on that fortune,' said Galaine, 'I'd simply have seen to it that my son married Élodie!'

'Married Élodie? Pooh, Monsieur! You make light of the precepts of our holy mother Church! A first cousin? And what's more, a girl who was about to have a baby . . .'

'And how do you know the child wasn't my son's?'

A deathly pale Jean Galaine now rose to his feet. 'No, Father, not that, not from you!'

'You see?' said Nicolas. 'Even your son, whom I've long assumed was in love with your niece, protests against that idea. Besides, did it never occur to you that the as yet unborn child could have refuted this suggestion?'

Monsieur de Sartine intervened at this point: 'What exactly are you trying to imply, Commissioner?'

'Simply, Monsieur, that although the baby could not have testified as to its origins, it would have become obvious as it grew up that its father could not have been Jean Galaine or any other young Parisian.'

'And what leads you to say that?'

Nicolas threw his first major card on the table. 'Because everything points to the likelihood that the father of Élodie's child was Naganda. A shared childhood, a long ocean voyage amid the perils of war and the sea, then the hostility they aroused in the Galaine household – all these things had brought them together. After all, she was not yet twenty and he is thirty-five. Do you see any overriding obstacle? More virtuous people than they would not have resisted.'

Nicolas and the two magistrates were the only ones to notice the tears streaming down the Indian's impassive face.

'We'll come back to that when we come to question Naganda and demand an explanation from him. But, for the moment, let's take a closer look at the Galaine family. We'll leave your case until later, Monsieur. Let us consider that of your son. Here we have the same vagueness, the same inability to provide a coherent account of that fateful night. First there's an adventure in the arms of a courtesan, then he spends time with some casual drinking companions, then there's a gap of several hours and, when he finally gets back home, it's late. So much uncertainty, so many grey areas that cannot help but arouse doubt and suspicion! I hear you thinking to yourselves, gentlemen, "But where's the motive, what could possibly have led this young man to cut short his cousin's life?" Motives do exist, and they are strong and significant ones. But, first, I'd like to ask the suspect a question. Jean Galaine, were you in love with your cousin? Take your time. Your fate depends on your honesty – unless, God forbid, I'm very much mistaken.'

Jean Galaine rose to his full height and replied in an almost inaudible voice, which cracked completely by the end of the sentence: 'Commissioner, I confess that from the very first day I was very much in love with Élodie, but that nothing and no one could have led me to do her harm.'

'And yet, Monsieur,' retorted Nicolas, 'what a situation is yours! As the eldest child, and the issue of a first marriage, you hate your stepmother, and the feeling is mutual, although she conceals it beneath a mask of indifference. Desperately in love with your first cousin, this impossible love eats away at you, destroying you. Your union, even if she agreed to look at you, would require the kind of dispensation sometimes granted to great aristocratic families with a prince of the Church among their members. An insane love, which lives on images and frustrated dreams! A love made all the more painful by the fact that you may have known, or at least guessed at the ties – assuming we are correct – that bind Élodie and the Indian. Passion is a powerful motive in itself, but when we add financial gain – for you had the same interest as your father in seeing her out of the way – anything is possible. In your defence, though, I did notice that you were the only member of the household – with one other exception – who was really touched by your cousin's death. I even knew what you were thinking when you looked at your father and suspected him of being responsible for the murder.'

'Commissioner,' cried Sartine, 'please confine yourself to the facts of the case, and spare us any personal observations!'

'I'll try to do so, Monsieur, but the truth can only be revealed through a fertile combination of rational facts and vague intuitions. Which means that doubts remain concerning Jean Galaine's role in this affair.'

Nicolas paused for breath, then crossed the room and approached Madame Galaine.

'Madame, mine is a thankless task at best, but you have certainly complicated it. What a destiny is yours! The house in Rue Saint-Honoré seems to encourage false positions. You are the *de facto* mistress of the household. You help your husband in his business and even deputise for him. You gave him a daughter. Yet you seem to be a stranger in your own home. You enjoy neither the affection nor even the indulgence of the other members of the family. Your stepson is hostile to you. Your sisters-in-law hate you. Naganda is just a piece of furniture to you – you don't even see him. As for Dorsacq, the shop assistant, you flirt with him and pretend to be a woman of learning, and he appears to be under your spell. What anguish there must be for you in that house! Every day you think about what the future holds in store for you, living with an insecure, spineless husband for whom you have no respect, and who is still under the pernicious influence of his sisters. You've discovered that, thanks to him, the business is on the verge of collapse, threatening your survival but above all that of your daughter, Geneviève, whose future is close to your heart, since you are a good mother. There is one hope, and that is Claude Galaine's fortune. But one thing stands between your husband and that fortune: poor Élodie. Once again, Madame, what are we to make of your stubborn and inexplicable refusal to account for your whereabouts on that crucial night? For the last time, I solemnly implore you to relieve your conscience.'

Madame Galaine looked at him and said nothing.

'Madame, please search your memory,' insisted Nicolas. 'You don't have to have studied at the Collège d'Harcourt, *or even the Collège de Presles*, to remember something so recent!'

'What's the Collège de Presles?' asked the Criminal Lieutenant. 'I've never heard of it.'

Madame Galaine stood there red-faced. Nicolas's ploy had hit home, and she had immediately grasped the implication of his enigmatic words.

'Madame, it's entirely up to you,' Nicolas went on. 'If you wish to confide in the Lieutenant General of Police, he may be willing to let you approach and speak to him.'

Intrigued, Monsieur de Sartine consulted his colleague and then gestured to Nicolas to join them.

'What's the meaning of all this, Commissioner? You've been so precise so far; we weren't expecting such ambiguity.'

Nicolas moved even closer to the two magistrates and they bent their heads towards him.

'The meaning of it, gentlemen, is that this woman has an alibi, but it involves a shameful occupation she cannot admit to publicly. That's why I'd like you to hear her in secret.'

The Lieutenant General requested Madame Galaine to come forward. She did so and, her eyes swollen with tears, revealed in a low voice what Nicolas had already discovered during his encounter with Restif de La Bretonne. As she went back to her place, her husband watched her with an intrigued look on his face, and her sisters-in-law eyed her suspiciously. At a sign from Monsieur de Sartine, the commissioner resumed.

'Gentlemen, after the confidence you have received, I am sure you realise that Madame Galaine cannot be materially suspected of the murder of her niece by marriage, although that does not rule out the possibility that she may have been an accessory in the planning of the crime. And, since we are talking about Madame Galaine, would this not be an appropriate moment to examine the case of Monsieur Dorsacq, the assistant in the shop on Rue Saint-Honoré, who openly proclaims himself the said lady's escort? True, he is not a member of the family, but as an employee he is required to share their meals. Here is a young man who apparently enjoys Monsieur Galaine's trust. He may harbour great expectations. He is intimate with his employer's wife, he goes to the theatre with her and gossips with her about the news of the city and the Court, and all with the tacit assent of her husband, whom he thus relieves of a role he finds irksome. Does he have some secret feelings for the mistress of the house? I don't think so. On the contrary, I believe they are birds of a feather, both equally duplicitous. He pretends to flirt with his mistress . . .'

'Monsieur,' cried Charles Galaine indignantly, 'this is an outrage! How can you imagine—'

'I said *pretends*,' replied Nicolas. 'Between appearance and actual fact there's a difference you seem not to grasp – but I do. As I was saying, he pretends to flirt with his mistress, all the better to conceal something else even less fit for publication. I assume he is involved in a number of adventures. Is he in love with Élodie, the young girl of the house? Is he aware that it would be to his advantage to plead his cause with her? That way he could become part of the family, and ensure his position. Has he had wind of Élodie's expectations? Anything is possible, and suspicion falls on him, too. In answer to our questions, he persists in claiming that his one concern is to protect a lady's honour. Does that make sense, coming from someone in danger of being charged with a capital offence and executed in Place de Grève? And yet he refuses to reveal his whereabouts on that same night. With your permission, gentlemen, I'd like to arrange a little confrontation that will, I hope, throw new light on the case.'

Nicolas called Bourdeau and gave him instructions. The inspector walked up to the youngest of the police officers, asked him to take off his wig and jacket, and positioned him facing the two magistrates. He then asked Jean Galaine and Louis Dorsacq to stand on either side of him.

'Gentlemen,' Nicolas resumed, 'if you'll allow me, I'd like to call a witness.'

The door of the courtroom opened and Old Marie, full of self-importance, admitted a puny, half-bald little man. He was wearing steel-rimmed spectacles, through which he contemplated the solemn assembly with frightened eyes. With his threadbare black ratine coat and overlarge, down-at-heel shoes with no buckles, the man presented a wretched picture.

'Please come closer, Monsieur . . .?' said Nicolas.

'Jacques Robillard, Monsieur, at your service.'

'Please tell us your occupation.'

'I'm a second-hand clothes dealer, in Rue du Faubourg-du-Temple.'

'Monsieur Robillard, you told Inspector Bourdeau that early on the morning of thirty-first May 1770, you received as security, for the sum of eighteen *livres*, five *sols* and six *deniers*, a number of garments and objects, some of which are on display in this courtroom. Is that correct?'

'Absolutely, Monsieur, that's the truth. Two identical outfits with a cloak and a hat, of good quality. I was surprised that the man accepted so little for them. And an apothecary's bottle. Obviously, I didn't argue. It was a good deal for me, because people never come back, and you can sell the things later.'

'Now, Monsieur Robillard, do you see these three men with their backs to you? I'm going to ask you to walk in front of them and tell me if you recognise your customer from the other day.'

Nicolas prayed to heaven that the witness didn't open his mouth and repeat what he had already told Bourdeau, which was that he had not paid any attention to the customer's face and so could not give a description. He hoped that some detail would come back to the man. This was a card he had to play, however doubtful it was. But even before Robillard had stepped in front of the three young men, Louis Dorsacq turned and walked up to Nicolas.

'Commissioner,' he said in a low voice, 'before this man recognises me, I'd prefer to tell you myself that it was I who pawned those things, to pay a gambling debt.'

Nicolas had the feeling that this was yet another attempt to pervert the course of justice. 'You've certainly changed your tune! Perhaps you could tell us exactly where you got hold of these odds and ends you pawned, without arguing or haggling, for the wretched sum of eighteen *livres*. And this confession of yours raises other questions. To whom did you owe this sum?'

'Some gambling friends of mine.'

'Well, that's very specific! But I insist, where did you find all the things you pawned?'

It was clear that Dorsacq was trying desperately to come up with a plausible story. Whatever it was would not be enough to deceive Nicolas, who knew the likely provenance of the apothecary's bottle and at least one of Naganda's costumes.

'In the servants' pantry.'

'What do you mean, in the servants' pantry?'

'Yes, I found them one morning in the servants' pantry, lying about on the floor . . .'

'Which morning was this?'

'The morning after the disaster in Place Louis XV. I thought they were being thrown out, so I picked them up. Now I'm sorry I did.'

309

'What about the apothecary's bottle?'

'That was on the floor, too.'

'So when you see things belonging to your masters lying on the floor, it seems normal to you to pick them up and walk away with them. A likely story! The court is impressed! What were you doing in the shop so early? You don't live there.'

'I'd come for the summer stocktaking.'

Nicolas did not want to reveal the rest of the cards up his sleeve just yet. For the moment, it was enough to let Dorsacq tell one patent lie after another. There was no point in rushing things until he had finished questioning all the suspects, so he did not press home his advantage. He dismissed Robillard, who bowed to all and sundry as he went out. The two young men returned to their places on the bench and the police officer put his jacket and wig back on. After a long, thoughtful silence, the commissioner turned to Naganda.

'Monsieur, I find your situation especially puzzling. Like everyone here' – with a broad gesture, he indicated the Galaines sitting opposite him – 'you lied to me. I know from experience that there are such things as white lies, lies told in a good cause. Be that as it may, you lied to me. Here you are, the child of a new world, uprooted and transplanted to the shores of an old kingdom, among people who are either curious or hostile – or who can't really grasp the idea that one can be anything other than Parisian – friendless, with no one to turn to but yourself. And again, here you are, locked up like a criminal, drugged, deceived and – the last straw – someone tries to kill you. How can one not feel the most basic compassion for you in your appalling situation? And yet, you lied. At the point we have reached, I beg you to consider what can still be salvaged. Remember that the only basis for justice is truth. If, as you claim, Élodie's memory is dear to you, take that last step for her. But, if you persist in your aberration, then you will merely feed every prejudice felt against you, you will increase the burden of suspicion under which you labour and finally, I predict, the inexorable march of the law will crush you. For we know that you, too, have a motive.'

The Indian made a gesture of denial.

'Let's think about it for a moment. Élodie was a girl with a reputation for being fickle and thoughtless – in a word, flirtatious – a girl who did not spurn the advances of young men. How could such an attitude not provoke you, you who I suspect loved her? It may indeed be that *the victim brought it on herself*. We have testimonies. Do my words leave you indifferent, Naganda? That's up to you. But these elements may indeed explain – I do you the honour of ruling out any thought of financial gain as a motive – why you had violent feelings of jealousy, all the more violent in that you come from a warrior tribe in which, if travellers' tales are to be believed, such an insult is repaid in blood.'

'In my tribe,' cried Naganda, lifting his head proudly, 'we don't kill young girls!'

'A remark I would welcome, if it were accompanied by the truth which I have been demanding of you for days.'

'Commissioner,' said Naganda, 'I'm going to answer as clearly as I can. I put my fate in your hands. You have always shown me the kind of consideration I expected from the subjects of a King I had dreamt about all through my childhood. Ask me your questions.'

'Good.' Nicolas smiled. 'You told me you were drugged and unconscious until the afternoon following the crime, in other words from the afternoon of thirtieth May until the afternoon of thirty-first May. Do you confirm that statement?'

'No. I was drugged with a drink served by the cook on the afternoon of the thirtieth. I slept very deeply for several hours. When I woke up, it was dark, I didn't have my talisman or the necklace on which it hung and my head ached. I was locked in and my clothes were missing. That was the first time I escaped by way of the roof. I wandered in the dark for several hours in the vicinity of the house. People seemed to have gone crazy and no one paid any attention to me. Everyone was shouting and running, and carriages were rushing past. I suspected that something serious had happened. I was especially worried because Élodie was supposed to be going to the festivities, as she'd several times expressed the wish to do, and the baby was due any day. Unable to do anything in the state I was in, I went back to the house. It was only the next day that I escaped for good, because I feared for my life.'

'Very well. In what you say, you admit the ties that bound you to Élodie Galaine, who, according to you, was pregnant with your child. Didn't you know that she had already given birth?'

'Not at all. For some days they'd been stopping me from seeing her. They said she was ill. I was worried sick just to think of it. So I don't know anything about the birth. I loved Élodie. We had plighted our troth on the ship bringing us to France. For months, she had been concealing her condition as best she could. Life in that house was becoming unbearable, and we were planning to run away as soon as the baby was born, back to New

France. She had pawned her jewellery and the few valuable objects she had from her parents . . .'

At last Nicolas understood why he had not found any of the young woman's personal belongings.

'She had no idea that she was due to inherit a large fortune,' the Indian resumed, 'and neither did I. I'm telling you the truth as if I were testifying before the apostle of justice, Monsieur de Voltaire, himself. I don't know anything else. I performed the rites of my people, so that the spirits should calm Élodie's soul and confound her murderer. I have spoken.'

Monsieur de Sartine made a discreet signal to Nicolas to pass over this particular point, which risked taking the proceedings on to the subject of Miette's possession.

'How did you feel about Élodie's reputation?'

'It was something we'd decided on together as a way of allaying suspicion. She was acting. She used to practise by reading the plays of Monsieur de Marivaux. We laughed together at the attempts by Jean Galaine and Louis Dorsacq to seduce her. Élodie also scandalised her aunts by making suggestive remarks, which probably confirmed them in what they already thought of her. Behind this screen of pretence, we were – at least, we thought we were – hidden and protected.'

'Is that all? Do you have anything else to tell the court?'

'I want to reveal everything to the man who saved my life!'

'That's not true; your wound was not fatal.'

'If you hadn't come upstairs, my life would have drained from me along with my blood.'

Nicolas glanced at Semacgus, who nodded.

'All right, I'm listening.'

'As the man of stone saved me, I saw Élodie killed by—'

Monsieur de Sartine intervened again and interrupted the Indian, much to Nicolas's despair.

'Commissioner, let's not wander off the point. Please continue.'

Naganda sat down. Nicolas picked up the apothecary's bottle and, holding the object between his fingers, he showed it to the suspects and observed their reactions. None of them batted an eyelid.

'Which of you has seen this bottle before?'

Jean Galaine raised his hand, as did Charlotte, the elder sister. Whom should he question first? He had a feeling he knew what Jean Galaine was about to say. He would confess that he had visited the apothecary in Rue Saint-Honoré. Nicolas therefore plumped for Charlotte.

'Mademoiselle, what can you tell us about this?'

'In all honesty, Commissioner, it was my sister, my sister Camille. She's not in her right mind; she doesn't sleep well. She takes potions which are prepared for her at the apothecary's in bottles identical to this one.'

'That's true, Commissioner,' Camille cut in. 'I sleep badly. Orange blossom helps.'

'Didn't you know that this product can be bought from any grocer? Why go to an apothecary?'

'Habit. And it's more effective. I fear the grocers adulterate it. For example, one day –'

Nicolas interrupted her. 'How long ago did you last buy it?'

'About three weeks, perhaps longer. I give milk to the cat and I take a little spoonful in my cup at the same time . . . but even so . . . not every evening.'

'Have you bought any other potions recently?'

Camille hesitated, and her sister cut in. 'Of course you did, Camille! You're really losing your head with all this hullabaloo! Jean went to fetch you a bottle from our neighbour, Master Clerambourg! It tasted so good, you wanted me to have some, too.'

Camille looked at her sister, at a loss for words. 'If you say so . . . I really can't remember. What difference does it make anyway?'

Nicolas turned to Jean Galaine. 'Monsieur, can you confirm this?'

'Of course. At the request of my aunts, I went out to buy a bottle of laudanum.'

'Your aunts, you say? Which one?'

'I don't know.'

'How can you not know?'

'The request was passed on to me by the cook and, in fact, when I brought the bottle back, that's who I gave it to.'

At last, Nicolas thought, a new piece of first-hand testimony. Marie Chaffoureau, who acted as if butter wouldn't melt in her mouth, had concealed her role in this business.

He turned to the cook. 'What's the meaning of this, Marie? Why didn't you mention it before? After all, we spoke for a long time about the bottle. Who asked you to fetch laudanum, which is a dangerous substance?'

'Don't ask me to betray the trust of my masters,' muttered the cook.

'Wrong answer, Marie Chaffoureau. Was it Camille or Charlotte?'

'There was a note in the servants' pantry.'

'And where is this note now?'

'I threw it in the stove. It's just ashes.'

They were getting bogged down in all this nitpicking by witnesses who might be guilty, and who were enjoying themselves muddling the workings of the law. Nicolas moved away from the witnesses' bench and stood for a moment contemplating the two dummies and the exhibits: papers, objects, clothes, the dress, the bodice, the corset. It suddenly occurred to him that Élodie's shoes had never been found. He noticed that Monsieur de Sartine's wig was swaying dangerously back and forth, a sign of great irritation in its wearer. He ignored this and looked in turn at each exhibit.

That was when he saw the light. Yes, that could be the way to the truth, unless, by some absurd coincidence, there were two identical examples of the same thing. The words of someone in this courtroom came back to him, words that left no room for doubt. He knew how he was going to be able to use them. It was a risky move, certainly, but a vital one. Like all last-ditch measures, it would be a kind of gamble. It wouldn't solve everything, but it would be a great step forward. Nicolas looked up and called Bourdeau, who approached. He whispered in his ear, and the inspector nodded and immediately left the courtroom. While waiting for his return, and to keep the court occupied, Nicolas had to continue questioning the witnesses, circling ever closer to the truth without arousing their suspicions. The Lieutenant General interrupted these reflections.

'Are we going to wait much longer, Commissioner, for you to conclude yet another of these pauses with which you see fit to interrupt the languishing course of this hearing? I'm suspending proceedings for a few minutes. The Criminal Lieutenant and myself wish to speak with you immediately in my office.'

The two magistrates went out through a door at the far end of the room, from where a small corridor led to Sartine's office. Nicolas followed them. No sooner had they entered than his chief, pacing up and down, addressed him in the cold, intense tone he liked to adopt when he was trying to control his temper.

'It's not enough, Commissioner, to regale us with these twists and turns that lead nowhere, these bottles, this Indian who rambles on, all the insane nonsense we've been hearing. Every one of these suspects is a potential culprit or a potential innocent, but so far, in your presentation of the disparate elements of your investigation, you haven't shown us the way to a solution. Where are you taking us?'

'Yes,' said the Criminal Lieutenant in support, 'where are you taking us? I thought you would get to the point more quickly, Monsieur. You disappoint me. These proceedings are taking a very leisurely and roundabout route. I'm sorry now that I gave in to pressure and—'

'Monsieur Testard du Lys is speaking sense,' Monsieur de Sartine cut in wearily. 'Either you finish within the next hour, or we send these people back to their cells and institute more normal and perhaps more effective proceedings.'

'Gentlemen,' said Nicolas, 'I am sure I can bring this to a conclusion.'

Monsieur de Sartine looked at him with a hint of affection. 'Given your past history, I'm inclined to believe you. Let's go back.'

XII

ENDINGS

To the unexpected, the gods give admittance.

Euripides

The hearing had resumed. Nicolas approached the suspects' bench, noting in passing that Bourdeau had not yet returned, and immediately declared, 'I'd like to look again at the whereabouts of certain members of the Galaine family on the night in question.'

He came to a halt in front of Camille and Charlotte.

'Do you confirm,' he asked Camille, 'that you did not leave the house on the night of thirtieth to thirty-first May?'

'Of course, Commissioner, and anyway the cat—'

'No, not the cat, Mademoiselle. I'm talking about you, and about two murders.'

Her bloodless little face seemed to shrink even more. She tried to catch her elder sister's eye, but Charlotte had turned her head away. Nicolas consulted his notebook.

'Both of you stated that you helped your niece to dress for the evening, because . . .'

They nodded with surprising unanimity.

'. . . you found what she was wearing too bright!'

'That's what we thought,' said Camille.

'But you let her go alone, in the end?'

'No, not alone,' said Charlotte. 'Poor Miette went with her.'

'It's sad indeed,' Nicolas remarked, 'that her condition does not allow the poor girl to confirm what you say.'

He took a few steps towards the assistant.

'Monsieur Dorsacq, I need your help. You claim you pawned a number of objects to pay this famous gambling debt of yours. You must have received a note for them. That's the law.'

'I don't know . . . Yes . . . Of course.'

'Who did you give it to?'

'I really don't know.'

'Yes, you do, you know very well. I found that note. It was given to the person who, contrary to what you told me earlier, asked you to take those clothes to the second-hand dealer in Rue du Faubourg-du-Temple. Will you now tell me that person's name, or would you prefer us to settle the matter by torture, as laid down in common law for persons accused of homicide?'

'Commissioner, I'm desperately sorry, but—'

'Come on now, make one last little effort to be honest.'

'I had no choice.'

'If you had no choice, that means someone exerted pressure on you. Who threatened you, and why?'

The young man seemed on the verge of tears. 'I had a bit of fun with Miette,' he blurted out at last.

'Meaning what, Monsieur?'

'I fear, alas, that she's pregnant with my child.'

'Were you in love with her? What were your intentions?'

'I had none. I told you, it was just a bit of fun.'

'Were you in love with someone else?'

'No.'

'I think you were. I think you were hoping, whether out of desire or for the money, to seduce Élodie Galaine. Come on, admit it. She scorned you, and you were angry that your chance of joining the family had slipped through your fingers. That's why you decided to kill her.'

Dorsacq took his head in both his hands and shook it frantically. 'No, no! Never!'

'So who was blackmailing you? Who? Who?'

'Mademoiselle Charlotte.'

'Mademoiselle Charlotte? On what pretext? Explain yourself.'

'She came to see me in the shop on the Thursday morning. I'd been wandering around all night. I'd wanted to speak to Élodie, but couldn't find her. I was angry and humiliated. Mademoiselle Charlotte told me what to do with the clothes, the hats and the bottle – take them to a second-hand dealer, pawn them and bring her back the note.'

'That way they wouldn't be found by the police, but could be reclaimed if need be. But how was she able to force you to do it?'

'She knew about Miette and me. She threatened to tell Monsieur Galaine everything and have me thrown out if I didn't obey. But if I did what she said, she'd use her influence to get me accepted as her niece's suitor. I don't know how she found out about my situation.'

'But I do,' said Nicolas. 'Through a witness who is too young to appear in this court, but who is the spirit of the Galaine house, circulates everywhere and is always listening at doors and searching cupboards and drawers. That witness – Geneviève Galaine, if I must name her – repeats everything she hears, reveals everything she discovers, sometimes to her father, but always to her aunts. Thanks to her, everything is known, everything is destroyed, everything is corrupted and, from her innocence, crimes are born. But we're getting ahead of ourselves. Charlotte Galaine, do you admit to blackmailing Monsieur Dorsacq?'

It was Camille who answered. 'No,' she said hurriedly, 'it wasn't blackmail. I'll tell you everything. I wasn't going to tell you the other morning, but you never listen, you always interrupt. Cats—'

'Oh, no, not the cats.'

'Oh, yes. At night all cats are grey.'

'What of it?'

'On the evening of the festivities, the thing my sister and I were afraid of was that the streets would be full of gallants who might importune our niece. So . . .' She burst out laughing, and her laughter echoed like the sound of a shrill rattle. 'We thought up something, a kind of carnival game. Yes, just an innocent little game. What we did was dress Élodie in Miette's clothes and Miette in Élodie's. As I told you, we had to stop the savage from going with her. After what we've just heard, I think we were right. Thanks to the cook, who's really devoted to us, we put him to sleep and took his clothes. We'd already got hold of a copy of his costume. The idea was that Miette would leave first with the cook disguised as Naganda, and the gallants would follow them. Then, a few minutes later, Élodie would go out with Charlotte, also dressed like Naganda. Two savages, two Élodies. Quite a trick, wasn't it?'

'But who were the two savages?'

'I just told you: my sister, Charlotte, and Marie Chaffoureau, the cook.'

'So your sister lied: she did go out with Élodie?'

'Yes, I keep telling you!'

Charlotte got to her feet. 'Commissioner,' she said, 'she's making it all up. She's the one who went out. Her poor head's playing tricks on her again. She has all these mad ideas. She's like a mechanical doll that's broken down, the poor thing!'

'What does Marie Chaffoureau have to say to all this?' Sartine interrupted. 'Commissioner, have you taken the trouble to check her alibi?'

'Of course, Monsieur, but only in connection with the presumed time of the murder, not for the rest of the evening. The two versions may coincide. Marie Chaffoureau, what do you have to say?'

'The little one had to be protected!' gasped the cook. 'The little one had to be protected!'

She kept repeating the same sentence, and he had to shake her. It was no use: they would get nothing more from her for the moment. What could he do to press home his advantage? The best thing would be to bombard the adversary with arguments that would leave him or her dazed. Then he would stake everything on his final card. He went back to his place beneath the narrow windows.

'Gentlemen,' he said, 'you have ordered me to bring this matter to a conclusion. I'm going to tell you a story, the story of a domestic tragedy set within the narrow confines of a merchant's house. Two people united by misfortune, cut off from their families in a land at war, where the English have taken our place and still pursue the children of our defeated nation and the Indians loyal to our King. These two people have no one left to whom they can give affection except each other. Which of us can possibly throw the first stone? They disembark in a hostile land, after a terrible crossing, which has decimated His Majesty's navy. They present themselves to a family who have previously been secure in the comforting knowledge that the elder brother and all his family perished in the downfall of New France. A strained welcome, feigned sentiments, incomprehension and contempt towards the "savage": everything conspires to bring these two people even closer together, if that's possible. The result: the promise of a child, the desire to flee a hostile family and marry, the desire, too, to finally open the famous talisman which Naganda wears round his neck, and which apparently contains a secret concerning Élodie's destiny. They talk about all these things, without suspecting that an innocent child is watching and listening, and reporting their every word, gesture and hope.'

'But who knew about Élodie Galaine's condition?' asked Sartine.

'I'm coming to that, Monsieur. First and foremost, Charles Galaine, the father. Does he tell his wife? I don't know. Charlotte and Camille, without any doubt. And the cook, that goes without saying. That makes a lot of people in on the secret. Two young men, Dorsacq and Jean Galaine, are pursuing Élodie. For tactical reasons, she strings them along. She in her turn is deceived by her aunts' apparent affection for her. What did she say about them, Naganda?'

'She thought they were very strange, but she admitted that they were the only ones who had really welcomed her.'

'In other words, Élodie thought she could trust them. The time comes for her labour, after a difficult pregnancy she has had to conceal. Who helps her in her labour? Miette? Alas, she can't tell us. The aunts? Let me ask them.'

'We knew vaguely,' said Camille, looking doubtful, 'but it all happened without our being informed.'

'My sister's right for once,' said Charlotte.

Nicolas decided to play a little trick. 'So,' he said, 'neither Élodie nor Miette told you about it. The birth took place in complete secrecy. You didn't even know it had happened or what the outcome was. You had no idea that the little girl who was born a few days ago was immediately taken by Miette to a nurse in Suresnes. The child is doing well, and since its mother died intestate, there's no question but that a court will recognise it as the rightful heir to your brother Claude's fortune.'

The two magistrates made no attempt to conceal their surprise at Nicolas's words.

Charlotte leapt to her feet. 'But that's false! Completely false! It was a bastard! What are you talking about?'

'What do you call a bastard? A daughter born out of wedlock?'

'No, no!' screamed Charlotte. 'A boy, the boy! It's a trick; she can't inherit. She isn't Élodie's daughter. Our niece gave birth to a son. I saw him, with my own eyes.'

'You saw him? How delightful. Tell us more. When did you see him? When he was taken to the nurse?'

'Yes. Actually, he was taken to a home for abandoned children.'

'Do you think it likely, after what I've said about Naganda and

Élodie, that they would have wanted to abandon their child?'

'It was Élodie who wanted it,' said Charlotte. 'A ribbon with half of a medal was attached to his swaddling clothes, and a paper stating that we planned to take him back soon.'

'So many details! You weren't informed of the happy event, and yet you know so much! What's the name of this home for abandoned children?'

'That was Élodie's secret. Only Miette knows it.'

'How unfortunate once again that she is unable to tell us. Or how convenient. So, gentlemen, Élodie gives birth to a child and then abandons it. I'm sure you find that very believable!'

Nicolas again went and stood in front of the two sisters. He saw Bourdeau enter the room, a packet wrapped in silk paper under his arm. 'If that's the case, then why did we find in your room, under your bed to be more precise, these strips of cloth which seem to have been used to squeeze Élodie's breasts and extract her milk?'

'Those cloths,' said Camille, 'were taken off when we dressed Élodie for the festivities.'

'Very well. Let me continue. This child – this son, in fact – this heir, this noble son of the Algonquin, has been found.'

The whole room seemed to be hanging on Nicolas's every word.

'Yes, found. Dead, murdered. Buried under the cellar floor at the Deux Castors, slaughtered in the most terrible manner, with the umbilical cord sliced off, not tied, the little body drained of blood . . .'

Madame Galaine burst into sobs.

'I hope,' said Nicolas, 'that those tears are the expression of a mother's horror. Gentlemen, I am now going to have to utter some grave words. I am going to have to make accusations.'

He again walked away from the Galaine family.

'I accuse Charlotte and Camille, one or the other or both, of having known all about Élodie's pregnancy. I accuse one or the other or both, probably helped by Miette and Marie Chaffoureau, the cook, of destroying the living fruit of the love of Élodie and Naganda in terrible conditions, draining him of his blood, as ascertained, without any possibility of error, by experienced practitioners and, finally, of burying him in the cellar, hidden beneath animal hides. But, you will ask, why kill this baby? Because it was a boy, and one or both of the sisters are afraid, before it has even been confirmed, that he might become the heir to a great fortune. Presumably they convince the unfortunate mother that her child was still-born or died of some disease. They also urge her to appear at the festivities a few days after the delivery, all the better to allay suspicions.'

'These are grave accusations,' said Monsieur Testard du Lys. 'Do you have evidence to back them up?'

'The testimony of little Geneviève, who sees a strange figure going down to the cellar with a shovel.'

'The testimony of a child!'

'A child who sees everything and reports it exactly.'

'And how do they make Miette go along with them?' asked Sartine.

'She's a poor girl, a little simple, and she's also pregnant, which means she could be thrown out onto the streets. That seems to me incentive enough. I also observe that, some days before thirtieth May, the sisters or sister get hold of clothes identical to Naganda's, with the intention of accusing the Indian of Élodie's death at a later stage. In fact, let's go back to Naganda. They have to steal his talisman, which contains a secret. It's child's play for the cook to drug the Indian. Once asleep, he's immediately stripped. His necklace is broken, the talisman is opened, and Claude Galaine's will is discovered – a will I later found in Camille's sewing egg – which stipulates that the fortune reverts to Élodie's first male child. On reading that, I'm sure they feel justified in having employed such extreme measures.'

'Where are you taking us with this, Commissioner?' asked Sartine. 'It's like something out of a novel!'

'To the festivities, Monsieur, to the festivities. Nothing makes sense without several persons being involved. Miette is dressed up in yellow satin, complete with bodice and corset. Élodie is dressed up in Miette's clothes. Camille – or Charlotte – lures the poor girl into a barn belonging to the convent of the Daughters of the Conception. I have two eye-witnesses who can vouch for that: two French Guards. Once in the barn, she is strangled. Miette is now on her own, Marie Chaffoureau having left. She goes to the barn as previously arranged, which, by the way, establishes premeditation. Now, consider this sordid scene. Miette takes off Élodie's clothes, removes her own from the corpse, and one of the Galaine sisters, whichever it is, dresses the poor lifeless remains. An obsidian pearl is placed in the victim's hand. Everyone goes home. A witness sees two Nagandas, which both confuses things and confirms my later suspicions. Then something unpredictable happens.'

'I have a question for you, Commissioner,' said the Criminal

Lieutenant. 'In your memorandum, there is an account of how the cook spent her day, and I observe—'

'That account is correct. She leaves the house with Miette, but she soon parts from her, comes back to Rue Saint-Honoré and runs off to play *bouillotte* with her friends, although she doesn't stay long.'

'I see.'

'The something unpredictable to which I referred is the disaster in Place Louis XV. The Convent of the Conception is not far from Rue Royale. Miette has already left. The sister, whichever she is, goes out and discovers what has been happening. She sees the lifeless bodies being laid out along the Garde-Meuble, but it probably doesn't occur to her immediately that she might be able to use this event. She returns home. There, she is told by the cook that Naganda has woken up and has probably gone out. It won't be so easy now to pin the blame for the murder on him as they had planned to do, claiming he acted out of jealousy. What has he done and what is he going to do? It's too dangerous. Early in the morning, before it gets light, the murderer and Marie Chaffoureau leave the house to retrieve Élodie's body. Luckily for them, the area around the convent is deserted. They carry the body by way of Rue Saint-Honoré to the Garde-Meuble. No one is surprised, no one even notices, there's so much panic in the area. The body is thrown on a heap of victims, and is later collected and taken to La Madeleine cemetery, where Charles and Jean Galaine will later go to identify it. But the night doesn't end there for you, Camille, or for you, Charlotte. You have to get rid of Naganda's clothes since you can't put them back in the attic. It's a terrible situation! What to do? To go out is to risk questions being asked. Louis Dorsacq arrives, for the reason he has told this court. The culprit or culprits, who know his secret, immediately use it and blackmail him into going to the second-hand clothes dealer in Rue du Faubourg-du-Temple.'

'Evidence, evidence!' cried Sartine impatiently.

'I'm getting to that, Monsieur. I haven't used all my weapons yet. In that fatal barn, apart from the hay found on Élodie's body, I picked up a handkerchief from the mud.'

Nicolas took it from among the exhibits and brandished it in front of everyone.

'The initials CG, finely embroidered. CG can stand for many things. Claude Galaine, Élodie's father, in which case the object might belong to his daughter. Charles Galaine. Charlotte or Camille Galaine. Who among those present recognises his or her handkerchief?'

He waved the little square of cloth. Charles Galaine stated that he did not own a handkerchief. At a sign from Nicolas, a police officer confirmed this statement. Charlotte took hers out: it was made of silk and did not bear any initials. Camille Galaine, in turn, held out hers. It seemed absolutely identical to the one discovered on the floor of the barn, the same kind, the same initials.

'Mademoiselle, how do you account for the presence of your handkerchief in that barn?'

'I can't.'

Monsieur de Sartine made a sign to Nicolas, who hastened to approach.

'That's quite a tall tale, Nicolas! First the strips of cloth under the bed, and now this. You seem to be constantly finding clues under your feet, like mushrooms after autumn rain. Don't you find that suspicious?'

'Indeed I do, Monsieur. These clues did not get there by themselves, they were put there to be found, as you will realise at the end of my demonstration.'

He went back to his place.

'I ask you, Camille Galaine, to come here.'

Camille stood up, throwing a terrified glance at her sister, who looked right through her. Bourdeau approached the two dummies. He removed the Indian's clothes, carefully opened the packet wrapped in silk paper, and took out two corsets, which he placed on the dummies.

'Observe these two corsets,' Nicolas said. 'They are worn over the shift, and cover the trunk from the shoulders to the hips. They are identical, with one exception to the corset found on Élodie Galaine's body. Gentlemen, I should like to ask Camille and Charlotte Galaine to come forward and lace up these garments.'

Camille took the two ends of the lace and calmly tied the first corset, then went back to the bench. Her elder sister stood up.

'I protest against this farce, which is unworthy of the memory of our poor niece!'

'Protest all you want,' said Monsieur de Sartine, who appeared increasingly intrigued by the turn this hearing was taking, 'but I strongly advise you to do as you are asked.'

Charlotte Galaine approached the second dummy and, after several unsuccessful attempts, tied the lace. Then she ran back to her seat. Almost respectfully, Nicolas picked up Élodie's corset.

'When we came to open up the body, I found this corset to be very tightly knotted, so tight that the laces had to be cut with a scalpel. I assumed that had been done in order to squeeze the breasts and extract milk. But now I understand how it was that the corset on Élodie's body could have been pulled so tight. It's because when it was tied, she was no longer breathing.'

At this terrible image, a sigh of horror went through the room. The two magistrates left their chairs at Nicolas's invitation and approached the two dummies.

'See for yourselves, Monsieur, whether the knots are similar or different. This is Camille's: it isn't identical to the original. Whereas Charlotte's is an exact copy.'

'I don't follow your argument, Commissioner,' said Sartine. 'What bearing does this have on the case?'

'I understand your perplexity,' replied Nicolas. 'It so happens that one of the witnesses, Marie Chaffoureau, who we now know to have been an accomplice, told me a great many things, certain that I would never suspect her. One of the things she told me was that for a long time Charlotte Galaine was unable to tie a knot.'

'And?'

'When she finally managed to tie this knot, it was upside down. There is only one conclusion I can draw. Charlotte Galaine, I have the sad privilege of accusing you of the murder by strangulation of your niece, Élodie Galaine.'

Charlotte stood up with a fierce look on her face.

'You who brought the devil into our house, don't you see it was my sister Camille who did it?'

Nicolas smiled. 'These words merely confirm my accusation. In trying to prove too much, you prove nothing. Getting the laudanum from the apothecary was Camille's idea. The ticket from the second-hand clothes dealer was found under Camille's bed. Whenever things look bad for Charlotte, it's always Camille who did it. I've just remembered something, a tiny detail from early in my investigation. When I first questioned you, Charlotte Galaine, you mentioned white Venetian masks. Unfortunately for you, your sister Camille didn't remember them and looked puzzled. If the two of you had been accomplices, you would never have contradicted her. I don't claim that Camille Galaine bears no share of the blame for this tragedy, but there is no evidence that she was your accomplice in the murder.'

Camille had started weeping.

'Why does my sister accuse me?' she asked with a sob. 'She assured me the poor child was still-born, that we had to bury it secretly, for fear of scandal. That was all.'

'We're getting off the point,' said Sartine. 'Please conclude!'

'Gentlemen,' said Nicolas, 'as a final proof, I recall that on the morning after the disaster in Place Louis XV, during my first visit to the Galaines, I found Camille fully dressed, whereas her sister had apparently not had the time to get ready. Of course, it had been a long and difficult night, lots of moving about, dressing and carrying a corpse . . . But what of the motives? you will ask. One, of course, is financial gain. Charlotte loves her brother, she's ready to do anything to help him out of a difficult situation. Élodie Galaine is a dangerous obstacle that has to be removed. But there's a second motive: revenge. The murderer has long harboured a desire for revenge, and this is her opportunity to finally take it. That same witness, whose loose tongue led her to come out with a great many compromising truths, told me that in their youth the two sisters were rivals in love. Their rivalry was so fierce that the suitor made his escape, rather than being forced to choose between them. Although Camille enjoys being a spinster, Charlotte has never become reconciled to it. She is the murderer of Élodie and her child, with the complicity of Miette and Marie Chaffoureau; it is she who planned the whole thing to the last detail. I should add that the cook not only helped Charlotte in the execution of the crime I have just mentioned, but is also the person responsible for the attempted murder of Naganda. On reflection, it seems clear that she was the only person with access to the Indian's room, and she went up there while we were involved with another matter of which you are aware . . . To her, Naganda was the evil genius who had brought disgrace on the Galaine house. His murder was also intended to again cast suspicion on Jean Galaine and Louis Dorsacq, who might be thought to have acted out of jealousy. At the same time, we need to ask ourselves about the role played by Charles Galaine. Is he not an unwitting culprit, an unwitting accomplice, an unwitting contributor to his niece's terrible fate? The law will have to decide.'

Silence fell on the courtroom, disturbed only by Camille Galaine's weeping and Charlotte's incoherent muttering. Marie Chaffoureau was smiling, as if she did not understand what was happening. After a sign of assent from Monsieur de Sartine, the Criminal Lieutenant stood up.

'I thank Commissioner Le Floch for his masterly demonstration, supported by sufficient evidence and necessary assumptions. At the end of this extraordinary hearing, I order, in the name of the King, that Charlotte Galaine and Marie Chaffoureau, both presumed guilty, and Charles Galaine, pending further inquiries, be incarcerated in the royal prison of the Châtelet. The normal procedure will run its course. I order that the girl Ermeline Godeau, known as Miette, be placed in a house of correction. If she ever regains her reason, she will have to answer for her actions. The other witnesses remain at the disposal of the law, but are free to go.'

Naganda was the only one to come and thank Nicolas. Madame Galaine seemed on the point of speaking to him, then changed her mind and smiled weakly by way of farewell. Père Raccard approached and put his hand on Nicolas's shoulder.

'Monsieur Le Floch, you have brought him down for the second time.'

'Who, Father?'

'He whose name is legion.'

Thursday 7 June 1770

Prepared the previous evening during a very alcoholic supper at Ramponneau's, in the hamlet of Les Percherons, paid for by Bourdeau, the arrest of Major Langlumé took place as planned. Dawn had just broken when a cab and four horsemen stopped outside a tall, opulent-looking house in the area around Saint-Gervais, in the Hôtel de Ville district of Paris. While a water carrier and a boy delivering a tray of *bavaroises* and *oublies* looked on in surprise, Nicolas, dressed in his commissioner's robes, walked in through the entrance archway with Bourdeau. On the first floor, they knocked at a heavy oak door decorated with brass nails. An old woman in a mantilla and a woollen shawl opened. She introduced herself as the major's mother, asked the new-comers the reason for their visit and told them that her son was still asleep, but that she would wake him. Nicolas, who was more of a horseman than a magistrate, kept shaking the wide sleeves of his costume, which hindered his movements. Shuffling footsteps were heard and the major appeared, looking haggard, his night-shirt only partly hidden by a white piqué housecoat. He jumped when he saw Nicolas.

'You? You dare to disturb me at this hour! What are you after?'

Nicolas waved a paper. 'Are you Major Langlumé of the City Guards?'

'Yes, and I'm going to make you pay for this!'

'That would be a pointless effort, Monsieur. By order of the King, we are here to take you to the Bastille. You can look at the *lettre de cachet*, if you want to.'

'A coward's revenge!' said Langlumé. 'And what is the charge?'

Nicolas took out one of the tags. 'Do you recognise this?'

'Yes, Monsieur, a very innocent practical joke played on a bastard whippersnapper of a police commissioner.'

'Please note,' Nicolas said to Bourdeau impassively, 'that the defendant has insulted a commissioner from the Châtelet in the exercise of his duties.'

'That's absurd.'

'Not at all, Monsieur, and you will answer for it. And, while we're about it, what can you tell me about this other tag?'

'Nothing. There are thousands like it in Paris.'

'Only a few of them were made by Master Vachon, tailor

and supplier to Major Langlumé. So we'd be grateful if you'd show us your uniform. Do not attempt to resist. We need it as evidence.'

Nicolas and Bourdeau followed the major into his bedroom, where he opened a chest. Bourdeau jostled him to hurry him up, and a fight nearly broke out between the two men. But, in the end, the inspector brandished the garment like a trophy, and Nicolas went closer to check the aiguillettes. Two tags identical to those in his possession were missing.

'By order of the Criminal Lieutenant, I inform you, Major, that a preliminary investigation has been opened against you for the attempted murder of Monsieur Aimé de Noblecourt, former procurator of the King.'

'You're joking, I hope?' cried the major. 'Who is this Noblecourt? Did I meet him in Vanves? Or Charenton?'

'Observe, Monsieur, that there are two tags missing from your uniform. The first was used to block the attic door of the ambassadors' mansion, an unworthy act that prevented a magistrate of the King from organising emergency help during the disaster in Place Louis XV. The second was found in the entrance to Monsieur de Noblecourt's residence in Rue Montmartre two days ago. According to witnesses, it was torn off one of the attackers as they were assaulting the victim.'

'Cowards deserve to be beaten, Monsieur!'

'Which presumably means that I was the target of the attack. But it was an old man who bore the consequences.'

The major rose to his full height. 'Monsieur Jérôme Bignon, provost of the merchants,' he said, 'will treat your accusation with the scorn it deserves, and I will take pleasure in your disgrace.'

'We'll see about that. In the meantime, Monsieur, Inspector Bourdeau will escort you to the Bastille.'

Nicolas went back to Rue Montmartre, where he told a delighted and sardonic Monsieur de Noblecourt all about the major's arrest. Towards the end of the morning, he received a note bearing the arms of Monsieur de Sartine, informing him that he was invited to supper in the King's small apartments that very evening. His Majesty wished to hear an account of the investigation from Nicolas's own mouth, especially a description of the exorcism. Nicolas devoted what remained of the morning to choosing his attire and getting ready. By one in the afternoon, his carriage had passed Saint-Eustache and was crossing to the left bank of the river.

His account finished, Nicolas fell silent. Every one of those present was looking at the King, who was smiling pensively. Nicolas had made an effort to keep it short, mixing amusing comments with graver observations and trying hard not to overdramatise the demonic manifestations in the Galaine house. He described them in the tones of a naturalist who has just discovered a new species. The ladies shuddered and the men grew sombre or gave rather forced laughs. With his usual penchant for macabre details, the monarch, listening attentively, had interrupted him several times to ask him to clarify certain points. But Nicolas's brisk narration had not dampened the King's spirits. Louis liked nothing better in the evenings than to escape the constraints of etiquette and spend time in these intimate surroundings with his friends. There, with nobody making representations to him, he could enjoy a few hours of peace, talk animatedly, encourage the freest conversations and provoke controversies, to which he reserved the right to put an end if they went beyond the permitted limits.

In his apartments, away at last from the constant pressure of public life, the King was free to reveal his true nature, that mixture of gaiety and melancholy, devoid of affectation or any artificial desire to please. What made these evenings so agreeable was the choice of guests and the atmosphere of exquisite and subtle urbanity. For all its violence and horror, Nicolas's story had, thanks to his moderation, his elegance of tone and his lightly ironic touch, made the moment even more precious.

'Monsieur de Ranreuil is a first-class storyteller,' said the King. 'That was the first impression I had of him back in 1761. It was quite cold . . .'

Nicolas admired the monarch's memory. It had sounded as though he were about to mention the Marquise de Pompadour, but had held back at the last moment. Those present, Madame de Flavacourt, Madame de Valentinois and the Maréchale de Mirepois for the women, and the Maréchal de Richelieu, the Marquis de Chauvelin, Monsieur de Sartine and Monsieur de La Borde for the men, were listening to the King with respect and affection.

'If the King will allow me to ask a question,' said Richelieu. He did not wait for a reply. 'Has the King ever seen the devil?'

The King started laughing. 'I see you every day – that's enough for me! However, when I was a child, I thought I saw the little man who was said to wander the corridors of the Tuileries. I talked about it quite innocently to my tutor, the Maréchal de

Villeroy. He was pleased that I had been afraid, since that was how he felt, too, and he strengthened me in my conviction that I had seen something. I was so terrified I couldn't sleep. I decided to open my heart to my cousin d'Orléans, who was then regent. He was furious.'

A door opened. The King turned, recovering his cold, distant air in a split second. Who had dared enter like this without being announced by an usher? Then his face relaxed and softened at the radiant sight that presented itself: a young woman whom Nicolas realised could only be the King's new mistress, the Comtesse du Barry.

How dazzling she was, thought Nicolas, and what a contrast to the good lady of Choisy, so sick and so ravaged at the end! The young woman was wearing a white dress with panniers, its satin threaded through with silver, decorated with pink and green sequins. Little embroidered roses were strewn over the body of the garment. She was covered in cascades of diamonds, and with each step she took, there was a glimpse of her lace petticoats.

'Oh, Madame!' said the King, leaning towards her. 'Roses without thorns!'

She made a low curtsey and sat down on a *bergère*. Her natural blonde hair framed regular, graceful features. There was a delicacy about her face, and at the same time a lustre discernible in her little mouth. Her narrow blue eyes were half-open, and yet her gaze was frank and forthright, and radiated a languid charm. The overall impression was one of youth and seductiveness. She was said to be kind and obliging. The fact remained that Monsieur de Sartine was still bitter about a quarrel he had had with the lady who, while apparently amused by some of the satirical songs of which she had been the target, nevertheless bore a grudge against the man whose task it was to prevent them from appearing, or to seize them when they had appeared.

'Madame,' said the King, 'you've just missed a tale beside which those of many authors would pale. Young Ranreuil, whom I mentioned to you, really amused us . . . or frightened us, depending on how you look at it.'

'If he amused Your Majesty,' said the countess, 'then he deserves my gratitude.'

The King stood up and urged Madame de Flavacourt, the Maréchale de Mirepois and Monsieur de Chauvelin to join him in a game of whist. The Duc de Richelieu took Nicolas by the arm and led him over to Madame du Barry.

'Madame, I advise you to win this heart. He is worthy of his father, even though he intends to remain a Le Floch.'

'In His Majesty's service, Monseigneur. The police – just think of it – would be a demeaning profession for the Marquis de Ranreuil.'

'Ho, ho!' said the duke. 'I'm going to tell that to Sartine; he'll be delighted. So, Madame, what is happening about your apartments?'

'I've abandoned the one on the Cour des Fontaines for one left by Lebel,[1] near the chapel, and I'm waiting for a small study. I collect, I gather and I scour the connoisseurs. Lacquers, ivories, minerals and bisques – which are my favourites – hold no more secrets for me.'

'Minerals? Diamonds above all, I assume.'

'They are made to run in rivers, Maréchal.'

'Quite an ambition! What does Choiseul say?'

'He turns up his ugly nose.'

'Did you know,' Richelieu went on, 'that our friend Chauvelin has abandoned his apartment in the chateau and that His Majesty has been so good as to grant it to the Maréchal d'Estrées? Not that Chauvelin has lost out, for he now has the Marquise de Durefort's apartment. Admittedly, he made the gesture of reimbursing her for all the improvements she made to it, as he was determined to retain it in all its finery.'

The comtesse turned to Nicolas, and the ardour in her eyes made him quiver. The King's hoarse voice could be heard commenting on his lucky cards and mocking Chauvelin.

'Monsieur,' she said, 'I've been told I can count on your devotion, and that nothing can equal the fervour with which you serve the King and those . . . who are close to him.'

'You are too indulgent, Madame.'

'I've also been told that you were much appreciated by a certain lady. And that the services you rendered her were fully commensurate with your loyalty.'

'Madame, the King's service is indivisible.'

'I'm convinced, Marquis, that one day you will wish to do something which is agreeable to me.'

'Everything I have I owe to His Majesty, Madame. So you can count on my zeal and my attachment to all those who are dear to him.'

The King's favourites came and went, he thought, but they all believed they could score points with him if they addressed him by his title – a title which he had renounced and which meant nothing to him. The evening passed like a dream and was an apt reward for his efforts. The King talked to him several times in private with that benevolent open-mindedness that made him so loved by those close to him. Nicolas would have liked to share his happiness with the whole of France. When he found himself in Sartine's carriage, he had the impression he was reliving a scene he had already lived through ten years earlier. The Lieutenant General of Police, who, beneath his cold, polite exterior, felt things deeply, smiled and said in his ear, 'May destiny always offer us such happy journeys home from Versailles!'

Nantes, 18 August 1770

A long, high-pitched whistle accompanied Nicolas as he descended the accommodation ladder of the *Orion*. He stopped for a moment. The skiff that was to take him back to the riverbank was moving up and down on the waves. He waited until the floor of the boat and the ship's gunwale were level, and jumped into the skiff. Naganda, leaning on the guardrail of the ship, his long hair floating in the wind, waved to him. Soon, a grove of trees on a little island in the Loire hid the ship from sight.

Since the conclusion of the Rue Saint-Honoré case, things had moved quickly. Charlotte Galaine and Marie Chaffoureau, both found guilty of the crimes with which they had been charged, would soon, according to the procedure, undergo the final interrogation before judgement on the 'saddle of infamy'. The rigour of the law left them no chance to escape the gallows, even after making amends. The other actors in the drama had been exonerated. Charles Galaine, who was strongly suspected of being complicit in the crime, whether passively or not, underwent torture without opening his mouth. Admittedly, he had lost consciousness even before the torturer had approached him and begun his work. His peers in the guild of furriers had interceded for him and, in the absence of hard evidence, he was released. He had immediately set sail for Sweden, where he planned to pick up the threads of his business and open a new shop.

The dishonoured Madame Galaine had broken off all relations with her husband and had retired to a convent in Compiegne. The nest egg amassed through her evil trade had opened the doors of this peaceful retreat to her, and there, sheltered from the world, she would oversee the education of her daughter. Camille Galaine had responded to both interrogation and torture with incoherent answers. She was now vegetating in the house in Rue Saint-Honoré. The strangeness of her character had become accentuated. She collected cats by the dozen and, all alone in the fetid mustiness of their excreta, spoke to the devil. It did not look as though Miette would ever recover her reason: her whole life would be spent amid the horrors of a house of correction. Dorsacq had promised to recognise her child. Made superstitious by the extraordinary events in the Galaine house, he claimed to have been touched by grace and wished to mend his ways.

As for Naganda, who was now free, he had decided to return to the New World in order to succeed his father at the head of the confederacy of Micmac tribes. Monsieur de Sartine had been surprised that Nicolas had not sufficiently pressed home his advantage by forcing the Indian to reveal information, which, apparently, could have helped the investigation to end sooner. 'What!' the Lieutenant General had exclaimed. 'You have a vital witness in your hands and you let him do as he likes in a garret from which he escapes at will, like an alley cat!' It had not been difficult for Nicolas to counter that, as the procedure had been exceptional and the whole case had an irrational side, putting too much pressure on Naganda would not necessarily have yielded much, and that his presence in the Galaine house had been one of the determining elements in the complicated alchemy of cause and effect in this domestic tragedy. Grudgingly, his chief had been forced to agree. Then, with another smile, he had added a cryptic comment to the effect that 'whatever we do, we always rebuild the monument in our own manner'.

Remarkably, the King, who forgot nothing and whose curiosity had been aroused by the commissioner's story, had ordered that the Indian be presented to him. Nicolas would long remember this astonishing conversation between the monarch and the Micmac, who still considered himself his subject, whatever the treaties said. The young Dauphin was also present. Much to his grandfather's surprise, he shrugged off his usual reticence, and without any shyness asked Naganda many questions, displaying real geographical and cartographical knowledge.

He was also kind enough to thank Nicolas for his investigation into the disaster of 30 May.

A second audience had followed, this time in the King's secret study with only Nicolas present. Soon afterwards, Sartine communicated to him the decisions the monarch had come to as a result of this extraordinary combination of circumstances. Charmed by Naganda's talents, the King had decided to use his services. He would set sail on a vessel as the ship's scribe, and would be secretly landed on the coast of the Gulf of Saint Laurence. Louis wished to be kept informed of events in his former possession. It was important to maintain links with the loyal tribes there, some of whom, like the Micmacs, were still fighting the English. A secretary from the Foreign Ministry initiated Naganda into the subtle mysteries of encoding, and he was given a personal code. An approximate calendar of meetings was drawn up to facilitate regular contacts with a fishing boat that travelled up and down the coast of Newfoundland. The King provided Naganda with all the equipment he needed, and gave him a tobacco pouch with his portrait. The Indian had launched himself enthusiastically into his preparations, overjoyed that he was still able to serve the old country.

On 10 August, he had left Paris with Nicolas. Sartine had duly provided his deputy with letters and orders from the Duc de Praslin, Minister of the Navy, introducing the Indian to the commander of the ship. They had reached Nantes in a rented berlin, after travelling along the Loire in small stages. Naganda had gone into ecstasies over the beauty of the towns they had passed through and the prosperity of the countryside. Their long conversations had drawn them together, and Nicolas never ceased to be surprised by his companion's knowledge and curiosity. But when he asked him about the vision he had had of Élodie's murderer, the Indian said nothing. Nicolas had the feeling that his reply would have been similar to the comment made by Père Raccard at the end of the hearing. He did not insist.

As soon as they arrived in Nantes, Nicolas was surprised by the dilapidation of the older districts, where the streets were so narrow that their berlin had several times to reverse in order to find a wider lane. High buildings, close together, with lattice windows, dominated the roadways. They put up at the Hôtel Saint-Julien on Place Saint-Nicolas. It turned out to be old, dirty and full of vermin, like most of the places they had stayed in since leaving Paris. An inn on the banks of the Erdre provided compensation with a tender roast duck, locally raised, washed down with a wine from Ancenis. The next day they boarded a two-decker whose appearance had been transformed in order to pass it off as a merchant ship leaving for the coast of Africa, and thus deceive the English fleet. Its fifty cannon had been loaded secretly at La Rochelle. They received a polite welcome from the commander. The farewells had to be kept brief. The Indian thanked Nicolas for his support, and expressed the hope that one day he would welcome him among his people.

Now, from the garden of the Capuchin monastery situated on a high rock overlooking the city and its surroundings, Nicolas contemplated the landscape. The river as it widened split into several branches, with a number of little islands, some deserted, others covered with tumbledown houses. Between them could be seen, here and there, the masts of a multitude of vessels. Ahead of him stretched a monotonous countryside of fields, flocks, mills, marshes and the dark masses of distant forests. To his left was the town, with its many steeples, the well-to-do merchants' districts, and the imposing silhouette of the castle of the dukes of Brittany with the cathedral towering over it. He thought with emotion of Guérande, so close to here, where he had spent his childhood, and this thought led him on to look back over his past. Too many of his friends, he told himself, had left him to cross the seas. Pigneau was continuing his mission in Siam, and now Naganda was going back to his own people. He searched for the *Orion* with his eyes, but it was nothing more than a toy in the distance. Nicolas filled his lungs with sea air, imagining that, one day, he too would take to sea, and slowly went back down to the town. Paris was waiting for him, with its crowds and its crimes.

Carthage, La Marsa, April–November 2000

NOTES

CHAPTER I

1. 'Here, there is nothing.'
2. Louis XV's eldest daughter (cf. *The Man with the Lead Stomach*).
3. The author cannot resist quoting this very eighteenth-century statement by Talleyrand, spoken when he presented to Emperor Franz of Austria the jewels originally given as a gift by Napoleon to Marie-Louise.
4. A net was stretched across the Seine at Saint-Cloud to collect the bodies of the drowned.

CHAPTER II

1. French baroque painter (1644–1717).
2. Cf. *The Châtelet Apprentice* and *The Man with the Lead Stomach*.
3. A name given to Madame de Pompadour, who owned this chateau near Paris.
4. Author of *Paradoxum médico-légal* (1704).
5. Author of *Vernünftiges Urteil von tödtlichen Wunden* (1717).

CHAPTER III

1. 'Beneath a mask of simplicity and modesty, he remained impenetrable, simulating a taste for letters and a love of poetry the better to conceal his soul.'
2. A casual garment worn in the morning.
3. This disaster had a long-term effect on the capabilities of the French Navy.
4. The largest and most important Indian tribe in the maritime regions of Canada. They were steadfast allies of the French against the English.
5. A women's prison.

CHAPTER IV

1. Cf. *The Châtelet Apprentice*.
2. The Duc de Richelieu.
3. The Treaty of Paris, which ended the war between the French and the English and enshrined the loss of New France.

4. 'The Lord having seen him, he was touched and said to him: Do not weep.' (St Luke's Gospel)

5. Racine's *Andromaque*.

6. Racine's *Britannicus*

7. It will be recalled that Nicolas, abandoned as a child, eventually discovered that he was the illegitimate son of the Marquis de Ranreuil (cf. *The Châtelet Apprentice*).

CHAPTER V

1. The Comtesse du Barry.

2. The month in which he died was in fact November.

3. A fashionable mixture of tea and orgeat.

4. The captain's quarters on a galley.

5. The King's eldest surviving daughter in 1770.

6. Contrary to received opinion, it was not Marie-Antoinette who introduced hygiene to Versailles. Quite the contrary, in fact.

7. Leather caskets for dispatches and files.

8. The Maréchal de Villeroy.

CHAPTER VI

1. Small, cone-shaped wafers.

2. Cf. *The Châtelet Apprentice*, Chapter XI.

3. Ibid., Chapter IX.

CHAPTER VII

1. Cf. *The Châtelet Apprentice*, Chapter IV.

2. Madame de Pompadour.

3. Cf. *The Man with the Lead Stomach*.

4. Three times, in fact.

5. Cf. *The Châtelet Apprentice*.

6. Ibid.

CHAPTER VIII

1. This expression was used for the marshals of France.

2. St Paul.

3. Cf. *The Châtelet Apprentice*.

CHAPTER X

1. Where banned works were printed.
2. This was done to distract the customer from the bitter taste of the medication.
3. A highly malignant disease that makes the skin appear dead.

CHAPTER XII

1. Concierge of the palace, who had recently died.

ACKNOWLEDGEMENTS

First, I wish to express my gratitude to Marie-Claude Ober for her competence, care and patience in preparing the final version of the text. I am also grateful to Monique Constant, Conservateur Général du Patrimoine, for her encouragement and unfailing assistance. Once again I am indebted to Maurice Roisse for his intelligent and detailed checking of the manuscript. Finally, I wish to thank my publisher for the confidence he has shown in this third book in the series.